SMALL MOVING PARTS

SMALL MOVING PARTS

D. B. JACKSON

TURNER

Turner Publishing Company
Nashville, Tennessee
New York, New York
www.turnerpublishing.com

Small Moving Parts

Cover design: Maddie Cothren
Book design: Glen Edelstein

Library of Congress Cataloging-in-Publication Data

Names: Jackson, D. B., author.
Title: Small moving parts / D. B. Jackson.
Description: Nashville, Tennessee : Turner Publishing Company, [2018] | Identifiers: LCCN 2018003410 (print) | LCCN 2018005936 (ebook) | ISBN 9781683367840 (eBook) | ISBN 9781683367826 (pbk. : alk. paper)
Classification: LCC PS3610.A347 (ebook) | LCC PS3610.A347 S63 2018 (print) | DDC 813/.6--dc23
LC record available at https://lccn.loc.gov/2018003410

9781683367826

Printed in the United States of America
17 18 19 20 10 9 8 7 6 5 4 3 2 1

To

MARY—THE LOVE OF MY LIFE
PAT LOBRUTTO—FRIEND AND LITERARY MAGICIAN

WITHOUT THEM, HARLEY AND DODGER WOULD BE WANDERING MINSTRELS IN A BORDER TOWN SIDESHOW.

THESE MORTALS DO CONCERN ME, DYING AS THEY ARE.

—Homer, *The Iliad*

NOTHING MUCH GROWS IN THAT HARD COUNTRY AROUND BUFORT, TEXAS. BUT A FEW THINGS DO.

—Thomas Morriset Washington

SMALL MOVING PARTS

CHAPTER ONE

BUFORT, TEXAS—THE SUMMER OF 1958

There he is. Watching him watch himself like some mute carnival barker in a dream. Sitting off in the moonlight. A .45 to his head. His reflection in the window glass the sole witness to the last of his undoing. He had come to this place stowed in the back of a wagon, an afterling born to a railroad tracklayer dead before the child's sixth birthday, a mother dead before his seventh. Passed from house to house. Working in the coal mines, a breaker boy at the age of twelve. A runaway road-kid hopping freights at fourteen.

"Harland Cain," he heard the doctor say, "there's nothing more we can do." That had been a month ago. The old man set the pistol down, rolled a cigarette, and struck a match. The flame flared. He held it to the paper and inhaled. He shook the match. The flame died. The cigarette glowed, then dimmed. He watched the smoke rise before his face and trail upward to the porch ceiling, where it stalled.

A final drag off the cigarette. Cain stared off into the gloom of the desert, ground the cigarette butt into the glass ashtray on the table before him, and then took up the pistol.

He watched the image in the window glass raise the .45 and edge the muzzle across the hollow of his cheek to the temple where his pulse throbbed against the smooth steel bore.

This was it.

First would come the explosion. The bullet spiraling down that empty corridor, twisting its way to him. The impact. The scattering of flesh and bone and gore that would follow. The shutdown of the cerebral cortex. All before the brain could process any sensation of pain. Then darkness.

He considered the after-journey. For the first time, it occurred to him that there might not be one. No matter. He had made his peace.

Cain squeezed the single-action trigger partway. A faint click at the first detent. There it was—that absolute and liberating shift of power as he took control over his destiny. Death was now his choice. His time. His place.

He eased up on the trigger, smiled, slipped his finger from the trigger guard, and set the pistol on the table with the hammer cocked. It was all done but the doing of it.

No urgency now. One more cigarette, a final cup of coffee. So simple in the end. He tapped the tobacco out onto the paper, poured himself a fresh cup of coffee, and then leaned back in his chair.

He closed his eyes and tipped his head back when he inhaled. He wondered how he had ever taken such a pleasure for granted. He lifted the cup to his lips, its aroma intoxicating.

Cain took another drag, flipped the butt into the yard, and then picked up the pistol and pressed it again to his temple. For all he had agonized over the right and wrong of it, the guilt, the shame—in the end it was an uncomplicated act. The fear in living was death. Now, so close to death, his only fear was living.

He leaned his head forward and held his breath. *God forgive me.*

The sky cracked like thunder, a howl coming in off the nearby blacktop road, ripping through the night like the onset of Armageddon. An engine roared. Tires screamed. Headlights pierced the emptiness like the fiery eyes of something from the inferno as they lurched and bounded out of the murky abyss and then dipped and went black. Shearing metal, exploding concrete—the final crescendo in an eerie quiet followed by the gasping, dying sound of radiator steam. The noise was coming from the direction of the bridge.

The old man dropped the pistol. He stared wide-eyed out into the blackness, expecting to see Satan himself come to collect his dues. He waited. He listened. There was no sound save that of the hissing, which sent a chill through him.

He waited. Nothing. He hurried off the porch and across the driveway, poking in his trouser pocket for the keys as he ran. He slipped in behind the wheel of the old ranch truck. The keys rattled as he thrashed about, searching for the ignition. It started on the second try. Gravel sprayed out from beneath the rear tires as he fishtailed out of the driveway and onto the blacktop.

He came upon the fresh skid marks first. Then, in his headlights, the smoking wreckage. Before him sat a half-ton pickup angled across the shoulder, its hood collapsed to the firewall, steam rising from beneath it. Both doors were sprung open and bent. The bed partially torn from the frame. The front fenders wrapped around the concrete bridge abutment. The entire scene covered with the broken glass of every window.

The old man stepped out of his truck and hurried to the driver's side of the wreckage. There, behind the wheel, sat a young boy, fifteen at best, staring through the missing windshield with eyes white and reeling. He was wearing an old felt cowboy hat, a threadbare shirt, and worn-out Mexican boots.

Cain leaned in, supporting his weight with one hand above the doorframe. "You okay?"

The boy, red with blood and reeking of alcohol, turned half toward him. His head bobbed and he coughed.

"I ain't sure."

Cain took him by the arm.

"C'mon, we gotta get you to the hospital before you bleed to death."

"Don't move me."

"You need looking after."

"I can't go to no hospital."

"Why can't you?"

"I said I can't."

"Well, can you walk?"

"I ain't tried."

The old man reached for the boy, pulled on him.

"Hold it, hold it," the boy protested.

"We gotta get you outta there."

The boy's head wobbled. He teetered side to side. "Okay, okay. Let me do it."

The boy swung his feet out with great effort. It was not clear if it was the alcohol or the injuries that impaired him.

Cain reached for him again.

"I'll take you to my place, and we'll see how bad you're hurt."

"I don't need your help."

The boy stepped out and then stood shaking while he held on to the loose door. He took one step and then another, limping noticeably on his left leg.

"That leg hurting you?"

"It ain't the leg."

The boy turned and began staggering in the direction from which he'd come, and then he collapsed to the pavement.

He awoke on the old man's sofa. His eyes darted wildly about the porch, and there was an unsettling fear in them.

"Where am I?"

"You're on my davenport. You're cut up some, but you don't look to be hurt too bad."

"I gotta get out of here."

"What's your hurry? It's two a damn clock in the morning and your truck's all tore to hell."

"It ain't my truck."

The boy stood. He tottered side to side and then sat back onto the deep cushions of the sofa.

"Whoa. You got anything to drink?" He slurred his words.

Cain regarded him with disdain. "Coffee."

"Got any beer?"

"Ain't that what got you here in the first place?"

"Probly—I'm drunker'n Cooter Brown."

The boy leaned his head back and held on to the sofa cushions. The old man poured him coffee in a tin cup.

"Here—drink this."

The boy sat up and took the cup. He sucked in a hot sip, then another, and handed the cup back to the old man.

His legs wobbled when he tried to stand again. He sat down and leaned forward between his knees.

"I'm 'onna puke."

The old man snatched the boy's hat from his head and held it in front of the kid.

"Puke in this then. There's gonna be a big enough mess around here as it is."

The boy's body convulsed as he heaved. The sour smell of half-digested alcohol made the old man turn away as he held the hat.

When the boy raised his head and wiped his sleeve across his wet mouth, the old man pitched the hat out into the yard.

"You're a sorry mess."

"Yessir, I know it."

"What the hell were you thinking?"

The boy spoke without looking up. "I was aiming to kill myself."

"You didn't do a very good job of it."

The boy shook his head. "That was my first go at it."

"That was a practice run?"

"No, sir. I didn't think it would take more'n one."

"Whose truck is that, if it ain't yours?"

"It's Eugene's. He's my momma's boyfriend. When he sees it, he's gonna off me himself."

The boy's eyes closed. His head dropped to the cushions, and he began to snore. Cain lifted the boy's feet onto the sofa.

He sat back in the rickety chair at the small table, glanced over at the boy, and then rolled his fingers over the checkered wooden grips of the pistol. He lit another cigarette, took two quick drags, flicked the burning fag out into the yard, and pressed the muzzle to his head.

He squeezed the trigger, and the pistol exploded with an awful roar as it spewed fire at the same instant the old man jerked his hand and sent the bullet ripping into the ceiling. Dust, wood fragments, and debris fell upon the table. When the dust and smoke cleared, the old man cursed.

He looked at the pistol and released the locked-back slide. He set the pistol down, rose to his feet, and went inside. When he returned he carried a washbasin of warm water, a small brown medicine bottle, and a handful of rags. He sat next to the boy and set to cleaning his wounds. The boy did not stir when he picked out the glass fragments, and he did not stir when Cain turned him over, but he sat bolt upright when the old man daubed the deep wounds with Mercurochrome.

"What the hell?"

The old man pushed the boy back down. "Be still."

The boy's eyes, bloodshot and feral looking, flitted about the room as he attempted to control the spinning sensation and remember where he was.

When the old man finished, he walked the basin to the edge of the porch and slung the bloody water over the railing, where it was absorbed into the dust of the driveway. He returned to the boy, placed the bloody rags into the washbowl, and then surveyed his work.

"You don't look too good, but you'll live," he said to the drunken mess of a boy.

The boy slept until late morning. When he awoke, he sat up and looked about. He heard the old man inside and smelled bacon cooking. He limped through the open door and said to the old man's back, "You the one doctored me up last night?"

Cain turned to assess the raggedy example of a boy standing

in the doorway. He appeared younger in the light of day. His wounds appeared more severe with their bruising and swelling.

"That's right. You want some breakfast?"

"No, sir. I don't feel too good." The boy leaned against the door casing. "You got any coffee?"

"Cup's on the drainboard. Pot's on the stove."

The boy filled a cup half full and sat at the table. He looked down at his shirt, stiff and dark from the blood that had dried on it. His blue jeans hung on him, bloody from belt to knees.

"Where's my hat?"

"Out in the yard."

The boy turned to look back at the door opening.

"It's a Resistol, you know. They ain't but one like it."

"You puked in it last night."

"It was my daddy's."

The boy shook his head and blew into the cup before taking the first sip. He studied the bandages and the bloodied clothes, then he looked up at the old man. "Thanks for what you done."

"I'd a done it for anyone. It had nothing to do with you."

"Well, thanks just the same."

The boy smiled a half smile. Cain did not smile back.

"Where's my truck?"

"In a pile where you left it."

"Bad, huh?"

The old man stared at the boy. "You don't remember?"

"I reckon I do—I was just hopin', I guess."

"It's a miracle you're still alive."

"Yeah, I wasn't countin' on that."

Cain nodded. "I know what you mean."

"Did the po-lice come?"

Cain turned and leaned back against the counter, and then he pushed himself forward and took a seat at the table across from the boy. "I don't see many cars come down that stretch of road. Unless someone calls it in, that truck could sit there a while before the police see it."

"I'm going to jail over that truck."

"Why's that?"

"I done stole it."

"From your stepdaddy?"

"He ain't my stepdaddy. He's just my momma's boyfriend, but he will sure as shit kill me when he finds out."

"You got a mouth on you for a kid."

"What do you mean?"

"Cussin' like that."

"I heard that before."

Cain looked up over his fork. "You still got time, you know."

"For what?"

"To kill yourself."

"Yeah, well, I ain't in the mood any more. I was fixin' to be drunk when I done it, anyways."

The old man finished his breakfast and watched the contemplative kid nurse his coffee. His expression dead serious, he held the boy in his eye. "I got a bottle of whiskey in the pantry if you're fixin' to take another run at it."

The kid looked up and smiled an uncertain smile. The old man stared at him with no expression at all. The kid watched him and waited for a change in the old man's appearance, but none came. The kid gave up and shook his head.

"I reckon I lost the taste for it."

The old man nodded but did not say anything one way or the other. The kid directed his attention to the plate of bacon and bread on the table. "Mind if I have me some of that?"

"Help yourself, but be quick. We got work to do."

"What kinda work?"

"We're going to burn what's left of that truck, then call it in."

"They gonna know I took it."

"How they going to know that?"

"Fingerprints."

"There won't be no damn fingerprints. Does your momma's boyfriend know where you were last night?"

"He thinks I went over to Bobby Washington's house."

"Who's Bobby?"

"He's my friend since fifth grade. He's a good fighter."

"Will Bobby vouch for you?"

"What do you mean?"

"Will he stick up for you if you ask him to say you were with him last night?"

"Yeah. He does all the time. Me and him's best buds. He's colored, and them other boys don't like me or him that much, so we look out for one another. He beat up a lot of guys bigger than him that was pickin' on me."

The old man looked at him and nodded toward the front door. "Eat up."

The boy followed Cain out to the barn. The old man motioned in the direction of a small shed off to the side of the main structure.

"Go in there. Get them two cans of kerosene. Bring them to my truck."

They returned to the wreckage and, for as bad as it had looked in the dark, the light of day painted a clear picture of the totality of the devastation and the narrow margin by which the boy had missed killing himself.

The boy whistled and his eyes widened.

"I prit'near got the job done."

"Douse it good, and hurry up about it."

When the cans were empty, the boy watched as the old man threw a match to it. The whole affair belched into flames amidst a cloud of black smoke that spiraled heavenward and could have been seen for miles had there been anyone looking to see it.

Back at the house, the old man made the telephone call. The dispatcher noted the information and thanked him.

"Now we gotta get you back to Bobby's house. When you get there, can you call your momma's boyfriend and ask him for a ride home?"

"Well, yeah, I can, but you know he don't have no way to give me a ride now that he don't have no truck." The boy's tone softened. "And he wouldn't give me no ride even if he did."

"That ain't the point. We just don't want him thinking you know anything about his truck."

"Oh, okay, I get it."

"Where does Bobby live?"

"In Bufort, same as me. I can show you if you can drive me there."

"That's thirty miles away. What you doing way out here?"

"I told you, I come to kill myself."

"Seems like you could have found a place closer to home and saved us both a lot of trouble."

"I didn't know it was gonna be this much trouble or I woulda."

"What's your name anyway?"

"Bodean Cleon Cooper. What's yours?"

"Harland—Harland Cain. Do they call you Bo?"

"No, sir, they call me Dodger."

"Dodger? What the hell kind of name is that?"

"It's what they called me since I was a kid."

"Dodger?"

"Yeah. I was born in the back seat of a 1937 Dodge."

The old man shook his head. "I reckon you're lucky. It could have been a Studebaker."

CHAPTER TWO

Dodger asked Cain to drop him off a block from Bobby's house.

"Thanks, Mr. Cain."

"Yeah. Good luck to ya."

Cain sat with the engine idling as he watched the boy hobble down the street, hauling the bad leg along like some ill-conceived inbred. Glad to be rid of him and ready to get back to the business at hand. He wondered if surviving the crash was more bad luck than good for the kid, but that was not his problem.

When the old man pulled off the highway back at his place, he sat in his pickup in the driveway and considered what forty years of working the unyielding West Texas land had given him in return for his efforts. A small herd of thin-ribbed cattle, a house that needed fixing, and a barn with the doors sprung and half the corrugated metal roof blown away by the wind. All defined by a wire fence with scarcely a tight strand among them. All signs of neglect, not for the lack of money, but for the lack of will—the more egregious of the two in his mind.

Forty years for what?

He slammed the truck door, noticed Dodger's hat in the driveway, and shook his head. *One of a kind—like hell.*

Cain stepped up onto the porch and hesitated at the top step. He turned and walked back to the hat. He picked the wretched mess up with his fingers, held it at arm's length, and walked it over to the water hose. He flushed out the vomit, carried the one-of-a-kind hat to the porch, and laid it on the table to dry. He knew the boy could not come after the hat once they located the pickup, but still he treated it as though it might somehow find its way back to him. Neither the hat nor the boy were of any further concern to him.

Cain figured that when they found the pickup and then came to the house and found his own gunshot body, there would be speculation that the two were related, and that should take the heat off the kid. The boy was no longer his problem. He sat gazing at the pistol lying on the table where he had left it earlier.

He rolled and lit a cigarette, crossed his boots on the porch rail, and stared off into the west where the sun began its descent and left the dry earth blurred in the heat that rose off the desert floor against a sky the color of blood orange and sapphire.

He wondered what could drive a boy to the edge at such a young age. It bothered him to know he could have done more but had not. It was out of his hands, and he accepted that as his fate—and the fate of the boy.

He picked up the pistol and, with no contemplation or hesitation, placed it to his head and pulled the trigger. *Click.*

He looked up at the hole in the ceiling and then back to the pistol. He shook his head and laughed. *I guess that's a sign,* he said to himself as he slipped the pistol under his belt at the back of his trousers and walked into the house. He packed the pistol away in the closet, swapped yesterday's shirt for a clean one, lifted his hat from the peg in the hallway, and walked out the door. On his way, he picked up Dodger's hat and strode across the gravel driveway to his truck.

He rolled up onto the blacktop highway, turned north, and

headed for Bufort with Dodger's hat on the seat beside him. The burned-out wreckage no longer smoldered and, for all appearances, could have been there a long time.

Cain drove back to Bobby's house. He knocked on the screen door that hung from a single hinge and was surprised when an attractive middle-aged woman appeared before him.

"Ma'am, I'm Harland Cain, and I was looking for Bodean Cooper."

"Dodger? He ain't here, Mr. Cain. Bobby and him said they was going to the Conoco down the street to get a pop. I give them a quarter. That was about two hours ago."

"Thank you, ma'am. I'll go look for them. If I miss him, will you give him my telephone number and have him call me?"

"Yes, sir."

"It's 9-7-8-0. Tell him I got his hat."

"I'll do that, Mr. Cain. 9-7-8-0?"

"Yes, ma'am."

Cain drove to the Conoco station but found no sign of Dodger or Bobby. He pulled up into the service area. A uniformed attendant walked briskly out to greet him. Behind him was a large glass window with DUANE'S CONOCO painted across its surface in bold red letters that hadn't changed in twenty years.

"Fill 'er up, Mr. Cain?"

Cain nodded. "Regular. Thanks, Duane. Hey, I was just wondering if you know a kid from around here name of Bodean Cooper."

Duane nodded to his left as he inserted the nozzle and began pumping. "Yessir. Him and that colored boy left here walking thataway 'bout an hour ago."

"Don't know where he lives, do you?"

"Yessir. Drive down here to San Antonio Street. Take a left at the stop sign. Just before you get to the hardware store, take another left and go one block. It's the first yeller house on the right—the one with the broke-down Indian motorsickle on the porch. You can't miss it."

"Much obliged."

"How's that oil?"

"Good, thanks. How much I owe you?"

"Two dollars and fifty cents, even."

Cain drove down as far as San Antonio Street. He stopped at the stop sign and, when he glanced into the vacant lot next to the hardware store, he saw Dodger sitting, straddling a wooden crate, blood on his chin, staring down the alley.

Cain pulled in and stopped near where the boy was sitting. He climbed down from the truck, and the boy looked up at him, his lips swollen, his nose bleeding.

"Now what happened?"

"Me and my momma got into a argument, and Eugene popped me."

"What was that all about?"

"They seen me cut up and figured I was out fighting."

"What did you tell them?"

"I told them I got jumped."

Cain looked at him. His expression asked the next question, and the boy answered without being asked to do so.

"I figured I'd ruther take a whupping for fighting than stealing a truck."

"Did he ask you about the truck?"

"No, sir, he didn't say nothin' about it."

"What did your momma say?"

"She's too drunk to say much."

"So what now?"

"I don't know. If I go back, he'll beat on me some more. I 'spect I'll just walk around 'til mornin', then go on over to Bobby's."

"Won't they come looking for you?"

"No. This happened before. No one comes lookin'."

"Get in the truck. You can come stay at my place until we get this figured out."

Dodger smiled a broken smile. "You sure that's okay?"

"It'll just be for the night 'til we get this sorted out for you."

The boy slid into the passenger side of the truck, slammed

the old door, and looked down at his hat. He looked up at Cain with a fat-lipped grin.

"That's my hat."

The boy pulled on his hat and leaned over to look at himself in the mirror.

"Minus the puke you left in it."

"Thanks, Mr. Cain."

"Look, just call me Harley."

The boy nodded, smiled, and sat back in the seat and stared out the side window. He fussed with his hat and sat up straighter because of it.

As they left town, the exhaust from the old truck rumbled and the tires hummed on the asphalt. Neither spoke as the roadside telephone poles blew rhythmically by the window. There was nothing to see but more of the same, and the boy stared out across that barren plain in the late afternoon heat a long time before he said anything.

"The radio work?"

"It quit some time back."

They rode in silence for several miles, the old man contemplating his circumstances and those of the boy, while the boy marveled at the quiet.

"So, what happened to your leg?"

"It ain't my leg. It's the ankle."

"How did it get that way?"

The boy looked up at the old man. He weighed his thoughts and then turned his head toward the side window when he answered. And when he did, he lied.

"My momma fell with me when I was a baby. We never got it fixed. It just healed crooked is all."

After a long silence, the boy looked at the old man.

"I don't know it to be any other way, so it don't bother me none."

"It would me."

"Well, it don't me."

The old man looked across at the boy. He turned back to gaze out at the open highway and did not respond or ask any further questions.

CHAPTER THREE

Here's a blanket and a pillow. You can sleep out here on the davenport. It's cooler than in the house."

The boy took the bedding and set it beside him as he sat on the sofa and laid his head against the back cushion and stared up at the ceiling. He looked over at the old man and then nodded in the direction of the bullet hole.

"What happened there?"

"That's a bullet hole."

The boy laughed. "You shot a hole in your ceiling?"

"A housefly was annoying me. I shot him."

The boy smiled. "You didn't shoot no fly."

"He's gone, ain't he?"

"I don't reckon there was one there."

"Suit yourself."

The old man did not smile. The boy's questioning gaze followed the old man as he walked back into the house.

When the morning sun inched its way up over the edge of the dry plain and began to heat up the day, the old man stepped out onto the porch. The boy lay on his back with a bare leg hanging out the side of the sheet that covered him, a foot resting on the floor.

Cain set out a clean shirt, an old pair of jeans, a pair of red boxer shorts printed with bird dogs in the hunt, and a clean pair of white socks for the boy.

He kicked the end of the sofa with his boot.

"Come on. Get up."

Dodger sat upright, covered his face with his arms as though he were about to be struck, and then turned his head from side to side as his eyes darted about and quickly took in his surroundings. He relaxed, yawned, and swung his legs out and placed both feet on the floor.

"A mite jumpy, ain't you?"

"I thought for a minute you was Eugene."

"He thump you around a lot?"

"Yessir. Some."

The boy looked down at his blood-soaked clothes and yawned. "It don't matter. I don't plan on being around that much longer anyhow."

"I brought you some clean clothes. Go in the house there and take a bath and put them on. I'll get you a belt to hold them britches up."

"You don't mind me calling you Harley?"

"Whatever suits you."

"Thanks—Harley."

The old man was standing before the stove in the kitchen when the boy limped into the room wearing the blue work shirt and the old jeans rolled up at the cuff.

"You seen my boots?"

Cain tipped his head in the general direction of the porch. "They're sitting on the step. I hosed the blood off 'em best I could."

The boy returned wearing the still-wet boots and sat down at the table, where Cain had a stack of pancakes waiting.

"You like griddle cakes?"

"Yessir."

"Pour yourself some milk. It's in the icebox."

"The 'icebox'?"

"What do you call it?"

Dodger laughed. "We call it a fridge."

The boy reached inside and pulled out a bottle of milk. He held it out to Cain. "You want some?"

"No."

The boy sat back down with his milk and picked up the sticky bottle of maple syrup sitting next to the butter. "You got any molasses?"

"There's a bottle up in the cupboard. Fetch it if you want some."

"I had it at Bobby's house a couple times. It's my favorite."

They sat in silence and ate. Aside from the swollen lips and the healing cuts on his face, the boy appeared none the worse for the wreck and the beating he'd taken.

The old man turned his gaze from the open door to the boy. "Where do you go from here?"

The boy looked the old man directly in the eyes. "Same place I was going when I got here, I reckon."

"You still aiming to kill yourself?"

"What do you think?"

"I think you do what you need to."

"You mean kill myself?"

"Sure. Why not?"

The boy looked at the old man and the old man looked back. No one ever looked the boy in his eyes when they spoke to him, and it made him uncomfortable, but at the same time it held an intimacy to which he felt powerfully drawn. He glanced down at the table. "One a my teachers told me one time I been dealt some bad cards."

The boy's expression was thoughtful. He paused and then looked back up at the old man. "He said you gotta play the cards you been dealt."

"So you lookin' to throw in your hand?"

"That was in the sixth grade. I'm still holding the same cards."

The old man studied the kid a long time. He contemplated his thoughts carefully before he spoke. The kid dipped his fork with no pancake on it into the molasses and then licked it clean.

Cain rolled and lit a cigarette before he spoke. "Truth is, you could be right."

"About what?"

"Throwing in your hand."

"Killing myself?"

"Yes."

"You really think so?"

"I do."

Cain took a drag and the boy poked at his pancake.

"You got any reason to think it's gonna get better?"

"No, sir, I don't."

"Well?"

"No, I see what you're saying."

"And?"

The boy gnawed the inside of his cheek as he contemplated Cain's words. "Well, now that I know I can do it, I guess it's my call, ain't it?"

The old man sat back in his chair. He almost grinned. "A course now you're out of trucks."

"It don't have to be no truck."

Cain studied the boy and then snubbed out the cigarette butt in the ashtray. "There's something to be said about having nothing left to lose."

The boy grinned through his swollen lips.

"Nothing I can think of."

After they ate, the old man stood, gathered up his plate and that of the boy along with the flatware, and put it all in the sink.

Cain pulled a rag from his back pocket and coughed into it. "Think I ought to have a talk with Eugene?"

"What do you mean?"

"Tell him to lighten up on you some?"

"That's not a good idea, Mr. Cain."

"Why not?"

"He's trouble with a capital *T*."

"You don't think he'd talk to me?"

"He might, but he won't take no talking to."

"From me, you mean?"

"From nobody."

The boy's expression was one of great concern as he looked up at the old man.

"He was a convict, Mr. Cain—I mean, Harley. I don't think he cares much if he goes back or not. He'd kill you if you messed with him. I mean seriously *kill* you."

The old man turned and walked out onto the porch as he contemplated some private thought he did not share with the boy. He carried a cup of coffee with him and set the cup on the porch railing. He leaned against the post at the top of the steps and gazed out upon the parched wasteland.

Nothing he tried to raise grew here. The garden his wife had tended year after year promised the possibility of corn, collard greens, and okra, but delivered nothing. The trellises and carefully shaped rows, still visible on the east side of the barn, stood as stark reminders of a crop and a marriage, neither of which had ever held any hope of survival.

He looked out at the barn and beyond across the poor section of land. Two horses. A handful of cattle, their ribs showing and their heads down. The house itself, more a part of the land than the man, stood handmade with adobe mud and used lumber. A testimony to his broken dreams.

The day his wife had packed up two cardboard boxes and a worn suitcase and left, she did so with an infant son and a traveling salesman bound for California. She wrote him twice. The first letter told him she was gone. The second requested his signature on the divorce papers from her lawyer. He never saw her or his son after that.

Harland Cain worked the land and wrung from its unwilling soil a modest living that tested his perseverance until that was all he knew. He sold calves and rode outside colts for thirty dollars a month until his knees gave out on him. On the seventh of every month a VA check arrived in his mailbox, a monetary apology from the government for the shrapnel he carried in his back from a World War I German hand grenade. The check covered his modest needs and living expenses. Everything else was a bonus, and he lived accordingly.

Twenty years earlier, Cain, half-drunk in a poker game, won a stack of penny Polaroid stock certificates he tucked away in a dresser drawer. The one thing in his life he had not worked for, and the only one that paid off. And he bought land—cheap West Texas dry ground no one else wanted—until he had amassed over fourteen thousand acres of sagebrush and desert with scarcely enough vegetation to keep his small cowherd alive.

He turned when the screen door opened and stayed that way as the boy stepped out onto the porch and watched the old man a long time before he spoke. "You okay?"

The old man nodded his head and then reached down for his coffee cup. He took a sip of the cold coffee and then slung the rest out onto the yard.

"Fine. Why?"

The boy shrugged and stood at the top of the steps, looking out at the horses.

"Them your horses?"

"Them and the cows."

"You reckon I could ride one of 'em?"

"I don't know—you ever rode a cow before?"

"You're funny, Harley. I meant a horse."

"I don't see why not. You ever rode a horse before?"

"Yessir. My real daddy was the cow boss for the Two Sixes up near Wheeler—I was horseback since I was three. I still remember everything he taught me, and he's a for-sure top-hand cowboy."

The old man looked at the boy and watched him standing there in his one-of-a-kind hat. He stared out past the boy at the vastness of the wretched land that was the landscape of his life.

"I used to cowboy some myself," Cain said.

His eyes looked out at the gauzy image of a life that had passed him by and slipped away without him ever knowing it.

He seemed to be gone, and then he was back. Dodger watched him as though the old man had passed through some sort of time portal.

"We need to figure out how to get you back home."

"If you can drop me off at Bobby's house, I can stay there tonight and go home in the morning."

"I thought you said you couldn't stay with Bobby."

"It's okay. They'll let me stay the night."

"You sure about that?"

"Yessir."

They drove in silence to Bufort. When they reached Bobby's house, Cain pulled up and stepped out of the pickup the same time the boy did. He dug into his pocket and pulled out three dollar bills and several coins. He extended his hand to the boy.

Cain turned away as he had a brief coughing fit. His eyes watered. He turned back to the boy. "Here, take this. Buy you and Bobby a pop."

The boy looked up at the old man. He stepped back, looked at the money, and then looked back up at the old man with an expression of uncertainty.

"That's a lot of money, Harley—why you giving me that?"

"I ain't giving it to you. It's a loan. You can pay me back when you get rich."

Dodger laughed. "When I get rich."

"It's a good idea to have a little pocket money."

The boy took the money, dropped the coins into the front pocket of his jeans, and straightened the three bills. He folded the dollar bills and slipped them into his shirt pocket and snapped the flap shut. He looked up at the old man.

"This is the most money I ever had at one time." He looked down at his boots. "Thanks, Harley."

Cain nodded, then climbed back into the truck. The three dollars eased his conscience some.

Dodger limped to the mailbox, stood near the street, and waved as the old man drove off. He waited until the pickup turned the corner and then hobbled off in the direction of Duane's Conoco with no idea what to do next.

CHAPTER FOUR

The sun traversed the Texas sky and settled behind the dark stitching of the distant mountains that outlined the fiery horizon. It dropped low and dissolved into a disappearing, red half-circle. Dodger checked his reflection and that of the sunset in the glass of the door before he opened it. When he pulled the heavy door to him, a bell rang, and the boy nodded at the man behind the counter of the store as he entered.

"How you doing, Dodger?"

"Hey, Leland."

"What can I do you for?"

The boy spoke over his shoulder on the way back to the coldbox. "I'm getting me a pop."

Dodger stood in front of the mist-covered glass doors, scanned the labels up and down the crowded shelves, and then slid one of the doors to the side. He reached in for a sixteen-ounce RC Cola. When he got to the cash register, he set the cold bottle down, smiled through his puffy lips, and pointed to the shelf behind Leland.

"Can I get me one a them Moon Pies too?"

Leland set the Moon Pie on the counter and tilted his head as he looked the boy over.

"Open that for you?"

Dodger nodded.

"That do it for you, then?"

"Yessir."

Leland punched the numbers up and pulled the handle on the side of the register. The cash drawer slid open, and Leland looked at the total in the display window.

"Fifty-three cents. Cash or charge?"

Dodger pulled out a handful of coins, picked out two quarters and three pennies, and then laid them on the counter.

"Cash."

"Whoa, Dodger—you just rob a bank?"

Dodger laughed.

The clerk took the coins and dropped them into the cash drawer. He then nodded toward Dodger's damaged face as he slid the drawer closed.

"What happened?"

Dodger blushed and looked down at his boots as he reached for the bottle and the Moon Pie. He headed for the door. He looked back at Leland and shook his head. "Some ol' boys jumped me."

Leland knew the boy was lying.

"You take care, Dodger."

"Thanks, Leland."

The boy walked slowly down through the shadows of the alley behind the hardware store, tipping the bottle back and eating the Moon Pie as he wandered aimlessly with no thought of going home. He dropped the empty bottle and the wrapper into a garbage can and then looked up at the sky with no daylight left in it. He found a corrugated box the size of a kitchen stove and curled up in it with his jacket pulled up around him to wait out the night.

Luanne Cooper raised herself up from the disarray of sheets on the bed upon which she had passed out earlier in the day. She sat on the edge of the mattress and reached across to the nightstand for a cigarette. She coughed, lit the cigarette, and looked toward the doorway leading into the small kitchen.

"Eugene, are you in there?"

She heard the radio in the background and raised her voice.

"Eugene, can you hear me?"

She stood slowly with her feet set wide apart and waited for the room to steady. Her bare legs carried bruises—some old, some new. When she was fully upright, her legs trembled and then steadied as her head cleared. She looked into the mirror above the bureau as she shuffled by and quickly turned her head away from the unflattering image reflected in its glass.

Eugene sat at the small chrome dinette table and looked up at her through bloodshot eyes as she stood in the doorway of the kitchen. He neither spoke nor acknowledged her presence beyond the turn of his head in her direction. She stood with the smoldering cigarette at her side and looked first out the window into the darkness and then casually around the room.

"Where's Dodger?"

Eugene nodded over his shoulder. "I guess he's spending the night with that colored boy."

"You didn't get into it again with him, did you?"

There was concern in her eyes, but her manner suggested the question was more out of curiosity than concern. Eugene took a long drink from the beer bottle he held and then stood and walked past her as he spoke. "He got mouthy with me again."

"Why can't you just leave him alone, Eugene?"

He ignored the question, but Luanne lacked the conviction for a confrontation. Eugene set the empty beer bottle down on the wooden arm of the old stuffed chair as he reached for the doorknob to leave. He shook his head in disgust. "I'll be back later. Put some clothes on."

When the door slammed shut, Luanne stuck her middle finger up in the direction he had just taken. She wanted to cry, but there were no tears left in her hard eyes. She sat down at the kitchen table and looked out across the room, relieved that he was gone. She saw past the dirty dishes piled high in the porcelain sink. She saw past the beer bottles piled on the counter and the one lying on the floor. She studied her nicotine-stained fingers, took the last drag off the cigarette that had burned down to a nub, and then turned it into the plate on the table as she exhaled into the stale air.

While her son curled himself into his thin jacket for warmth, Luanne Cooper stood before the open door of the refrigerator and cursed Eugene for drinking the last beer.

Eugene Cazares and Rolando Barone waited in the dimly lit parking lot at the rear of the Sundowner Lounge until past midnight. They drank beer, smoked, and waited. The back door opened, casting a soft yellow light onto the pavement, and an elderly patron staggered toward his pickup. Rolando nodded in the direction of the man. "There he is."

Eugene quietly opened the car door on his side and exited Rolando's vehicle at the same time Rolando slid out of the driver's side and called to the man. "Need some help there, partner?"

The man ignored the question, wobbled, and then braced himself with one hand against the side of his pickup as he dug into his pockets, searching for the keys.

Eugene carried a four-inch section of galvanized pipe wrapped in his big-knuckled fist. He rushed in behind the man before he could react and dealt him a crushing blow to the side of the head. The man slumped to the ground. His eyes rolled back and stared upward with no life left in them.

Rolando stood guard while Eugene held his fingers to the man's neck. He looked up at Rolando. "He's dead."

"Get his shit and let's go."

Eugene slipped the man's watch from his wrist, took the wallet from his pocket, and then stood with the man's keys in his hand as he fumbled with the lock on the pickup door.

He searched the glove box and under the seat. "There ain't nothin' in here."

Rolando turned his head but kept his eyes focused on the back door of the lounge. "Check behind the seat."

Eugene leaned in through the driver's side and tilted the seat back forward. The reflection of the streetlight illuminated the walnut stock and blue steel of a rifle and a box of .30-30 ammunition. Eugene lifted the rifle from behind the seat and grabbed the box of ammunition. "Let's get out of here."

Rolando positioned the body next to the open door of the pickup, laid the keys near the man's hand, and stood back to survey the scene. He looked across at Eugene. "They'll think he fell and hit his head."

Eugene removed the bills from the wallet and handed it back to Rolando. "Put this back in his pocket."

"How much was in it?"

"Twenty-three bucks—hurry up." He got in the car.

Rolando slid the wallet back into the man's pocket and looked around before he returned to his car and drove slowly to the side entrance of the parking lot. No other cars had passed, and not another person exited the bar. Rolando glanced at Eugene, who examined the rifle and checked the chamber before laying it in the back seat.

"What do think we'll get for the Winchester and the watch?"

Eugene shrugged and shook his head. "I don't know—maybe fifty for the Winchester and ten for the watch."

Rolando pounded the heel of his fist against the steering wheel. "He was supposed to be carrying a couple hundred bucks."

Rolando pulled the car out onto the street and into the darkness, unhurried and unconcerned, leaving behind the crumpled body of the intoxicated man and, across the vacant lot, a lone pair of eyes watching from the cover of an empty appliance box.

Dodger hunkered against the back of the box and buried his face in his hands. When he closed his eyes, all he could see was the fierce blow from Eugene's huge fist and the limp body of the man slump to the pavement.

At the same instant the boy pushed out the flaps on the

box to go check on the man, the back door of the lounge swung open, casting a light onto the parking lot as three people staggered out laughing and talking loudly. A woman screamed at the sight of the man afloat in a black pool of his own blood. One man rushed back inside the bar.

Within minutes, the patrons from the bar crowded around the pickup. The flashing lights of an ambulance and a police cruiser turned the scene into a brightly lit spectacle that sent the boy retreating to the shadows of his box. He crowded as deeply into the corrugated shelter as the small space allowed and watched the rotating red beacon from the police cruiser travel across the dirt-stained leg of his jeans as the light circled in the darkness and back again in a mesmerizing rhythm upon which he fixated, waiting for it all to go away.

Under the parking lot lights, Dodger had recognized Rolando's familiar brown-and-tan–colored sedan and he recognized Rolando. However, the sickening image of Eugene rubbing the scarred knuckles of his fist as he stood over the body of the dead man was a horrifying reminder of the confrontation he knew lay before him. He tucked his head between his arms, closed his eyes, and attempted to shut out the sounds coming from the parking lot.

The boy did not remember sleeping. He awoke and opened his eyes. He shivered and looked out onto the vacant parking lot. The Sundowner Lounge stood dark and solitary, and the night was void of all life save the bare-ribbed dogs that slunk among the garbage cans.

Dodger trembled, crawled from the box, and stood in the predawn cold with his hands in his pockets.

CHAPTER FIVE

Dodger walked the streets the rest of the night and waited for daylight, his shoulders hunched and his thin jacket zipped to the top to try to ward off the chill. He walked in the shadows and avoided the main street, and he walked in the opposite direction of the police station. When the sky changed from black to gray, he walked to Duane's Conoco and glanced through the glass before he entered. The bell on the door jingled, and the clerk looked up from his girlie magazine. He nodded.

"Hey, Dodger."

"Hey, Mickey."

"You're up early."

"I spent the night at Bobby's, but my momma wants me home early."

"She got chores for you today?"

"No, she just wants me to go with her to maybe get me some new boots," he lied.

Mickey looked down casually at the boy's boots. "You looking to get you some nice lizard ones this time?"

Dodger laughed.

"No, I reckon we'll stick with these Mexican boots if they got any brown ones my size."

Dodger walked back to the cooler, fetched a sixteen-ounce RC, and walked back to the counter. He set the bottle next to the register. He pointed his chin at the shelf behind Mickey.

"Can I get me one of them Slim Jims?"

"Leland said you got in a fight."

"I got jumped."

"I hope you give him a whuppin'."

Dodger laughed but had to check the smile because of the scabbed-over crack in his bottom lip. He laid a dollar bill on the counter and shrugged. "I gotta get going—my momma's waiting on me."

Mickey opened the cash drawer without ringing up the sale, slipped the dollar bill in his pocket, and handed Dodger the change. He did not look up from the magazine when the boy opened the door to leave.

"See ya, Mickey."

"See ya, Dodger."

When the boy turned the corner, the first hint of sunlight brightened up one side of the street and he could see that his house was dark inside. He prayed Eugene would not be there. He stood on the porch a long time holding the bottle in one hand, his other hand on the doorknob. He turned the knob slowly, and the door opened with a creak and a scraping sound where it dragged across the buckled linoleum. He crept into the kitchen. The house reeked of stale smoke and old beer bottles. He quietly set the bottle and the Slim Jim on the table among the dirty dishes and hung his jacket on the back of one of the chrome chairs.

He tiptoed quietly down the narrow hallway and looked in through the open door of his mother's bedroom. With the shades drawn, his eyes adjusted slowly to the darkness. He could see she was alone. Her bare leg hung with the dingy sheet twisted around it, and a foul-smelling ashtray full of burned-out cigarette butts stood on the nightstand near the bed. The room smelled of stale smoke, like the rest of the house, and her clothes lay on the floor where she had dropped them two days earlier.

Luanne mumbled in her sleep, a slumber that appeared more like a coma, and she rolled over, facing the boy. The single button holding her shirt was misaligned and exposed her bare breast and the bite marks on her neck, a reminder of Eugene's jailhouse version of passion that kept the boy up through those nights when they were not fighting.

He reached down to the pile at the foot of the bed, pulled a sheet up over his mother, and left the room to the heavy breathing sounds of her fitful sleep.

Dodger ate the Slim Jim, finished the cola, and went to his room. The door, which Eugene had kicked off the hinges months ago, was missing. From the hallway the boy could see that someone had torn his room apart, apparently looking for something. He moved the clothes and his baseball glove from the bed and lay down on the covers with his fingers laced behind his head and his eyes rimmed red and tearing up.

He closed his eyes, his chest rose and fell, and he lay there in the dark. He saw the lights of the pickup swerve across the highway. He saw the bridge abutment rushing at him. He saw everything grow dark and, for that moment, he was free. He opened his eyes and stared at the ceiling, the familiar cracks and stains, the cheap light fixture.

He closed his eyes again and this time he walked through a valley of tall grass, beside a cool river, down a path in the warm sunlight. A band of wild horses lifted their heads and watched him, and when he walked he did so with no limp and no sign of the cripple he knew himself to be. He stopped, breathed in slowly and deeply. He slept and dreamed himself a long way away from where he was.

He awoke when he heard the front door slam hard against the wall, and he heard Eugene stagger in, drunk as usual. He sat upright in his bed when Eugene's voice boomed from the kitchen.

"Luanne! Get out here!"

He slurred his words and his tone was hateful and dangerous. Dodger recognized the drunken manner and the abusive mood, and he swung his legs off the bed and sat there waiting.

"Luanne!"

"I'm coming."

Dodger heard his mother's bed creak and groan. He heard Eugene slam himself down in one of the kitchen chairs. He heard his mother's bare feet padding across the hall. He heard his mother's voice.

"Eugene, it's almost nine in the morning—where have you been all night?"

A chair slid across the linoleum and an awful slapping sound followed it. Dodger heard his mother stumble and fall and, when he heard her pleading and crying, rose to his feet and rushed to the kitchen. She stood holding her face. Eugene sat down, his eyes heavy, his head unsteady. He looked over at the boy who stood glaring at him from the doorway.

"What are you doing here?"

The boy's expression grew dark, his eyes filled with hatred. "You hit my momma again, I'm gonna kill you."

Eugene rocked back and forth in his chair. He began to rise. Luanne shouted at the boy, "Now listen here, you show some respect!"

Dodger looked at his mother and back at Eugene.

Eugene slumped back into his chair, too drunk to react.

Luanne crossed the room, took the boy by the arm, and led him into the hallway. She leaned against the wall and Dodger stood staring down at the torn carpet.

"Honey, I'm sorry. Look, you know how he gets when he's been drinking. I just didn't want him to hurt you."

"Yeah, well what about you? He treats you like shit, and you just take it."

Luanne tucked a wisp of hair back behind her ear and held up her chin as though she still had some remnants of self-respect about her. Then she broke, her dignity and her pride long past her ability to retrieve either. She covered her face with her hands and shook her head. She didn't need the boy to remind her of what she had become, and she had neither the will nor the resolve to defend herself.

Dodger watched her. She had driven his father off, taken up with one after another of an assortment of slobbering drunks, and then settled on the worst of them. He looked at her with disgust and pity and then put his arm across her shoulder.

"It's okay," he said. "It's not your fault."

And then he cried when she looked up at him, broken and beyond repair.

"You're a good boy, Dodger. I don't deserve you."

She held him close, and he felt her tears on his arm. For that moment he was again a child in the protective embrace of its mother. He held his eyes closed tightly and knew he would never be this child again.

"You were a beautiful gift when you was born," she said. "You're the only thing I ever loved, and I never could do right by you."

Dodger pushed her away gently. "You did the best you could."

She looked at him. Her eyes had no hope left in them. She shook her head almost imperceptibly as her soft voice cracked when she spoke.

"Things will be different. You'll see. We're gonna get out of this. Get us a nice little place up in Norman soon as I get back to work. I promise."

She smiled and the smile made her words a lie, and the boy dropped his hands from her shoulders as he smiled a lie back at her.

"Everything will be perfect when we get to Norman."

He hugged her, aching to feel like her child again, but it was a stranger that hugged him back.

He followed her into the kitchen where Eugene sat almost comatose staring across the room. She fetched her purse and handed Dodger a one-dollar bill.

"Will you run down to Duane's and pick your momma up a pack of Luckies?"

Dodger left without saying good-bye. Ten minutes after he'd left, Eugene stood and motioned Luanne toward the kitchen window.

"Go see who just drove up."

Luanne walked across the kitchen and peered just past the curtain to look out to the street. “It’s the po-lice.”

Eugene bent low, rushed out of the room, and called back from the hallway. “Tell them I ain’t here.”

Luanne buttoned her shirt and waited for the knock on the door. She stood half-concealed behind the door when she opened it.

“Yes?”

“Is this the residence of Eugene Cazares?”

“Yes, it is.”

“Is he in?”

“No, he ain’t here right now. Can I help you?”

“When he comes back, will you tell him we recovered his stolen pickup?”

“Is it okay?”

The officer shook his head. “What’s left of it is in Lamont’s salvage yard. It was a total loss from the wreck and the fire.”

“Where did they find it?”

“About thirty miles south of here . . . almost to the border.”

“Did they catch the ones that took it?”

“No, ma’am. No witnesses, no fingerprints, and no clues. They hit a bridge, and the truck caught on fire. Ain’t nothing left of it.”

“Okay, thanks. I’ll tell him when he comes home.”

Dodger, on his way back home from Duane’s, watched from the corner until the police cruiser pulled away. His heart pounded, and he secretly prayed that Eugene was in the back seat.

He made short work of the trip and, when he returned to the house, his mother met him at the door and rushed him inside.

Dodger handed her the cigarettes and her change.

“Why was the cops here?”

“They found Eugene’s truck.”

“Where was it at?”

“South, almost to Mexico.”

“Did they catch who took it?”

"No—no they didn't. It was wrecked and burnt up. They didn't find nothing."

"Was Eugene mad?"

"I didn't tell him yet."

Luanne padded down the hall and looked in at Eugene, passed out on their bed, fully clothed and snoring loudly. She returned to the kitchen, sat in one of the chrome chairs, placed her elbows on the table, buried her face in her hands, and began to sob. Dodger stood beside her and gently placed one hand on her shoulder, his mind a million miles away.

CHAPTER SIX

Eugene awoke from his drunken stupor just before dark, foul-tempered and predictably combative. He swung his booted feet from the bed and sat there holding his head, fighting the urge to vomit. He took a deep breath and stood.

Luanne heard him stirring and braced herself. She waited for him to come out from the bedroom, watching the hallway from the torn sofa with a beer in one hand and a cigarette in the other, a movie fan magazine folded beside her. She looked up when he entered the room.

Dodger sat outside on the front step. The evening sun lingered at the edge of the earth. He stared down at his scuffed boots with the run-over heels.

He imagined himself in the desert riding, riding, riding. The world behind him dwindling away in the dust. He saw himself alone, and then an old man appeared on one side. The farther he rode, the more ghostly the old man became until he faded from the dream altogether and he was alone again.

It was always the same. Still the desert drew him to it.

When he heard his mother's voice inside the house, he sat up straight and waited.

"They found your truck," he heard her say to Eugene.

The boy held his breath and listened.

"Where's it at?"

"It's at Lamont's—it's totaled."

"So now I don't have no truck?"

"No . . . it burned up."

"Do they know who stole it?"

"No, they said they didn't even have a clue."

"Now how am I supposed to look for work?"

Luanne regarded the question as a genuine interest in her opinion.

"Maybe Rolando could drive you," she said, hoping to engage him in any exchange that resembled a civil conversation.

Eugene's expression was hateful and cold. Luanne regretted responding at all.

"You stupid . . ."

Eugene slapped her hard and she fell from the chair, spilling her beer and gashing her leg on the bottom edge of the table as she toppled to the floor.

"He's got more to do than taxi me around every day."

Luanne pressed her hand to her bleeding leg and pushed herself up on one elbow. She looked up at Eugene and then over at the front door as it swung open. The boy stood glaring at Eugene.

"Leave her alone."

Eugene swung his fist. It caught the boy on the jaw, sending a tooth flying and slamming the boy against the wall bleeding from his nose and mouth.

"Shut your gimpy ass up."

Luanne stood and shuffled to the boy's side. She reached up for the dishrag draped over the sink. She pressed it to his bleeding lips and looked back at Eugene, who stood before the refrigerator looking for a beer.

"Look what you did. His tooth is gone. You didn't have to hit him so hard."

Then she looked back down at the boy.

"Can you spend the night with Bobby? I don't want you here when he's like this."

The boy gave her a blank look and nodded. He rose to his feet, limped to the door, opened it, and then looked back at Eugene. Just before he ran for the street, he shouted at Eugene, "Fuck you!"

He stopped running and looked back at the house when he got to the corner. The door stood closed, the house was quiet with a soft light showing from the kitchen window, and, from all outside appearances, the place was as docile and normal as any on the block.

Dodger stood on the sidewalk looking in at Bobby's house. Through the window, he could see the family sitting at the table. He saw their bowed heads, and he knew Bobby's father was saying grace over a modest meal set upon a sparse table and served on chipped and mismatched dishes—a poor man's meal that appeared to the boy to be nothing short of a royal feast. There was no empty chair at the table. The boy knew not to impose himself. He turned and began to walk with no plan at all for what he would do next.

He ran his tongue over the vacant spot where there had recently been a tooth. He stopped at the first car he came to and bent over to look in the side mirror. His jaw was bruised and swollen, his lip puffy and split. When he smiled, the dark gap of the missing tooth made him appear as someone he no longer recognized.

He walked a long time before he found himself at the phone booth on the corner near the Conoco. Leland stood inside the station and tipped his cowboy hat at the car leaving the island. The slender hand of a young girl waved back at him through the open window as she bumped across the driveway and out into the traffic lane. She flashed her lights, honked, and was off.

Dodger turned his back to Leland and reached into his pocket. He picked out a dime and dropped it into the slot. He waited for a dial tone. He listened to the tone and then hung up. The dial tone stopped, he heard a click, and then he heard the dime make its way down the chute into the coin return.

He stood there several minutes with the dime clenched in his fist. He leaned back against the glass wall of the booth and imagined another night in the appliance box. He dropped the dime in the coin slot, waited for the dial tone, and then dialed . . . 9 . . . 7 . . . 8 . . . 0 and waited.

"Yeah?" the voice said.

"Harley, it's me—Dodger."

"Hey, Dodger."

"Hey, Harley."

There was a long silence, and finally the old man spoke.

"Did you steal another truck?"

Dodger laughed. "No . . . I was wondering if I could maybe sleep on your porch tonight."

A long pause. "I wasn't counting on any company."

"Okay. That's all right. Bobby's waiting on me anyhow."

"Hold on a second." A long pause. "Where you at?"

"I'm at the Conoco in the phone booth."

"It'll take me about forty-five minutes to get there. Are you okay?"

"Yessir . . . I'm fine. Thanks, Harley."

"Go inside and get something to eat. Tell Duane, or whoever's there, I'll pay them when I get there."

"It's Leland—you sure?"

"Yeah, yeah. I'm sure."

"Okay, then. Thanks, Harley."

He hung up the phone, walked to the store, and listened for the familiar bell when he opened the door. Leland stepped out from the men's room drying his hands on a red mechanic's rag. They met near the coldbox.

"I thought that looked like you out there, Dodger."

"Hey, Leland."

Leland stopped drying his hands, and his expression became one of serious concern. "What the heck happened?"

Dodger shook his head. "Can I get me something to eat and wait 'til Mr. Cain gets here in a little bit to pay you?"

Leland nodded in the direction of the hotdog cooker on

the side counter. "Sure, I just put on some fresh dogs this morning. Help yourself."

Leland followed the boy back and watched as Dodger pulled a bun out of the warming drawer and used the tongs to slide a hotdog off the chrome spike that held it. He squeezed on mustard from a yellow bottle and ketchup from a red one. He spooned on a layer of relish and then wrapped the dripping affair in a square of waxed paper and made his way to the cooler. Leland followed him.

"Did Eugene do that to you?"

The boy ignored the question, but his expression revealed the answer.

"That ain't right, Dodger . . . someone needs to call the cops on that sumbitch—excuse my French."

Dodger smiled a half smile and limped in the direction of the register. "It was my own fault. I back talked him and shouldn't ought to have, I guess."

Leland offered Dodger one of the two folding chairs set up behind the counter. "Have a seat. I'll ring up your food when Mr. Cain gets here."

Dodger set his cola on the shelf behind him, took a seat, and unwrapped the hotdog. Leland watched the boy devour the hotdog and wash it down with a long pull from the bottle.

"I guess you like them hotdogs, huh, Dodger?"

Dodger grinned and nodded. "I'm still runnin' on that Slim Jim from this morning."

"Go ahead, get yourself another one."

"I can't. Mr. Cain's paying, and I don't want to make a hog out of myself."

"Go on—it's on the house. They can only be out there eight hours, then I have to throw them out."

"How long they been there?"

Leland laughed. "Some of them's been there since yesterday . . . they'll probably kill you anyway."

Dodger finished a second hotdog. He sat while Leland ran the register and wrote up replacement inventory orders in between customers.

"How do you like working here, Leland?"

"Hey, it's a job. I was out of work almost six months after I blew out my knee framing houses. I'm glad to have the work. Duane's as good a boss as I ever had."

"Do you reckon I could get a job here?"

"I don't think Duane's looking for any help right now. He's got me and Mickey, and we ain't going nowhere."

"I could clean up around here and do the stuff y'all don't have time to do."

"You'd have to talk to Duane, Dodger. I know you'd be good help . . . I just don't think he's looking for nobody right now."

They sat and exchanged small talk. The boy looked around the place and imagined himself working there. The shelves needed facing and restocking. The floor needed a good mopping, and he would keep the magazines all in order and straight after every customer came in, looked at them, and put them back in the wrong spot. There was a lot a boy with no experience could do.

Three quarters of an hour later, the door opened and the bell jingled. Harland Cain looked over at Dodger and Leland.

"You boys sitting there getting drunk, are ya?"

Leland and Dodger both laughed. Leland spoke first. "We tried Mr. Cain. This pop don't have much kick, though."

Cain laughed.

"How much I owe you, Leland?"

"Twenty-five cents and call it good."

"You sure?"

"Yessir—that'll cover it."

Dodger grinned. "I had me one good hotdog and one that'll probably kill me before the night's through."

On the way out the door, Dodger stopped and looked back at Leland.

"Thanks, Leland. See ya."

"See ya, Dodger. See ya, Mr. Cain."

Cain drove through town, out onto the highway, and deep into the darkness of the barren country before he spoke.

"Did Eugene do that to you?"

Dodger nodded but did not elaborate.

Cain stared at the white lines coming at him. He squeezed the steering wheel, gritting his teeth at the thought of the beating the boy had taken and the helplessness he felt for not being able to deal with Eugene man-to-man.

They drove the rest of the way in silence.

CHAPTER SEVEN

Early the next morning, Cain swung the screen door open to the porch and was surprised to see the boy up and dressed, sitting on the front step. "Mornin'," he said.

Dodger turned and stood. "It sure is pretty out here, Harley."

"It does grow on a man, I suppose."

He coughed deeply, turned, and spat from the porch. Dodger looked at the old man with great concern and waited for the coughing to subside.

"I watched the sun come up."

Cain cleared his throat and spat again. "Couldn't sleep?"

"I slept good. I guess I was just anxious to see everything in the daylight is all."

"So what do you think?"

Cain daubed his watering eyes with his handkerchief.

Dodger smiled. All Cain could look at was the gap the missing tooth had occupied.

"I was thinking you and me should saddle up them horses of yours and take a long ride out there sometime." He pointed generally to the wide expanse of bleak land leading up to a dark blue stretch of mountains that defined the horizon to the east.

The old man leaned up against the post of the porch, his eyes taking in the broad landscape. He took the last draw off the hand-rolled cigarette and flipped the butt out onto the gravel of the yard. He nodded approvingly and smiled.

"We can do that. I got some things I can show you out there."

"When can we go?"

"When do you have to be back home?"

Dodger's expression darkened. He dropped his gaze to the deck boards of the porch. "I don't reckon I got a time to be back."

"Why's that?"

"I back talked Eugene. He knocked my momma down, and then he hit me and did this." Dodger pointed to the gap in his teeth. "And he called me a gimp."

"You want me to see if I have an extra bullet for that pistol of mine?"

Dodger laughed. "No, but if you could let me have a bottle of whiskey and the keys to your pickup, I promise I'd do a better job of it this time."

The old man and the kid both laughed.

"All right, look," Cain said. "We'll leave in the morning. There ain't nothing better than watching the sun come up ahorseback. We'll ride one day out and one day back. I know a place we can pitch our bedrolls."

"Do you have an extra gun so maybe we could shoot some stuff while we're out there?"

Cain smiled. "I have a couple of .44-40 rigs we can strap on and make us look like sure-enough cowboys."

Cain wasn't sure if he was beginning to take a liking to the kid or if it was the distraction of his presence that he found a welcome reprieve from the dark thoughts that stalked him.

Dodger grinned, and Cain nodded toward the opening in the boy's teeth. "The more I look at that gap in your teeth, the better I'm thinking it makes you look. It gives you kind of a manly appearance."

Dodger grinned again and stuck his tongue through the gap. "You mean like this?"

Cain shook his head. "That ain't exactly what I had in mind."

They both laughed. Dodger looked up at the old man and wondered what it was about him that made conversation so easy.

The next morning, the old man and the boy stood in the barn under the light of the bare bulb that hung from a wire. The bulb swayed slowly in the cool draft that flowed from one open end of the breezeway to the other.

In that void between night and day, the scent of the desert hung over the land like it had since the beginning of time.

The shadows of the horses swung back and forth on the wall behind them, moving in time with the hanging light bulb blown by the intermittent breeze. The barn air, heavy with the sweet-smelling scent of dust and horse and saddle leather, stirred within the boy some ancient calling he'd inherited from his father or his father's father before him. It seemed to transport him back to a time to which he felt more suited.

Dodger watched the old man brush the back and underside of his horse, and he did the same with his. When the old man picked up first one hoof, then another, and cleaned out the hollows between the frog and the sole, he took the bent flathead screwdriver the old man had given him and did likewise.

The horse stood calm under his touch, but when he leaned in against its shoulder, he could feel the power and the strength that resided beneath a hide so sensitive, it could feel the weight of a fly alight upon it. He spoke into the horse's ribs where his head rested as he held a front foot aloft and picked at it with the screwdriver.

"You reckon a horse does what we want because we make him, or 'cause he wants to?"

Cain coughed and dropped the rear foot of the horse, stood, and stretched his back and then slipped the screwdriver into his back pocket. "Generally, a broke horse does what we want because we give him choices and point him at the one we want him to make."

"I don't get it."

Cain thought for moment. "Well, it's like this. Say I want this horse to turn to the left. I'll lay the reins up alongside the right side of his neck and put some pressure against his right side with my knee. It's a horse's nature to move away from pressure, so when he does, he's going to the left, like I wanted, and I let up on the pressure. His reward is the pressure goes away, and mine is he turned to the left."

Cain bent over, picked up the saddle blanket, and laid it across the back of the horse. He smoothed out the wrinkles and continued.

"The whole while we're thinking we taught that horse to turn, the truth is he just did what he's known to do since horses ever came to be—that's to move away from pressure."

Dodger dropped his horse's foot, stood, and adjusted his hat. "There ain't nothin' about horses my daddy don't know."

"He have a way about him when it comes to horses, does he?"

"Yessir, he does. He was a top hand on the Two Sixes and some other big outfits up north. They pay him good money to cowboss on 'em."

"You ever hear from him?"

"I do." Dodger took some pause at that one. "At least I used to. He's been pretty busy lately though, I guess."

"So, it's been a while?"

Dodger nodded and smiled a fake smile. "I guess it has."

The boy stood near his horse and looked over at the old man. "All I've ever known is cowboy horses. My daddy rode 'em hard. It always looked like they did what he wanted 'cause he made 'em do it."

"Most horses, at least around here, are made like that," Cain said.

Dodger patted his horse on the rump. "Ever have any problems with this one being sound?"

"No, not really. Why?"

"Feels like he's got a little bow to that tendon on the off-front."

Cain appreciated the boy's astute observation. "That's been like that since he was a colt. He'll walk this one down every day of the week."

The boy stood at the horse's side with the saddle blankets ready to swing up. He looked across the back of the horse at

Cain and smiled his new gap-toothed smile. "I like him a lot."

Cain did not respond, but the boy was beginning to grow on him, and he wasn't sure how he felt about that. Nothing about the old man's plans had changed, and the last thing he wanted was another complication to consider.

Cain bent over to pick up his saddle, but then he let it drop and stood up straight with his arm at the small of his arched back as he grimaced.

The boy watched as Cain let the cramp run its course. "Can I get that for you, Harley?"

"I don't need any help saddling my own damn horse."

Dodger backed off and slowed down getting his rig set and tightened so as not to offend the old man further.

They got the horses saddled and bridled, tied on the bulging saddlebags, and laced their bedrolls over them.

Cain pointed at a row of canteens hanging on wall pegs across the breezeway. "Fill two of them up and hang one on each saddle."

The boy filled the canteens from a hose in front of the barn and hung them, first one on the saddle horn of Cain's horse and the second on his own. Cain stepped out of the small room with the padlocked door, carrying two pistol belts. He handed one to the boy and hung the other over his own saddle horn. He stepped back into the room and came back with a box of .44-40 ammunition. He opened the box and set it down on the small table near the wall. "Put six rounds in your pistol and fill the loops on the belt. When you get done, make sure the keeper is over the hammer so you don't lose your gun."

The moon had set low in the sky by the time they rode out across the gravel yard and up across the blacktop highway near the bridge that bore the scars of the wreckage that seemed to have happened a lifetime ago. There was no sound save the rhythmic footfalls of the horses, the cadence of their breathing, and the creaking of the saddles. Dodger buttoned up his jacket and looked up at the black sky alive with stars. The air smelled sweet and fresh, and the weight of the pistol belt promised the power he wanted to feel when he pulled the trigger for the first time.

They rode south without speaking. When Dodger turned to see how far they had come, everything behind them appeared as everything before them. For the first time in his life, he felt free. He looked over at Cain in the darkness. The old cowboy sat easy in the saddle and, to the boy, appeared younger and stronger, as though this was the world to which he'd been born.

They rode the sun up. It brought with it the heat of the day, and the pace of the horses slowed accordingly. The dark silhouette of the mountains ran red and lit the horizon up with fire as the sun crept up from the dark side of the earth. The morning sky, moments earlier black and hollow, flared up in a spectacle of turquoise, aquamarine, and all shades of blue and gray streaked with a thin line, deep crimson in color.

In the distance to the west stood another band of mountains, and before them lay nothing but barren desert and, beyond that, Mexico.

As the sun lifted, Dodger's thoughts of cigarette butts, beer bottles, and back alleys lifted with it. He could not imagine himself anywhere but where he was.

CHAPTER EIGHT

Out on the flatlands rode a pair of horsemen, their presence as transitory and insignificant as anything that had crossed that infinite wasteland since the beginning of time. A low-lying trail of dust followed them as they rode—two shimmering images distorted by the rising heat of the desert floor, fading to the south until the men, their horses, and everything about them merged into the gauzy skyline.

Overhead, a doublet of harrier hawks rode their outstretched wings upon a rising thermal column until they appeared high above the riders. Dodger watched them a long time. When they began to disappear from sight, he wished he were with them. "See them hawks, Harley?"

Cain held his hat with one hand and tilted his head back. "I don't see them."

"They're up there. Or, they were."

Cain dropped his free hand to his side. "Where do you suppose they went?" the old man asked.

The boy looked up and then looked at the old man and shook his head. "I reckon they just went higher."

"I expect you're right."

The boy's eyes took on a contemplative look. "You think they could just keep on going?"

"You mean getting higher?"

"Uh-huh . . . just higher and higher without stopping."

The old man shrugged. "I think the spirit of the hawk can go on. The body of the hawk, like that of man, is subject to the laws of physics."

"What's *physics*?"

"The physical nature of things. Touch a hot horseshoe, you get burned. Things that you know from experience never change, no matter how much you wish them to."

"Like my foot, you mean?"

"Yep. Just like your foot. Until you do something about it, it's going to cause you to limp. It's not good or bad, it just is."

"I know what you mean, Harley. For a long time I would wake up each morning after I dreamed it better—it never got better."

"Most things are like that."

The boy rode a long time without responding. Then he looked over at Cain and Cain looked back at him. Dodger smiled a half smile with the missing tooth now a dark gap that commanded the attention of the looker.

"I guess I know what you mean. Nothin' is simple anymore, is it?"

Cain shook his head. "Don't seem to be. But then again, I ain't sure it ever was."

They rode up game birds and watched rabbits and squirrels scurry from cactus to sagebrush and back again. A coyote slunk off into the shadows, and a lizard looked out from the hollow eye socket of a cow skull and watched them pass by.

"There's a lot more going on out here than you can see from the road, ain't there, Harley?"

"That's the thing about this country . . . it's like some people—you got to get to know them to like them."

"You been here a long time, Harley?"

"It don't seem like it, but yeah . . . I been here a long time."

• •

After a while, they stopped to water the horses where a spring ran and green grass grew between a small stand of stunted trees. A scattering of small yellow flowers blossomed in the sunlight and grew down to the water's edge. They dismounted in the shade, sideline hobbled the horses, and let them graze while they sat.

Dodger took off his hat, laced his fingers behind his head, and lay back in the grass. Overhead, blackbirds massed into a choreographed sheet that twisted and folded as it swept across the sky and then turned off and vanished.

The boy appeared to be deep in thought. He finally spoke without turning his head to look at the old man. "Remember that day you told me you set out to kill yourself the same night I did? Would you still do it if you had it to do over?"

The old man looked at the boy. He thought about it a long time before he answered.

"It wasn't something I decided to do for no reason."

"But would you?"

Cain was slow to answer. "For me, it was the right thing to do, given my circumstances."

Dodger sat up, wrapped his arms around his knees, and leaned his chin on his arms. "What about now?"

"Some things are a little more complicated right now."

"Do you mean me?"

"Yeah, that's part of it."

Dodger stared off across the desert. "Same here. I don't know why for sure, but I feel like there might be some hope for me."

"You don't want to kill yourself?"

"No, sir. Not now."

Cain felt himself push back from the conversation. Nothing had changed for him, and there was nothing he had to look forward to that gave him the hope he saw igniting in the boy. He rolled a cigarette and sat with his back to a thick willow. He took a long drag and let the smoke out slowly before he changed the subject.

"Your momma's boyfriend ever say anything to you about that pickup of his?"

"Not to me, but to my momma. He was mad when she told him it was totaled and all burned out."

"So he never figured you took it?"

"Nope. That was a good plan you had, Harley."

The boy was silent then. Cain watched his expression change, and he waited for the boy to decide whether or not he wanted to share whatever it was that was on his mind. The boy leaned up on one elbow and stared off toward Mexico.

"That truck might still be the end of me."

"How so?"

"Well, now Eugene's got no way to get to work, and he'll take that out on me and my momma. He's crazy to kill me."

"He may beat on you some, but I ain't sure he'd kill you."

"Yes, he would, Harley. He would for sure."

"What makes you think that?"

"I just know, that's all."

There was a long pause, and Cain took a deep breath before he spoke. "Eugene's a lot of things, but I don't think a killer's one of them."

Cain could see by the concern on the boy's face that his fear ran much deeper than another beating.

"You got any family around you can stay with?"

"No, sir, I ain't. My real daddy's family is somewhere up in Oklahoma, but I never hear from any of them."

"And your daddy?"

"He'd take me with him if he could, but he can't."

"Can you get ahold of him?"

The boy shook his head. "No, not really."

"How long's it been since you heard from him?"

Dodger agonized over his answer. "I guess I was eleven last time."

"How about on your momma's side?"

Dodger looked at the old cowboy, and this time his eyes were rimmed in red.

"They done wrote me and her off a long time ago. I don't care. I'm through with all of them too."

Cain raised his eyebrows and held his cigarette midway to another drag.

"Why would you be done with your family?"

"They ain't really my family." He stared off into the desert. "I heard my grandma tell my momma I was trouble, just like my daddy."

"I thought you said your daddy was a good man."

"That was her talking."

The old cowboy looked away. He could not respond. The cigarette smoldered between his fingers, and he finally flicked the butt into the sand. He looked over at the boy and slapped him on the boot. "The hell with all of them. We came out here to have us some fun. Is your gun loaded?"

Dodger grinned. "Yeah, it's loaded."

They both stood. Cain walked off twenty feet to a green sapling growing twisted and bent to the ground. He hammered in three pennies with the butt of his pistol, returned to where the boy stood, and scratched a line in the dirt with his boot heel.

"We'll take turns. First one to hit two pennies wins—loser cooks supper."

Dodger tilted his head and fixed his eyes on the targets. "Can you see that far, Harley?"

"Don't worry about me. Just remember I like my Vienna sausages well-done."

Dodger stood at the line. "Me first?"

"Hell no, not you first." Cain withdrew a silver dollar from his pocket and nodded at the boy. "Call it."

When the coin reached its apex, Dodger yelled "Heads."

The coin landed in a burst of dust. When the dust cleared, Harley bent down over the coin without touching it.

"Heads it is."

Dodger stepped to the line, drew his pistol from its holster, and ratchetted back the hammer. He settled the front blade sight on the center penny and lined it up with the rear sight. He took a deep breath, released half of it and squeezed the trigger. The .44-40 bucked in his hand and fire exploded from the barrel, followed by a high-pitched pinging sound as the penny whistled off into the air.

Cain approached the line. With the deadly air of a gunfighter, he drew and fired in one quick motion and sent a penny spinning off into the heat.

Dodger smiled at him. The old cowboy stepped back as he let the pistol drop smoothly back into the holster.

"*Uno mas*," he said.

Dodger stepped up to the line, took the pistol in his left hand this time, and squeezed the trigger. The bullet slapped into the wood of the sapling and nicked a small circle out of the edge of the penny, but the penny stayed in place. Dodger smiled at Cain. "You gonna give me that one?"

Cain fired from where he stood and the penny disappeared. Without looking at the boy, he replied, "Life ain't about what they give you—it's about what you earn."

They ate and sat in the shade and talked a long time. Then Cain tipped his head to the south and they caught up the horses and rode out. The sun bore down upon them from the west, and they came to a highway that faded in both directions into a horizon interrupted only by the mountains that resided there.

"Where does that go?" Dodger asked.

"A little border town called Los Caminos. It ain't no place for a couple of gringos, especially an old man and a kid."

"You reckon we could end up in old Mexico and not know it?"

"I suppose, but the place I got in mind is still in Texas, or at least it was last time I was there."

"When was that?"

"About eighteen years ago."

Dodger laughed.

"Seriously?"

Cain nodded. "The desert don't change much in eighteen years. A couple more miles and we'll be there. See them trees way off yonder? That's it."

CHAPTER NINE

They rode into camp with two hours of daylight left, unsaddled the horses, and hobbled them to graze. On one side, a creek ran through the trees and divided the oasis north to south where it dumped into a river that marked the southern US boundary.

"How far do you reckon we are from Mexico?"

Cain tipped his head. He cleared his throat and broke out in a coughing fit before he could answer.

"That cough don't sound too good, Harley."

Cain waved it off. "That's it right there, just the other side of the river."

"You mean that's it? You walk up out of the water and you're in Mexico?"

"Yep, just like that."

"I never been to Mexico."

"Mexico's a foreign country. You're supposed to use a regular border crossing to go there."

"We could cross right here."

"Aren't you supposed to be cooking supper?"

"I will, but I want to say I was in Mexico. Can we go across?"

"Let's sleep on it. Right now, I'm hungry."

That night, Dodger lay in his bedroll and looked up at the stars. He wondered what it had been like a hundred years earlier. Then he saw the lights and heard the far-off sound of a commercial airliner streaming across the night sky. He wondered what it would be like to fly, to have somewhere to go and a reason for going.

"Hey . . . Harley?"

"Yes?"

"You know what I'm gonna do?"

"Swim across to Mexico?"

Dodger laughed. "No. I'm going to get a job working for Duane and save up my money to buy a place like yours someday."

Cain listened.

"I'm always nervous at home. When I'm at your place or out like this, there's something special about it. This is the same sky we got in Bufort, and I never looked at it before."

Cain sat up to begin to speak, but then he hushed the boy. "There's someone out there by the horses."

The old man pulled on his boots and dug the pistol out from inside his bedroll. Dodger watched him. He pulled on his own boots and fetched his pistol. Cain touched the boy's arm. "Stay with me."

They circled the clearing where their hobbled horses were grazing. Staying out of the moonlight, they approached under the cover of the trees. Two swarthy men were leading the horses quietly away from the camp. Cain and the boy followed. When they came to a rutted dirt road, the men, speaking only in Spanish, walked the horses over a small rise where a '49 Ford half-ton pickup with a two-horse trailer sat parked with the trailer doors open.

As they approached the trailer, Cain told the boy to wait in the trees and stepped out into the moonlit clearing with his pistol in hand.

"Back off them fucking horses," he commanded.

The two men stopped. Dodger watched from the trees. One man spoke to Cain in Spanish, and Cain answered him in Spanish. Cain fired a shot into the air at the same time a third man, armed with a rifle, stepped out from the front of the pickup and fired at Cain. The bullet took Cain's leg out from under him. He went down hard and lost the pistol.

Dodger watched the horses bolt back toward camp. He saw the two horse thieves disappear into the brush on the opposite side of the pickup.

The man with the rifle closed in on Cain and stood over him with the rifle trained on his chest. He levered in a round and put the rifle to his shoulder.

From the cover of the brush, the boy hunkered down on one knee with his pistol leveled on the rifleman. The pistol rattled in his grasp as he tried to squeeze the trigger but could not bring himself to do it.

Cain, unable to rise to his own defense, waited for the explosion and the rip of the bullet. When the crack of a gunshot echoed in the darkness, Cain squeezed his eyes shut. When he opened them, he saw the man's shirt blossom with a red circle. He watched the circle grow until the man tottered and fell onto his back.

Dodger rushed from the trees, his pistol still smoking, and stood at the back of the trailer wildly firing into the darkness where the two men had disappeared. All Cain heard was one click after another as the hammer fell upon spent rounds.

The boy returned to Cain's side. "Harley?"

"It's nothing. See if you can find a flashlight in their truck."

Dodger returned with a flashlight and held it while Cain pulled down his trousers and examined the wound.

"Barely grazed it."

Cain stood, and Dodger looked at him. "Now what?"

"See if you can find the horses and get them tied up. I got a first aid kit in my saddlebags at camp." He nodded toward the body. "We'll come back for him."

Cain lifted the hood of the pickup, ripped out the distributor wire, and then took the keys from the ignition and threw everything into the swift current of the river.

By the time Cain limped into camp, Dodger had the horses caught and tied and had begun to saddle them.

"We have to get everything cleaned up like we were never here," he told the boy.

"What about the dead one?"

"We'll drag him into the river and hope he ends up in Mexico."

"Shouldn't we call the cops?"

"What's done is done. We'd never get a fair shake down here."

Cain had no intention of letting the boy get caught up in a legal system that could ruin what little life he had going for him.

The boy finished saddling the horses and waited for Cain to make sure they were leaving nothing behind. Cain walked back to the boy and touched his shoulder. "Come on, we got work to do."

They walked back to the scene of the shooting and found no sign of the body, only a circle of blood-soaked sand and drag marks leading off into the brush. Cain seemed nervous, and he spoke quickly.

"Look for the rifle."

They made a fast search of the area. Dodger picked up the spent cartridge from the man's rifle, but the gun itself was missing. Cain gazed off into the darkness where the drag marks faded into the brush, but saw nothing. He stopped abruptly and grabbed the boy by the arm.

"The horses!"

They both limped back to the campsite. The moonlight reflected off the empty ground where the horses had stood tied moments earlier. Cain stopped and swung his arm in front of the boy and then put his finger to his lips. Dodger's stomach knotted when he looked through the brush and saw that the horses were gone.

Cain dropped down into a crouch, and Dodger did likewise. In the distance, over the sound of the river and beyond the sound of the wind traveling across the treetops, they heard a horse whinny and a man's voice. Cain set off in that direction, with the boy following.

Under the light of the full moon, Cain followed the tracks of two men and two horses in the soft sand following the river to the west. Cain and the boy jogged to keep up. When the tracks of the two men no longer appeared alongside those of the horses, Cain called off the pursuit.

"They're mounted," he said, and then he bent over with his hands on his knees and tried to catch his breath. Dodger walked in a circle, limping badly and trying to walk out the pain.

"What do we do now, Harley?"

Cain coughed and wheezed and then looked up at the boy and shook his head. "Now we got no choice. We gotta go to Los Caminos and report this."

They returned to the disabled pickup and found an expired registration paper and a recent letter in an envelope in the glove box. Cain folded the letter and the registration and put them in his pocket. He figured the names and addresses would make short work of identifying the horse thieves.

By dawn, they stood on the shoulder of the highway with their gun belts concealed beneath their coats and their thumbs out. By all accounts, they appeared as two vestiges of the past in their leather leggings, frayed coats, and battered hats pulled down low over their eyes.

They both limped when they walked. The few vehicles that did pass gave them a wide berth. The drivers watched them in the rearview mirror without slowing.

The sun had risen halfway up the morning sky when a flatbed truck pulling a gooseneck trailer full of Corriente cattle stopped for them.

"Where you boys headed?" the driver asked through the passenger-side window.

"Los Caminos."

"Get in."

Dodger slid in first and sat next to the driver. Cain climbed in beside him, slammed the door, and nodded his thank you to the driver.

The driver shifted through the gears until he reached sixty, and then he looked up at Dodger in the rearview mirror and over at Cain.

"Gonna be a hot one again today," he said.

"I reckon. We appreciate the ride. That was beginning to look like a long walk."

"It's none of my business, but why were you boys out there walking anyway? I didn't see your rig broke down nowhere."

"We rode down yesterday. Last night a couple ol' boys stole our horses—saddles and all."

The driver shook his head.

"Now days, it seems, you gotta have a lock on everything. I don't know what this world's coming to. I'm going right by the police station, if that's where you're heading."

"Much appreciated."

At the station, Cain and Dodger shook hands with the cowboy and thanked him, and then they stood out on the street looking at the adobe brick building.

"Los Caminos Police. I guess that's it," the boy said.

Cain's eyes were hard, and there was no humor about him. "Keep your jacket buttoned. We don't want anyone to see these gun belts."

Dodger did not say a word. He checked the buttons on his coat and looked down to make sure the weapon was properly concealed. Then he followed Cain inside.

The desk sergeant instructed Cain and the boy to follow him to a private office after he heard the nature of their business. The sergeant carried a clipboard, a ballpoint pen, and several forms he proceeded to complete as they spoke. Between questions, he clicked the pen and then reclicked it to continue.

"So, let me get this straight," he said. "After the unknown assailant discharged his weapon, you went down, wounded in the upper thigh of your right leg. Is that correct?"

"Yessir."

"Have you had anyone take a look at that leg yet?"

"No. It's just a scratch."

The desk sergeant, a bit skeptical, looked up over his reading glasses at Cain. "Mind showing it to me?"

Cain shook his head and stood. He pointed out the hole in his trousers and the dried blood around it.

"You want me to drop my trousers?"

"No, that's good enough. I can see it's a bullet hole."

The officer resumed his questioning as he took notes.

"And you said he stood over you with his rifle and was preparing to shoot you again, yes?"

"Yes."

"This is off the record, but how do you know he was going to shoot you again?"

"He levered in another round, called me *pendejo*, and was squeezing the trigger."

"You said it was dark—how do you know he was squeezing the trigger?"

"He wasn't backing off, and I wasn't waiting to find out for sure."

The officer sat back in his chair and then leaned forward, clicked the pen again, and began writing.

"And that's when you pulled your pistol and shot him."

"That's correct."

Dodger's heart raced, but he sat completely still and showed no reaction to Cain's version of what had happened.

"At that point, do you know if the man you shot was dead or alive?"

"No, sir, I have no idea."

"Well, was he moving?"

"No, sir. If he'd of moved, I'd a figured him to be alive."

The desk sergeant cleared his throat. "Well, all right then."

The officer slipped the ballpoint pen into his pocket and then looked at his watch.

"The chief will be back soon. He's going to want you to go with him and the detective out to the scene."

Cain stood.

"What are the chances we'll get our horses back?"

The desk sergeant gritted his teeth and sucked in air as though Cain had touched on a sensitive subject.

"I wouldn't count on seeing them horses again."

"This kind of thing happen a lot around here?"

"This is a poor town, Mr. Cain. Half the people who live here don't speak English, and half the stuff stolen never gets reported. What does get reported ends up there." The officer pointed to a tall stack of papers sitting atop a file cabinet too full to contain them.

"If you're hungry, there's a café down the street where you can get some lunch while you wait for the chief to come back."

The old man and the kid walked to the El Agave café. Cain picked a booth in the corner and sat facing the door. Dodger stopped in the men's room. When he returned to the table and sat down, the sunlight from the window shone like a spotlight on the cuts and bruises on the boy's face and the dark circles beneath his eyes.

Cain spoke without looking up from the menu. "Pretty rough night. How you holding up?"

"I ain't sure."

Cain's eyes moved up from the menu to look directly into the boy's eyes, which bore into him with great intensity.

"I killed a man, Harley. That don't make me any better than Eugene."

"What are you talking about?"

"Killing. I'm talking about killing."

"Nobody knows what happened last night."

"Yeah, well, nobody knows what happened Sunday night, neither."

"What are you talking about?" Cain focused all his attention on the boy.

"I saw Eugene kill that man."

Cain's expression changed to one of surprise and concern.

"The one behind the Sundowner?"

"Yes. Now me and Eugene got the same secret."

"You saw him do it, or you heard he did it?"

"I seen him." Dodger bit his inside cheek and stared down at the table. "Eugene hit him. Then him and Rolando robbed him and drove off. I was across the street. No one seen me."

Dodger's eyes narrowed, and there was fear in them.

"I told you Eugene wasn't to be messed with," he said. "Now you know."

He paused a long time.

"And now I ain't no better than him."

CHAPTER TEN

Detective Spiotto, well dressed and clearly not a Texan, drove the Chevy station wagon while Chief Flores studied the notes taken by the desk sergeant. Cain and the boy rode in the back seat, and Cain directed them to the scene of the crime. Spiotto shifted into compound low and followed the trail back to the campsite.

Cain leaned forward with his arms resting on the seat back between Spiotto and Flores. He saw the vacant spot where they had left the truck and trailer. The rig was gone and, with it, much of the credibility for the rest of his story. He slumped back into the seat.

"They came back and got their rig."

Spiotto parked the vehicle away from the campsite. They walked back to the crime scene, with Cain pointing out all the key locations while the detective took notes.

"We had our bedrolls here. The horses grazed over there. The pickup was parked here. The shooting took place in a clearing through those trees."

Spiotto and Flores walked the area. The tire tracks of the truck and trailer stood out in the soft sand. Spiotto confirmed the tracks of two horses.

"Did you get the license number of the truck?" Spiotto asked in a distinctively New Jersey accent.

Cain shook his head.

"Take us to the shooting site," Flores instructed Cain.

They found tire tracks and hoofprints, but there was no sign of blood and no sign of anything to suggest anything unusual had taken place there.

Spiotto snapped a few pictures of the scene with the same enthusiasm the desk sergeant had displayed when faced with another theft report to add to his stack.

"Is that it?" the chief asked.

"Pretty much," Cain said. "And this."

He handed Flores the expired registration, but withheld the letter.

Flores stared at the name on the registration, and his expression changed as his tone became somewhat dismissive.

"Manuel Delgado," he said, under his breath.

"So, we have the license number here and the last registered owner," Flores said. "But it's a couple of years out of date and may not be much help."

Dodger stepped forward with the spent rifle casing in his upturned palm.

"This came from his rifle."

The chief examined the casing.

"Winchester .30-30. That narrows it down to about eighty percent of the rifles in the county."

They sat in the Chevy, waiting for the chief to review his notes. Flores and Spiotto exchanged a few cryptic comments, and then the chief turned in the seat and addressed Cain.

"Assuming what you told me is true, and I have no reason to doubt you at this time, unless a body shows up or these men turn themselves in, we have nothing to go on here."

"That's it?"

"I'm sorry, Mr. Cain. We'll follow up on the expired registration but, as you can see, it is two years old. Even if we find the truck, we still have no body, no weapon, and no crime."

"I understand. Any chance you could give us a ride back to my place? I'm just south of Bufort."

"Detective Spiotto will drop me off at the office and give you a lift home."

They arrived at Cain's place with less than an hour of daylight left. Cain thanked Spiotto, and Spiotto told him he would do what he could. Dodger followed Cain into the house. Cain took the pistols and gun belts and put them up high in a closet. He returned with the .45 automatic and a box of ammunition.

"Will you be okay here by yourself for a couple of days?"

"Why, where you going?"

"Back after my horses."

"I want to go with you."

"Can't do it, Dodger. I want you to stay here."

"Come on, Harley. I can help."

"I know you can—I'd just feel better about it if you were here."

Cain left the boy standing in the kitchen while he hooked up the two-horse trailer and packed an ice chest with food and water. He packed a canvas bag with socks, underwear, and an extra shirt.

"I'll be leaving at first light. You take the bed in my room, I'll take the davenport for tonight. I'll call you if I need anything once I get back down there."

That night they ate and talked and studied a map of the area. Cain memorized the names and addresses from the envelope and the names in the letter. He handed the letter to the boy.

"Looks like we're dealing with a whole damn family here."

"Who are they?"

"The Delgados."

"Ever hear of them?"

Cain shook his head. "If anything happens to me, I want you to get this to Chief Flores, you understand?"

"Yessir."

"This letter was postmarked earlier this month, so we know the names and addresses are good ones. It was mailed from an address in El Nogal, Mexico, to County Road 37 in Los Caminos, Texas."

Cain did not sleep much that night. He arose an hour before dawn. He looked in on the boy from the door of the bedroom, and the boy, bundled in his blankets, did not stir. Cain left without waking him. He wore the .45 under his vest in a shoulder holster and carried an extra magazine and the ammunition in the canvas bag.

Cain concluded the thieves had hid the horses out and then returned for their rig. They'd taken the time to rewire the truck and clean up the site before they left with the body and the rifle.

At the first light of dawn, he stood at the location where the shooting had occurred and found the tracks of the horses where they disappeared into the brush heading toward the river. The thieves had made no effort to cover the trail, and Cain followed it in his pickup to a wide, shallow sandbar that made a natural crossing into the Mexican border town of El Nogal.

The shoreline on both sides of the river had long since been worn down to dirt from the traffic of those who passed back and forth between the two countries at will. Cain glassed the collection of run-down shacks along the river, but he found nothing unusual.

He tossed the binoculars in on the seat and headed for town.

He drove back into Los Caminos and stopped at the town's only auto-supply store. Inside, he waited at the counter while the clerk finished a telephone call. If the thieves had purchased a replacement distributor wire, this was the only auto-parts store within fifty miles; it was worth a try.

"Good morning. What can I help you with?"

"Morning. I was wondering if you got a distributor wire for a '49 Ford half-ton."

The clerk smiled. "They must all be wearing out at the

same time. I sold the only one we had yesterday."

Cain laughed an engaging, country-boy laugh. "Just my luck. Who got that one?"

"Manuel Delgado came in all in a rush for it and got my last one."

Delgado, the name on the envelope. Cain remained expressionless. "That sumbitch. He still living over there on County Road 37?"

"Yeah, him and his brothers."

"All right then. I'll just have to make the old one do for now. Thanks."

County Road 37, the address on the letter, was just off the main highway where it ran parallel to the border for two or three miles before it ended at a "T" intersection. He attempted to read the numbers on the mailboxes as he drove by, but many were illegible or missing altogether.

He tried to calculate the missing numbers by those he could read. He repeated the numbers in his head: 1-2-1-1-4. He passed 10065, two with no numbers, and there it was, 12114. At the end of a long, rutted drive sat several buildings, patched and in disrepair, but clearly lived-in. On the porch of what appeared to be the main house, two men sat smoking and drinking beer. There was no sign of the pickup or the trailer, and no sign of the horses.

Cain continued on past and watched the place in his rearview mirror. He pulled over at the end of the road, far past 12114, and then made a U-turn. He pulled onto the shoulder of the road and turned off the engine. Cain contemplated his options and realized he had no workable plan. His vision of finding the horses tied to the side of the trailer and getting them back at gunpoint had vaporized.

A face appeared at the passenger-side window, and a knock on the glass startled Cain. His hand went instinctively for the .45. Then he relaxed and reached across to open the door.

"Dodger, what the hell are you doing here?"

Dodger grinned and climbed up onto the seat. He was

wearing the gun belt, and it hung heavy on his narrow hips.

"I came to help you get them horses back."

"How did you get here? You were sleeping like a baby when I left."

"I was in the trailer the whole time. That was my pillow all wrapped up in them blankets. I like to froze to death last night."

"Look, this could get real Western down here. They tried to kill us once. I'm sure they wouldn't think twice about doing it again."

Dodger's expression was serious, and he stared out the window when he spoke.

"So far, we ain't been real good at getting dead."

Cain looked across at the boy, but Dodger did not turn his head at first. When he did turn to face the old cowboy, the kid gnawed at the inside of his cheek as though he were processing some deep thought.

"How 'bout I walk back to their place?" he asked. "I seen you looking at it. I'll tell them we broke down and need a jump. I can get a closer look and see if I can spot the truck or the horses."

Cain thought about it a moment, and then he nodded.

"They never saw you. I doubt they would recognize me, and they've never seen this rig. That just might work."

Dodger climbed out of the pickup, and Cain stopped him. "You don't think the gun belt might make them suspicious, do you?"

Dodger laughed, unbuckled the belt, walked to the driver's-side door, and handed it to Cain. "I reckon I could have shot my way in and out if I had to."

Cain watched the boy limp down the road. He waited until the boy looked very small against the landscape, and then he got out, raised the hood of the pickup, and waited.

The boy was gone a long time, and Cain felt uneasy about the whole plan as he waited.

Fifteen minutes later, he watched an old sedan come over the rise in the road ahead, traveling slow and bobbing up and down on worn-out shocks as it approached. It pulled in bumper-to-bumper with Cain's pickup. Dodger came out of the back seat, and two overweight men emerged from the front, one carrying a set of well-used jumper cables.

"Dead battery?" one of the men asked without saying good morning or smiling.

"It won't hold a charge."

Cain hooked up the cables to his battery, did the same with theirs, and then climbed back in his pickup. One of the two men stood back from the sedan while the driver revved the engine and signaled for Cain.

"Try it."

Cain turned the key, the engine started, and he gave the other driver a thumbs-up. He thanked the men and waited for them to pull out and turn around, and then he followed them and honked as they pulled into the driveway. The men neither waved nor acknowledged Cain and the boy.

"They got the horses in the barn," Dodger said.

"You saw them?"

"Yessir . . . and the rigs. They had the saddles and bedrolls slung across the hitch rail just as bold as you please."

"The truck and trailer?"

"If they was there, I never seen 'em."

"Do you think they suspected anything?"

"I don't know. What now?"

Cain pushed the speed up to sixty once they reached the highway.

"We're going to the police and see if we can get this done right."

After hearing the full report from Cain, Chief Flores and Detective Spiotto pulled out from the Los Caminos police station bound for the Delgado place with the lights flashing, but no siren. Before they departed, Flores instructed Cain to stay close by until they returned.

CHAPTER ELEVEN

Cain and the boy sat at the corner table in the El Agave café. Cain faced the door. The boy sat across from him. A jukebox in the corner played Mexican music as Dodger flipped through the song selections in the modern-looking box attached to the wall at their table. He took a dime from his pocket, dropped it into the slot, and pressed two of the large red buttons.

Cain watched him with interest but made no comment on the money the boy had just wasted.

"Which one did you play?"

"You'll see."

Dodger watched the machine in the corner pick up the 45-rpm record from the turntable, invert it, and slide it into an empty slot. The arm moved down the lineup of records and then retrieved a new record from the slot marked E-4 and placed it on the turntable.

In a moment, the voice of Marty Robbins came over the jukebox speaker.

"'A White Sport Coat,'" Dodger said. "It's my favorite song."

"You still got that letter I gave you?"

Dodger reached in his back pocket, retrieved the folded paper, and handed it across the table to Cain. Cain read the letter for the fifth time and then folded it and placed it back inside the envelope.

The waitress, a dark-haired girl not much older than Dodger, stood at the table with her small order pad and yellow wooden pencil in hand. She looked from the boy to Cain and back to the boy, her eyes dark as a crystal-clear night.

"Hi. What can I get for you cowboys?"

Dodger grinned. Cain studied the menu and then looked up at the girl, a little surprised at the confidence she displayed for a girl as young as she appeared.

"How's the chorizo here, Elena?" Cain asked.

She rolled her dark eyes and feigned an expression of exaggerated disapproval. "It's sooooo greasy, but all the cowboys seem to love it."

"Well, then, it must be good."

She smiled. "If you like chorizo," she said, pronouncing *chorizo* in her perfect Mexican accent.

Dodger watched the exchange, mesmerized by the easy restaurant banter between the two.

"Can I get the chorizo with two eggs, sunny-side up . . . and coffee, black?"

Elena made the expression of disapproval again, and when she smiled, Dodger was sure he was in love.

"I was just kidding. I can't stand eggs sunny-side up—but it's okay if you want them," Elena said as her head bobbed and her ponytail swished from one side to the other.

She turned toward Dodger and fluttered her eyelashes at him as he had seen it done in the movies. He stared at her without speaking.

"Hello?" she said.

Dodger came to and sat back in his chair.

"Oh, sorry. I'll have a hot roast beef sandwich with gravy, and a chocolate milkshake, please."

"How would you like that roast beef cooked?"

"Huh?"

She smiled. "I was just kidding. It only comes one way."

Dodger grinned.

"*Gracias,*" he said as he began to get a better grasp of the verbal exchange.

"*De nada . . . hablas español?*"

Dodger tipped his hat back, looked over at Cain and then back up at the girl, who waited as she tapped the eraser end of her pencil against the order pad. He smiled up at her. "Enough to get by, I reckon."

She pointed the pencil at Cain and said, "Okay, I have two eggs and chorizo for you. Coffee—black." Then she pointed the pencil at Dodger. "And a roast beast and a chocolate shake for you. Will that be it?"

Cain said yes. Dodger just nodded. Elena slid the pencil behind her ear and walked away with her ponytail flipping side to side in rhythm with her steps.

"Did she say roast *beast*?" Dodger asked.

"I believe she did. You better hope it comes with the hair off."

They both laughed, and Dodger leaned forward and whispered.

"How did you know her name was Elena?"

"It's on her name tag."

Dodger shook his head and laughed.

"Oh."

Elena returned with their orders. She set the plates on the table, leaning across Dodger to do so. She smelled of sweet flowers, and the closeness of her took his breath away. With everything in place, she stood and put her hand on Dodger's shoulder as she surveyed the table.

"You're all set. Enjoy your food . . . it's really good. I was just kidding you earlier."

"Thank you, Elena," Cain told her. She waited while he wrote out a check.

"Okay if I make this out for ten dollars over? We need some change."

She nodded.

He paused, slid the old envelope across the table, and pointed at the name on it.

"Do you, by any chance, know this man?"

Elena backed away from the table. Her expression ran cold.

"Manuel Delgado," she said. "He's my uncle."

She took the check, turned, and quickly walked away.

Nearly three hours later, Flores and Spiotto met Cain and the boy at the station, and there was nothing encouraging about their report. The Delgado brothers denied any knowledge of the incident, there remained no sign of the horses, and they claimed Manuel Delgado was in El Nogal, where he had been for the past week. They were convincing in their statements and concluded the questioning saying they had no idea when Manuel planned to return to the US.

"The horses were there on County Road 37," Cain told them.

"Well, they're not there now," Flores said. "If they were there at all, they're probably in Mexico by now."

Cain and the boy drove to the small border crossing at Paradero and waited until the long shadows of evening lay across the river and the bright inspection lights shone down upon the uniformed officers on both sides as they checked each vehicle through. Cain pulled off the road, and they sat there a long time watching as the few cars they saw moved easily through the process.

"They're checking IDs . . . no chance of us getting across there with no ID for you."

"How far is it to El Nogal, you reckon?"

Cain shrugged his shoulders.

"Maybe fifteen or twenty miles—at the most."

"Any chance we could cross at the sandbar where we were?"

"Maybe, if we drop the trailer."

They returned to the campsite, dropped the trailer and chained the axle to a tree, and then drove upstream to the sandbar. The light of a full moon reflected off the rippling water where it ran wide and shallow over the sand. Cain sat, pulled off his boots, and waded in calf-deep water until he was two-thirds of the way across, and then the current pulled stronger and the water reached over his knees until he emerged on the other side. Dodger waited on the US side of the riverbank. By the looks of the tracks on both sides, they were not the first ones to consider crossing here.

Once Cain was back in the truck, sitting at the water's edge, Dodger readied himself.

"Gonna make a run for it?" he asked as he held on tight.

Cain turned off the headlights and shifted into compound low. The truck groaned as it inched forward into the black water.

"We're just going to try to ease it on over."

The truck gurgled through the water and rolled up onto the Mexican shore dripping and rumbling. Cain looked up into the rearview mirror and watched the water settle behind them. He grinned at the boy in the dim light of the moon where it came in low through the side window.

"Welcome to Mexico. We're now criminals with no rights in a country that doesn't want us here."

The boy grinned back. "It's kinda scary, Harley—but this is the most excitement I've had in my whole life."

The moonlight reflected off the lines in Cain's face. His eyes were alive and determined, and his whole expression added to the mystery of it for the boy.

"Let's go get them horses," he said.

A quarter of a mile away, Cain drove out of the brush and up onto the blacktop heading south. He turned on the headlights, and for the next twenty minutes they never saw another vehicle. Cain lifted his foot from the accelerator when they passed the El Nogal city limit sign.

"All right, this is it. Now all we got to do is find the Delgados on Monterrey Street."

Cain pulled out the letter, unfolded it, and then reread the return address.

They drove the streets, many of which had no signs, but they were unable to find Monterrey Street. The haphazard layout of the small town suggested that city planning had never been a priority and putting up street signs was, at best, an afterthought. Finally, they stopped at a service station with a map posted on the wall. Cain found that Monterrey Street was actually a short stretch of rural roadway just outside what appeared to be the city limits. He recited the directions and told the boy to remember them.

They located Delgado's place, a double-wide mobile home that sat right on the road. There were lights on inside but no sign of activity. Behind the rusted mobile home sat a small barn constructed of scrap wood sides and a salvaged sheet metal roof of multiple colors. They drove by slowly. A quarter of a mile down the road, Cain made a U-turn, pulled over, and turned off the engine and the lights.

"Here's where it gets tough."

Cain glassed the place and then handed the binoculars to the boy.

"You got better eyes than me. See if those are our horses right up there behind the barn with them others."

Dodger took a quick look and lowered the glasses. His voice shook with anticipation. "It's them."

"You sure?"

"A hundred percent."

Dodger adjusted his hat, sat forward in the seat, and looked into the side mirror to see if there was anything behind them. "How we gonna get 'em out of there?"

"Can you drive a truck?"

The boy laughed. "I was driving one when you met me."

"Yeah, that's what I was afraid of. Look, one of us has to go in there and get them horses. The other one needs to get this truck back across the river. You think you can find the way back?"

"I think I can find it. I'd like to be the one to bring the horses if it's all the same to you."

Cain thought about it a long time. Neither option was better than the other, so he agreed.

"We'll slip in there together, on foot. We'll get the horses caught up and saddled and back here, then you ride like hell for the crossing. I'll duck out the other direction and get their attention if anyone shows. I'll lose them and meet you in the US of A, back at the trailer."

Dodger was in the process of strapping on his gun belt when Cain reached out and took hold of it.

"Whoa, what you doing there, cowboy?"

Dodger jerked the gun belt back. "I ain't letting it come down to an argument."

Cain paused and pulled back his hand. "Did you reload it?"

"It's the first thing I done."

They crossed the empty field on the east side of the house, and Cain used wire cutters to open up the first of the two fences between them and the horses. They passed through the second fence, cutting all but the top wire. If the horses bolted, the top wire would contain them until they got them caught.

They walked beneath the light of a full moon. The light shone down upon Cain's two horses standing at a hay feeder alongside the smaller Mexican-bred horses.

"That's them," Cain whispered.

"I'll go in the barn and see if I can find the saddles and bridles," the boy said.

Cain approached the horses and quietly stood among them while he waited for the boy.

Inside, the barn was a dark void, and nothing there was familiar. Dodger worked his way down one wall by the indirect moonlight that lay across the floor from a side window with no glass in it.

Past the stalls and against the opposite wall he saw saddles and ropes and bridles sitting on racks and hung on wall pegs. He started across the stretch of light and then heard voices approaching. He backed into a narrow gap cluttered with old wagon parts and broken implements and hunkered down.

A man's voice and the voice of a girl spoke in Spanish. A light hanging from the crossbeam above the center of the barn came on, lighting the entire area and compromising the boy's position to anyone inclined to look his direction.

The two spoke again. The man left, and the girl pulled a saddle down from the rack and hung it over the hitch rail. She turned and spotted Dodger. She stifled a scream with her hand over her mouth. Her dark hair was down and hung loosely over her shoulders. She wore tight jeans, a white western shirt, and boots, and when she smiled, Dodger smiled back.

"Hey, Elena. Can I get another roast beast sandwich and a chocolate shake?"

She laughed, and he stood up.

"What are you doing here? I just left Los Caminos an hour ago. Did you follow me?"

"No, I came for our horses."

"Your horses? Those two new horses are yours?"

"They was stole from us."

"If my uncle finds you here, he'll kill you."

"You're not going to tell him, are you?"

"No, I'll help you. I just knew he stole them. He's a very bad man—and I'm serious, he will kill you."

"Do you know what he did with our rigs?"

She opened the door to the small tack room and led him inside. They picked up the saddles, blankets, and bridles and hurried out the back to the horses. When they got to Cain, Elena shook her head.

"Oh, my gosh, not you too. Hurry, we have to get you out of here before my uncles come out."

They saddled and bridled the horses, Cain cut the top wire on the fence on the way out, and they walked the horses through the opening. Elena disappeared into the barn, and the light went out. When they arrived at the truck, they unsaddled one horse and threw the extra saddle in the bed. The boy mounted up, nudged his horse into a trot with Cain's horse in tow, and rode off alone into the night.

Cain turned the truck around and waited with the lights off and the engine running. He watched the house for almost fifteen minutes with no sign of activity coming from it until he saw the shadow of one man walking toward the barn. Moments later a yard light went on, the light in the barn turned on, and soon every light in the place was on.

Three men stomped down the steps of the double-wide, carrying rifles and shouting. Cain edged the truck forward, passed the driveway, continued another hundred yards, and then turned on his lights and accelerated away, showering the blacktop with gravel from the shoulder and drawing the attention of the men at Delgado's.

Cain had a mile lead when he saw the headlights lurch into his rearview mirror in pursuit. He took the first right turn onto a main road leading back into town, and then a left and another right. He waited at a stop sign with his lights off. Nothing appeared in his rearview mirror. He took a deep breath and another and began to relax.

Out of nowhere, the sedan sped by in front of him from right to left with its headlights off and three rifles jutting from the windows. He heard the screaming of the tires braking on the pavement. He floored the accelerator pedal and shot across the intersection with his lights off and his heart pounding. He entered El Nogal from the south and took the first left turn behind a series of abandoned buildings where he pulled into a large warehouse, turned off the engine, and waited.

He heard the sedan speed by on the street out front, and he heard the open exhaust as it rumbled farther into town and slowed and then finally disappeared altogether. Ten minutes later, he heard the unmistakable sound of the sedan coming his direction and moving slowly.

Through the cracks of the building in which he was parked, he saw the spotlight from the car searching the shadows as it inched closer. He waited when they turned down the narrow street leading to the warehouse, and he waited when he saw the lights turn in behind the abandoned buildings. But when the lights stopped and pulled in behind him, Cain started the engine, shifted into reverse, slipped his foot from the clutch and floored it. The big truck roared in reverse, and the impact of the heavy bed sent steam spewing from the sedan's fractured radiator. Cain continued pushing until he had clearance to turn, and then he shifted into first gear and accelerated around the corner and into town.

No shots came from the sedan and there was no pursuit, but Cain drove like the devil was after him.

CHAPTER TWELVE

The boy pushed the horses as hard as he dared for the better part of two hours, following the back roads and attempting to return to the river. He lost his way on the outskirts of town. He rode through a neighborhood marked with graffiti and stripped cars sitting up on blocks. When he rode up on a gathering of beer-drinking young men with tattoos and long hair combed into slick, black pompadours, he knew he was in trouble.

"Hey, *pendejo*," one of them called out.

"What you doing here, white boy?" another said.

They gathered about him and stood alongside a parked car with spinner hubcaps on the wheels and a pair of fake Appleton spotlights mounted near the front doorposts.

"Hey," Dodger said, ignoring the challenging remarks. "How do I get to the river from here?"

They laughed and one flipped a cigarette at his horse. The horse jumped. Dodger caught it up short and glared at the man. "Don't do that again."

"Or what?"

Dodger pulled his pistol, pointed it at the man, and cocked the hammer back.

"Or I'll shoot you in your face."

The men backed off. One gestured to the left. "Go there and turn right on Second Street, man. It will take you to the crossing."

Dodger nudged his horse forward with his heels and the horses stepped out while the men behind him shouted obscenities in Spanish and one threw a beer bottle.

He found Second Street, rode it to the end, and started down toward the sound of the water. He looked about and nothing was familiar to him at all. At the water's edge, he could see in the bright light of the full moon what appeared to be a crossing. It was not the one he and Cain had crossed earlier, and he had no idea what lay in between or on the other side.

He had no idea where he was, and he had no idea in which direction they had left the trailer, but he did know that every minute he was in Mexico put him one minute closer to more trouble than he could handle.

Dodger coaxed the horses up to the bank. They balked at the rushing water, swirling and loud in the dark. He nudged his horse forward and it reared, turned, and thrashed at the surface with its forefeet as it fought the bit and resisted the boy's urging into deeper water. Under the light of the moon that now rode high in the sky, the boy could see the roiling water before him. He had no sense of the depth or the nature of the bottom. He turned his horses back up onto the solid bank on the Mexican shore.

He sat still in the shadow, concealed in the heavy brush, and watched the lights of a police car as it moved slowly in his direction on the nearby street. Its spotlight scanned the shadows along the river as it passed by and continued westward.

Now I'm the horse thief, he thought as he watched the taillights of the police vehicle disappear into the darkness. He followed the river downstream, stayed off the highway as much as possible, and searched for anything that appeared familiar—thus far, nothing did.

• •

Cain had to force himself to slow down as he sped through town, attracting more attention for his reckless speed than for the out-of-place appearance of his pickup. He watched the rearview mirror and listened for the open-exhaust sound of the sedan, but he neither saw nor heard anything of the pursuing vehicle.

He found the highway that ran parallel to the river, and he waited to turn onto it when he saw a police car approach with its spotlight burning into the darkness of the brush between the road and the river. He held his breath as it approached. The officer ignored him as he passed Cain's position and continued searching the brush along the river. Cain allowed the police cruiser to get a half mile down the road before he turned and followed it.

When the police vehicle arrived at the crossing point, it slowed and then stopped. The cruiser backed up and then turned and followed the trail to the water. Cain pulled over, turned off his lights, and waited. He watched the rearview mirror and sat listening with the window down.

The lights from the police vehicle lit up the trail as they bounced back toward the highway and turned west to continue the search. Cain waited until the taillights faded into the darkness, and then he raced to the turnout and slid to a stop at the crossing. He shifted into compound low and then inched his way across the river and up onto American soil.

Cain backed up to the trailer, hitched it to the pickup, and threw the chain into the back. He positioned the truck and trailer facing the highway, and waited for the boy. He checked his watch. It was almost midnight. He walked around the pickup and back down to the river. There were no sounds beyond those of the crickets and frogs and the night birds, and he began to worry.

At two thirty, he took to the trail on foot and followed it upstream. He watched and he listened, but he neither saw nor heard anything that sounded like the boy or his horses. He returned to the pickup and waited.

He checked his watch again at a quarter after three. Moments later, he heard gunshots and the pounding of the hooves of horses and an awful crashing through the trees on the Mexican side of the river. Out of the black void of the heavy brush and into the silver-lighted water there came charging two horses, their eyes red in the night, their forefeet reaching across the roiling current.

On one of them sat a boy, wild-eyed, with his legs flailing and his free arm whipping the reins over and under. The horses—their ears laid back, their necks stretched forward, and their nostrils flared—thrashed across the water running like death was upon them.

The boy shouted, "Open the trailer!"

The horses came high-legged out of the water, glistening in the moonlight, dripping sweat and river water, and they rode up a vortex of dust that followed them across the American side of the grassless crossing and into the clearing where Cain stood near the trailer. In the dark, there was a muzzle flash and the crack of a rifle, then another and another behind the boy who rode out of the darkness, his good foot in the stirrup and his bad leg slung over the back of the horse.

The boy swung to the ground and stumbled forward, and the horses bounced to a stop as they pranced and tossed their sweaty heads.

Cain took hold of the lead rope on the spare horse and drove him into the trailer. The boy loaded the horse he rode and they slammed and latched the trailer doors. They heard the men splashing across the river behind them, levering in round after round as they sent the bullets whining indiscriminately past them into the night.

Inside the pickup, Cain ground the transmission into gear and accelerated across the rough ground. They heard two rounds ping into the metal of the left rear fender over the sound of the pounding of the horses' hooves on the bare boards of the trailer floor.

They drove without lights, and the dust that followed them up onto the blacktop hung in the still night air a long time after they were gone. They drove until they could see no lights behind them and none before them before either spoke.

"What happened?"

"I got lost in town."

"Did you see who was shooting at you?"

"No. I seen some lights coming and I run for it."

The boy looked over at Cain. "I seen a cop car before. You think it was them?"

Cain shook his head. "Those were rifle shots. It wasn't the police."

The boy slumped in his seat and tipped his hat forward. "The Delgados."

"Yeah, that's my guess. You okay?"

"I'm okay."

"Well, you done real good."

The boy looked in the side mirror and rolled down the window.

"You reckon they can find us?" he asked.

"I don't think so. Why?"

The yellow light of the speedometer cast the old cowboy's face in dark shadows so only his outline was clear, and the boy sensed a dangerous air about him.

"One of them's dead. They don't seem the kind to take that lying down."

"They don't know who we are."

"The girl does. She had your check with your address on it."

The cowboy's eyes narrowed, and he nodded.

Dodger set his hat on the seat between them, not certain about anything. He rolled up the window, laid his head against the glass, and slept.

CHAPTER THIRTEEN

The next morning, Dodger sat at the kitchen table, his hands around a cup of coffee, watching Cain's back as the old cowboy stood before the stove with two black skillets splattering hot grease and drifting the smell of bacon across the room.

"How'd you sleep last night?" Cain asked.

"I had dreams," the boy said.

"What kind of dreams?"

"Bad ones."

"About the one you shot?"

"Yessir. Him laying dead, and them others showing up here to get even."

"You concerned that the girl will say something?"

"She's kin."

Harley shook his head to make his point. "She helped us steal our horses back."

"That's true—she coulda give us up, and she didn't."

Dodger thought about it a long time, but the conversation ended there, and Cain convinced the boy he had more pressing problems to deal with back in Bufort.

• •

By late afternoon, they had all but decided it was time for the boy to face up to whatever it was awaited him at home. The telephone rang. Cain answered and spoke in a low voice. Dodger was unable to hear most of the conversation from the porch where he was sitting.

"That was Chief Flores," Cain said when he stepped out onto the porch.

The boy waited with doubt and apprehension in his eyes.

"They got a man in the hospital was chest-shot. He wants me to come down and identify him if I can."

"He ain't dead?"

"He's got a hole in his chest, a collapsed lung, and a bad infection, but he's alive. His brother told Flores he fell with his gun."

"Is it Delgado?" the boy asked.

Cain nodded. "Jorge Delgado."

The boy sat back, his expression relaxed, and he took in a deep breath. "I didn't kill nobody," he said, grinning.

"No, you didn't."

"When's he want you to go look at the man?"

"He said I just needed to identify him from pictures. He doesn't want the man to know who shot him just yet."

"I want to come with you."

"No harm in that, I guess. He wants us in Los Caminos at ten tomorrow morning."

The boy tipped his hat back and grinned. "Guess there ain't no rush for me getting back to Bufort, then."

"Not just yet," Cain said.

The next morning, Cain and the boy stood in front of the police station fifteen minutes early. Cain motioned toward the El Agave café and handed the boy a ten-dollar bill.

"Why don't you go get yourself something to eat, and I'll meet you over there when I'm done."

Dodger folded the bill in half and stuffed it into his shirt pocket hoping, by chance, to catch up with Elena.

• •

Inside the police station, the duty clerk directed Cain to a small conference room.

"Chief Flores will be with you shortly," he said with no further direction.

When Flores entered the room, they shook hands and said good morning. Flores laid a book of photos in front of Cain and asked him to look through them and to let him know if he saw the man he shot. After several pages Cain paused and studied one picture and then marked it with a scrap of paper before moving on to the others. When he finished, he slipped his nicotine-stained finger in between the pages and opened the large book to the paper-marked page.

"This looks like him."

The chief turned the book around, looked momentarily at the photo, and then back up at Cain. "Jorge Delgado. That's the one we have in the hospital. Sounds like your story may have some merit to it, Mr. Cain."

"It's the truth."

"But there is a problem. His brother told us it was an accident. Jorge was conscious when they brought him in, and he corroborated the story."

"Where's that leave me?"

Flores sat down and pushed the chair back on two legs. "Well, we have no complainant and no apparent crime. What we do have is a very unusual set of circumstances that leads me to believe there is more here than meets the eye. Be that as it may, our legal system isn't designed to keep the world in balance."

Cain hoped the issue of the horses would not come up. Flores folded his arms and appeared to be disappointed.

"I'm afraid there is nothing we can do about your horses. You do have a right to file charges with the Mexican government if you decide to pursue it that far. My advice to you is to let it go."

"So, we just leave it like this?"

Flores's expression left Cain with some concern.

"For now," he responded.

• •

Dodger waited until Cain entered the police station. Then he crossed the street and headed for the El Agave, nervous and excited at the same time. Inside the entrance, he noticed that the corner table was empty. He took a seat and sat there facing the door as Cain had done. He noticed a young, dark-haired girl with her back to the counter and grinned while he waited for her to acknowledge him.

He studied the menu in an attempt to appear disinterested as she approached the table. He turned his eyes up toward her and noticed the name tag first. *Gabrielle*, it said.

He looked into the smiling face of the girl and smiled back at her.

"May I help you?"

"Yes, ma'am. Can I get a hot roast beef sandwich and a chocolate milkshake, please?"

"One roast beef and a chocolate shake. Will there be anything else?"

"Um, yeah. Is Elena working today?"

Gabrielle looked back at the big round clock on the wall.

"She'll be in at ten thirty. Are you a friend of hers?"

"No, not really. I just know her from here, is all."

Dodger nursed the chocolate shake, waiting for his food order as he counted each sweep of the second hand on the wall clock. At ten twenty-nine, the door swung open and the boy looked up to see Cain enter.

Cain pulled out a chair and sat across from the boy.

"Was it him?"

"It was him. They said it was an accident."

"So what happens now?"

"That's it. It's over."

The door opened and closed, and Elena stood there a moment before she disappeared into the kitchen. Gabrielle came out without her apron and waved to Cain and the boy on her way out the door.

"Elena will be right out with your order," she said before she closed the door behind her.

• •

Elena set Dodger's order before him without looking at him and then, when she finally recognized the two, her red-rimmed eyes widened and she drew in a sharp breath before she spoke.

"What are you two doing here?"

"We had business in town," Cain told her.

"Did you report my uncles to the police?"

"We got the horses back—that's all we wanted."

"I'm sorry," she said. "I know what they did is wrong, but they are poor people."

"That ain't no excuse for stealing," Cain said.

"I know, I know. I'm so sorry."

She touched the corners of her eyes with a wadded tissue from her pocket. Her voice cracked when she spoke. "Everything is just so messed up."

"You okay?" Dodger asked.

She nodded. "I guess. My father's in the hospital. They said he should be okay, but I just don't know how we're going to pay for it."

Dodger wanted to take her hand, to put his arm around her, but all he could do was sit there and try to understand. She seemed to calm some.

"He fell and his gun went off on accident. Now he has a bullet in his chest, and they're going to do surgery today to remove it. I have to be back at the hospital at three."

CHAPTER FOURTEEN

Dodger sat up straight in the seat and rested one hand on the dash of Cain's pickup as they entered Bufort. He pointed to the side of the street.

"Pull over here. I'll walk the rest of the way," Dodger told Cain when they reached the intersection near Duane's Conoco.

Cain nosed the pickup into a diagonal parking space shaded by a purple-flowered jacaranda tree and turned off the engine.

"You sure you don't want me to come in with you?"

The boy stared down between his boots and shook his head slowly.

"You got my number," Cain said. "You call me if you need to."

The boy nodded he would, and he reached for the door handle. He looked back over his shoulder at the old cowboy.

"That was the most living I ever done, Harley."

Cain put his hand on the boy's arm, and the boy slid off the seat and shut the door behind him. He waved back as he limped down the street, shuffling slowly, dreading what was to come. Cain sat there and watched a long time after the boy turned the corner.

• •

Dodger hesitated on the front porch at the sight of the door hung slightly open and no sounds coming from inside. He pushed the door open just enough to pass through and left it that way as he walked softly down the hall, listening and making no sounds of his own.

His mother's room stood dark and stale, the shades drawn, clothing strewn carelessly about. He waited for his eyes to adjust to the darkness. When they did, he saw the arm of his mother, white and motionless where it extended from the sheets, palm up and an empty prescription drug container below the fingers on the floor where it had come to rest when she released it.

He knew instantly. His stomach twisted and the knot in his throat made it impossible to breathe. He rushed into the room. He shook her and called to her. He pressed his fingers to her wrist and then to her carotid artery.

He wept when he laid his hand gently onto her cold cheek, and then he closed her half-open eyes. He stood to his full height and tucked her arm in beneath the sheet.

He picked up the container. *Dexedrine Sulfate* the label said above the bold-print warnings for inappropriate consumption and overdose. He sank to his knees and cried a long time before he called for help.

Mrs. Washington stood on the porch of Luanne's rental with Bobby and Dodger when the coroner and the ambulance left. She told the police officer the boy could stay with her family until they could make other arrangements. She helped Dodger pack up his things into two brown grocery bags.

She was there later to clean up when Eugene stopped by and told her he could not pay the rent and had to let the place go. Eugene did not ask about the boy, and he offered nothing to her for her kindness.

Bobby and his eight-year-old brother shared a bed. They made one for Dodger on the floor next to theirs in a room converted from a one-car garage. The room, split by a tarp hung from a cross wire, housed the boys on one side and Bobby's two sisters on the other.

When they sat down to supper that night, they did so as a family. Dodger felt his throat tighten when Thomas Washington blessed the food and the boy and the soul of the boy's departed mother.

Bobby, his younger brother, and two younger sisters looked from their plates to their mother and back to their plates when she set the small servings before them, proportionately smaller by the addition of a new mouth to feed. When she set Dodger's plate before him, they understood and no one commented. They drank water from jelly jars and none of the children mentioned Dodger's mother or the circumstances that had brought him to their table.

Mr. Washington brought up the subject in his normal unassuming manner.

"I shore am sorry about your mother, Dodger," Mr. Washington said.

"Thank you, sir."

Mr. Washington poked at the macaroni and ground meat with his fork, looking for the right thing to say next.

"You got family anywhere?"

"None to speak of."

Mr. Washington tipped his head back and nodded in the affirmative.

"None to speak of," he repeated in a slow, contemplative drawl. "I see."

Bobby kept his head down but turned his eyes to his father and waited for what felt like a final decision coming next.

"We can put you up here a spell."

Bobby grinned and nudged Dodger with his elbow. Mrs. Washington put her hand on the arm of her husband and smiled. Dodger took a deep breath, but there was no relief in his expression.

"Thanks, Mr. Washington. I don't want to be no trouble."

Mrs. Washington smiled at the boy. "You ain't no trouble at all, Bodean Cooper."

After supper, Mr. Washington unfolded yesterday's newspaper, procured that evening from the trash can in the elementary school teachers' lounge where he worked as the school custodian. After the meal, he read the news of the day to the children, as he did every evening.

"It says here," he said to no one in particular, "they still ain't found the one who killed Al Sawyer at the Sundowner. Says his wife and three kids are gonna lose their home now."

Dodger waited until Mr. Washington laid down the newspaper.

"Is it okay if me and Bobby walk over to the Conoco for a pop?"

Mr. Washington looked over at the clock on the counter.

"My treat," Dodger added, knowing the money might be an issue.

"That'd be fine—get back before dark."

The boys walked to the end of the block and turned the corner before either spoke.

"What's up, Dodger?"

Dodger stopped walking, and Bobby stopped with him. He looked at Bobby with fear in his eyes. "You gotta promise not to say anything to anybody."

Bobby appeared puzzled. "About what?"

Dodger took a deep breath, unsure whether or not to say anything. Finally, he blurted it out.

"I know who killed Mr. Sawyer."

"How do you know that?"

"I seen it."

"You seen what?"

"I seen who killed him."

"Why didn't you tell the cops?"

"I can't."

"Why not?"

"If I tell the cops, he's gonna kill me."

"Who is?"

"Eugene."

"Eugene done it?"

"I swear, Bobby. I watched him do it."

"Man, that ain't good. Does anyone else know?"

Dodger nodded. "Mr. Cain is the only other one. But that ain't the half of it."

Bobby dropped his eyes and then looked back up at Dodger.

"What do you mean?"

"I shot a Mexican man. And night before last I helped Mr. Cain steal back his horses in El Nogal, Mexico. I got chased and shot at by the brothers of the man I shot."

Bobby laughed and shook his head. "You're as fulla shit as a Christmas goose, Dodge."

"I swear. It's true—all of it."

"Seriously?"

"Seriously."

"What happened?"

Dodger explained the circumstances, elaborating on the details of the trip and the horse rescue in El Nogal.

Bobby sat there wide-eyed and slack-jawed.

"Did you kill the guy you shot?"

"I thought I did. He's in the hospital with the bullet still in him."

Bobby sat down on the curb. Dodger leaned against a sign pole and waited for Bobby to say something, anything, just some small clue as to what he should do next. Bobby just shook his head.

"Dodge-man, I don't even know where to start, but you got yourself a world of trouble."

Dodger nodded and his expression was grave. "I got troubles you ain't even dreamed of."

Bobby stood, and they turned and continued walking. Bobby adjusted his pace to Dodger's limp, as always.

"I'm sure sorry about your momma, Dodge."

"Thanks, B-Bob." B-Bob was Dodger's usual nickname for Bobby. "I guess I knew it was coming. I just didn't expect it."

Later that night, Bobby and Dodger slipped out the side door of the converted garage and sat on the curb, where they watched traffic drive by on the main street down at the end of the block. They talked until there was no more traffic and no lights on in any of the houses around them. The summer sky blinked with stars scattered to an infinite darkness and far beyond to a universe the two boys could not begin to imagine. They watched the beacon light of an airplane crossing silently between the stars.

"B-Bob, I met me a girl," Dodger said without shifting his gaze from the lights of the airplane.

"Really? Where did you meet her at?"

"A café in Los Caminos. She works there."

"Is she good-looking?"

"Whoa, buddy. She's primo . . . and smart."

"Does she like you?"

"I doubt it. She could have anyone she wanted. I don't think she'd settle for a limper."

"Even if you didn't limp, she'd probably still want somebody good-lookin'."

"Hey, nice talk, Bobby. It wouldn't work, anyway. The man I shot is her daddy."

Bobby's eyes widened. "Oh man. Does she know?"

"She don't have no idea, and I ain't about to tell her."

"Does anyone else know, besides you and Mr. Cain—and now me?"

"Her father and her uncles."

Bobby rocked back and forth absentmindedly on his haunches. "She's gonna find out, you know."

"I know it."

They sat with their arms over their knees and their chins resting upon their arms, neither ready to call it a night. Dodger was running on sensory overload, and Bobby refused to leave him alone.

The moon rode high in the sky, and the air that came in from the south cleared out the city smells and replaced them with smells of the desert. In the still of the late night, the breeze brought no sounds with it. The boys watched the stars and everything they imagined beyond the stars.

"What do you suppose happens to us when we die?" Dodger asked.

"If we lived good, we go to heaven."

"And if we didn't?"

Bobby waited a long time before he answered. "Then I guess we don't."

"Do you believe there's a hell, B-Bob?"

"I reckon if you believe in one, you got to believe in the other."

"Yeah—maybe."

"You don't believe in hell, Dodge-man?"

"I sometimes wonder if this ain't already hell, and dyin' is the only way to escape it."

Bobby put his hands on the sidewalk behind him and leaned back, still looking up at the sky. "That's one way to look at it."

"B-Bob, do you believe knowing something makes you part of it?"

"You mean about Eugene?"

"Uh-huh."

"I can see where it could."

"What do you think I ought to do?"

"What do you want to do?"

"I think I want to do what's right."

"And tell the po-lice?"

"Yes."

"You said Rolando Barone was with him?"

"Yeah."

"What if Eugene goes to jail and Rolando don't?"

"Even if they both went, they got friends here, and I'm done in either way."

"You best let it be, Dodge. You ain't gonna see him again, are you?"

"You mean Eugene?"

"Uh-huh."

"No reason to. I ain't nothing to him, or him to me."

Two days later, Dodger, Harland Cain, and the Washington family stood over the county-paid casket at the graveside memorial for Luanne Cooper.

Dodger watched a pickup drive up. He saw a wiry man in a cowboy hat slide out from behind the wheel. Dodger's hopes soared at the thought of his father come to pay his final respects and to take him away with him. Then the cowboy turned off and joined another group of mourners across the way. The boy bit down on his bottom lip and turned away.

The burial service itself was little more than a formality, with no speaker and no clergyman to offer a few kind words for the departed. They stood in uncomfortable silence as the groundskeeper and the gravedigger waited at the crank to lower the plain gray casket into the dark hole beside which they stood.

Mr. Washington bowed his head and recited the Lord's Prayer from memory. He asked blessings on Luanne's soul and on the boy. They all said amen. The groundskeeper lit a cigarette and then began to turn the crank.

Dodger stood there after the others returned to their cars. He watched the casket until it settled at the bottom of the hole. The gravedigger watched him. The boy did not move. The gravedigger tossed in the first shovelful of dirt, then another and another.

When the dirt finally covered the casket top, Dodger turned and walked away, with no sign of emotion on his face and nothing in his eyes.

CHAPTER FIFTEEN

Elena Delgado sat in the hospital room with her back to the curtain room divider. She watched the IV drip into her father's arm as he lay comatose, an esophageal tube taped to his mouth and his head tilted to one side. Her mother stood in silent vigil near her husband. The Delgado brothers huddled outside the open door, whispering in Spanish and smoking unfiltered Faro cigarettes as they gestured with their hands.

The girl listened to their talk of infidelity as they laughed and boasted of their machismo conquests. She ignored their profanity and she ignored their business talk; but when the talk turned to that night on the river and the shooting, she held her breath and listened to every word.

They spoke of an old man and a boy. They spoke of the horses. When they spoke of the shooting and the boy who'd fired the pistol, she felt sick.

She held the hand of the unconscious man and whispered "*padre*" before she laid the hand down softly and turned and walked out into the hall. Her uncles stopped talking but did not address her, nor she them, as she passed by without looking in their direction.

Outside, she stood in the evening air and wept.

• •

The next morning, as Elena prepared to leave the house to visit the hospital before reporting to work, a police car pulled up and stopped. Chief Flores walked slowly to the door and knocked.

Elena swung the door open. Her eyes widened, and she shook her head as though to deny his presence.

"No, *Tío*, no. Not *mi padre*."

Mrs. Delgado appeared behind her daughter with tears on her face and her hands covering her mouth.

Flores stepped forward and put his arm around the sobbing girl.

"*Lo siento, mi sobrina. Lo siento, mi hermana*."

He held Elena while she cried, and he patted her back. The girl's mother slumped in a soft chair near the door and stared vacantly across the room. It was the advanced infection, he told them, but they refused to hear him. When he left, they held one another, rocking back and forth trying to comprehend what had happened.

At noon, when most of the staff had gone to lunch, Chief Flores sat in his office. He dialed Cain's number on the telephone and waited.

"Mr. Cain, Chief Flores here. Thanks. Yes, there is a bit of a problem. Uh-huh. Jorge Delgado died this morning."

After a long pause, Flores continued.

"According to the doctor, it was an infection resulting from a failure to get prompt medical attention for the damage caused by a potentially nonfatal gunshot wound."

Flores shook his head as he continued.

"No, the cause of death is recorded as an accidental self-inflicted gunshot wound at this point. Well, that's the complicated part. You reported a shooting, which technically is a possible murder or manslaughter charge."

A long pause.

"I'm no lawyer, Mr. Cain, but I am sure there would have been no infection if there had been no gunshot wound."

Another long pause.

"I know—I'm just telling you. No, no need for a lawyer at

this time. That's right. Look, can you and the boy come down sometime this week so we can get a follow-up statement from you both?"

Flores wrote on the calendar on his desk as he spoke.

"Friday is fine. Yes. Anytime in the morning."

A dry wind carried the heat of the West Texas desert through the open windows and into the cab of Cain's pickup.

"We'll get us a cold drink in Los Caminos," Cain said.

"What are we going to tell them?"

Cain drummed his fingers along the top edge of the steering wheel without taking his eyes off the road. He coughed deeply and then spat out the open window.

"Same as before. Nothing's changed," he said, still wheezing.

"Why don't we just tell them we was mistaken and we never shot no one?"

"I identified Jorge Delgado in a picture and I told them I put a .44-40 bullet in the man's chest—and that's damn sure what they pulled out of him. The man himself said he fell on his own gun and his brothers told them the same thing when they finally took him to the hospital. If it comes down to it, they can match the bullet up with my gun. If I change my story now and Flores thinks I'm playing him, he might decide to take it up a notch. As it is, he just has one less criminal to worry about."

"What do I tell them?"

"Same as what you saw from standing in the brush when me and him went at it. He shot me once, stood over me, chambered another round, and aimed to shoot a second time. I fired my handgun once, and that was it."

Thirty minutes later, they sat in the police chief's office, somber and uncertain.

"Mr. Cain, I'm going to need you to sign this testimony as you gave it and as it's written. You must acknowledge that you swore, under oath, that everything you said is true."

Cain signed his statement, and Dodger signed his. The

demeanor of Flores was cold; if he was relieved to have one more criminal off the street, as Cain had suggested, there was no indication of it in his attitude.

"If we need anything further, we know where to reach you," Flores said.

Cain and the boy turned to leave.

"Oh, there is one more thing," Flores said as he tapped his desk with the pen he held. "We're going to need a ballistics test on that pistol of yours. Can you get the weapon to me on Monday? They'll need it a week or so for the tests."

"I'll bring it over Monday morning."

Cain and the boy were standing on the front step of the police station when Cain noticed a gray delivery van with Mexican license plates idling behind his pickup. The driver leaned out the window and pointed at the two bullet holes in the rear fender of Cain's pickup. Then the driver turned to speak to the two men on the seat beside him, and they leaned over to look.

Cain took the boy's arm and ushered him around the corner. They stood there and watched as the driver of the van backed it into an alley across the street and turned off the engine.

"It's them, ain't it?" Dodger said.

Cain nodded.

"Wait behind those cars, and keep an eye on them."

Cain crossed the street and slipped into a telephone booth in front of a convenience store. He picked up the telephone book suspended from a chain, found the number he wanted, and dialed.

"Yes, I just saw three men break into a gray van in the alley beside the auto-parts store across the street from you. They're sitting in it now. Yes, ma'am. Thank you."

Cain and the boy watched until two uniformed officers approached the van, removed the occupants, and walked them into the police station. Cain and the boy waited. When the door of the police station closed behind the last officer, they headed for Cain's pickup.

"Them boys will be there a while getting that sorted out."

He pulled the pickup around to the side of the auto-parts store and parked it between two bobtail trucks.

Dodger appeared confused.

"Why we stopping here?"

"I want to pick up something to fix those bullet holes. There's no point advertising what happened. You wait here."

He entered the store. The door slammed shut behind him. The clerk looked up and nodded to Cain.

"Hey, bud, how'd that coil-wire problem work out for you?"

"I managed to jury-rig it. What's all the action with the police out here?"

"I ain't sure, but the three they hauled in won't be in there long."

"Why's that?"

"That's the Delgado brothers. They're in town for their brother's funeral. The dead one's wife is the chief's sister."

"Elena's mother?" Cain asked.

"Yep . . . I guess that makes them husbands-in-law with Flores."

Cain attempted to appear nonchalant. "You got any Bondo and some primer?"

"Third shelf up, right behind you."

Cain checked the labels and settled on a small can. He picked up a can of gray primer and set them both on the counter.

"This'll do."

Cain pulled a ten-dollar bill from his wallet, laid the wallet on the counter, and read the label on the can again as he waited for his change.

The clerk returned from the register and counted out the old man's change.

". . . eight, nine, and thirty-two makes ten."

Cain closed the money in his fist and shoved it into the front pocket of his trousers. He nodded at the clerk, picked up the receipt and his purchases, and hurried out the door, leaving his wallet lying on the counter.

The country north of Los Caminos stretched to Bufort flat and barren. The afternoon heat shimmered up from the desert floor, distorting the edge of the earth so the mountains on the horizon seemed to move and not hold their shape. The old man and the kid, each with an arm postured in an open window to catch the wind, sat in silent contemplation of circumstances spiraling out of control.

Cain's tone was slow and thoughtful.

"You know them bad cards your teacher told you about?"

"Yeah."

"We just been dealt a handful of them."

The boy did not respond for a long time. When he did, his voice was low and subdued.

"When they test your pistol and it matches the bullet, they ain't gonna have no choice but to know it was the one killed that man."

"Well, that's a fact, and no matter what they heard from him and his brothers, my story is the one they'll be forced to go with."

"Then they're gonna arrest you for murder, Harley—and I'm the one that shot him."

"Maybe they will, Dodger . . . maybe they won't."

CHAPTER SIXTEEN

Late Saturday, with a half-moon hung low in the sky over Cain's place, the old cowboy rode more than an hour into the desert. His saddlebag contained a .44-40 revolver, oiled and wrapped in heavy Cosmoline-soaked canvas and bound in a burlap sack. A small miner's shovel was tied behind the cantle of his saddle. When he arrived at a place where nothing much grew, he dismounted and buried the burlap sack with the pistol inside.

When he finished, he brushed the burial site clean, scattering it with loose rocks and debris like he'd found it. He stood there a long time in the moonlight, trying to reconcile exactly what it was that had gotten him to this place in the universe at this point in his life.

Control of his own destiny had been a long time coming; he wondered if it was now in his hands or those of the boy—or, worse, in the hands of a legal system that seemed bent on extracting an eye for an eye regardless of the cost. He rode off into the evening, leaving no sign of his ever having been there and wondering if he shouldn't have, instead, simply finished what he'd started on the porch that night that seemed like a thousand years ago.

• •

Monday morning, Cain delivered a .44-40 to Chief Flores as promised. Flores accepted the pistol into evidence, as documented by a clerk with a clipboard. As a matter of routine procedure, Flores removed the pistol from the holster, opened the loading gate, and spun the cylinder.

"It's empty," he said to the clerk, but his gaze remained fixed on Cain. He then held the barrel to his nose and inhaled. "And it has been fired recently."

The clerk completed the property slip and handed a carbon copy to Flores. Flores glanced at it and then handed the paper to Cain.

"We'll be in touch," he said with a steely look in his eyes.

Cain hesitated at the front door of the police station before he exited and crossed the street to the auto-parts store. When he stepped inside the store, the clerk waved him over.

"Hey, bud, you left your wallet last time you were here. Hold on. I'll go back to the office and get it for you."

"Yeah, I know. I didn't miss it until I got home."

The clerk disappeared into the narrow gap between the backroom storage racks and returned a few minutes later.

"It was in the safe. Everything's still in it," he said when he handed the wallet to Cain.

"I appreciate it. Thank you. Whatever become of those three they pulled out of the van last week?"

"Like I said, they was back out in twenty minutes. One of 'em stopped in here and asked about you. Acted like he knew you. I give him your address off your driver's license. I hope that wasn't no problem. He called you by name."

Cain shrugged. "No problem. Do all three of them still live in El Nogal?"

"Manuel still lives out on County Road 37. I ain't sure about the other two."

Cain laughed to take the edge off his next question. "Them boys staying out of trouble with the law, are they?"

The clerk laughed in return and then dipped his head and shrugged his shoulder in a so-so gesture. "Well, you know how that goes."

"I reckon. Well, hey—thanks for looking after my billfold.

Take care now."

"Any time, bud."

Across the street in the police station, Flores and Detective Spiotto sat in Flores's office with the door closed. Flores poked his finger in the air to make his point.

"I want Cain in jail for the murder of Jorge Delgado. Do you understand?"

"Yessir, I do, but the deceased said, in his own words, it was an accident. His brothers all signed statements to that effect. So far, all we got is the word of an old man who said he shot someone that looked like one of the photos in a book of mug shots."

"Coincidentally, the same man in the picture shows up two days later with a bullet in his chest the same caliber as Cain claimed he shot him with," Flores countered.

Spiotto nodded his agreement. "And the .44-40 is not a common round these days, so Cain's story actually squares with what happened," he added.

Flores stood, walked around from behind the desk, and looked down at Spiotto. "The second we get the ballistics test back, I want you to have Cain in custody."

"Just give me the word."

Spiotto slid his chair back and looked over the papers he held.

"Any chance you can get the Delgados to recant their statements and tell us what really happened?"

Flores walked over to the window, looked out onto the side street a long time, and then turned to look back at Spiotto. "What really happened is they got caught stealing Cain's horses. I suspect they're going to want to settle things their way."

Spiotto tapped his finger on the original statement Cain had made. "It says here they got away with two bay horses, the saddles, and the bridles. You know, we never verified that those horses are actually missing. It says here he only owned the two."

Flores checked his watch. "You've got time—why don't you take a drive up to Cain's place and check that out?"

• •

Less than an hour later, Detective Spiotto drove by Cain's ranch and spotted two bay horses in the small field north of the barn, but he did not stop. He pulled in four miles up the road, where Cain's nearest neighbor was working under the open hood of his pickup alongside his adobe-walled house.

"Excuse me," Spiotto called through the open window of his unmarked car.

The man looked out from under the hood and reached for a rag lying on the fender. He walked over to Spiotto's car as he attempted to clean the grease and oil from his hands.

"Yessir?"

"Do you know if those are Harland Cain's two bay horses in the pen up by his barn?"

The man nodded. "Same ones he's had there for ten years."

"Well, thank you, sir."

"You bet."

Spiotto drove off without another word. When he got within radio range, he keyed in the station and asked the dispatcher to patch him through to Chief Flores.

"Chief, I just confirmed that Cain's horses are here. No one stole them. You want me to bring him in?"

The radio crackled, and the chief's voice sounded hollow but clear. He spoke as though he were talking to himself in a subconscious attempt to square the facts with the stories.

"If the Delgados didn't steal his horses, then none of this makes sense."

"No, sir, it sure doesn't. Want me to pick Cain up?"

"No. We'll just leave it be until we get the ballistics results back on that handgun of his."

Manuel Delgado sat with his deceased brother's wife and her daughter when the other visitors departed after two days of paying their condolences. Elena never asked about her father, she never mentioned the conversation she'd overheard in the hospital, and she did not confide in her mother. She had seen Cain and the boy twice enter and leave the police station from the front window of the El Agave café, and that was enough evidence for her to believe what her uncles said was true.

The days that followed came dark and brooding to Elena. The girl's visions of her father came to her in sleepless nights like some hellish nightmare in which she reached out to him with unmoving arms and cried out to him with no voice. And, in that nightmare, the image of a boy-child arose from the ground, draped in grave clothes, its eyes on fire, bearing a great sword with which it smote the old man until the old man was gone and all that remained was his blood-soaked shirt. She would sit upright in her bed and her hands would shake. Each night, the dream came back to her.

On the day the priest came and blessed the house and prayed over them, her mother tendered the last boxes of her father's clothes to him. Elena stood at the door and watched the clergyman and the parishioner who accompanied him as they loaded the last of the boxes into the trunk of the car. She bowed her head. "*Que Dios me perdone*," she whispered as she crossed herself and vowed to kill the one who had killed her father.

At Sunday mass, Elena and her mother prayed in black mourning garments and shook the hands of those who paid their respects with insincere offerings, saying, *You just let us know if you need anything*. Elena looked out at them through the crosshatch of the black veil that covered her eyes and hid her thoughts and concealed the tears that ran bitter with hatred.

She stepped back from the small flock of worshippers and sought out her police-chief uncle standing alone, smoking a cigarette in the shade at the side of the church.

"Are you okay, *Sobrina*?" he asked as she approached him.

"*Sí, Tío*, but I need to speak with you."

"What is it?"

"I think you know something I need to know."

Chief Flores shifted uncomfortably from one foot to the other.

"And what do you think that is?"

"I think my father did not shoot himself."

Flores held the cigarette behind him and leaned in toward the girl. He put his hand on her shoulder, and when he spoke, his tone was very paternal and very authoritative. She looked up at him with all the respect his manner implied.

"Elena, listen to me. You may be right, but this is a police investigation and you must leave it to me to handle. Do you understand me?"

She lifted the veil and stared at him, her black eyes cold and hard. "He killed my father."

Flores patted her shoulder but did not respond.

CHAPTER SEVENTEEN

Dodger hung around outside the mechanic's bay while Duane finished checking the oil and lowering the hood of the pickup at the gas pumps. He thanked the driver and smiled. The driver smiled and thanked him back. Duane waited until the pickup accelerated away down the quiet street before addressing the boy.

"So, what's shakin', Dodger?"

Dodger followed Duane into the store, and they stood near the checkout counter.

"I was wondering if I could get a job working here for you, Duane."

Duane grimaced. "Jeez, Dodger."

"I'd work hard. I could be here every day or at night if you want."

"I don't know."

"I could clean up, stock shelves, change them hotdogs in the rotisserie—anything you need having done, I'd do it."

Duane looked down at the floor and shook his head, and then he looked up at the boy whose eyes pleaded with him.

"I'm just barely making ends meet now. If things don't pick up, I'll have to cut Leland's hours as it is."

"I wouldn't need to make what Leland and Mickey make. Just anything will help." He took a deep breath and spoke in a voice just above a whisper. "Mr. Washington can't afford lodging me, and I ain't got a lot of choices right now."

They stood in silence. Duane agonized over the only choice he had. He walked behind the counter and took a twenty-dollar bill out of the register and offered it to the boy.

"I'm sorry, Dodger. I can't put on any more help right now. Take this. It'll get you by a little while."

Dodger shook his head.

"I appreciate it, Duane, but I ain't looking for no charity. I'm looking for a job."

Duane watched the boy limp out past the pumps and stop. The boy looked to the left and to the right and, when he shuffled off down the street, he appeared, of all God's creatures, to be one of the disposable ones.

Bobby met Dodger at the corner two blocks from the Washington house.

"Mr. Cain's at my house talking to my daddy."

"What about?"

"He asked my daddy if you could come work for him at his place for the summer."

"He did? What'd your daddy say to him?"

"He told Mr. Cain he don't have no say in the matter. That would be up to you."

"I'll tell you one thing, B-Bob—there ain't nothing slow about life around Mr. Cain." He grinned and then added, "But there sure enough is lots that needs done around his place."

Cain was sitting at the kitchen table with the Washingtons, where they were drinking sweet tea out of Mason jars. They stopped talking when the boys entered the room.

"Hey, Harley," Dodger said, smiling.

"Hey, Mr. Cain," Bobby said at the same time.

"Hey, Dodger. Hey, Bobby. You two staying out of trouble?"

The boys looked at one another.

"Yessir," Bobby answered.

Mr. Washington sat up straight in his chair, and all eyes turned to him as though he had asked for the floor and been granted sole authority to address those in attendance. He rose from his chair and stood tall and straight, with all the elegance of his African heritage, and pushed the chair back to the table.

"We'll leave you two gentlemen to talk," he said as he looked first to Cain and then to the boy. He held the door for his wife and son and then closed it as he followed them from the room.

Cain leaned forward and held the Mason jar in both hands with his elbows resting on the table. He spoke to the boy, one man to another—a friend to a friend. The boy sat up straighter because of it.

"Dodger, I'd like you to come work for me for the summer."

"Thanks, Harley. But I ain't looking for pity work."

"Pity work would be if I didn't need the help and you couldn't do the work and I hired you anyway. That's not the case here. It don't pay that good, and I'm going to work your ass off."

Dodger laughed. "I believe you, but I don't work cheap neither."

"How much you looking to make?"

"I don't know. More than minimum wage."

"Minimum wage is a dollar. I'm offering a dollar five."

The boy stuck out his hand and Cain shook it.

"When do I start?"

"I'll come get you tomorrow. I'll run the mice and raccoons out of that extra room and set you up a bed in there."

Dodger looked over at the old cowboy and tried to thank him, but the words stuck in his throat and all he could do was nod. Cain saw the look in the boy's eyes. He stood and pushed his chair to the table. He cleared his throat.

"Well, that's that then. Be ready about noon."

Dodger sat at the table and watched Cain shake hands

with Mr. Washington as the two men stood on the porch. He watched him walk to the street, and he watched until the old pickup with the primer-painted fender rumbled out of sight. He rubbed his eyes with the sleeve of his shirt and swallowed hard.

Bobby was the first to reenter the room, and, when he looked at Dodger, he chose not to speak but sat next to the boy and put his arm on his shoulder. Bobby's parents stood looking out from the porch, holding hands with their fingers interlaced, comfortable with the silence that comes from a relationship long past the need for small talk.

Dodger sat there a long time without speaking or acknowledging Bobby's presence. Finally, he took a deep breath and let it out slowly.

"I don't reckon there's any way I can ever pay your folks or Mr. Cain back for everything they done for me."

"They ain't none of 'em looking for any payback, Dodge."

Dodger looked down at his hands folded before him on the plastic tablecloth. He let his eyes take in the details of the room for the first time since he had been there. The faucet dripping into the rusted sink, stress cracks where the old walls met the ceiling, linoleum worn through to the black underlay, the mismatched dishes drying on the rack on the counter, and the stack of coupons clipped from yesterday's newspapers all looked like a home to him. Dodger turned to Bobby. His expression softened, but he did not smile.

"You sure got it good here, B-Bob."

The next morning Dodger lay on his blankets with his hands behind his head, staring up at the ceiling while he waited for the sun to come up. The two grocery bags of his belongings sat near the door and, next to them, his boots with his hat resting atop one of them. He listened to the steady cadence of the breathing of Bobby and his brother. The peacefulness of the sound of undisturbed sleep comforted him and made him feel part of something he could not define. He closed his eyes and imagined death was like sleeping.

• •

After breakfast, Dodger thanked Mrs. Washington and then helped Bobby with his chores before they walked to the back of the hardware store and stood in the alley looking across at the parking lot of the Sundowner Lounge.

Dodger pointed to a spot near the dumpster.

"I was right here in one of them big boxes."

"Sleeping?"

"Trying to."

Bobby shook his head and looked across the alley.

"Where was they?"

Dodger led Bobby across the alley and into the empty parking lot. They stood on the spot where the intoxicated man had fallen. He then pointed back to the side street.

"They was parked over there, waiting."

He then turned and pointed at the back door of the lounge.

"The man came out of that door all by himself."

Bobby raised his eyebrows and whistled. "Man, and you saw all this?"

"Ever' bit of it."

Bobby's eyes widened and he grew silent as the sound of an idling engine rolled in behind Dodger. Dodger turned to face the approaching vehicle, and his expression flushed cold and fearful. He recognized the car before he saw Rolando Barone's face clearly through the windshield.

Rolando rolled up, stopped, and cranked down his window. His narrowed black eyes, punctuated by two teardrop tattoos beneath the left one, bore into the boys, hot and menacing. Bobby hung back, and Dodger stepped forward near the driver's-side door.

"Hey, Rolando."

Rolando's eyes did not move for a long time. His gaze finally shifted to the back door of the lounge and then to Bobby and back to Dodger.

"What are you *cholos* doing here?"

Dodger tilted his head in Bobby's direction. "I'm showing Bobby where that man got killed."

"What do you know about what happened here?"

"Just what Duane told me."

"Are you lying to me?"

"About what?"

Rolando did not answer, and he sat back in the seat with his hand draped over the steering wheel.

"What if I tell Eugene I saw you here?"

Dodger shrugged his shoulders. "I ain't nothing to him, but tell him I said hey."

Rolando nodded that he understood. He pulled slowly out of the parking lot sitting low behind the wheel, leaving Dodger feeling very much like the mouse watching the cat leave. His hands shook when he turned to Bobby. "Do you think he knows?"

"He was just trying to scare you."

Dodger's face was drained of color. "He did a pretty good job of it."

CHAPTER EIGHTEEN

The Delgado brothers, bold and belligerent from the local beer they were drinking, held private and treacherous court at a back table in a neighborhood cantina in El Nogal. Undeterred by the loud music from the jukebox and the drunken bar talk of the late-night patrons who crowded the small establishment, they exchanged dangerous talk while Manuel Delgado flipped a bottle cap between his fingers and listened as he weighed his thoughts.

Anger, fired by the death of their brother, came hot and vengeful in their talk. But when they spoke of the horses, the matter cut deep into their ancient sense of Mexican honor. They argued the right and wrong of killing el niño, but there was no argument concerning the horses, and there was no argument that both the boy and the old man had gutted the machismo of the three men from whom they stole the horses—in their country, on their land, and under their noses. For that, there could be no acceptable retribution short of death.

They slammed their empty beer bottles down hard against the wet-ringed table and called for shots of tequila in a boisterous manner of celebration of an event that was yet to happen.

• •

Across the border, under the same stars that shone down upon El Nogal, Cain and the boy sat at the kitchen table and talked about the day's work they had done and the work yet to be done. Talk ran low and Cain tipped his chair back, held his coffee cup in both hands, and yawned. Hard work suited Cain. New fences felt like a new beginning. He couldn't remember the last time he'd looked forward to tomorrow. He couldn't recall the last time he'd sat at that table looking across at someone he cared anything about. It was as close as he had come to smiling in a long time.

The boy, his face streaked with the dried sweat of the day, his hands fresh with the cuts from the barbed wire he'd strung, appeared worn out. He also appeared anxious. The old man sensed it.

"What's on your mind?"

"Nothing, really—I just ain't had this much to do maybe ever in my life."

"You going to be able to keep up?"

"I can keep up."

Cain dropped his chin and looked over his nose at the boy. "But?"

"Well, I was thinking . . ." He sat back in his chair and took a deep breath. "They ain't gonna let it go, you know."

"The Delgados?"

"Uh-huh."

"I don't reckon they are."

"So, what are we going to do about it?"

"It's their play. We got no choice but to wait it out."

"I'd feel better about it if I had a gun."

Cain looked at the boy as one generation looks upon the other with all the hope wrung out of it. He shook his head.

"No guns."

Three days later, Cain's telephone rang while he and the boy were eating breakfast. When Cain returned to the table, he appeared unsettled.

"I need to take a run into Los Caminos this morning," he told the boy.

The boy stood, collected the plates from the table, and walked them to the sink.

"Was that the po-lice?"

"Flores wants to talk to me. He didn't sound happy."

Less than an hour later, Cain sat in the police station conference room waiting. When Chief Flores and Detective Spiotto entered the room, Flores chose not to sit and instead stood behind the high-back chair at the end of the long table. Spiotto took a seat across from Cain. Flores started in on Cain with no pretense of formality.

"I don't know what kind of game you're playing here, Mr. Cain, but I promise you, if you are lying to me, I will make sure you are prosecuted to the full extent allowed by the law of the State of Texas."

Cain frowned. "I don't know what you mean."

"I mean, the bullet removed from the body of the deceased did not come from that gun you brought in."

Cain raised his eyebrows and sat back in his chair, attempting to appear surprised.

"Well, it was dark and I was close, but maybe my shot missed and he was telling the truth. Or maybe one of the others shot him, trying to hit me."

Flores's face flushed red, and his breathing became more rapid as he fumed. He considered the possibility. His demeanor settled as he pulled out the chair and took a seat. He turned toward Detective Spiotto. "What do you think?"

Spiotto shrugged. "It's possible. The problem is we don't have the weapon that fired the shot, but we do have an admission from the victim. Maybe Cain here did miss and it happened just like he said."

Flores nodded, his eyes narrowed. "That's a possibility. And it is the only one that makes any sense."

Spiotto threw down his pen.

"The problem is everything else tends to back up Cain's version of the story—a shot at near point-blank range, the caliber of the bullet, the horses. If anyone is lying, no offense, but it seems to be the Delgados. I've heard of men confessing to crimes they didn't commit, but this don't seem to be one of those."

"You think the Delgados are lying because they were stealing the horses in the first place?"

"Exactly. Or because one of them shot his own brother."

Flores pushed his chair back from the table. "That could be. But how could they steal horses that haven't been stolen?"

Spiotto shook his head and looked across at Cain.

"Because I stole them back," Cain said.

"You what?"

"I crossed into El Nogal, found my horses at their place on Monterrey Street, and brought them back."

"Just like that?" Flores asked.

"There was a little more to it."

"I know the place," Flores added. "You expect us to believe you just walked in there and took your horses?"

"No, sir, it was more complicated than that. But I did get the horses back."

Spiotto looked over at Flores. "That does make some sense. Without the horses to tie the Delgados to Cain here, we have nothing."

Flores's expression was one of skepticism, but it was clear that he was measuring the facts carefully as he nodded without commenting.

They returned Cain's pistol to him. After Cain left, Flores and Spiotto remained in the conference room.

"I think he's telling the truth," Spiotto said.

"I reckon he is, because if he's not, I sure don't know what the justification would be for him to go through all this. There is no logical reason for a man to work this hard confessing to a shooting everyone else denies."

Flores thought about it as he examined the file and reread the reports.

"I think I'll try to get Manuel aside and talk to him

man-to-man and see what he says. I know he's as bad as his brothers, but I have always been able to talk to him."

Spiotto stared out the window as he spoke. "What we now have is an accidental gunshot case—open and shut. Are you sure you want to turn it into a killing?"

"It needs to be what it is, Detective, and that's our job to find out."

"Family or no, huh?"

"That's not our call."

That evening, Flores arranged to meet with Manuel at his sister's place. He arrived there to find Manuel, Teresa, and Elena waiting for him in the small living room of the house made uncharacteristically empty with the absence of Jorge from it.

They spoke of family and they spoke of the weather, and they smiled at one another. Manuel, his brooding dark eyes shaded by the white straw cowboy hat he wore, sat back and offered nothing. Elena nervously chewed the inside of her cheek and appeared to want to get to the matter at hand, but she restrained herself. Only Teresa regarded the gathering as a social call. She offered more coffee and then sat at the table, deferring to the police chief, who sat there in full uniform.

He apologized first to Teresa.

"I'm sorry to have to bring this up, but we have reason to believe that the shot that led to Jorge's death may not have happened as we heard it."

Manuel stared at his boots, but his expression remained unchanged as he listened.

"We know three men stole the horses of two Americans near the crossing. There was trouble. One of the Americans was shot in the leg, and one of the thieves was shot in the chest."

Manuel sat emotionless, and Teresa held her hand over her mouth as she listened in horror of what was coming next. The look in Elena's eyes was hard and hateful, and Manuel avoided looking at her.

"Manuel, I need to know what happened," Flores said.

Manuel raised his eyes but did not respond.

"Look, from the sounds of it, the whole thing could have been an accident. Jorge may have fallen, as you said, or one of you could have accidentally shot him trying to defend him. Whichever way it went, I need to know."

"Are you asking as family, or are you asking as the police?" Manuel asked.

"Both."

Manuel shook his head and returned to staring at his boots. "I don't know about no horses. Jorge fell with his gun, and it went off."

Flores looked at his sister.

"Teresa, can you bring me Jorge's *pistola*?"

Teresa shook her head, and her eyes were red-rimmed. "No—he kept his guns at the house in El Nogal."

Manuel spoke up quickly. "He lost the gun in the river. We never found it."

Flores sat with a silence that ran cold and disputed the words of Manuel as effectively as if he'd called him a liar.

Elena leaned forward in her chair and glared at Manuel. With no regard for her disrespect, she slammed her hand down hard on the table. "You know that's not true!"

Manuel shot her a devastating look, but she stood her ground. Her mother sat back and watched wide-eyed and disbelieving.

"I heard you and your brothers in the hospital say the boy shot my father—did you not?"

Flores turned to Elena. "The boy?"

"Yes. They said a boy shot my father."

"Not the old man?"

"No, the boy."

Flores turned to Manuel. "Is that true?"

"No, she misunderstood. That was not our conversation, and she was not part of it."

"I know what I heard."

"Look, Manuel—family to family now. Is that true?"

"I'm telling you, it is not true."

Elena's eyes narrowed and bore into those of her uncle.

"The old man and the boy took their horses back from you when I was in El Nogal. Is that also a lie?" Elena asked.

Manuel's expression darkened, and he stood and glared down at the girl. "That's enough of your insolence." He stood, turned, and slammed the door behind him as he left the house.

Flores asked, "Elena, are you sure about the horses?"

"Yes, I'm sure. I was there. Go see for yourself. The fences are cut in two places. The man and the boy came in at night."

"Are you sure the boy was with him?"

"Yes. I spoke with them both, and I helped them get the horses back."

"Why did you help them?"

"I didn't know they'd shot my father then."

"That explains a lot. Please say no more about this to anyone. I'll handle it."

"Okay, but you know *Tío,* Manuel is lying."

Flores rose, hugged his sister, patted Elena on the shoulder, and then stopped at the door. "It seems that several people are not telling the truth."

CHAPTER NINETEEN

The midday heat rose off the parched ground and lifted to the sky. An invisible thermal column carried a hawk resting lazily on outstretched wings as it soared higher and higher into the cloudless blue canopy overhead. It made no sound as it studied the earth below with ancient eyes that measured everything that moved except time itself.

Dodger tilted his head and pushed his hat back. He squinted and watched the hawk and then ran his shirt sleeve across his forehead. He hammered the last staple into the newly set fence post and checked the wires for tightness. He stood back and surveyed his work from the barn to the corner of the pasture and nodded his approval.

Cain stood on the loading chute at the side of the barn and waved him in. Dodger loaded the posthole digger, fence stretcher, bucket of staples, and extra roll of barbed wire into the back of Cain's pickup. He drove across the irrigated pasture to the barn.

"What's up, Harley?"

Cain climbed down from the loading chute and leaned against the top of the driver's-side window. He coughed into his rag, bent over, and held his hand up as if to dismiss the coughing when Dodger's expression turned to one of concern.

"I need to be in Houston day after tomorrow. Probably be gone a day or two. You be okay here by yourself, or do you want to go back and stay in Bufort with the Washingtons until I get back?"

"I'll be fine here. You gonna drive or fly?"

"It's a ten-hour drive. I'll fly."

"I got lots to do while you're gone, so I'm good."

"You drive me to the airport, and I'll leave my pickup with you in case you need it."

Dodger grinned. "What if I get some beer and decide to take another run at that bridge?"

"You best make sure you're going fast enough this time, or I'll kill you myself when I get back."

They both laughed, and then Dodger stopped smiling.

"Is it okay if I have Bobby over?"

"That's fine. Put him to work and keep track of his hours. I'll pay him same as you."

Dodger's expression changed. "You going to the doctor in Houston?"

"The medical center. I've been there before."

The boy saw the expression of uncertainty on the old cowboy's face and knew to let it go at that. "I should be able to get quite a bit done around here without you interrupting me all the time."

"Yeah, well, I may just put a big knot on your head before I go."

"Bring a lunch."

"To the airport?"

The boy laughed again. "No, to the fight, 'cause it's gonna take you a while."

Cain was on a commuter flight out of Bufort before daylight. The boy stood on the blacktop and watched the cowboy take a seat near a window over the wing as the engines revved and the propellers chopped into the morning air. The pilot jockeyed the small airplane around. Dodger waved at Cain, and Cain waved back. He waited while the aircraft taxied from the short apron to the runway and then sped down the center of the short strip until it lifted off. The airplane banked into a sharp turn to the east. The boy watched until the rotating tail beacon disappeared into the black predawn sky.

Dodger slid in behind the wheel of the pickup, adjusted the seat and the rearview mirror, and then looked around, grinning. His first stop was a block down from Bobby's house. He pulled in next to the curb, turned off the lights and the engine, and waited a long time. When the lights came on in the windows of the Washington house, he waited until he was sure everyone was up, and then he stepped out of the pickup and limped along the sidewalk to the front door.

Mrs. Washington opened the door when he knocked.

"Well, hello, Dodger. What are you doing here so early?"

Dodger stood with his hat at his side and smiled up at Bobby's mother.

"Me and Mr. Cain are in town on some business, and I was wondering if Bobby could come stay with us until tomorrow. We'll bring him home."

Mrs. Washington looked out past Dodger as Bobby walked up behind her. "Where is Mr. Cain?"

"He's taking care of some stuff, but we'll be heading back to his ranch pretty soon."

Bobby stuck his head around his mother. "Hey, Dodge. What's up?"

Mrs. Washington stepped aside. "He wants to know if you would like to spend the night at the ranch with them," his mother answered.

Before he could respond, Dodger chimed in. "You'll have to help us put fence up, though. Mr. Cain will pay you."

"Can I go?" Bobby asked.

"Go ask your father."

Bobby sprinted around the corner into the kitchen. His voice and that of his father drifted back to the front door in quiet talk. Bobby returned, grinning.

"He said I can go. Wait up while I get my things."

Bobby's mother kissed him and told both boys to stay out of trouble. They said they would, and Bobby walked alongside his friend at Dodger's hobbled pace until they got to the pickup.

"Where's Mr. Cain?"

Dodger grinned and slid in behind the wheel.

"On his way to Houston. It's just me and you, B-Bob."

"Noooo . . . are you serious?"

Dodger nodded. Bobby's expression was one of disbelief as Dodger checked the mirrors and settled in behind the wheel.

"Can I drive?"

"Are you nuts? This is a four-speed. It takes lots of practice to drive one of these."

"Come on, Dodge-man. I've driven a four-speed."

Dodger turned the key, and the engine fired up. "This ain't exactly a four-speed."

"What is it, then?"

"It's a three-speed with compound low."

Bobby held up a fist then let his fingers rise one at a time as he counted.

"So, you have first, second, third, right?"

"Right."

Bobby raised one more finger. "And compound low."

"Right."

Bobby held his hand in front of Dodger.

"That makes four . . . so it really is a four-speed."

Dodger shook his head. "Compound low don't count. It's like an extra gear, but they don't count it."

"That don't make any sense, Dodge, and you know it."

Dodger sat up straight and grinned as he pulled away from the curb.

"How about when we get to the ranch then, Dodge—can I drive then?"

Dodger looked in the mirrors again and raised himself high to look out over the hood into the gray of the new day.

"Okay, maybe then."

"Let's listen to some music."

"The radio don't work."

"How fast will this thing go?"

"I don't know, B-Bob, but I gotta take care of it. Harley trusted me with it."

Bobby settled back, rolled his window down, and pulled his hat low to shade his eyes against the rising morning sun.

"I only been down this way one time—and I ain't never been to Mexico before, not that I ever wanted to," Bobby said as he looked south into the horizon, with Mexico just beyond it.

At the highway, Dodger slowed for a cattle truck that pulled onto the blacktop in front of him. He downshifted and let the compression of the engine slow them until there was room to pass. He accelerated into the other lane and pulled ahead of the truck.

Outside of town, the highway stretched out straight and flat. Dodger leaned back in the seat, glanced over at Bobby, then back out the windshield. Dodger rolled up his window to reduce the noise in the cab, and then he spoke to Bobby in a slow manner. Bobby crossed a boot over one knee and turned to listen.

"I don't know what's up with Mr. Cain," he said, his voice subdued and serious.

"What do you mean?"

"That cough of his keeps getting worse, and now he's going to Houston to the medical center, but he didn't say what for."

"It ain't no cold, is it?" Bobby asked as he sat up straight and looked across at Dodger.

"No, it ain't. And you don't go to Houston for a cold anyway."

"You think it's serious?"

"Yeah. Don't you?"

Bobby nodded. "It sure sounds like it."

Dodger looked worried. "I hope it ain't."

"Me too."

Dodger slowed and stuck his arm out the window to signal a turn to the car tailgating the pickup. The sound from the tires changed from pavement to gravel, and he pulled the pickup in alongside the house and turned off the engine.

"This is it—this is Harley's ranch."

He swept his arm in the general direction of miles of wire fence in varying states of disrepair.

"And that's the fence we gotta fix."

By early afternoon, the boys had the worst of the fences around the barn and the horse pens mended with new wire and new corner braces, as well as a line brace in the long stretch between the highway and the back pasture. They stood back shirtless, soaked in sweat, and pulled off their gloves while they surveyed their progress.

"It ain't real straight," Dodger said, "but it's tight as a guitar string."

Dodger pointed to a section between the driveway and the nearest cross fence.

"Let's finish that one, then it will be time to knock off for the day. We'll take us a ride down to Los Caminos."

Bobby lifted his hat off and rubbed his gloves across his forehead. "You think that's a good idea?"

"Sure, why not?"

"From what you told me, you might not be too welcome around there."

Dodger put up his hand in a dismissive manner.

"That ain't no problem—give you a chance to see a place you never seen before. I'll show you where everything happened at the river crossing too."

The air began to cool as the sun traversed the sky. Dodger pulled the pickup into a dirt parking spot in front of a small country store, a Mexican *mercado*, just off the highway midway between the ranch and Los Caminos. The boys stepped inside, and Dodger addressed the man behind the register.

"*¿Cerveza?*"

The man pointed to the rear of the store. The boys returned with two chilled longnecks.

"*¿Es todo?*"

Dodger looked at Bobby, and Bobby nodded.

"*Sí. Es todo.*"

They entered Los Caminos, and Dodger avoided the police station, circled the block, and approached the El Agave café from the alley that ran behind it. He pulled into a vacant lot at the end of the block and saw Elena walking in their direction from the café.

"Hey, there she is. That's Elena. Wait here."

She stopped at the side of an older Ford 2-door, lowered in the back and missing half of the right taillight lens. She put her hand on the door handle and paused after she opened it.

She heard Dodger's voice but did not immediately recognize him as he crossed the street.

"Elena, hey, Elena. Wait up!"

She glared at him as he approached her.

"Please, Elena, I gotta talk to you."

Her hands trembled and her voice choked with anger. "What do you want?"

He stopped and held up a hand.

"I know what you're thinking, and I just want to tell you my side of it."

"You don't have a side. You shot my father, and I hope you go to hell for it."

"It wasn't like that. Can I please tell you what happened?"

Her expression changed and the look in her eyes changed, but there was nothing soft there. She set her jaw, folded her arms, and listened.

The boy told her everything as it had happened. She thought about it a long time without speaking, and she seemed to understand. When he told her that her father had shot Cain and would have killed him, she looked away and drew in a deep breath before she spoke.

"I know they did things that weren't right. And I know they stole those horses, but I need to think. How can I find you if I need to talk to you again?"

Dodger gave her Cain's address and directions to the place. He gave her Cain's telephone number and told her he would like to talk to her again. She looked into his eyes, and her look was disarming.

"I don't even know your name."

"It's Bodean Cooper, but everyone calls me Dodger."

She slid into the seat of the car and brought her legs in slowly, and then she closed the door and rolled down the window.

"I just need to think about all this, okay?"

Dodger nodded. "I understand. And I am really sorry about everything."

She backed out of the parking space and left without looking at the boy.

By the time Dodger pulled off the road and drove through the brush and trees on the north side of the river and stopped near the crossing, Elena was at home on the telephone.

"Uncle Manuel, this is Elena. The boy is here. In Los Caminos. No. I just talked to him. He's with another boy."

Elena told her uncle everything, including Cain's address and telephone number. When Manuel told her he would call his brothers in El Nogal, the girl hung up the telephone and crossed herself.

CHAPTER TWENTY

This whole place looked bigger at night," Dodger explained to Bobby as they surveyed the campsite and the area near the crossing.

Bobby pushed his hat back with his index finger and walked to the river's edge. "Is this where you crossed?"

"Yep . . . and that's Mexico right over there."

"It looks just like Texas."

Dodger smiled and shrugged his shoulders.

"It don't look like Texas when you're trying to get out of there at night."

"How deep is that river?"

"It ain't. There's a sandbar goes right through almost to the other side. It drops off not quite belly-deep on a horse about halfway across. We made it in the truck."

Bobby pointed out several sets of tire tracks leading in and out of the water. "It looks like some others have made it a time or two by them tracks."

"Yeah, I reckon this is a regular crossing for them that know it."

"How far is it to El Nogal?"

"Not far. Why?"

"I ain't never been to Mexico. I'd like to see where the Delgados live."

"No way, B-Bob. If we get caught over there, we're done."

They walked back to the pickup and sat gazing across the river. Bobby sat in the seat and crossed his boot over his knee.

"We wouldn't need to stop, just drive by, keep going, and come back here and head home. Wouldn't even take an hour, would it?"

Dodger grinned. "It might take an hour."

"We going to do it?"

"Hell yeah, we're going for it. This might be your only chance to see Mexico."

Dodger edged the pickup up to the water and coaxed it in slowly. The truck's exhaust rumbled and then gurgled when it dropped below the surface of the water. The front of the vehicle dropped off quickly, but Dodger held it steady. When it came sloshing out on the other side, both boys yahooed and Bobby slapped the outside of the door.

"We're in Mexico, Dodge-man!"

Dodger looked about nervously as he pulled out of the heavily treed area and up onto the blacktop. He looked over at Bobby, his expression serious and his eyes darting from mirror to mirror and window to window.

"Sit back and try to look like you belong here. We don't want no extra attention."

Bobby looked over at Dodger, and he held his hands out in front of him and shrugged in his best *what-are-you-thinking* gesture. "Do I *look* like I belong here?"

Dodger laughed. "I guess neither one of us is going to fool anyone. Just keep your eyes peeled."

Bobby sat up straight and rested his arm in the frame of the open window. "Do you know how to find their place again?"

"I'll know it when we get on the other side of El Nogal. We got jacked around trying to find it the first time, so I ain't altogether certain how to get there."

In the waning light, the town appeared smaller and dirtier than the boy remembered it. They passed the filling station with the map on the wall. Dodger pulled over, made a U-turn, and parked near the map. He and Bobby found Monterrey Street.

"Okay, I remember now," Dodger said. "We go by one time then head back to the crossing and back into Texas."

Bobby agreed. Both boys remained silent until they turned onto Monterrey Street.

Dodger slowed the pickup and pointed up the road with a shaky finger.

"It's up there on the left. A light green double-wide with a old whitewashed barn in the back. I ain't stopping, and I ain't slowing down."

As they approached the place, they saw no sign of activity. The truck continued to pick up speed until Bobby leaned over and looked at the speedometer.

"Slow down, man—you're going almost seventy."

Dodger watched the rearview mirror for any sign of the Delgados. At the first intersection, he applied the brakes hard, downshifted, and accelerated toward El Nogal, traveling west on the same road Cain had used. He reached up and pulled the visor down against the setting sun.

"It'll be dark soon. We gotta get back across that river."

"You best slow down when we get in town. We don't want to get stopped."

A beat-up pickup driven by an old man with three young children riding in the back entered town ahead of them. Blue smoke rolled out of the exhaust, and the rusty pickup labored into town at twenty miles an hour with the two nervous boys following and wishing them off the road.

At the first stop sign in town, the old pickup stopped and sat at the empty intersection a long time while the driver and the person next to him spoke, waving their hands and ignoring the vehicle behind them. Dodger honked. The driver flipped him off and continued arguing.

"Go around him," Bobby said.

Dodger hesitated, looked over his shoulder, and was starting to pull out when the old pickup ahead of him made a left turn, cut him off, and crept away ahead of the smoke cloud that followed it.

• •

There was a sky full of stars and half a moon hanging over the trees by the time Dodger turned off the highway and rolled slowly into the underbrush at the crossing. He eased up to the water's edge and noticed lights bumping their way toward them on the other side of the river. He turned his own lights off and waited.

"What do you suppose that is?"

Bobby's eyes widened. He shook his head. Dodger turned off the engine, leaned his head out the window, and listened.

"It's a car."

"Border Patrol?"

"Or someone coming back."

Then the lights went dark. The engine stopped. The boys faced the darkness and silence with no good choices left to them.

"What do you want to do, Dodge?"

"We have to wait him out. If it's someone trying to get back across, we might have to leave so they know the coast is clear."

"We could turn on our lights and head down the road a piece."

The boys' hearts pounded in their ears. They stared across the river into the darkness.

They watched the crossing and listened, but neither boy heard the sedan behind them turn off the pavement, its lights off, rolling silently up on them.

Bobby turned in his seat when he heard the gravel crunch behind them. He saw the moonlight reflect off the windshield of the car as it crept through the trees.

Suddenly, the interior of Cain's pickup was awash in light as the sedan's headlights lit it up.

"Hang on!" Dodger yelled.

The engine fired and roared. Dodger ground it into first gear and made a run for the water. The truck faltered in the drop-off, lost traction, and then grabbed again and climbed the shallow bank up onto Texas soil. The lights from the car on the American side flashed into the cab. The vehicle sat blocking the road—the only way out.

Dodger turned off the engine and the lights and handed the keys to Bobby.

"It's the Delgados. Put these in your pocket. When I get out, you stay low and run that way as hard as you can."

"But . . ."

Dodger threw open the door, exited the pickup, and then ran thirty yards into a clearing. He heard men splashing across the river on foot. He heard the Delgado car doors open and slam shut. He prayed that Bobby was getting out.

He heard cursing in Spanish, and he heard angry voices. He stopped, raised his hands.

"*¡Me rindo! ¡Me rindo!*" he screamed.

He recognized Manuel Delgado coming out of the dark, felt a heavy blow on the back of his head, and saw a flash of white light before everything went black.

Bobby ran. No one followed. He stopped, caught his breath, and then turned and watched. He saw Dodger go down. He saw the two dark shadows of men who carried the boy and laid him in the back seat of the sedan. Bobby turned and ran again, staying close to the river and running upstream. This time he did not stop until his lungs ached and his legs collapsed beneath him. He lay where he fell and stayed there a long time waiting and listening. He pushed himself up on one elbow and gazed into the darkness downstream.

He heard men splashing across the water. He saw the headlights of the vehicle on the Mexico side as it backed and turned. He watched the Mexican taillights disappear into the trees in the direction of El Nogal.

He watched the lights from the car on the Texas side eventually begin to move, backing and turning. The lights appeared to move in the direction of the highway, but Bobby could not tell if the vehicle stopped or continued up onto the roadway.

He crawled and clawed his way through the brush and stopped before he reached the clearing at the crossing. He stood to look over the low-growing thicket before him and saw Cain's pickup where they had left it.

Bobby dug his hand deep into the front pocket of his jeans and wrapped his fingers around the keys. He held his breath and listened. His mouth was dry and his lungs burned. Searching the darkness, he neither saw nor heard anything, save the chirping of the crickets and the sounds of tree frogs. He skirted the clearing and waited under the cover of the heavy brush and the black sky with the half-moon now dropping toward the horizon.

He resisted the temptation to run to the truck. He hid out and watched it for more than an hour. Then the headlights of the sedan came on and lit up the pickup. He heard the sedan start up. Two men's voices, angry and brusque, spoke in Spanish. When he heard the car doors slam shut and watched the vehicle roll slowly toward the highway, he sat back against a willow trunk and closed his eyes. His hands shook and his breathing came in rapid, shallow bursts. He waited until dawn before he moved again.

Bobby stood, looked about, and then sprinted in the direction of the truck. He stopped and took cover at the edge of the clearing and waited there before he continued, this time stopping only to pick up Dodger's hat from the ground where an obvious struggle had taken place. He tossed the hat on the seat and slid behind the wheel.

The keys rattled in his trembling hand as he poked at the ignition switch. He steadied his hand enough to insert the key. The engine turned but did not fire. Bobby held the clutch pedal to the floor, turned the key off, and then tried a second time. Nothing.

He slammed the steering wheel with the heel of his hand.

"Dammit!"

On the third attempt, the engine fired.

Bobby's eyes darted from shadow to shadow to the reflection of the river crossing in the rearview mirror as the truck bounced up onto the blacktop, and he accelerated north.

His imagination ran wild with thoughts of Dodger dead or seriously hurt. Either way, Bobby knew he had to help. He did not notice the distant headlights in the mirror creeping up on him until they filled the glass and shone in upon him like the hot eyes of some evil predator. When the lights reflected from the mirror to his face, he panicked, choked the wheel, and stared.

His first impulse was to lock up the brakes and hope to disable the trailing vehicle. His second was to swing wildly off-road into the desert, where he hoped the car could not follow. He waited for the right moment, unsure of his next move. Then, on a remote stretch of highway, the sedan swung into the other lane and crept up on the driver's side of the pickup as Bobby tracked it in the outside mirror.

Bobby prepared to turn into the sedan and run it off the road. He waited to see their faces and to time his maneuver before they got off a shot.

He braced himself and gripped the steering wheel as he looked across with his hands shaking uncontrollably. The driver, a state trooper, motioned a *slow-down* gesture to him and accelerated ahead in his ghost-chasing patrol of the highway.

Bobby pulled over onto the shoulder, swung open the door, leaned out, and vomited. He walked around the truck and breathed in the cool morning air as he regained his composure.

When Bobby entered Cain's house, he glanced up at the wall clock on his way to the refrigerator. It was early morning. He felt as though he had been up for days. He reached in for a milk bottle, his hands still shaking. He set it on the counter, pulled the paper cap off, took a deep breath, and then drank directly from the bottle.

Bobby sat at the kitchen table and set the milk bottle down next to the telephone. He stared at the telephone a long time before he dialed home.

"Hi, Momma. Uh-huh, it's me. I know it's early. I am. Yes, I will. No, I just wanted to ask if I can stay until Sunday. I know, but we got so much fence to fix, and they need me—plus, I need the money."

He nodded, then he shook his head, and nodded again.

"Okay, thanks, Momma. I can just borrow some from Dodger. We wear the same size."

Bobby ended the call and then rose from the chair, proceeded down the hall to the closet, and took out the .45, an extra magazine, and a box of ammunition. He picked out an army holster with *US* carved into the flap and laid it all on the kitchen table. He mentally replayed the instructions he had received from Dodger during a moment that, at the time, seemed nothing more than reckless child's play. He loaded the first magazine. When he slammed the magazine home and felt the heft of the combat-ready weapon in his hand, the weight and seriousness of it stripped the boy of any bravado he expected when he held it at arm's length and brought the blade sight over his reflection in the mirror.

He loaded the second magazine, holstered the pistol, laid it on the table, and contemplated his next move. He picked up the milk, chugged what was left, and then walked over to the sink and looked out the window. The view captured the highway and the bridge in the distance and, beyond that, the flat desert that ran uninterrupted to the base of the blue silhouette of the mountains on the horizon.

He held out his hand, and it still shook. He was unsure which or how many of the Delgados resided in Los Caminos. He was equally unsure which of them stayed at the place in El Nogal. He was sure that, regardless, he had to find Dodger fast.

The telephone rang, and Bobby jumped. He spun around and stared at it as it rang a second and third time. On the fifth ring, Bobby lifted the receiver and put it to his ear. He waited before he spoke.

"Mr. Cain's residence. No, this is Bobby. Oh, hi, Mr. Cain. No, he's way out back. Uh-huh. By the bed? Okay, hold on a sec."

Bobby set the receiver on the table, went to the nightstand by Cain's bed, and retrieved an envelope from the top drawer.

"I'm back. Okay, it says 12114 CR 37. I know—Dodger told me. Three more days? I will. See ya, Mr. Cain."

Bobby repeated the address to himself as he sat down to think in Cain's overstuffed recliner chair, the only sign in the house of any concession to the old man's age.

• •

He stood up quickly and fetched three cans of Vienna sausages from the cupboard and a cola from the refrigerator. When he opened the truck's door, his gaze fell on Dodger's crumpled hat, and his entire body trembled. He pulled out of the driveway heading south with the .45, the cola, and the three small cans on the seat beside him. He had no idea what was to come next.

CHAPTER TWENTY-ONE

Dodger awoke lying wire-bound by the wrists and ankles in a room void of all light but for a narrow crack at the bottom of the door. He heard voices. Two men, maybe three, muffled and speaking Spanish.

He lay on his side. The surface of the floor felt cool and smelled of linoleum. His head throbbed and his ribs ached. He remembered the blow to the head and assumed the bruised ribs had come later. He sat up and blinked as his eyes adjusted to the darkness.

The room seemed small. It reeked of mildew and disuse. He used his feet to push himself back up against one wall, and then he maneuvered himself along the perimeter of the room. By the dim light, he could make out images of boxes piled with clothing and other household clutter. A spare room of some sort.

He sat back and listened. The footfalls of the men outside the door reverberated with a hollow sound as they strode throughout the flimsy structure that felt to Dodger to be very much like the mobile home he remembered as a child.

He could not move his hands. He had no feeling in his feet. The realization of those two facts alone unnerved him. The boy worked his way close to the door and swung his boots near the light source to reveal the insulated copper wire twisted around his boot tops, where it dug deeply into his ankles. He imagined the same wire bound his wrists, for there was no give to it.

With his head tipped back against the wall and his eyes closed, he tried to envision dying. For the simplicity of the concept of death he'd entertained as he careered toward the bridge abutment, the idea of dying at the hands of another extended far beyond anything he imagined. He vowed not to leave that undertaking to the Delgados.

The boy sat there a long time before he heard a hand on the door handle. The door opened slowly, and the dark silhouette of a man stood framed by the doorjamb. He looked in without moving or speaking. He swung the door fully open. The morning light flooded the room. The boy's eyes narrowed, and he looked up at the man looming over him.

"Where's the old man?" the man said.

The boy glared up at the shadowed face of Manuel Delgado. He set his jaw without answering. He did not see the boot coming, but when the impact of it doubled him forward and forced the air from his lungs, he gasped and choked and tried not to vomit.

"I asked you a question."

The boy's voice was airy and raspy. "He's in Houston."

"When will he be back?"

"I don't know—he's supposed to call me from the airport."

"Call you where?"

"At his place. I'm staying there."

"Alone?"

The boy nodded. "Yes."

Manuel Delgado turned, left the room, and stood outside the doorway with his brother. They spoke in Spanish and, of the few words the boy understood, *muerto* and *el viejo* hung in the air like a threat.

Manuel returned to the room. He leaned over the boy and cut the wire from his boots. "You're going with Umberto."

He stood the boy up, and the boy's legs buckled beneath him, driving him to his knees. The man grabbed the front of the boy's shirt in both hands and stood him up again. This time the boy tottered but stayed on his feet.

Umberto followed as Dodger limped across the yard. When they got to the sedan, Umberto roughed him up as he pushed him into the back seat. Dodger slumped against the seat with his hands wired behind him. The ponderous Umberto waved a pistol in his face and motioned him to swing his legs inside, and then he slammed the door.

The boy judged the time to be early morning by the slant of the sun in the sky and the shadows it cast. He judged their destination by the northerly direction in which they traveled and the familiar landscape between the border country and Cain's place.

Dodger watched each of the few southbound vehicles they passed. When he saw Bobby drive past them in Cain's pickup, he held his breath and resisted turning to confirm his observation. He glanced up into the rearview mirror at Umberto. There was no reaction from Umberto. Dodger sat back in the seat, out of Umberto's line of sight.

He arched his back and twisted his hands to give relief to his aching wrists. Bound and helpless, he closed his eyes, and the full realization of his circumstances overwhelmed him.

He imagined Bobby driving blindly to his death in the Delgado compound. Dodger figured Umberto would keep him alive as bait for Cain. He wondered if Bobby might be the better off of the two of them.

Dodger's thoughts blurred. The Delgados would leave no loose ends this time. Now Bobby was becoming as much a loose end as he was.

Dodger was certain Bobby would not notify the police. He would go straight to the Delgados, prepared to do whatever it took to rescue his friend. That meant he had the .45. Dodger refused to entertain what might happen after that.

Umberto drove unbearably slowly. The sun burned in through the side windows and drove the heat up inside the car. The portly man nodded, and then his head jerked back—he was struggling to stay awake. Dodger watched him in the mirror. Umberto never looked back at him.

Moving slowly and with great deliberation, Dodger turned sideways in the seat and brought his legs up. He slid his hands beneath him, inched them down behind his legs, and, finally, over his boots. With his bound hands free, he lowered his legs and sat directly behind Umberto, out of his line of sight in the mirror.

He sized up the thick neck of the nodding man. The head was enormous. He envisioned his hands dropping over the big head, the wire cutting into the bull-neck, his knees dug into the seat back while the man thrashed about. He imagined Umberto's fingers clawing at the wire, the car drifting off the road and out onto the flat of the desert as it crawled to a halt while the big man's fingers relaxed and his shoulders drooped.

The boy tipped forward and balanced himself against the seat back. He looked into the reflection of Umberto's half-closed eyes and changed his mind about the strangulation.

"Hey, I gotta pee. Can you pull over?"

Umberto's head snapped upward, and he looked back at the boy. He pulled sharply onto the dirt shoulder without signaling and slid to a stop. He exited the sedan and walked around to the passenger side and opened the back door for the boy. When Dodger exited the vehicle, Umberto took no notice of the boy's repositioned hands.

Dodger walked several yards into the desert and stood with his back to Umberto, who unzipped facing the highway and relieved himself with no regard for any passing traffic. Still exposed, he leaned against the front fender. A semi-truck passed on the highway, and the driver sounded his air horn. Umberto turned and flipped him off.

When Umberto diverted his attention to the passing trucker, Dodger bolted. He ran blindly into the cactus and sage, searching frantically for cover in the thin and scattered vegetation.

The lumbering Umberto took up the chase but soon fell, winded and wheezing. He cursed the boy and stumbled back to the sedan. He over-revved the engine and spun the sedan around in a vortex of dust that followed the vehicle into the desert in pursuit of the boy.

Dodger hunkered down in the small boulders in the underbrush. Umberto scanned the flat landscape through the windshield of the moving automobile, hoping for a quick recovery of his escaped prisoner. No sign of the boy. He slammed on the brakes and slid to a stop.

Umberto turned off the engine and walked around to stand at the front bumper. He leaned back against the hood and took a long drag off the cigarette he held.

He shouted into the hot wind coming in off the desert. "Hey, kid—come on back. I ain't going to hurt you."

He tilted his head and listened. Nothing. He shaded his eyes and looked off across the desert floor in a wide, sweeping gesture. He saw nothing but the barren landscape. He turned and cursed beneath his breath as he slid behind the wheel.

Dodger lay where he had dropped among a scattering of rocks barely large enough to cast a shadow. His chest ached. He lay without moving, certain that Umberto would spot him huddled there with his body shaking. He waited a long time after he heard the sedan pull out onto the blacktop before he lifted his head to look about.

He stood and gazed off into the heat blazing up from the sand. He pressed the sleeve of his shirt against the sweat around his eyes. His wrists ached. He glanced up at the sun and, for the first time since the river crossing, he missed his hat.

Dodger paralleled the highway and stayed in the cover of the taller vegetation that grew in random patches. He worked his way south, always watching the highway for the sedan.

Dodger looked up at the sun again and then ahead at the long stretch of roadway. He brought his hands up to his face and attempted to twist the wire free with his teeth. He stopped and studied the skeletal remains of an ancient ocotillo plant with its spiny canes outstretched like the arms of some long-dead supplicant to this desolate place.

The boy circled the brittle framework, separated the whiplike canes, and broke off the one sturdy enough to work the twists from the wire that bound his hands. He steadied the cane between his knees and picked at the thorns with the wire. When the last twist gave, he jerked his hands free and cast the wire into the brush, rubbing his wrists and flexing his knotted fingers.

He had not seen a vehicle in two hours. At the crest of a rise in the highway he saw the distorted image of the *mercado* shimmering in the rising heat off the horizon far ahead. It seemed like a hundred years had passed since he and Bobby stopped there for a beer.

When he was near the store, he crossed the hot blacktop and stood on the shoulder looking across the parking lot. A one-ton truck with a stock trailer sat off to one side. The store owner's pickup stood in its usual place alongside the store. No other sign of life anywhere.

Dodger looked up and down the highway, and then he looked over the parking lot a second time for any sign of Umberto's car but saw nothing unusual.

He paused before he swung open the screen door to the entrance and stepped inside.

The same man stood behind the counter. Dodger nodded, and the man shifted his eyes but did not nod back.

"*Buenos dias*," Dodger said as he passed on his way to the coldbox at the rear of the store.

"*Buenos dias*," the clerk mumbled back.

Dodger stood with his face pressed against the cold glass of the cooler. He heard the front door open and close. He listened and heard the familiar voice of Umberto. Dodger slipped away from the coldbox and positioned himself behind the long shelves and looked out to see Umberto gesturing and speaking with the clerk.

His stomach knotted. Dodger bent down low and hurried to the corner of the store. He glanced into the back room, saw it was his only option, and stepped inside. He tried the door to the restroom.

"It'll be a minute," called a voice from inside.

He found a back door to the outside behind a stack of empty beer bottle cartons. He turned the doorknob hard one way, then the other. Locked.

He looked up. Light shone in from a window high above the full cases of beer stacked below it. Dodger made his way up the stack to the window and struggled with the paint-stuck slider lock. Unable to force it open, he descended the cases, heard the voices of Umberto and the clerk moving closer, and picked up a No. 2 can of peaches from the stocker cart behind him.

Back up at the window, he slammed the can against the lock, breaking it free. He set the peaches on the sill and pushed the window open wide. He climbed down from the stack, still inside the back room, and concealed himself between two pallets of canned goods as Umberto and the clerk rushed into the room.

Umberto tried the back door. The owner pointed at the open window, spoke urgently in Spanish, and they turned and ran for the front door. Dodger waited until he heard the voices of both men outside below the open window at the back of the building. He sprinted for the entrance.

On his way to the front door, the boy stuffed his pockets with beef jerky and grabbed a warm bottle of cola from the counter. He exited through the open door and raced in a lopsided gait for the cover of the truck across the parking lot.

Dodger climbed up onto the running board of the trailer, hunkered down holding onto the side bars, and waited while Umberto and the store clerk searched the area behind the *mercado.* He hung there a long time. When he heard the sedan accelerate northbound on the highway, he eased himself down.

He sat on the running board of the trailer, tore open a bag of beef jerky, and then popped the bottle cap against the side of the trailer while he ate and contemplated his next move.

A young cowboy ambled across the parking lot with the rowels of his spurs spinning in the dirt with each step he took and his jingle-bobs ringing every time a boot hit the ground. He turned the corner and looked down at the boy sitting on his haunches in the shade of the wheel.

"I heard the commotion inside. You the robber they was lookin' for?"

"No, sir. I ain't no robber."

"Then why you hiding?"

"I did hijack this stuff, but it ain't nothing like you think."

"You need a ride?"

"Yessir, I reckon so. You headed south?"

"Other side of Los Caminos."

"That'll do."

They were a mile down the road before either spoke. Dodger reached across the seat and offered the cowboy a piece of beef jerky.

"Jerky?"

The cowboy looked at him and grinned.

"Don't mind if I do. Where y'all headed to?"

"County Road 37."

The cowboy turned his head and looked at the boy with his eyebrows raised.

"Who you looking to see there?"

"I got some business with the Delgados."

The cowboy's expression hardened, and he looked askance at the boy.

"The *Delgados*?"

"Uh-huh."

"That was one of 'em back there."

"I know."

"It ain't none of my business, but it didn't look like he was fixin' to do you any favors."

"That's a fact too."

"You need to be careful around them boys," the cowboy said.

"Yeah, I know all about that."

The cowboy studied the road ahead and refrained from asking the questions he pondered as they rode through an awkward silence until Dodger offered an explanation that he knew fell short of the one the cowboy considered.

"My business ain't exactly with the Delgados. I'm just meeting my friend Bobby near there. He's got my truck."

The cowboy glanced over at Dodger, not at all convinced the boy was being straight with him.

Dodger chose to change the subject. He sat back, raised a boot, and sat cross-legged. He tipped back his bottle, burped, and wiped his mouth on his sleeve.

"You live around Los Caminos?"

"About five or six miles west of there—been cowboying for the Tumbling T going on three years now."

Dodger took another pull on the bottle.

"My daddy was the cowboss up north on the Two Sixes."

"The Two Sixes?"

"Yessir."

"That's a big outfit. I dayworked for 'em some last year at branding. What'd you say your daddy's name was?"

Dodger squirmed in his seat, but he never missed a beat. "He was gone before you got there, I reckon."

"I might have heard of him, though."

"Bo Cooper. Ever hear of him?"

"Can't say I ever did. Lot of 'em come and go."

"Well, my daddy's a top hand. Everybody knows him."

The young cowboy let it go at that. Then he looked over at Dodger, still trying to feel him out. "You ever think about cowboyin' for a livin'?"

"I thought about it."

"Change your mind?"

"No, not really. I got this bad foot. They don't hire limpers."

"I know a few stove-up pretty good been doin' it all their lives."

Dodger stared out the side window. "But they didn't start out that way."

The cowboy pushed his hat back and draped a wrist over the top of the steering wheel. "No, I guess they didn't. So what are you going to do?"

"You mean now, or later on down the road?"

"Down the road—for work."

"I'd like to be a vet."

"You good around animals?"

Dodger smiled. "They don't mind a limper."

"Vet school takes some money, don't it?"

The boy nodded. "That's why I reckon I'll end up working in a gas station or something. I'd like to buy me a place like Mr. Cain's someday."

"Harland Cain?"

Dodger turned to look at the cowboy. "Yeah, you know him?"

"Known him most of my life. Him and my daddy rodeoed together."

Dodger sat up straight. "He never told me he rodeoed."

"Roughstock rider. There's probably a lot of things he ain't told you about."

The cowboy held out his hand.

"Name's Rob Crow."

"I'm Bodean Cooper—they call me Dodger."

"Good to meet you."

"You too."

The cowboy rested his arm on the sill of the open window, settled back in the seat, and nodded generally up the road ahead of them.

"You sure you just want me to drop you off when we get to 37?"

He turned toward the open window, spat, repositioned the wad of tobacco that caused his bottom lip to bulge, and turned back to Dodger. The boy looked out at the long road ahead.

In the vastness of that bleak landscape, he reckoned himself to be of little consequence.

"You done enough getting me that far."

CHAPTER TWENTY-TWO

Harland Cain," the nurse's voice called out to the small waiting room where a dozen people sat thumbing through magazines and shifting in their seats.

Cain held up his hand, stood, and nodded at the nurse, who smiled a quick smile with no meaning behind it.

"Doctor will see you now. Please follow me."

She carried a folder, pushed open a heavy swinging door, and held it for Cain.

"Room two, on the left. Have a seat. The doctor will be right in," she said as she followed him in and closed the door behind them.

"Thank you," Cain said, with the same absence of sincerity as her smile.

Cain watched the nurse arrange the folders and papers before her. She turned and exited the room with no further conversation, leaving him with the distinct feeling he had become an investment in which they expected no further return. He stood between the chair against one wall and the paper-covered exam table next to it. A small desk and a roller chair occupied the other wall. He took a deep breath and studied the chart on the wall showing the heart and its complex system of veins and arteries depicted in shades of red and blue.

The focal point of the entire human graphic came down to a single muscle the size of a fist—keep it beating and you have life. Cain smiled at the irony.

A light knock on the door, and the doctor entered. He carried no folder and had no stethoscope draped around his neck, which Cain found unusual. He extended his hand, and Cain shook it. Both men stood through a moment of awkward silence.

"How are you feeling, Mr. Cain?"

Cain shrugged. "A little wore out, but nothing I can't deal with."

"All things being equal, you're in reasonably good shape for your condition and your age."

Cain did not respond. He watched the doctor and waited.

"You know surgery isn't an option, and you decided against radiation therapy. You are aware of the implications of that decision. Have you changed your mind or had any second thoughts?"

"No, sir."

The doctor turned and took a seat at the desk. He flipped through the folder left behind by the nurse. It was apparent to Cain the doctor already knew what was in it.

Cain quickly grew impatient. "So how much time do I have?"

The doctor closed the folder and leaned forward in the chair.

"We can treat the pain, as it escalates—to a point. Certain functions may begin to fail before others. Without going into specifics, we're looking at two stages: a somewhat normal life and, eventually, acute care to manage the pain."

"How long can I get around on my own?"

The doctor looked up, his expression cold and matter-of-fact. "A month, six months, maybe a year—it's hard to say."

Cain left the hospital and returned to his motel room. He sat on the edge of the bed brooding for a long time, thinking about the good and bad of not pulling the trigger when he'd had the chance. It had taken him a lifetime to come to terms with that decision only to have it pulled away by some obscure quirk of circumstances, and he was going to die anyway.

He glanced at the brand-new Gideon Bible atop the lowboy dresser, probably never opened, and wondered if this was all a test or maybe just God's way of paying him back for wasting the life he had been given in the first place.

Maybe it was nothing more complicated than a harsh reminder of the delicate balance between free will and predestination. Whatever it was, Cain knew the final choice was ultimately his, and that gave him comfort. He thought about the boy and the long road the kid had ahead of him. No question, the kid had detoured his plans. As much as he wanted to help the boy, he felt he had to keep his endgame option open at all costs, and that bothered him.

He thought about it a long time, and then he reached for the telephone, phoned his ranch, but got no answer. He arranged a flight for the following morning and spent the rest of the day taking care of business—wrestling with how to wrap up seventy-eight years of living in a few short weeks.

Dodger sat up straight in the seat, and Rob Crow slowed the truck as they approached the intersection of CR 37. A quarter mile ahead, a pickup sat parked off the side of the highway.

"What the heck? Hey, can you pull in up there? That looks like Bobby."

Rob shifted gears and slowed as he approached the pickup. He pulled in behind it, and Bobby stepped around from in front of the parked truck.

Dodger, surprised to see Bobby there, swung the passenger-side door open and limped up to where Bobby stood.

"You been here the whole time, B-Bob?"

"I been driving everywhere. I just ran out of places to go and decided to come here and wait. I just been here a few minutes."

"You okay, B-Bob?"

"I'm okay. I been looking all over for you."

Rob stood at the front of his idling truck. Dodger pulled Bobby by the arm and introduced him to the cowboy. The three stood there as Bobby and Dodger filled in the blanks of the last day and night for each other.

Rob pulled his hat down over his eyes. "Like I said, it ain't none of my business, but it sounds like you two are in a little over your heads."

Bobby looked at Rob and then over at Dodger, and shook his head. "You ain't heard the half of it—and it ain't my place to tell it."

Rob understood and did not press the issue. He looked the two boys over and reached in his back pocket. He withdrew a small round can and dipped out a pinch of chew, tucked it behind his bottom lip, and offered the can to the boys. They shook their heads.

"I've known the Delgados a long time. They ain't totally bad people—they're just old country. But if you get sideways with them, there ain't much they won't do to settle a score."

Dodger shook Rob's hand. "Thanks."

Bobby shook the cowboy's hand, they both said *good to meet you*, and then Rob pulled his rig back out onto the highway heading south.

Bobby and Dodger watched Rob's truck and trailer until it vanished into the heat. Bobby turned to Dodger.

"Now what?"

"We gotta get out of here. Umberto's in his car and on my tail somewhere. I outfoxed him on the road and at the *mercado*. There ain't gonna be a third time with him."

They walked back to Cain's pickup.

"You drive," Dodger said. "I can duck down if we see Umberto. He don't know you."

Both boys closed the truck doors at the same time, and Dodger looked down at the seat and whistled.

"Looks like you aimed to make a stand of it, B-Bob."

Bobby grinned. "I wasn't sure what to expect."

Dodger smiled as he picked up his hat and reshaped it the best he could.

"You pick this up at the river?"

Bobby nodded.

"It was laying in the dirt. It made the whole place look bad."

They drove without speaking until, finally, Bobby said what they were both thinking.

"They could be waiting for us at the ranch."

"I know it."

"Maybe we should go to my place."

Dodger shook his head. "I can drop you off there, but I have to be at the ranch when Harley calls."

"He called when you were gone. I told him everything was okay here."

"He say when he was coming back?"

"Three days, he thought, but he wasn't sure. We need a plan, Dodge-man."

Dodger swung his arm wildly about. "Turn around and drive by the Delgados'. Let's see if Umberto's car is back there yet."

"Why?"

"If he's there, we have time to go to the ranch and get ready for them when they do come."

"Man, I don't know, Dodge."

"You got any better ideas?"

Bobby slowed the pickup, looked behind him, and made a quick U-turn.

"Nope."

They approached the lane leading into the Delgado place, and Bobby slowed the truck. Both boys studied the yard and the area behind the mobile home. Bobby reached across and slapped Dodger on the arm.

"There it is! See it, right behind the house? That's it, right?"

Dodger strained to get a better look.

"Yeah, yeah . . . that's it. Let's get out of here, fast."

The ride back to Cain's seemed short. When they arrived at the ranch, it was with great dread. The wire marks that crossed his wrists and the thought of waking up bound and caged in a dark room by men with malicious motives unnerved Dodger.

"Keep going," Dodger said.

"Why?"

"Something ain't right."

"You see something?"

Dodger shook his head. "No, I just got a feeling, that's all."

Bobby continued past the ranch without slowing and pulled off the road a quarter mile north at a cutout.

Bobby watched nervously as Dodger picked up the .45, pressed the release, and caught the magazine in his free hand. Dodger flicked the bullets out of the magazine with his thumb and counted as he reloaded.

"What are you thinking?"

"I ain't getting whupped no more."

The boys left the pickup, set out cross-country, and came onto Cain's place from the pasture behind the barn. They entered the barn through the slider door at the back, climbed the ladder to the loft, and took up positions at the front where they could watch the house through a paned glass window.

"Them fences look good, huh, Dodge?"

Dodger nodded and whispered back. "We're a couple of fence-building fools, all right. Harley's gonna be pretty happy."

Dodger tried to see through forty years of haze and flyspecks on the small glass window. He spat on the glass and rubbed it with the heel of his hand. They both looked through the tiny smudged area.

"It looks like someone left that front door cracked, don't it, B-Bob?"

Bobby buffed the glass with the elbow of his shirt. He moved back from the window and nodded at Dodger.

"I'm positive I closed it when I left."

Dodger reached around and lifted the .45 from the rear of his belt. He jacked the slide back, chambered a round, and set the safety.

"Let's go see if anyone's in there," Dodger said in a voice that was neither confident nor convincing.

"Shouldn't we wait to see if anyone comes out?"

"This won't be any easier come dark," Dodger said as he nodded toward the sun hanging low in the afternoon sky, and then he turned and started down the ladder.

They exited the barn through the door where they'd entered and skirted past the woodshed to the back door of the house. Dodger turned the knob, and the door creaked open when he pushed it slowly. He turned and whispered to Bobby, who stood near the corner of the house, "Go on over to them trees and watch the front door. Give me a whistle if anyone comes out."

Bobby nodded and hurried into a concealed position behind the largest of the three ancient trees that stood like skeletal sentinels with their gnarled and twisted limbs stretched and reaching out across the evening sky. He waved at Dodger and hunkered down.

Dodger's mouth was dry and a shudder ran through him when he slipped into the gloomy corridor and stood waiting for his eyes to adjust to the darkness. He passed the spare room and crossed into the small living room with its woodstove in the corner and an old newspaper on the small table by the window. Nothing appeared out of place, but nothing felt right. The boy moved quietly into the kitchen and out into the hall. He stopped outside the closed door of the bathroom and tilted his head to listen.

He heard nothing, took a deep breath of relief, and then heard the faint rustling of a magazine page. His heart pounded. He stood back from the door and held his breath.

He heard a page turn, and then he heard the sound of a man clearing his throat. Every instinct in him told him to point the gun at the door and start squeezing the trigger. His face flushed hot, and he began to breathe faster. He resisted the urge to overreact, took a deep breath, and then reached over with his free hand to steady the shaking gun hand.

He stepped back into the shadow of the corner and waited. He heard the water flush and saw the doorknob turn. When the door swung inward, a great flood of light lit up the hallway and silhouetted the dark shape of a large man Dodger did not recognize. The man stepped forth, and Dodger reacted without thinking.

He fired a shot into the ceiling and yelled out in a voice fearsome in its desperation, "On your knees . . . now!"

The man threw down the magazine, dropped to his knees, and pleaded. "*No disparar*."

Dodger shifted back and forth across the narrow hall like a trapped animal, his eyes wild, his movements jerky and erratic. The man held his hand up to shield his face from the bullet he feared was coming, and he shook his head in protest.

"*No disparar—por favor*."

Then, in English, he said it again when the front door exploded open.

"Please, señor, do not shoot."

Bobby turned the corner and stopped at the end of the hall, his eyes wide and his chest heaving.

"You okay, Dodge?"

Dodger nodded but did not take his eyes from the big man kneeling before him. "Get some wire from the barn—hurry up."

Dodger motioned with the pistol to the man. "Lay down flat on your stomach."

The look in the man's eyes turned to contempt.

"*Dos hijos*," he said as he pulled one leg under him and prepared to stand with no regard for the boy or the gun.

Dodger squeezed the trigger of the heavy pistol drooping in his grip. Fire and smoke filled the narrow hallway. The bullet ripped into the floor near the man's feet, sizzling the carpet and splintering the wood with an intimidating slap. The man splayed himself prone with his arms stretched above his head.

"Okay, okay, okay," he said, clearly surprised at the boy's dangerous behavior.

Bobby burst through the door carrying two lengths of insulated wire that he dropped at the entrance when he heard the shot.

"What happened?" he asked as he looked from Dodger to the man and back again.

"He tried to get up. He ain't shot."

Dodger stood over the intruder while Bobby fetched the wire and bound the man's hands behind him, wrapping and crossing the wire over the thick wrists until the wire cut into the skin and the man protested. He wrapped the man's ankles with the second wire and stood over him admiring his work.

"See if he's got a gun, B-Bob," Dodger said as he stood with his back against the wall and the pistol trained on the nervous man.

They sat the man upright and Bobby located a pistol under his loose-fitted shirt. He lifted a short-barreled .38 revolver from the waistband of the man's trousers and then turned and looked at Dodger.

"Now what?"

CHAPTER TWENTY-THREE

The rest of that day and late into the night, Harland Cain replayed the doctor's words over and over in his mind.

"We can run other tests," the doctor had told him.

"Will that buy me more time?"

"No, but that's not the point."

"Time's all I got left."

"You choose to forego further testing then?"

"I choose not to rob Peter to pay Paul."

When they shook hands, the doctor's grip told him he had made the right decision.

Late the next afternoon, Cain stood with the others when the attendant announced his flight. When he stepped aboard the airplane, he checked the seat numbers against the number on his boarding pass and took his seat next to the window. He kept his hat on and watched the luggage handlers through the thick double glass as the remaining passengers stuffed the overhead compartments with bags that were too large and eventually took their seats. The last of the stragglers worked his way down the aisle behind a well-dressed woman in a business suit who stopped and looked up at the number on the overhead compartment and then over at Cain.

"14-C?"

"Yes, ma'am."

She smiled, sat down, and slid the canvas shoulder bag she carried beneath the seat in front of her. She buckled her seat belt and removed a dog-eared magazine from the seat back holder at her knees.

"Business or pleasure?" she asked Cain.

"Beg your pardon."

"Are you traveling on business, or is this a pleasure trip for you?"

She smiled an apology for catching the old man off guard.

Cain smiled back.

"Well, it's not much of a pleasure but, then again, it's not business."

She nodded.

"More of a *have to* than a *want to*, it sounds like."

"How about you?" Cain asked.

"Business. I'm in pharmaceutical sales. The Houston Medical Group is one of our biggest clients. They have a very extensive research facility there for terminal diseases, and they are making wonderful progress."

"They about to get a handle on any of the bad ones?"

"You mean like cancer?"

Cain nodded.

She smiled again.

"Oh, absolutely. With the new drugs they're testing and the new procedures and technological advances coming on board, the next ten to fifteen years are going to revolutionize the medical world as we know it."

Cain leaned forward and then turned and looked directly at her, his expression sincere as he patted her arm, signaling the end of the conversation. "Well, keep up the good work. There's lots of folks waiting on that revolution."

She smiled and thanked him. Cain leaned back with his hat pulled over his eyes and contemplated the irony of being the last casualty before the war ends. Last or not, Cain felt like he was in a race to give the boy as much time as possible before the inevitable caught up with him and deprived him of the only true option he controlled.

• •

The desert wind blew in hot and dry through the open door of Cain's house, where the two boys stood over the man with his hands wired together.

Dodger, emboldened by fear and the urgency of the coming confrontation he dreaded with Umberto, pressed the man.

"What's your name?" he asked as he waved the pistol about.

"What?"

"Your name—what is it?"

"Luis."

"Delgado?"

"No, no. Luis Ramos. I am only a friend, no family to them."

"Why are you here?"

Ramos shook his head.

Dodger kicked Ramos's immobile leg, and Bobby watched wide-eyed at the act of brazen disrespect.

"Why are you here?"

Ramos looked away from the boy as though to dismiss the conversation and ignore the question. This time the walls shook when the .45 exploded, and Ramos felt the heat of the blast as the bullet ripped through the drywall and splintered the two-by-four stud behind the gaping hole it left.

Luis Ramos tilted his head to favor the ringing ear and looked up at the boy. Dodger's expression was clouded with bad intent and left no room for further negotiation, nor any tolerance for a lie.

"Umberto told me to hold you until he gets here."

"For what?"

"You killed his brother."

"That was an accident—they was stealing our horses and he was going to kill Mr. Cain."

Ramos shook his head slowly side to side, and his eyes narrowed. "Don't you know nothing?"

"What do you mean?"

Ramos breathed in deeply and exhaled slowly. "You disrespected the man whose brother you killed. You cut his fences, and you stole those horses from him."

"They was our horses."

"No, when you took them they were his horses."

Dodger looked at Bobby, and Bobby shrugged his shoulders. Ramos turned away. "Now it is your debt to pay."

"And he wants to kill me for that?"

"It's his honor—he must kill you for his honor."

"Ain't there no other way?"

Ramos did not reply. He gazed down the narrow hallway toward the door and stared a long time before he shook his head.

Dodger set his jaw, released the half-spent magazine into his hand, and shoved the pistol into his waistband.

"I need more bullets and that other magazine, Bobby. Go to the closet and get you that .44-40 and a shotgun—and more ammunition."

Bobby stood without moving, as though this was all a nightmare from which he could escape if he just refused to acknowledge its existence. Dodger waited. Bobby did not move or respond.

"Bobby?"

Bobby shifted his gaze to Dodger but did not move his head.

"What are we gonna do, Dodge?"

"Go get them guns, then go get the truck. We're getting out of here, and we're taking him with us."

Bobby hesitated and watched as Dodger slammed the magazine back into the pistol and looked down at Ramos.

"It don't have to be like this," Ramos said.

His voice was soft and almost prophetic.

Dodger glared down at him. "It is like this."

The telephone rang. The boy jumped back and swung around to face the direction from which the sound came. He limped to the kitchen and watched the telephone as it rang two more times, and then he picked up the handset.

"Hello."

Dodger waited. When he spoke there was great relief in his voice.

"Oh man, Harley, we got trouble. Yeah, we're okay for now. No . . . the Delgados. They're coming to kill me. Bobby's with me. Okay, I'll be there."

The boy stood there holding the telephone, looking down at the table, deep in thought. He did not see the shadow behind him, but he lurched forward when Ramos hit him with his clenched hands and sent the .45 flying across the linoleum.

Ramos took the boy to the ground. Dodger lay pinned to the floor, immobilized beneath the ponderous weight of Ramos. Dodger felt the man's hands on his throat. His arms flailed helplessly. He tried to scream but could not. He felt himself relax and begin to lose consciousness. He heard Bobby's muffled voice a thousand miles away.

"Git offa him!"

Bobby swung the butt of the shotgun up in a brutal, arching upstroke. Ramos's big head snapped to the side, gushed with blood, and then tipped limply forward. Ramos rolled over, his eyes turned back in their sockets.

Dodger stood, sucking in air, his hands on his knees.

Bobby stood over Ramos, the 12-gauge in his hands, the gun belt slung over his shoulder. His pockets bulged with ammunition.

"What happened?"

"I don't know. He jumped me from behind. He almost killed me, Bobby."

Dodger knelt before the man and slapped him hard across the face.

Ramos stirred.

"Get up."

The man attempted to stand, fell back, and nodded to his ankles and waited for Bobby to remove the wire.

Dodger, his eyes hot with rage, held the .45 in the man's face.

"Any more shit like that and I'm gonna shoot you in your face."

Ramos kept his eyes down. He shook his head. "I'm sorry. I'm sorry."

"Bobby, go get the truck, fast. Mr. Cain will be back in Bufort in two hours."

Bobby exited the house at a run, carrying the shotgun and attempting to hold the gun belt in place as he sprinted down the driveway and out onto the blacktop highway.

Bobby reached the pickup a quarter of a mile away, gasping

for air and dripping sweat. He leaned against the tailgate, rested his head on his forearm, and held the shotgun hanging at his side. He did not see the beat-up sedan slow as it approached Cain's house and then pause at the driveway before it continued in his direction.

Bobby lifted his head at the sound of the approaching vehicle and recognized Delgado's sedan as he instinctively moved around to the passenger side of the pickup, hunkered down, and waited. The sedan inched past at an idle, and Bobby knew the driver was looking. He prayed Delgado would not stop. He did not move. When he heard the sedan accelerate, he waited until it disappeared around the turn. He opened the passenger door and threw the shotgun and the gun belt down on the floorboard. He slid across the seat and put the key in the ignition, the keys rattling as he did so.

When Bobby pulled into the yard of Cain's house, he spun the truck around and honked for Dodger. Before the dust that hovered around the truck began to dissipate, Ramos exited the house with Dodger prodding and pushing him with the barrel of the .45.

"Hurry up, Dodge. Delgado's right behind me."

Dodger stepped around Ramos, lowered the tailgate, and motioned him into the bed with the pistol.

"Get in." His voice left no room for compromise, and Ramos did not hesitate or protest as he slipped backside-first onto the bed of the pickup.

Dodger carried a roll of black tape with which he bound the man's ankles and made half a dozen hasty wraps over the man's mouth and around his head. He looked at Ramos, and Ramos looked back at him.

"You try to jump or cause a fuss, I will shoot you."

He pushed Ramos into a lying position, and Ramos complied without an argument. Dodger slammed the tailgate and then climbed into the passenger side. He shouted at Bobby, "Get out of here!"

Bobby bounced up onto the blacktop with the tires squealing and turned to the left, heading south.

"Where you going, Bobby?"

"Delgado will be coming back from the north in just a few minutes. I didn't want him to see us."

Dodger nodded.

"Good thinking, man. We can circle back around on Old Presidio Road and take the back way into Bufort."

When they turned off the highway and turned north onto Old Presidio Road, the boys sat back and relaxed some. Dodger turned halfway in his seat, looked out the back window, and watched Ramos, who lay without moving.

Bobby glanced into the rearview mirror and then looked over at Dodger.

"What are we going to do with him?"

"I don't know, B-Bob—I don't even know what we're going to do with us."

Dodger sat back with one leg crossed over the other and his arm resting on the open windowsill. He stared out across the desert and saw himself floating there.

The hot air smelled of dust and ancient vegetation as old as the parched ground upon which it grew. Dodger's thoughts wandered and spun off back to some far time where he imagined himself in a strange land. He saw himself whole in body and whole in spirit and saw himself astraddle a horse the color of burnt mahogany, outfitted in the rigging of a working cowboy.

He saw himself mounted against a fading sun that made his horse appear to be the spirit of a horse and himself the spirit of a man. Both a hundred years into a journey with no end and no beginning. He could not envision his origin or his destination, or whether there was a destination at all. There were no others in his vision. As much as he wished others into it, he could not dream them there—and for that, he felt an emptiness he could hardly bear.

Then it was gone. He turned to Bobby. His voice was hollow, cold.

"Stop at the end of your street when we get there."

Bobby glanced over at him and then quickly returned his eyes to the highway.

Bobby hesitated, put off a bit by Dodger's cold tone. "I reckon I'll just stick it out with you and Mr. Cain."

Dodger sat up straight with his arms folded. "Me and him have to go to the po-lice. Ain't no need for you to get messed up in it. Your daddy don't need no trouble like that."

Bobby stuck out his jaw, offended by Dodger's exclusion. "Neither do you."

"I already got it—he don't."

Bobby remained silent a long time.

"Will you come get me if you need me?" Bobby asked.

Dodger softened some.

"I will, B-Bob. I promise."

They rode in silence, and Bobby hung his right hand over the top of the steering wheel in a casual manner.

"We been friends a long time."

"Yeah, we have," Dodger replied.

"Remember the first time we met?"

Dodger laughed. "Yeah, I do."

"Curtis Holloway said you called me a *spear-chucker*."

"He said you called me *hopalong*."

"I remember I whupped you good for that," Bobby said.

"That ain't how I remember it."

"Well, who ended up with a broke nose and a loose tooth?"

Dodger grinned. "That was just a lucky punch. I wasn't even ready."

"You gave me a black eye. You was ready," Bobby said.

They both laughed, and then Dodger smiled and added, "I do remember we both ended up in the principal's office and Holloway didn't even get called in."

Bobby grinned. "And I do remember we both kicked Holloway's ass for it later."

Dodger's expression turned serious and he gnawed at the inside of his cheek before he spoke. "You and your folks have pretty much been the only family I've ever known."

Bobby stuck out his hand, and Dodger shook it.

CHAPTER TWENTY-FOUR

Dodger dropped Bobby off and drove to the small airport with its part-time control tower and one-room terminal. The building and the tower sat like solitary tributes to an aviation world that barely acknowledged the existence of this remote West Texas town. Dodger parked the pickup out of the way on the grass-covered apron near the runway, where he waited and listened for the whining sound of the propellers of the twin-engine plane that was now running ten minutes late.

Dodger turned to check on Ramos, his hands wrapped with wire, his ankles bound with the same black tape that covered his mouth. The sinister appearance of it all struck the boy with the grim reality of his circumstances. His mouth was dry and he drummed the steering wheel with his fingers as he waited, watching the sky for Cain's airplane and the rearview mirror for Delgado's sedan.

A door at the terminal opened. A man exited the building, looked across the empty lot, and began to walk in the direction of the pickup. Dodger watched him in the mirror as he strode authoritatively in his direction.

Panicked at the thought of having to explain Luis Ramos to the man, the boy slipped out the door, hobbled toward the man, and intercepted him twenty yards from the truck. Dodger glanced over his shoulder and prayed Ramos would remain concealed as the man spoke in a challenging tone.

"What are you doing over there?"

"Waitin' on a airplane."

"Flight 112?"

"The one from Houston—I don't know the number."

"That's flight 112. They had a delay at Mueller Municipal in Austin. It should be here shortly."

Dodger heard Ramos shuffle in the bed of the pickup, and he glanced over his shoulder.

"Everything okay?" the man asked as he raised his head slightly and looked in the direction of the pickup.

"Yessir. Just waitin' on Mr. Cain."

"Harland Cain?"

Dodger nodded.

The man smiled and seemed to relax.

"You tell ol' Harley, Ben Pepper said hello."

"Yessir, I will."

"Shouldn't be much longer. You can wait inside if you've a mind to."

"I'm okay . . . I'll just wait in the truck. Thanks."

The boy returned to the truck, and the man departed the now-empty lot in a new black pickup that appeared oddly out of place for its undamaged and unspoiled condition in a land where pickups were either beat-up oilfield vehicles or old ranch trucks.

Dodger stopped and leaned over the bed of the truck.

"You okay there?"

Ramos looked up at the boy with eyes that bore no hatred and asked for no quarter. Something about the directness of the man impressed the boy, but the man did not favor him with a nod one way or the other.

Dodger remained leaning over the bed of the truck, his boot resting on the tire rim and his hat pulled low over his eyes. He looked up at the sky, now red with the colors of the setting sun, and watched the sun as it slipped down behind the dark horizon from a sky with no clouds in it anywhere.

Cain stared down upon the scattered lights of Bufort, the main street, the highway—familiar and welcoming in the way inanimate things can be when you have nothing else. This trip reconciled it for him. When the time came, the end would be his call. Now he struggled with the timing of it all and the weight of a load he was not sure he could carry the distance. It was no longer just his life on the line. A fraction of a second sooner, and none of this would have been his problem.

He smiled a half smile. The cowboy in the seat across the aisle looked over at him when Cain shook his head and muttered to himself, "Three strikes against him, and the damn kid's still up there swinging at everything that comes across the plate."

The pilot announced the descent as the airplane entered the pattern and made a wide banking turn for the approach. Cain acknowledged the cowboy across the aisle, who nodded when their eyes met.

"How many really good horses you reckon a man will own in his life?"

The cowboy grinned, angled his head, and thought a moment.

"Maybe one," he said before the grinding sound of the landing gear ended the conversation.

Dodger heard the engines before he saw the plane. The aircraft dropped down in a steep approach before the pilot expertly brought the wheels into contact with the tarmac without a bounce. The plane rolled up, the engines slowed, and the propellers continued spinning even after the door opened and a man lowered the stairs.

A young cowboy carrying a tattered canvas bag was the first to deplane. He stopped, lit the cigarette he carried clinched between his teeth, and walked toward the terminal building.

Cain appeared in the doorway of the plane and nodded to Dodger, who waved from the edge of the grass. Cain descended the stairs and hurried to join Dodger. They walked briskly to the truck.

When they got to the pickup, Cain tossed his bag in the bed and jumped back at the sight of the man who, at first glance, appeared to be dead.

"What the hell is this?" Cain asked as he stood back and looked at Dodger.

"He's our prisoner. Me and Bobby got him."

"Prisoner? Prisoner for what?"

"His name is Luis Ramos. Umberto Delgado got him to help kill me."

"How do you know that?"

"He told me."

"Where's Bobby?"

"I took him home."

Cain motioned toward the passenger-side door.

"Get in."

Before he got in, Dodger handed Cain Ramos's pistol.

"What's this?"

Dodger pointed his thumb at the truck bed.

"It's his. I told you this was serious."

Cain turned onto Old Presidio Road to avoid going through town and drove south.

"Where to now?" Dodger asked.

"We're taking him . . ." he nodded toward the back window ". . . to the police in Los Caminos."

"What do you expect they'll do, Harley?"

"I don't know, but we gotta do something or we're going to have a war on our hands."

Dodger sat back and chewed on the end of his thumb as he stared out the window and watched the last light of day fade from the heat-seared desert landscape. The boy's thoughts drifted and floated out across the sparseness of the dry land. It seemed like a hundred years ago now. He remembered the bridge abutment and hurtling full-speed toward it with his eyes closed and his fingers clutching the steering wheel before everything went black. He understood the right and wrong of it and wondered if he had actually died and found his way into purgatory without knowing it.

He spoke in a soft voice without turning his gaze away from the darkening shadows of the barren tract of wasteland that bordered the highway.

"Harley, do you suppose we could already be dead and this just be our new lives without us knowing it?"

Harley looked over at the boy and stared without answering. He turned back and pulled on the switch for the headlights and watched the lines in the road as they approached in a rhythmic pattern that silently slipped by on his left.

"I reckon we could be. Seems like I'd remember dying, though."

Dodger nodded. "I remember dying."

"You do?"

"Yessir. I knew what I was doing when I hit that bridge. I closed my eyes, and it was all over. I felt myself moving—and that was all there was. When I woke up, I expected there would be angels or the devil, or something."

"And?"

"And nothing—there was just a old man pulling on me, and that was you, Harley."

"I don't reckon you died then."

"Why not?"

"Because I didn't. Seems like, for your idea to work, everyone has to be dead or everyone has to be alive."

Dodger smiled a weak smile and turned to look at the old man. "That makes pretty good sense."

The boy turned back to gazing out the window. "Well, Harley, if we was already dead, this all would be a whole lot easier."

Cain laughed. "It ain't over yet—you might get your wish."

The pickup crested a hill, and the lights of Los Caminos flickered on the horizon like some lost outpost where the last of humanity gathered to wait it out. Cain pulled over to the side of the road.

"Why you stopping?"

Cain stepped out of the truck, and the boy did likewise.

"We can't take this man into town like some wild hog we just shot."

Cain leaned over and removed the tape from Ramos's mouth.

"You okay?"

Ramos nodded, and Cain removed the tape from the man's ankles but left his hands wire-bound.

"Come on, get out. You're riding up front with us."

Ramos eyed the old cowboy suspiciously.

Cain gestured toward the situation in the pickup bed with a broad sweep of his hand. "You don't deserve to be treated like that."

"Thank you, señor."

"Dodger, throw them guns and all that ammunition behind the seat. He'll sit between us."

When they arrived in Los Caminos, Cain pulled into a diagonal parking space directly in front of the police station. He and the boy walked Ramos inside with his hands still bound by the wire.

The desk sergeant on duty behind the counter stood when they entered and looked immediately to the bound hands of Ramos.

"What's going on here, Luis?"

"We need to see Chief Flores," Cain interjected before Ramos could respond.

The officer's expression showed his impatience. He leaned over the counter and pointed at Ramos's tied hands.

"Why is this man tied up like that?"

"It's a long story. This man—"

"Take that wire off him now. He ain't going anywhere until we find out what this is all about. The chief is at home having his supper, so how 'bout you tell me the long story?"

Ramos extended his hands, and Cain removed the wire. The desk sergeant waved Cain and the boy back away from Ramos and spoke directly to him, ignoring the old man and the kid.

"Luis, this better be good. What happened?"

Ramos rubbed his wrists and avoided eye contact with Cain. "I was hitchhiking home from Bufort, and they stopped to give me a ride. He asked me where I am from." He tilted his head toward Cain. "I told him, and he asked me if I knew Umberto Delgado. I told him I did, and they drove me to a ranch and took me inside a house. They had guns, so I didn't argue. They took me inside and shot the gun at me twice and asked me more questions, but I didn't know nothing to tell them, so they brought me here."

The desk sergeant leaned forward on his hands as he looked over the counter at Cain and the boy.

"I expect you're going to tell me a different story—am I correct?"

"Yessir, you are."

Cain explained what happened as he knew it and as it had been explained to him by the boy. When he finished, he waited for a response from the desk sergeant. The desk sergeant walked from behind the counter and approached Ramos.

"I'm familiar with this incident with the Delgados, and I ain't saying you have anything to do with it, Luis, but I'm going to hold you in one of our detention cells until Chief Flores can sort it out."

The sergeant stood behind Ramos, and Ramos automatically spread his legs and lifted his arms without being asked to do so. The sergeant lifted the man's shirt and removed a snub-nosed revolver. Cain looked at the weapon and then over at the boy.

"Didn't you search him?"

Dodger's face flushed red, and he nodded his head. "Yessir. That was his .38 I give you. We didn't know he had another one."

The desk sergeant stood back and turned Ramos to face him. "What's this?"

"It's for protection when I'm hitchhiking."

"Lotta damn good it did you."

The desk sergeant addressed Cain and the boy. "Are either of you two armed?"

Dodger shook his head.

"No," Cain said.

"They have guns in their truck," Ramos said, as though to defer his own culpability.

"There ain't no law against that," the desk sergeant said.

The desk sergeant escorted Ramos to the holding cell and then returned to talk with Cain and the boy. His demeanor was matter-of-fact, but not apologetic. He stood at the front of the counter with them and wrote on a clipboard in cryptic notes as they answered his questions.

"I expect Chief Flores will want to see you both first thing in the morning. If what you said is true—and I'm not saying it is or isn't—you might want to stay in town tonight to avoid any trouble at your place. There's the Econo Inn down the street. I can call and have them hold a couple of rooms for you."

Cain's voice sounded tired.

"That's probably not a bad idea. Tell them we'll be there after we get some supper. Much obliged."

Cain and the boy walked across the street to the El Agave café and took up seating at the booth in the corner. A man in a sweat-stained cowboy hat sat at the counter with his back to them, talking in whispers to the middle-aged waitress, who smiled and busied herself with a cleaning rag as they spoke. The cook worked at scraping the griddle-topped stove on the kitchen side of the open service window that divided it from the dining room. When the waitress looked up at Cain and the boy, she smiled, laid down the rag, and dried her hands on the wrinkled apron she wore.

She approached the table and stood there with an order pad in one hand and a pencil in the other.

"What can I get for you boys tonight?"

The man at the counter watched the reflection of the old man and the kid in the wide mirror that made the selection of pies appear much larger than it was. He studied their faces and then abruptly laid down a five-dollar bill and departed without waiting for change or saying good night to the waitress.

CHAPTER TWENTY-FIVE

Cain and the boy sat at the corner table at the El Agave waiting for their order. Cain felt uneasy watching three Mexican men who came in, sat at the counter eyeing him and the boy in the mirror, and carried on a guarded conversation in Spanish. They spoke in hushed tones and looked into the mirror frequently to check on Cain and the boy.

After they ate, the waitress refilled Dodger's cola and poured Cain another cup of coffee. She asked them if there would be anything else, thanked them, and laid the check facedown on the table.

The three Mexican men finished their coffee and departed quickly.

When the door closed behind them, Cain waited a few minutes and then stood abruptly.

"Let's go."

Dodger stood and followed Cain. When they reached the pickup, they neither saw nor heard the beat-up gray van idling, concealed by the building across the street. The man with the sweat-stained hat sat behind the wheel, smoked a cigarette, and waited. When Cain pulled out and proceeded down the street, the van gave them a long lead before it pulled out, inconspicuous in the light traffic that was behind Cain's pickup.

In the parking lot of the two-story Econo Inn, Cain wrapped the shotgun, the ammunition, and both pistols in a saddle blanket and carried them in with him. He and the boy had checked into adjoining rooms on the second level with windows overlooking the parking lot.

The man in the sweat-stained hat watched from across the street, made note of the room numbers when they entered, and then accelerated out of town in the direction of CR 37.

Cain laid the guns out on the bed in his room, unlocked the pass-through door on his side, and instructed the boy to do the same on his side. With the pass-through doors open, Cain braced a chair under the handle of the outside door in his room and did the same in the boy's room.

"You expecting trouble, Harley?" Dodger sat on the end of his bed and spoke through the connecting doorway.

"It's like waitin' on rain—you never know if it's coming, and you never know when."

Dodger removed his hat and laid it on his pillows. "Did you see them three watching us in the café, Harley?"

"You getting a little jumpy?"

The boy smiled. "I guess I am. Especially down here."

Then he stood and nodded in the direction of the guns on the bed. "Can I take the .45?"

Cain laughed. "A little partial to it, are you?"

"I do like the feel of it."

Cain picked up the .45, checked the magazine, and handed the weapon to the boy. Then he handed him the extra magazine and a box of ammunition.

"Well, I hope we don't need these, but load up both clips and keep the gun under your pillow just in case."

Cain stretched and yawned.

"Keep an eye on the doors. I'm going to take a quick shower."

Dodger turned out the lights and sat on the bed while Cain showered. The only light in the room was that reflected under the door of the bathroom and the yellow glow through the curtain from the streetlight in the parking lot below. He leaned back against the headboard on his rolled-up pillow with the .45 on his lap and his eyes heavy as he focused on the backlit curtain and listened.

The soothing sound of the shower lulled Dodger into a sleepy state, and he began to nod off. He heard footsteps outside the window. The shadows of two men passed in front of it. The boy's head jerked up with a jolt. He listened. The steps stopped at the door. The two men exchanged a few unintelligible words. A key rattled in the lock.

Dodger sat up straight and trained the .45 on the door.

Come on, Harley—please hurry, he pleaded silently.

The doorknob twisted and shook but the door didn't open, and then everything out front went silent. Dodger hurried to the window and looked out from the edge of the heavy curtain to see the men stagger away into the darkness. He let out a deep breath. His knees felt weak and unsteady as he returned to the bed and resumed his vigil.

Cain exited the bathroom fully dressed, drying his still-wet hair with a thin white towel long past its peak of serviceability.

"I feel like a new man."

Dodger told Cain about the two drunks. They both laughed, but there was no dismissing the fact that it was still a long way until morning. Anything could happen.

The boy showered in his bathroom. When he returned to his bed, he heard Cain snoring across the way.

He dressed and pulled on his boots. He propped the pillow up against the headboard of the bed and pressed his back to it as he tried to sleep sitting up, facing the door, with one hand on the .45 beneath his leg.

The boy did not remember falling asleep, but he sat up with a start as Cain kicked the bed and stood over him with his finger to his lips and pointed at the door. Cain trained the shotgun on the door. Dodger gripped the .45 and rolled off the bed near the wall. Cain stood on one side of the bed, the boy knelt on the other, and they waited.

Before he could question Cain or further get his bearings, the window exploded from its frame, sending shards of splintered glass across the carpet and onto the bed, and a concrete block bounced in behind the glass. Cain dove for the floor to his left, and the boy dropped flat alongside the bed on the floor.

The star-shaped muzzle flash of two high-powered rifles lit up the room from the outside. Bullets whined through the air, digging out holes in the walls and filling the room with dust and smoke. Cain returned fire with several blasts from the shotgun as he sprayed the gaping hole with buckshot. The shooting stopped. Cain dry fired three more times on the adrenaline-charged reflexes that refused to quit. Then, like some nightmarish dream, everything blurred into a gray, cloudy darkness and there was no sound save the heavy breathing of Cain and the boy and the distant wail of a siren.

Cain turned and looked across the room in the boy's direction. "Are you okay?"

Dodger's voice rose weakly above the smoke and dust in the room. "Yeah, I'm okay. You think they're gone?"

Cain slid the shredded curtain to one side and looked out across the parking lot to see two Mexican men in the gray van as it bounced over the curb and out onto the street and then away into the darkness. The sound of the siren and the flashing red lights of the police cruiser rounded the corner, and the vehicle slid to a stop near the reception office below.

Cain looked back at the boy, who stood in the darkness with the light from the window reflecting off the pistol he held at his side. Standing in the dim light amidst the glass shards and splintered wooden window casing, the boy appeared unshaken. There was a hard look about him. Cain turned to the parking lot below.

"Yeah, they're gone. Better put that thing away—we got company," he said.

They wrapped the guns in the saddle blanket, and Cain slid the bundle under the bed in his room.

He and the boy stood outside the splintered door and looked in through the cavernous hole where the window had been in the wall of the boy's room. Cain nodded toward the damage as Detective Spiotto and a uniformed officer ascended the stairs and waved their service revolvers about.

"They're gone," Cain said.

The detective pulled back his jacket and snapped his weapon into the worn leather holster beneath his arm. The uniformed officer held his as though he was poised for a shootout.

The detective admonished the officer with a nod and a glance, and the officer holstered his weapon. They stepped into the room. Detective Spiotto flipped the light switch near the door and looked at the devastation.

"Holy shit! This kind of thing happen to you all the time?" he asked, looking back at Cain.

"Just around here. Los Caminos seems to have more than its share of bad guys."

Spiotto raised his eyebrows. "Point taken," he said, as though he had just surrendered a bishop to a cleverly played pawn. "Any idea who did this?" he asked.

"Two Mexicans in a gray van."

"Did you recognize them?"

"No, sir. Never really got a good look. We saw them pull out in the van when they high-tailed it out of here heading that way."

Cain pointed in the direction of the highway.

Detective Spiotto questioned Cain's answer, but he did not say anything as his eyes bore into the old cowboy.

Cain stared back.

"So you think it was the Delgados?" Spiotto asked.

"You think it wasn't?"

Spiotto nodded as if to say *of course it was*. He looked over at the boy.

"Are you all right, kid?"

The boy nodded.

Spiotto sent the patrol officer out to cruise the surrounding streets on the off-chance the gray van had stayed in the area. He questioned Cain and the boy. After twenty minutes of routine interrogation and a brief examination of the crime scene, he folded his notebook and motioned toward the door with his hand.

"Go on downstairs and get two new rooms. I'll have an officer parked outside for the night. I don't expect they'll be back. But with your luck—who knows?"

Cain's expression was one of skepticism. He took a deep breath, exhaled impatiently, and nodded his agreement.

CHAPTER TWENTY-SIX

In her room at the back of her father's house, Elena Delgado stirred in her bed and listened as her mother answered the late-night knock at the front door. The muffled voices of two men exchanged a few words in Spanish with her mother. Her mother's voice was soft, but her tone reprimanded them in the same familiar way it had scolded her for her own misdeeds as a child. She sat up in her bed, tipped her head in the direction of the voices, and clutched her blankets to herself as she listened.

From what she could hear, she concluded that Cain and the boy were alive and the police probably had a description of the van. She heard them say they would cross the river back into Mexico and not return. They made excuses but promised that the death of Mrs. Delgado's *esposo* would not go unavenged.

Elena dropped back onto her pillow, stared up at the dark ceiling, and lay wide-eyed for a long time before she slept.

In the morning, Elena questioned her mother about the late-night visitors. Her mother dismissed her questions without a clear answer.

On her way to work at the café, Elena drove past the Econo Inn and paused on the street to view the damage to the second-floor room, from which two workers dropped the splintered door and the shattered window frame over the balcony railing into a dumpster below.

When she observed Cain and the boy exit their rooms and walk to the office to check out, she hurried away unnoticed.

Elena sat in her car and stared out across the sidewalk at the El Agave for a long time as she contemplated the circumstances in which she felt the weight of vengeance fall heavily upon her. That which compelled her to take up where her uncles failed ran far deeper than the machismo that drove them. Hers was a primal obligation to family, passed down through a thousand years of matriarchal duty that not even she understood.

She had no brothers, and the brothers of her mother had failed. She had watched her father die. The bullet that killed him had come from the reckless hand of a boy who had no regard for him or the family he left behind.

The thoughts that ran through Elena's mind left her trembling. Contrary to her nature, she found the thoughts of revenge strangely comforting—and disturbing. She looked up into the rearview mirror, touched the tears on her cheek with a paper napkin, and then took a deep breath. She exited the vehicle wondering what to do next.

Cain and the boy met with Chief Flores. They completed the report on the shooting incident at the motel and reviewed the details of the case from the beginning. When they concluded the meeting, Flores pushed his chair back and laced the fingers of both hands together, with his index fingers extended and resting on the bridge of his nose. He looked over the tented fingers at Cain and spoke in a quiet and deliberate tone.

"Mr. Cain, there are the facts, and there are the official reports on what happened. I believe what you told me is mostly the truth."

He looked over at the boy, who sat back in his chair with all the color drained from his face.

"I believe you have your reasons for not divulging the entire truth of the matter." He looked back at Cain, and the boy sunk back farther into his chair.

"Fortunately for you both, we have sworn testimony from a reliable witness as well as from the victim himself. Regardless of what I think, I am obliged by law to accept that reported testimony in the absence of anything conclusive from you or anyone else."

Cain sat up straight and addressed Flores in a direct manner. "So that's it? We're free to go?"

Flores nodded. "As far as the law is concerned, you are."

"But?"

"You have made problems here, over which we have no control."

Flores paused a long time, still looking over the tented fingers.

"You need to stay away from Los Caminos . . . and you must remain vigilant."

Cain took a deep breath and stood. "I understand."

"I'm not sure that you do," Flores said, and he laid the palms of his hands flat upon the tabletop with much the same effect as the dropping of a judge's gavel.

Dodger noticed Elena's car parked across the street as Cain backed out of the parking space and turned in the direction of the highway. He started to say something to Cain, but he thought better of it and sat in silence as they drove through town and headed north.

They passed the *mercado*, and the boy's head filled with kaleidoscopic images of the past few days. He looked over at the old cowboy as though searching for answers. Cain navigated his own maze of thoughts. When the boy could finally get above his own concerns, he turned toward the old man and spoke in a quiet voice.

"What did the doctor say?"

Cain looked over at him and then turned his eyes back to the highway.

"He said no more tests."

"So everything's okay?"

Cain smiled a half smile and nodded. "Pretty much."

Dodger stared at Cain, but Cain did not elaborate and he offered nothing more in the way of explanation. Dodger grinned and slapped Cain on the arm.

"Way to go, Harley. Mind if I ask what was wrong with you?"

Cain checked the rearview mirror and looked down at the speedometer before he answered. "No, I don't mind."

The boy waited.

"Well then, what was it?"

Cain did not answer, and the boy grew impatient.

"You said you didn't mind me asking."

"But I didn't say I'd tell you."

The boy turned toward the window.

"No, I guess you didn't."

He stared out the window a while, and then he turned to face Cain again.

"Me and Bobby got all the fences around the barn mended while you was gone."

"Did you get them wires stretched good and tight?"

"Yessir—tighter than a guitar string, just like you said."

"Did you use all new staples?"

"No, sir—we straightened the old ones and used as many of them as we could first."

"What did you do with the stretcher?"

"It's in the barn with all the other fencing tools. We 'bout run out of wire, though."

"How much you got left?"

"Maybe a roll and a half."

"We'll run into town and pick up more. Is Bobby going to help you again?"

"I'd like him to, if that's okay with you, Harley. He's real good help, and his family sure needs the money."

Cain coughed into his rag. His eyes watered, and he coughed again. He let his throat clear before he continued.

"That's fine with me. Tell you what, though . . . how's about you and me saddle up them horses and take a ride out toward the mountains tomorrow? The break would do us both some good."

"I'd like that just fine," Dodger said.

Cain looked across at the boy. "You want to bring them guns?"

Dodger hesitated. When he answered, he did so with great apprehension in his voice.

"I was thinking I might be done with guns, Harley."

"I understand . . . well, you think about it anyway."

"Are you bringing one?"

"I never ride out without one."

Dodger thought about it a long time before he responded.

"I reckon there's more good than harm can come from it. I'll take one too."

They drove without talking. The silence suited them. Neither felt the need to fill in the gaps. It appeared they both appreciated not having to explain themselves. That was new for Dodger. He rested his chin on his fist and smiled.

Dodger's mind wandered, and he contemplated thoughts he could not reconcile about the old cowboy at the wheel and the quiet strength of his demeanor. The boy spoke with candid confidence.

"You don't look all that good, Harley. You sure there ain't something you need to tell me?"

Cain stretched his arms straight against the wheel and flexed his shoulders as he slowly rolled his head in a circular, relaxing motion. He looked directly at the boy, and there was no apology in his voice when he spoke.

"The only thing wrong with me is I got old."

CHAPTER TWENTY-SEVEN

In that early part of morning, with no clear line between night and day, Cain and the boy walked beneath the stars from the small horse pasture to the barn, each leading a horse and neither inclined to say much. The cool air of the predawn sky and the harsh landscape at rest had a quieting effect on everything about them, and neither chose to breach the solitude of the moment.

Their boots trod softly upon the dry grass through which they walked. The shuffling of the horses' hooves struck the ground in a hushed cadence that somehow made the world feel oddly and temporarily back in balance.

They crossed the yellow light cast on the ground from the bare bulb hanging in the barn as they approached the wide opening of the sliding door. The boy slowed, and Cain led his horse in first. The boy paused before he entered. He gazed skyward among the stars. *If that's where heaven is, I don't know no one up there*, he thought to himself.

He led his horse in behind Cain, and they tied both horses to the hitch rail near which the saddles hung suspended from a beam in the tack room by old catch ropes looped through the gullets and over the saddle horns.

The boy picked up and cleaned the feet of his horse with a bent screwdriver while Cain brushed and checked his horse for hot spots and stickers. Cain smoothed the saddle blanket across the spine of his horse and, when it was just right, leaned across with his arms on the back of the horse.

"Ain't nothing better than cowboyin'," he said to Dodger, as though it was a known fact and he was thankful to be a part of it.

The boy looked up as he dropped the last foot. He smiled. "No, sir, there ain't."

They finished saddling the horses, and Cain handed the boy a full set of old, worn saddlebags.

"Here's something for you to eat—a couple of steak sandwiches, some biscuits, Fig Newtons, and a handful of pecans from that ol' tree out back—and a box of shells for these *pistolas* in case we get to shooting for money again."

"Thanks, Harley. You got the same in yours?"

"That and a pint of I.W. Harper."

The boy laughed. "We gonna get drunk?"

Cain smiled. "I was thinking more about snakebit, but you never know."

Cain nodded in the direction of the canteens hanging on wall pegs on the other side of the breezeway. "Fill a couple of those up for us from that hose out yonder in the yard."

They both tied on a bedroll, and Cain stepped up into the stirrup. He seemed to hesitate before he swung his leg over the back of the horse. The boy watched him but chose not to say anything.

The old cowboy sat upright and relaxed in the saddle, his heels down and his spurs close but not touching the horse. He lightly lifted on the reins held between his fingers and his thumb, and the horse stepped out with no apparent signal from the rider. The horse stopped, backed, and turned in a tight circle to the left and again to the right and then stood firm in the same hoofprints from which he'd started, all with no noticeable cue from the old cowboy who sat back in the saddle and gazed out into the darkness with a satisfied look about him.

The boy stood at the side of his horse with his arm looped over the saddle as he watched without comment. Cain reached into his shirt pocket, retrieved his tobacco and papers, and rolled a cigarette while he waited for the boy to fill the canteens. He pulled the tab on the small tobacco sack with his teeth and slid the papers and the tobacco back into his pocket with one hand while he held the makings in his other hand. He rolled the paper around the tobacco, wet the glue seam with his tongue, and pinched the ends together.

Dodger returned with the canteens, hung one on his saddle horn and the other on that of the old cowboy. He looked up at Cain. "You ready?"

Cain nodded and the boy stepped up into the saddle, pulled his hat down, and buttoned his jacket. Cain pulled the long string hanging down from the light bulb, and they sat there in the dark a moment until Cain nudged his horse forward out into the moonlit desert and the boy followed.

They heard no other sounds beyond those of the footfalls of the horses and the creaking of the saddles. They crossed the highway and followed their moon-cast shadows across the hard-crusted earth and sparse vegetation. The sky turned gray, and then the sun began to rise behind the mountains until it shone fully down upon them. They rode toward the mountains until there was nothing man-made to be seen in any direction. Not a fence, not a telephone pole, not a track anywhere.

The boy pulled up and fell in behind where the trail narrowed. He watched the old cowboy, the easy way Cain sat in the saddle, the fluid way his body rocked in rhythm to the movement of the horse.

Watching Cain ride put him to mind of his father—easily twice the cowboy as the old man, but on his best day not even half the man.

For all the signs of age Cain showed afoot, mounted he appeared with all the immortality of his youth intact.

Dodger compared the image of Cain riding before him to the image he carried of men like Eugene. He realized that becoming one or the other came down to the decisions he made along the way. How a boy could end up like Eugene worried him. How a boy could kill a man and not end up like Eugene, troubled him even more.

By midmorning what trail there was broadened out into chaparral country with no borders and no clear path upon which to set their course. They reckoned their bearings by the sun and the black silhouette of two mountain peaks that rose up on either side of a canyon far in the distance.

They rode with little talk between them. When Cain slipped off his jacket and tied it on behind his saddle with his bedroll, the boy did the same. Sweat ran down the boy's back, but he never commented on the heat. Cain sat up straight and stretched his back. He unbuckled the keeper on his catch rope and held the coils in his left hand as he casually built a loop in his right hand.

"You gonna rope us a rabbit for supper, Harley?"

The old cowboy looked over at the boy and grinned.

"Shake out a loop, kid. We got a long ways to go . . . might as well learn something."

Dodger grinned. "So, what do you want me to teach you, Harley?"

"See that stubby cactus there?"

Cain pulled his horse up, and Dodger did likewise.

"Yeah."

"See if you can drop a loop on it."

Dodger held the coils and the reins in his left hand and spun an ever-widening loop over his head with his right hand until the loop was just the right size. He took the shot. The loop sailed flat and smooth through the air and then died midway, where it fell to the ground.

Cain took the same shot and his loop settled expertly over the cactus and tightened around it when he jerked the slack.

"What'd I do wrong?"

"You didn't drop your extra coils—you ran out of rope."

Dodger pulled his rope in and recoiled it. Cain attempted to shake his free of the cactus, but it hung there on the spines. He motioned toward the boy.

"You mind jumping down and shaking my rope loose?"

Cain pulled in the slack after the boy freed his rope, and then he waited for the boy to remount.

He showed the boy how to handle the coils in his left hand, explained the importance of dropping the extra coils to give him enough rope for the long catch, and waited for the boy to take another shot.

His next shot and those that followed all sailed smoothly through the air and circled down around the thick cactus without a miss. On the last shot Dodger dallied the rope around his saddle horn and nudged his horse around as though he was dragging a calf to the fire.

"Watch him now," Cain warned.

The rope tightened and the horse, expecting the pullback of a heavy calf, lunged forward and jerked the cactus from the ground. Before the horse could stand clear, the airborne cactus catapulted up from the ground, flew between the two startled horses, and came to rest at the feet of Cain's horse. The horse lurched sideways. The boy's horse bolted, with the cactus following it across the desert.

"Drop your dally," Cain shouted.

The boy spun off the two wraps he had taken around the saddle horn earlier and cast the rope aside as he circled his horse and brought him quivering back to the rope. He dismounted and removed the loop from the cactus. When he got back up into the saddle, he calmed the horse and walked him back to Cain. The old cowboy bent over the saddle horn with his head resting upon his crossed arms. Even though he could not hear it, the boy knew he was laughing.

Dodger sat and watched Cain. His anger grew, until he found himself caught up in Cain's infectious laughter. They both laughed, and Dodger's eyes watered. When the old cowboy looked up at him from under his hat, the boy just grinned.

"That was a pretty good catch, huh, Harley?"

Cain caught his breath and leaned back in his saddle. "Yeah, that was real good."

"Think I'll make a calf roper?"

Cain nodded. "If you buy the right rope."

"What kind should I get?"

"Get you one of them with the calf already in it."

They rode and laughed as they coiled their ropes. Dodger wrapped and fastened the keeper, and then he sat back in his saddle and surveyed the land about them.

"Every direction you look, it just goes on forever, don't it, Harley?"

The old cowboy, in the process of tapping a line of tobacco onto the paper he held, did not respond until he clenched the finished cigarette between his teeth and fished a wooden match out of his shirt pocket.

"I reckon it looks that way . . ."

Dodger looked over at him.

"But nothing goes on forever."

They rode without speaking for a long time. The boy, unsettled by Cain's words, tried to make sense of a world in which some people fit better than others, and some did not fit at all. The boy turned his head, spat, and looked over at the old man.

"Remember that teacher I told you about, Harley? The one said I was dealt some bad cards?"

Cain nodded.

"He said, 'The world's a tuxedo, and you're a pair of brown shoes.'"

"What's that mean?"

"I guess it means I just don't fit nowhere."

"You believe him?"

"I don't know . . . I guess."

"Truth is, it don't matter what he thinks. What matters is what you think."

"Really?"

Cain thought a moment.

"If you think you can't do something because everything ain't just right, that's exactly what you'll do—nothing."

"How'd you figure all this out, Harley?"

"I didn't figure nothing out. I just quit doing the same

wrong things over and over. You don't have to eat the whole egg to know it's rotten, and you don't need to pick up too many hot horseshoes to know you'll get burned."

"How long did it take you to learn all that?"

The old man took a long drag off his cigarette and let the smoke out slow. "I'm still learning it."

The boy furrowed his brow and tilted his head. "When will you be done learning?"

"Never, I reckon. Things go by pretty fast. You know, a week goes by, then a month—by the time you see everything slipping away from you, you're an old man."

He paused. The boy waited.

Cain continued, "I don't know what's worse—quitting too soon, or hanging on too long."

He took another drag and blew the smoke out of the side of his mouth, which the boy found oddly intriguing.

The boy smiled. "You ain't clearing things up much, Harley."

Cain laughed. "It seems to come down to each man deciding for himself, when you think about it."

He straightened his back and looked directly at the boy. "You sure you want to hear all this talk that don't go nowhere?"

"Yessir. This is all new to me. It makes me think."

Cain found himself at odds with his rambling conversations with the boy. He was as insecure as he was drawn to tell the boy things he hadn't shared with anyone—including himself.

Dodger wanted to tell Cain about his father, his feelings of being abandoned along with his mother, the poor father his dad had really been, the lies he'd kept telling himself until even he believed them. Dodger figured he had said as much as he cared to for now.

And there they sat, one on either side of a wall neither was ready to scale.

CHAPTER TWENTY-EIGHT

The pace of the horses slowed as the temperature continued to rise. The old man and the kid went on with their conversation.

"When I was a young man, I married a homely girl—I was no prize myself—who said she wanted to live in the desert and raise her own food. I cowboyed, worked in the feedlot, and even had a painting business at one time. I got a few dollars ahead and bought us the ranch. We had a baby, a son. And then one day she told me she wasn't happy."

He took another drag, ground the butt out on the sole of his boot, and then flipped it out into the desert.

"She couldn't tell me what she wasn't happy about. I guess I never thought about it enough. One day she just up and left. Took the baby. Run off with another man—a damn traveling salesman at that. That was the last I seen of her or the baby boy."

"You never seen him again? The boy, I mean."

"No, never did. He's a grown man now. I never left. He could have found me had he looked. I reckon she never told him about his daddy."

"That make you sad, Harley?"

Cain shook his head in a dismissive manner, and then he nodded almost imperceptibly. "Some," he said.

The boy stared off ahead into the broad expanse of country before them. He spoke without looking over at the old man.

"So where does the good part come in?"

"That was the good part."

Then he smiled.

"It comes in every day. Right here. Right now. That's all we got for sure."

Cain pulled his horse up, and the boy stopped with him. He looked around him and, in the silence that followed, one by one, sounds began to filter through. The wind, the birds, cicadas, squirrels, the snuffling of a horse and, from high above, the sound of a hawk—all part of the world they missed by their inattention to it.

"Hear that?"

The boy nodded.

"See that cactus?"

The boy nodded again.

"It's likely over a hundred years old and still living."

He pointed to the skeletal remains of what appeared to be a coyote.

"And that?"

Again the boy nodded without answering.

"Maybe two years old. There ain't no rhyme nor reason for where things fit or where they don't—or how long they last."

The boy gestured toward the coyote and then the cactus. "Seems like the coyote would like to live a hundred years and the cactus don't care one way or the other."

"And there you have it," Cain said.

The sun rode high overhead when they dismounted and tied their horses in a small willow break where a spring pooled up into a grassy water hole.

"Did you know this was here, Harley?"

"Yeah, there's a few like this out here. If you're going to

ride this desert, you need to know that. You also need to know they dry up from time to time. I've never known this one to go dry, though."

"Do you have all this on a map?"

"No, it's in my head. You just get to know it after a while."

The boy thought about it for a moment as he looked across the miles of ground that all looked the same to him.

"I don't think I know much about anything compared to this."

"Maybe you do. You know how to get by in Bufort. You learned that by doing."

"That ain't the same, though."

"Why isn't it?"

"Bufort is just a town, and it's small."

"Maybe so, but it is your world and you know it well. It would be the same if you spent the time out here."

Dodger grinned.

"You really think so, Harley?"

"It's a fact. If you're a pair of brown shoes, then you need to know where it is in the world brown shoes are in style."

Dodger laughed and shook his head.

"I might be a pair of black boots, but I damn sure ain't no brown shoes."

The boy knelt beside the cool water and drank from the surface of it without disturbing the water itself. Cain stood in the shade and smoked another cigarette. There was no hurry about either of them. The boy stood and wiped his sleeve across his wet mouth.

Cain coughed into his hand. The boy waited to speak.

"You like the desert, Harley?"

"I do like most things about it. It could do better with crops if we had more water, and it takes a lot of ground to run cows, and the brush is hard on a horse and a man, but yeah, I like it."

Cain lifted one boot and rested it on the deadfall of an ancient tree.

"How about you?"

The boy stretched out on his back and laid his hat beside him.

"I like it a lot. It feels to me like it makes you earn your spot out here, and I don't know why, but I kind of like that."

"I know what you mean. A thing you work for seems to hold more value than a thing you're given, with nothing of you invested in it."

Dodger nodded, although he wasn't exactly sure what Cain meant.

"I guess it's the way I see the fences around your place, Harley. I notice the ones me and Bobby did first, and I feel good about 'em."

The boy sat up and pulled his knees to him as he wrapped his arms around his legs and stared into the spring water.

"What do you suppose guys like Eugene feel good about?"

Cain switched boots on the log and took off his hat to run the sleeve of his shirt across the sweat on his forehead, as though he had not heard the boy. The boy looked over at him and waited. Cain stared out at the desert, and then he shrugged.

"I expect even guys like Eugene have a few things they feel good about. But I don't imagine there's much they feel proud about. You ever see one of them big ol' perfect spider webs strung across a corner somewhere?"

"Yeah?"

"Know what happens if you knock it down?"

"Uh-huh . . . the next day you come back, it's built again."

"That's right. But do you know what happens if you knock it down again?"

The boy nodded. "Sure—the spider builds it back again."

"Exactly. But if you knock it down every day, each time you come back it will be a little less perfect until, before you know it, that ol' spider's just throwing up a half-built web 'cause he just don't care no more."

The boy thought about that a long time. He lay back in the grass, laced his fingers behind his head, and gnawed the inside of his cheek as he watched the thin clouds drift across the sky.

"That's Eugene," he said. He closed his eyes, and the gentle sounds of the desert seemed to float far away. He took a slow, deep breath and let it out softly as he felt himself relax at the edge of sleep.

The sounds of the desert seemed distant as they receded to the outskirts of the boy's consciousness. He felt himself drift off. Suddenly an explosion at his feet jarred him from his reverie. His stomach knotted, and he sat bolt upright. He jumped to his feet. His heart pounded as he reached for the pistol hanging loose at his side. He looked to the left and to the right, and when he saw Cain standing nearby holding a smoking pistol, he stared at him.

"What the heck's wrong, Harley?"

Cain nodded generally in the direction of hundreds of miles of wasteland before them.

"See that red-barked bush out there with the forked branches?"

"You're shooting at a bush?"

"Yeah. You see it?"

"That dried-up one?"

"Yep. Think you can take off the right fork?"

"That's pretty far, Harley. Did you hit it?"

"I wasn't aiming at it."

The boy laughed.

"I reckon you were aiming at the dirt, huh?"

The boy drew his pistol, cocked the hammer, and fired.

"You missed."

The boy looked over at Cain.

"I wasn't aiming at it neither."

Cain laughed, and the boy laughed with him.

They holstered their pistols, caught up the horses, and remounted.

"How far we going?"

"We'll ride 'til dark, wherever that finds us," Cain replied.

Cain's expression softened some. Dodger held his horse up and looked across at the old man.

"You know, Harley . . . beside Bobby, you're the best friend I ever had."

He turned away, half embarrassed by having said it. Cain sat there an uncomfortably long time, and then he leaned across in the saddle and extended his hand to the boy.

"Well, Bodean Cleon Cooper, you're damn sure the best friend I ever had."

"You ain't gonna give up on me, are you?"

Cain shook his head slowly. "No—no, I ain't."

Dodger shook the old man's hand harder and longer than would be deemed appropriate, and then he sat up tall in the saddle.

"It ain't gettin' any lighter," he said. He nudged his horse forward, and Cain did likewise.

The terrain began to change as they approached the foothills of the range that now appeared varied and steep. The prehistoric landscape was cut deeply into the granite from which nature had carved it before there was ever a horse or a man, or anything to disturb it. The rugged harshness of the topography appeared to be the careless work of the hand that had created it. But the mountain itself stood as an artistic accomplishment, stunning in its magnificence in contrast to the stark land that surrounded it.

"They call that one El Viejo," Cain said to the boy, who stared at the vertical face that rose high and flattened to a great plateau at the top. "All the gringos call it Table Mountain."

"Are we going up there?"

"No, we'll ride into the canyon between El Viejo and the one on the left they call Sangre de Cristo."

They rode three quarters of an hour, with Cain taking special care to choose the path that left the least sign of their having been there. He seemed wary and avoided unnecessary conversation. The boy watched him. Cain's change in disposition caused the youngster to pay close attention to the trail ahead and behind with some apprehension.

Cain reined in his horse, and the boy stopped with him.

"What's wrong, Harley?"

"Someone's been following us."

"Maybe he's just out here like we are," the boy said.

"Maybe . . . but not likely. I saw the sun reflect off his scope or binoculars this morning when we stopped. I saw it again just a minute ago."

"You think it's the Delgados?"

Cain dismounted and leaned over his saddle as he watched the trail behind them. "Could be."

"Are we going to wait for them?"

Cain shook his head and remounted.

"Not here."

They long-trotted for the next hour and reached the entrance to the canyon when the sun was barely visible in the late afternoon sky. Cain had second thoughts about the wisdom of bringing the boy into what could be another problem.

"We should have a good moon tonight," Cain said. "We'll ride to where the canyon splits."

"Then what?"

He looked over at the boy, and there was no humor in Cain's expression and nothing reassuring about the look in his eyes. He contemplated turning back, but changed his mind. He sensed in himself a more cautionary side, and it disturbed him that he might be losing ground to the big gray wolf of old age nipping at his heels. His response was more uncivil than he intended.

"Then nothing. We'll see when we get there."

He nodded toward where a narrow trail split off and ran slightly upward along one edge of the rift.

"You ride that side," Cain said. "I'll stay on this side. No point giving them an easy shot if that's what they're looking for."

The boy sat up straight in the saddle. "Ain't no point giving them a shot at all, if you ask me."

They rode until the sun was fully down, the sky was black, the moon not yet up. The two trails merged. Cain and the boy met at the confluence. Cain pulled his horse up, and the boy stopped with him.

"We'll wait here," Cain said as he dismounted. "Give your horse a rest. We'll have moonlight here to see by soon."

The boy dismounted, unhooked his canteen from the saddle horn, and drank while he held the reins looped over his arm. He walked around the horse and checked its feet and legs. He stood up straight and patted the horse on the neck.

"You're a pretty tough ol' boy," he said in a voice barely above a whisper. The horse dropped its head. The boy sat cross-legged on a flat rock and waited.

The moon came up red and full. When its color changed to crystal white, Cain said, "Mount up." The boy stepped up into the saddle and turned his horse to follow the old cowboy and his moon-cast shadow into the gaping jaws of the canyon.

They rode single file until the trail split again. Cain motioned for the boy to continue riding the left fork, while he turned his horse onto the right fork.

"Stay on the trail," Cain said. "When it forks again, stay right . . . wait at the creek when you come to it. I'll meet you there."

The boy nodded. He had an uneasy feeling but said nothing about it. He touched the horse with his spurs and looked over his shoulder. He watched Cain until there was nothing left to see and nothing left to hear but the footfalls of his own horse and the pounding of his heart.

He rode a long time in the still of the dark. He listened and he watched over his shoulder. He imagined himself in the crosshairs of a riflescope. He turned in the saddle, expecting to see the moon reflected in the glass and the fire of the muzzle flash before he heard the explosion of the bullet as it buffeted the soft night air on its way to him.

He thought about death, and he thought about his drunken journey to meet it. The thought of it brought him no comfort. He observed the trail in the moonlight until it became no trail at all. There was no left fork and no right fork, and if he'd strayed from it earlier, there was no clear indication that he had done so.

The boy pulled his horse up, dismounted, and led the horse back down the direction from which they came. When they found the trail, he remounted and turned the horse back up the canyon. He retraced his steps until there was no more trail and no one choice that made more sense than another. He let the horse have its head. The horse plodded on with no concern for the right or wrong of the direction in which it chose to travel.

As the moon rose higher in the sky, it appeared smaller, its light more intense. The boy watched the shadows move and felt a thousand eyes upon him as he and the horse intruded upon this primitive world where no man and no horse were meant to be. In the great distance a coyote raised its voice to the moon, and soon after, another—closer—and another, until the canyon echoed with their sorrowful cries.

To the boy, the calling of the coyotes sounded as though they mourned something that had happened a hundred years before or, perhaps, something that had not yet come to pass. Whatever it was, it chilled him to the bone.

CHAPTER TWENTY-NINE

Cain rode the right fork of the trail until it fanned out onto a massive granite debris field. He turned his horse up onto a lightly timbered bench and then crossed over to come in below the boy on the trail he was riding. He shook out a loop in his catch rope, dropped it over a fallen creosote bush, and dragged it up behind him, clearing both his own tracks and those of the boy.

He counted on the light cloud drift to mask the moonlight enough to cover his deception. He crossed the scree and followed the tracks to where the boy had dismounted and led his horse. He saw where the boy had remounted. He nudged his horse forward to follow the boy off-trail.

Dodger leaned forward in the saddle, searched the ground before him, and looked over his shoulder at every new sound. His horse came to an abrupt stop, cocked its ears, and bowed its neck. The boy sat upright in the saddle. He looked about nervously and listened. He pushed the reins forward, and the horse stepped out.

He dismounted near a slow-moving creek and led the horse into a thicket. He waited there with the horse grazing at the end of the reins.

He stood without moving, alert to the sounds and the quiet. He heard the mournful call of a coyote as it yipped at the moon. A distant coyote yipped back at it. Then the boy heard the snuffling of a horse. The footfalls of a single horse approaching. Then another.

Two horsemen entered the clearing, speaking Spanish and leaning over their saddles searching the ground in the moonlight.

The boy reached down and cupped the muzzle of his horse with his hand. He held his breath and waited, watching the two men close in on him. The riders stopped at the creek, where they dismounted and watered their horses.

Dodger felt his legs tremble. One of the Mexican horses lifted its head from the water and stared with its ears pitched in the direction of the boy's horse. The Mexican horse stood fixated on the shadowed spot in the brush that concealed the boy and his jigging horse. Dodger frantically stripped the rig from his horse and slipped the bridle over its ears. He held the horse with the reins hung over its neck, and he waited.

When the Mexican horse whinnied and the boy's horse answered, Dodger slipped the reins free and stepped back as his horse trotted stiff-legged out into the clearing, flagged its tail, and then galloped back down the trail.

Both Mexican riders spurred their mounts after the runaway. The boy dragged his gear into the brush and concealed himself among the rocks, cursing his bad luck. He waited until he could no longer hear the pounding hooves that disappeared into the darkness, and then he sat and leaned back against his saddle, spent.

The Mexican riders followed the runaway for the better part of a mile before they gave up the chase. Their horses bounced to a stop, and the two riders let them blow.

"That was some nice horse," the younger one said.

"It was no shitter. He run off from somewhere," the older man said.

Cain, on his way up the trail, stopped when he heard the approaching sound of the boy's horse. He unwrapped the keeper on his catch rope and positioned his horse in the brush near a bend in the trail while he shook out a loop. The approaching horse pounded closer in the moonlight, its cadence slowing as it neared the cowboy and recognized the horse.

The old man coaxed his horse out into the trail slowly and spoke softly to the runaway.

"Whoa, Poncho," he said to it in a whisper. "Whoa, buddy."

He dropped the loop over its head.

Cain knew no good reason for the boy's horse to be loose and unsaddled. He urged his horse up the trail at a long trot, led the boy's horse, watched over his shoulder, and rode without caution. He slowed for a sharp turn in the trail, crested a steep rise, and came head-to-head with two Mexican riders who sat on their horses with their rifles laid cross-saddle and the moon at their backs.

He stopped and looked from one featureless face to the other. One of his hands held the reins, the other the lead rope of the boy's horse. His pistol hung out of reach at his side.

One of the Mexicans nodded at the horse.

"Is that your horse?"

Cain looked back at the horse and then at the man who had spoken.

"Yeah. He run off before I could get him hobbled for the night."

The two Mexicans looked at each other. The first one spoke again.

"He come from up there. How did you get ahead of him?"

Cain's mind raced. "I followed him up. He must have turned to come back down."

The Mexican nodded again, but he was skeptical. Cain knew the silence that followed was a negotiation for power. He looked from one man to the other, their faces shadowed and backlit by the moon, rendering them unrecognizable. He did not speak, and he did not neutralize his position.

"Where is the boy that was with you?"

"In camp, why?"

"We seen him with you earlier. We hadn't seen no one else up here."

"That don't surprise me. This ain't a likely place to run into another person less he had a specific reason to be here."

Neither man responded.

Cain continued, "So, I ask myself—what are the odds of running into two others up here?"

"And what did you come up with?" the older Mexican asked.

Cain nodded toward the scoped rifles.

"Seems plain, you're hunting something."

The men bristled. The younger man smiled, and then he laughed. The laugh seemed inappropriate to Cain. Finally, the older man spoke.

"You got a problem with us hunting out of season?"

Cain shrugged. "Do I look like I got a problem?"

The man smiled, shook his head, and he laughed as well.

"No, I don't suppose you do."

The Mexican sidestepped his horse. Cain walked his horses past the two. With the moon to his back, Cain stopped and turned in the saddle. The Mexican horsemen watched him. Cain studied both faces, but he did not recognize either.

He turned back in the saddle, pulled his horse up after it took a step, and then turned back to the men.

"You don't by any chance know the Delgados over in Los Caminos, do you?"

The men looked at one another, then both shook their heads. One spoke.

"No, we're not from around here. We just come down from San Elizano to hunt."

Cain stared them down. They both braced for trouble. Then the old man tipped his hat.

"Well, y'all take care," Cain said.

He turned and trotted his horses up the trail and listened as the two riders waited. When Cain and his horses disappeared over the crest in the trail, the two Mexican hunters maintained a distance and followed him back up the mountain. Cain waited until he was sure they were following, and then he pressed the horses forward.

Cain watched the trail for signs of the boy. The loose horse running free with no saddle and no bridle could mean a lot of things—none of them good.

By the time the old cowboy reached the grassy meadow and the creek, he could no longer hear the sounds of the Mexican riders behind him.

He rode to the edge of the creek and looked about as he watered the horses. He whistled the sound of a night bird and waited. He repeated the whistle and heard a whistle come back to him from the shadow of the trees in the granite rocks downstream. He dismounted and walked the horses that direction.

Cain stood at the edge of the moonlit clearing and waited as the boy made his way over the rocks and out from the shadows.

"I got your horse."

"Thanks."

Cain handed the lead rope to the boy.

"What happened?"

"He give me away to a couple of Mexican riders that came by. I choused him down the trail so they wouldn't find me."

Cain nodded. "Good thinking. Where's your rig?"

Dodger pointed over his shoulder with his thumb.

"Hid in them trees."

"Saddle up. We ain't rid of them two ol' boys yet."

"What do you mean?"

"I run into 'em down the trail. They're right behind me. It ain't thc Delgados."

"Did you recognize them?"

"No. Said they was from San Elizano."

"You believe them?"

"I believe they're from where they say they are. They said they was hunting—I believe that too. I just don't believe it's game they're after."

Dodger furrowed his brow.

"Why not?"

"They got no packhorse, no gear, and they're riding at night when they should be in camp."

He touched his horse's neck, stepped around, and looked back at the boy.

"If things don't add up, there's usually a good reason for it."

Dodger saddled and bridled his horse. He and Cain retreated deeper into the willow break and waited. They stood concealed in the darkness alongside their horses and watched the Mexican riders approach the clearing in the moonlight. Cain and the boy watched them ride through looking for signs and continuing upcountry with their rifles laid across their saddles.

Cain whispered, "That look like deer hunters to you?"

The boy shook his head. "No, sir, it don't."

They waited a long time before Cain turned and walked his horse downstream, and the boy followed without asking where they were going.

Cain looked back over his shoulder at the boy, and then he stepped up into the saddle.

"There's a good place to camp back in here. We'll spend the night."

The boy nodded, threw his leg over his saddle, and followed without speaking. Behind them, the moon sat high in the black sky above the tops of the trees. They rode for most of an hour before Cain pulled his horse up and dismounted. He looked over the precipice of an ancient granite rockslide and tipped his head in the direction of a narrow game trail that led into the darkness and toward the sound of water roiling over the rocks somewhere below.

"Yonder's the trail. Let your horse have his head," Cain said over his shoulder as he remounted.

They began the descent to the river. The horses picked their way down the talus to the steep drop-off to the river, cautiously placing one foot before picking up the next. The murky trail lay washed in the tree-filtered light of the full moon and criss-crossed by the lattice of shadows from their branches.

The boy rode with great caution, sliding his feet back in the stirrups and carrying the weight of his legs on the toes of his boots. He looked down into the dark void that pitched off below them and made up his mind to swing off on the high side of the trail if the horse lost its footing. He shut out the sound of the river and listened only to the grinding footfalls of the horses.

They continued the descent until the air cooled and the sound of the rushing water filled the air. Cain pulled his horse up in a small clearing and leaned back with one hand on the horse's rump.

"This is it. We got water, grass, and no way for anyone to surprise us down here."

"Looks like a good spot, Harley. How'd you know about this one?"

Cain swung his leg slowly over the saddle and stood beside the horse. He untied his saddlebags and dropped them to the ground behind him as he leaned across his saddle and spoke to the boy.

"I been in this country more than half a century. There ain't much of it I haven't seen."

The boy dismounted, walked his horse around the clearing, and watered him at the river's edge. Cain had the beginnings of a camp set up when the boy returned to the clearing. He unsaddled his horse and hobbled him to graze.

"Want me to water that horse of yours, Harley?"

Cain nodded without looking at the boy.

CHAPTER THIRTY

Upstream, the two Mexican stalkers urged their weary mounts into a swale near the summit, where they dismounted and made camp. The younger of the two tended the horses while the other built a fire and then filled a coffeepot and a small pan with water from the river.

They hunkered near the fire and watched their shadows moving against the trees as the flame flared and burned. They sat cross-legged with the bean pot between them, taking turns dipping into it with folded tortillas they carried wrapped in cloth.

"That was them," the younger man said.

The older of the two looked across the fire with eyes that told you nothing of the man and nothing of what he thought. He nodded.

The younger man waited a long time before he spoke again.

"How do you want to handle it?"

"We wait."

"Wait? For what?"

"For daylight. They will come by here early in the morning. We'll be up there." The older man nodded into the darkness at the towering granite escarpment above them.

The younger man turned his eyes up to the moonlit precipice that loomed above them, an ancient formation carved by millions of years of erosion at a time long before man appeared on earth. He dismissed it with a shrug.

"No problem."

Sometime in the night, Cain nudged the boy's foot with the toe of his boot. Dodger sat upright and gazed quickly about.

"It'll be daybreak soon. Get your boots on and water them horses. Coffee's hot. We'll eat a little something before we go."

The boy rubbed his knuckles into his eyes and yawned.

"It seems like I just got to sleep."

He slipped on his boots and stood by the fire as he pulled on his jacket and picked up his hat. He grinned at the old man.

"This is a good-lookin' hat, ain't it?"

Cain laughed. "It suits you."

They broke camp and led the horses out of the clearing and back up the treacherous talus until the footing improved. Cain stopped, mounted his horse, and nodded back at the boy to do likewise.

Cain and the boy pushed on, following the river and the tracks of the Mexicans upstream to the higher elevation. The breath of the horses smoked out before them in heavy clouds of mist synchronized to the steady rhythm of each step they took. Dodger held his elbows in tight and shivered.

"It's a little chilly," he said through the jacket pulled up over his chin.

Cain glanced back at him and then turned back to study the trail they followed.

"It'll warm up soon."

The breaking sun began to light up the mountain ridges in a soft light the color of fire. Through the trees, the river reflected the morning light. Long, slanted shadows fell across the water and gave an uncertain appearance to the brush where nothing stood out clear and a man might hide unnoticed if he did not stir. Dodger sat straight up in the saddle and watched the shadows, waiting for something or someone to move.

At a spot where the trees thinned and grass grew in the passing sunlight, Cain pulled his horse up and turned to face the boy. He held his hand up, and the boy stopped. He looked up the trail and studied the tracks of the two Mexican horses where they left the path and began the upward climb to the escarpment above.

He quietly turned his horse and rode in next to the boy.

"Them two sure wasn't huntin' no deer, were they?" the boy said.

"That's for certain."

"Why do you think they went up that way?"

Cain tipped his head in the direction of the outcropping high above the trail.

"My guess is they're up there waiting for a shot. You wait here in the trees and watch for a muzzle flash. If you see one, fire two rounds up as close as you can to where it comes from."

"What if they get you, Harley?"

"Then you turn your horse down that trail and ride like hell."

Dodger shook his head. "No, I'm going with you."

Cain looked out from under the brim of his hat, and his eyes bore into those of the boy.

"I told you what to do—do it."

"Well, then, you fire off a shot if you ain't hit, so I know you're okay."

Cain nodded. "I'll be all right."

The boy moved into the cover of the trees, dismounted, and scanned the length of the escarpment for as far as he could see. Cain rode the fringe of the tree line, trying to offer no clear shot to the hunters if there was to be onc. He looked in the direction of the rising sun and calculated the angle of it to be in his favor as it crossed the trail from behind him and lit up the granite-boulder fortress.

The boy watched the rocks with great intensity. As his eyes moved along the ridge, he picked up a fleeting reflection, much closer than he anticipated. He imagined the reflection to be from the front lens of a riflescope. He tied his horse and braced his pistol in a tree fork. He set the sight on the spot where he'd seen the reflection and added extra elevation to compensate for the long distance.

He waited, but did not move or divert his eyes from the location of the reflection. When he saw the light for the second time, he saw the muzzle flash before he heard the report echo down from the rocks and repeat itself in the trees as the sound echoed quickly down the mountain. He squeezed the trigger, and when he saw the dust from the impact of the bullet low on the granite rock, he readjusted and fired again. The second round cleared the rock and whined as the bullet ricocheted off the granite walls that concealed the shooter.

A second rifle shot cracked the air from somewhere up in the boulders, but the boy saw no muzzle flash. He waited, but there was no confirming shot from Cain. His eyes bounced from shadow to shadow, looking for anything that moved, a glimpse of Cain, some idea of what was going on up there. There was none.

Dodger holstered his pistol and swung up into the saddle. He started up the steep trail, following the tracks of Cain's horse where they lay fresh and clear upon the earth and then faded into the rock and gravel.

The trail turned, and Cain's horse stood in the shadow of the turn, ground-tied and riderless. The boy lifted the reins, and his horse stopped. He stood in the stirrups and looked about for Cain's body, but there appeared to be no blood and no sign of the old cowboy.

Dodger dismounted and tied off his horse. He circled the trail on foot as he made his way through the brush. Cain's tied horse raised its head. The boy passed it and found Cain's boot prints, clear in the damp soil and leading up to the summit of the escarpment.

The boy returned to Cain's horse and waited. When he heard a solitary shot ring out from above, he hurried up the same path Cain had taken. He reached the high-level plateau, out of breath, to find Cain holding the two Mexicans at gunpoint.

"What happened, Harley?"

Cain looked from the two disarmed men to the boy and back to the men.

"They weren't watching this game trail—I got up on 'em while they were trying to get you sighted in."

"Is anybody shot?"

"Not yet."

Cain tipped his head back toward the trail. "Get down there and fetch them piggin' strings off our saddles."

When the boy returned, he stepped up next to Cain and bent over to catch his breath. He leaned down with his hands on his knees and looked up under the brim of his hat at the two men, who watched him intently but did not speak. He studied first one face and then the other. He stood up straight and looked at Cain.

"Them's the two from the café."

Cain furrowed his brow. "The Delgados?"

"No. The other two. It was them and another one. They was sitting there up at the counter that time we were in there."

Cain took the strings and bound the men's hands behind their backs. He stood the older man up and walked him into the trees, out of sight.

"If that one moves, shoot him," he said to the boy.

The boy sat cross-legged on a boulder with his pistol cocked and lying across one knee, its barrel in line with the man's chest. He stared into the dark eyes of the man.

"How come you lied to us?"

The man glared at the boy but did not respond.

When a shot rang out from the trees and echoed across the canyon and down to the river, the man's eyes widened. The boy's head snapped around. He watched the brush where Cain emerged, his pistol still smoking.

Cain sat down in front of the younger man, who stared at Cain. Cain cocked the pistol, leveled it at the man's face, and stood over him.

"I ain't got the time or the inclination to mess with you, so I'm only going to ask you once. If you want to live, you will answer my questions."

The man nodded. "*Sí, señor. Comprendo.*"

"Who sent you?"

The man dropped his head, and his voice was submissive but firm.

"Antonio Flores."

"Flores—the police chief?"

The man nodded. "*Sí.*"

Cain glanced at Dodger, who stood. Cain glared at the man.

"He wanted you to kill us?"

The man nodded again.

"Why would he want us dead?"

The man allowed his eyes to make contact with those of the old cowboy standing over him. He then lowered his head and spoke slowly.

"He said you killed the husband of his sister and you dishonored his family."

The man hesitated before he continued.

"He had no choice."

"Well, he did have a choice. Just like I do. I got a choice whether to kill you or not. Do you think you should die?"

"No, *señor.* I have a family. I do not wish to die."

"But you had no problem with killing us?"

The man shook his head. "I owe him."

"What's Flores to you?"

"*Familia.*"

Cain raised his head.

"Are all of you damn Mexicans related?"

The man shrugged.

Cain turned to the boy.

"Take the bolts out of their rifles and throw the rifles over the rocks. Then gather up their horses—we're getting out of here."

The boy picked up the rifles, removed the bolts, and pitched the rifles over the ledge.

"Them was nice scopes," he said to no one in particular.

The boy picked up the reins of the two horses and led them out of the trees to where Cain stood. He looked beyond the old man and nodded in the direction of the brush.

"What about the body?"

"What body?"

"The one you just shot."

"I never said I shot him."

Cain walked into the brush and returned, prodding the man at gunpoint.

Dodger grinned. "I thought you killed him."

The second man shook his head and looked down at his boots as both men preceded Cain down the narrow trail while the boy followed, leading the horses.

CHAPTER THIRTY-ONE

The four horsemen descended the trail as the sun passed overhead and sank to the edge of the earth, where the color of it blurred the flatland below them in all shades of crimson and gold. The temperature dropped, and soon it was dark but for the light of the small fire around which the four gathered where Cain chose to make camp for the night.

Cain untied his prisoners, fed them, and allowed them to relieve themselves before he retied them, hands behind their backs and the leg of one bound tightly to the leg of the other.

"We can't sleep like this," one complained.

"I don't give a shit if you can sleep."

Cain watched them through the night. When the sky began to turn from black to gray, he awoke the boy.

"Get a fire and some coffee going."

The two bound men appeared haggard and worn. They watched Cain from the corners of their eyes, not at all certain of the old man's intentions. Cain untied their hands and offered them coffee and a biscuit.

Cain retied their hands, and the boy helped them mount. When they lined out on the trail, Cain led one man's horse with the second horse tethered to its tail. At the rear of the procession the boy rode, discarding the two empty casings from the cylinder of his pistol as he replaced them with fresh rounds.

He watched the actions of the two men he guarded and wondered, if it came down to it, if he would shoot to kill. He hoped it would not come down to that.

By late afternoon, they were riding into the yard of Cain's place, where they halted the worn-out mounts at the hitch rail near the barn. Dodger turned Cain's two horses out and then loaded the two Mexican horses in the trailer. They then headed for Los Caminos with the two hunters in the pickup bed, bound and blanketed.

Dodger sat sideways in the seat and watched the two men in the bed as he spoke.

"You think this is a good idea, Harley?"

"No, it ain't a good idea. It ain't like we got a lot of good ones to choose from. It's not an idea at all—it's the only choice we got."

The boy appeared contemplative. "You know, they ain't no one on our side now," he said.

Cain's eyes never left the road. "There never was."

Dodger nodded and took off his hat. He leaned over and looked at himself in the rearview mirror. He ran his hand through his thick hair and stared at the image staring back at him.

"I think I'm getting gray hair, Harley."

The old man laughed. "Well, it was bound to turn eventually. You know, they say a man's hair will turn—it'll either turn gray or it'll turn loose."

Dodger laughed. "It looks like yours done turned gray *and* loose."

Cain smiled. "Keep an eye on them boys back there."

Cain pulled up near the phone booth in Los Caminos and spent several minutes on the telephone before he returned to the truck.

"Flores will meet us alone at the park in ten minutes."

"Does he know what it's all about?" Dodger asked.

"No, not for sure. But he did seem nervous and surprised to hear it was me."

"Do you trust him?"

"I don't see no reason to trust him—he just tried to kill us. But we do have to deal with him . . . one way or the other."

Cain found a spot on the street and turned his rig around facing the incoming traffic, what little there was of it. Flores arrived in the police vehicle, pulled in front of Cain's truck, and waited with the red lights on, shining into the cab.

Cain sat there until Flores turned out the lights and reached out the window to motion him forward. Cain opened his door and spoke to the boy before he stepped out.

"Get out and unload their horses and wait. If this turns bad, mount up and ride like hell."

"And then what?"

"And then nothing—just keep going."

The boy unloaded the horses, tied one, and saddled the better of the two.

Cain looked inside the police vehicle before he opened the passenger door and slid into the seat.

Flores spoke first, his voice tired and impatient.

"Why did you call me here?"

"I think you know."

"What do you think I know?"

"Flores, I'm about up to here with you and the Delgados. This whole mess is fixin' to turn into a war, and you're fixin' to find yourself right in the middle of it."

"Are you threatening me, Mr. Cain?"

"Yessir, I am. You better decide right now where you stand, because I'm getting very close to not having anything to lose. When that happens, you go first."

Flores, disturbed at the unanticipated turn of events, glared at Cain, his expression dark and menacing as he wrestled with his newfound dilemma. He thought a long time before he spoke.

"Mr. Cain, this is a very unusual set of circumstances, and you have become very troublesome for everyone concerned, particularly me." He looked absentmindedly into the rearview mirror and then back to Cain.

"You can change that, Flores. What you decide right now will change it—I promise you."

"And how do you propose to make it better?"

"I didn't say I'd make it better. I said it will change. For you, it could get much worse."

"Are you prepared to kill me?" Flores asked, his question more of a threat than a question.

Cain looked him straight in the eye.

"Whatever it takes."

Flores took a slow, deep breath and exhaled louder than normal. Cain's eyes caught the reflection of the service revolver Flores had covered with his hand where it lay between his legs. The old cowboy reached inside his jacket and wrapped his fingers around the butt of the pistol he wore under his arm. When he cocked the trigger in the dead silence that hung over the two men, Flores smiled as an old chess master smiles at the student.

"What if I didn't come alone?" Flores asked.

Cain shrugged.

"It don't matter if you did or not. If you decide wrong, you're just as dead either way."

Flores looked at Cain with tired eyes. He slowly slid the revolver from between his legs and holstered it with great resignation. He placed both hands on the steering wheel.

"So, Mr. Cain, what is it you want of me?"

Cain opened the passenger-side door and spoke over his shoulder as he exited the vehicle.

"Come on back here. I want to show you something."

Flores followed Cain to the back of the pickup. Cain pulled back the blanket. The two men laid bound and embarrassed. The three spoke briefly in Spanish, and Flores made no pretense of his intentions or his familiarity with the two men.

"I could have shot them and left them in the mountains," Cain said. "And then come back for you."

Flores stood burdened by his duty as a police officer and his obligation to the blood of his family. He spoke again to the two men, and the two men nodded. Cain leaned over the pickup bed, retrieved the knife from his pocket, and cut the strings.

"I'm giving you their lives. I'm giving you your life," Cain said. "And in return, I'm asking you to settle this with the family—all of them. Can you do that?"

Flores looked at Cain. There was an air of defeated defiance about him.

"And if I am unable to do so?"

Cain's expression grew hard and resigned.

"Then a lot of people are going to die for no reason, beginning with you."

"You knew these two men came to kill you?" Flores asked.

Cain nodded. "They tried."

"Why did you not kill them?"

"Because I want this over. Now they owe me and you owe me. If that's not enough, then I guess none of this matters."

Flores motioned the two men out of the bed of the pickup. Cain told the boy to bring them their horses. The police chief offered Cain his hand.

"You're an honorable man, Mr. Cain. We have all let this go too far, myself included. It's time to call it off before anyone else is hurt. I will speak to the family."

Cain was unsure if Flores was sincere or if this was his way of setting him up. He remained skeptical.

Flores paused while the two men checked the cinches and adjusted the headstalls. The older of the two men addressed Cain.

"This was not personal."

There was no give in Cain's expression.

"Maybe not for you."

For the next two days, Cain and the boy busied themselves at the ranch, with no talk of the Delgados and no talk of a plan one way or the other. When the telephone rang late in the evening, the boy sat with his elbows on the table and listened as Cain spoke. He sat upright when Cain paused a long time and nodded.

"Okay, we'll be there," he said. Cain hung up the telephone and looked across the table at the boy.

Cain's eyes were cast in doubt, and his expression showed no sign of encouragement.

"Well?"

Cain sat back in his chair. "Flores wants us to meet with the family at his house in Los Caminos tomorrow evening."

"Do you think it's a trap?"

"It might be."

"What are we going to do?"

"If we don't show up, it's like calling the whole deal off. If we do, and it is a trap, it might be the last thing we do."

The boy set his jaw and stood leaning against the wall, his eyes dark with concern and his expression one of defiant aggression.

"I'm getting tired of getting pushed around, Harley."

"Yeah, me too, Dodger. Me too."

The boy stood up straight with his thumbs looped in the front pockets of his jeans.

"I say we go in armed and dangerous."

Cain looked at him and laughed. "Armed and dangerous?"

Dodger smiled. "They said that in a movie one time—I liked the sound of it."

"The truth is," Cain said, "that might not be a bad idea."

The following evening, when Cain and the boy departed for Los Caminos, Cain carried the .45 holstered beneath his jacket with a full magazine and a round in the chamber.

Dodger sat slumped in the seat as they pulled onto the highway.

"I don't see why I can't have a gun too, Harley."

"We ain't going down there to start a war." He patted the bulge beneath his jacket. "This one's just for insurance. It might be enough to even the odds if things get tense."

The boy sat up and leaned on his arm against the window as he gazed out onto the desert and wished himself to be horseback, lost among the shadows and riding with nowhere to be and no concern for the time or day. He looked up at the sky cast in the gray flatness of twilight and tried to make sense of it all. He turned to the old cowboy.

"Who do you suppose goes to heaven, Harley?"

Cain looked at the boy a long time, and then turned his attention back to driving.

"They say only the righteous."

"Is that what you believe?"

"Well, I'd say that was right. I also like to believe there's a place for those who didn't get it quite right down here and just needed a second chance."

"Like my momma?"

Cain smiled and nodded. "Like your momma."

Dodger smiled. He was quiet while he contemplated the mental list of those he knew.

"What about bad guys like Eugene?"

Cain shook his head. "Some use up all their chances."

"Do you reckon a person who kills himself uses up all his chances?"

"Yeah, I reckon I do. There's no way to make up for that one."

The boy crossed a boot over his leg and gnawed his bottom lip.

"I guess you and me got lucky, huh, Harley?"

"I suppose, in the long run, we did."

Dodger thought a while before he spoke again. He seemed to be thinking his way through another of life's great mysteries.

"You know, once I made up my mind to do it—before I got all drunked up—it was the happiest I ever felt."

"How so?"

"Well, it was like I was in charge and life couldn't push me around no more—you know what I mean?"

Cain nodded. "I know exactly what you mean."

"I wonder if it would have been worth it."

"I don't know, Dodger. I wasn't thinking about that—were you?"

"No, sir. I just wanted to be done with it."

"How about now?" Cain asked, genuinely interested in the boy's answer.

"Now I ain't sure. Seems like we been working pretty hard to stay alive. I guess that means something."

Cain took a deep breath. "Yep. I reckon it does."

"Before I met you, I never had been down this way, Harley. Now I believe I could make the trip with my eyes closed."

"It's good for a young person to see some of the world before he gets too old."

"Have you been a lot of places, Harley?"

"I covered a lot of ground in my time. There ain't much left I'd like to see, but I would like to see Fiji."

"Where's Fiji?"

"It's an island in the middle of the ocean, by Australia. It stays warm all the time, everything is green, and they live in grass huts with no windows. The people fish and swim in the ocean, and they don't have wars or government to worry about." Cain grinned and looked over at the boy. "The ladies there don't wear no tops because of the weather, and no one thinks a thing of it."

The boy sat up and looked directly at the old man.

"Serious? They don't wear nothing on top?"

Cain laughed. "It's a fact. Haven't you ever seen a *National Geographic* magazine? There's a number of places in the world the women don't wear tops."

Dodger shook his head and grinned.

"It's sure educational hanging around with you, Harley."

Then the boy sat back in the seat and turned to gaze out the side window.

"Fiji sounds nice. Is it a long ways from here?"

"It's on the other side of the world. You have to fly or take a ship to get there."

Dodger leaned his head back, let his hat slide forward over his eyes, and dreamed he was afloat on a crystal sea. It was the first peaceful dream he could remember having.

CHAPTER THIRTY-TWO

Cain slowed, checked the address, and parked the pickup at the end of the street where they had easy access to a quick getaway if it came to that. He muffled a coughing fit and then nudged the boy.

"We're here."

Dodger sat upright, looked around, and set his hat. He was edgy.

"You shoulda woke me up."

The Flores house appeared to be the largest one on the street. It sat far back into the cover of the trees that surrounded it. A large porch wrapped around the front and both sides, and bright floodlights illuminated everything around it. The yard appeared well maintained. A police vehicle sat in the driveway. Elena's car sat parked on the street behind a sedan that the boy recognized as Umberto's.

"Looks like they're all here," the boy said in an uncharacteristically critical voice.

Cain coughed into a rag he pulled from his pocket. He and the boy stood in the shadows at the front of the house and waited before they stepped up onto the porch. He turned to the boy and handed him the keys to the pickup.

"You go on back to the truck and wait. If something's not right, hotfoot it on out of here."

The boy began to protest, but the look on Cain's face convinced him otherwise. He took the keys and turned back toward the truck.

"I got a right to be here too," Dodger said, offended by what he saw as being brushed off.

"This ain't no time to argue. Do like I said." Dodger went.

Cain, uneasy and a bit put out at Dodger's resistance, glanced at the button for the doorbell but decided to knock instead. The door swung open. Flores stood before him, his expression hard, his demeanor strained.

"Mr. Cain," Flores said as he looked beyond the old man. "The boy is not with you?"

Cain looked into the eyes of the police chief and then into the room behind him, where he saw Elena's mother sitting in a hardback chair. He heard voices speaking in Spanish, out of his line of sight. He shook his head.

"This ain't his concern."

"Please come in."

Cain followed Flores into the large but modestly appointed living room. He quickly looked about. The two brothers, Umberto and Manuel, stood smoking near a doorway that appeared to lead down a dark hallway. Elena sat on the sofa near her mother's chair. A strikingly handsome woman Cain assumed to be Mrs. Flores entered from the kitchen with a tray of *mollete dulce* and coffee. She smiled at Cain as she set the tray on the table. Cain relaxed as Flores began the introductions and asked the old man to sit.

Out of uniform, Antonio Flores appeared to be a man of status and dignity as he stood before the small group and weighed his words before he spoke. He took his time and made eye contact first with his sister, Teresa Delgado, then with her daughter, and finally with her husband's two brothers, both of whom stood withdrawn and dissident in their attitude. Then he turned to Cain as a great silence hung over the room.

He began to speak with the quiet power of a man of authority. His manner, direct and unyielding, reflected his genuine concern for correcting the dangerous course upon which everyone in the room was cast.

"This all stops here. Now."

He paused, defying an argument or a protest from anyone.

"Jorge is dead. His death was caused by more than just a bullet. It was caused by thievery, and it was caused by careless neglect."

He glared at Umberto and Manuel and pointed to Cain as he continued.

"You chose to steal this man's horses. He did the same as you would do in his place. Jorge made the same decision you did, and now he is dead, God rest his soul."

He gazed around the room at the silent faces.

"There is more than enough blame to go around, myself included. That's not the point."

Flores paced from one end of the carpet to the other and back.

"Vengeance and killing have no stopping place. I know that now. I wrongfully sent a father and his son to end this for the family. They are only alive today because Mr. Cain here spared them so we would end this once and for all."

Flores looked across at Elena. Her brooding eyes stared coldly at the carpet.

"That means all of us."

Manuel twisted his cigarette out in the ashtray near where he stood, but he did not look up at Flores and he did not respond. Teresa Delgado's head nodded in agreement. Umberto stared blankly at the space in front of him.

Flores walked a circle around the room and shook his head. He turned his attention to Cain. Flores appeared to become impatient.

"It's over. Everyone in this room bears the responsibility of what has happened. *Gracias a Dios* no one else has been killed."

Flores swore them collectively and individually to a truce and, while agreement was unanimous, the pledge from Manuel was hollow and came begrudgingly. They sealed the pact with shots of tequila poured from a bottle with no label.

The conversation that followed was awkward and civil, but strained.

Elena, still wrestling with her emotions, stepped outside onto the porch, staring into the night. Dodger saw her in the rearview mirror and stepped out of the pickup. He did his best to conceal his limp as she watched him approach.

"Hey," he said.

She didn't smile, but her expression appeared softer than the last time he had seen her.

"Hi," she replied.

"How'd it go in there?"

Elena leaned on the heavy railing but did not look directly at him. "It's all just talk."

Dodger stood with his head down.

"It won't bring my father back."

He looked up into her defeated eyes.

"If there was a way for me to make it all go away, I would."

Elena clinched her jaw. Her eyes rimmed with tears.

Dodger's voice was hushed.

"I don't know why it all had to happen like it did."

He put his hand on her arm. She pulled away and glared at him.

"Tell me the truth. What happened to my father?"

Dodger turned away from her, sat on the step, and wrapped his arms around his knees. He shook his head.

"I shot him."

His voice cracked, and he choked on the words.

"I didn't mean to."

Elena's fury erupted. She stood over him, pounding him with her fists.

"You didn't mean to—*stupido, pendejo*. You killed my father, and you didn't mean to? I hate you!"

She turned and stormed into the house.

Dodger limped back to the pickup, tears streaming down his face. He sat a long time wishing Cain had left the pistol there.

The door opened, and light from inside spilled out onto the yard. Cain and Flores stood on the porch. They shook hands.

Dodger watched as Cain walked in his direction. He ran his shirtsleeve across his eyes.

Cain slid behind the wheel, and neither spoke until he pulled onto the highway where it ran through the center of town.

"I saw you talking with Elena. What happened?"

Dodger shook his head, his eyes fixed on some distant spot in the night.

Cain pressed him.

"She didn't talk much inside, but I could see it wasn't because she didn't have anything to say."

He waited. "Look, if she hurt your feelings, that's one thing, but if we're going to get this over and done with, we need to deal with it."

Dodger sat tight-jawed. Cain waited, and then everything came at once as the boy didn't seem to know where to start.

"I killed her dad—she ain't never gonna forget that."

His eyes were wet, but he didn't cry. His voice cracked when he spoke again.

"She told me I was stupid, and she was right. Fuckin' gimp. She don't have to settle for no half a man."

Cain coughed into his rag, and this time there was blood in the phlegm. He folded the rag and glared across at the boy.

"You don't know the first thing about being half a man."

The boy's eyes were on fire. "None of this woulda happened if we wouldn't'a rode to the river that night."

"You saying this is all my fault?"

"It was all your old-ass idea."

"I should have followed my instincts about you from the get-go."

"And what?"

Cain stared out the window ahead and did not respond to the boy. He shifted in his seat, and neither of them spoke, but the tension in the air was at the breaking point. A few miles down the road, Cain leaned forward, reached behind his back, and removed the .45 from his belt. He laid it up on the dash.

Dodger looked at the .45, then at the old man, and back to the .45. His thoughts were dark, his mood somber. A pair of oncoming headlights loomed in the distance, grew closer, and then passed, casting the truck and the highway in darkness.

In the gloom of the dimly lit cab, Dodger looked across at the old man and then reached furtively for the pistol, laid it on his lap, and covered it with his hat.

"It ain't loaded," Cain said without shifting his gaze.

Dodger sat brooding a long time before he set the pistol back where it had been and turned away from the old man.

Another half dozen miles in silence down a road with no lights and no traffic and lots of time to think. Cain's voice was firm, his manner direct.

"You reckon she'd think better of you, knowing you blew your own brains out?"

"What do you know about anything? Your wife ran off and didn't even tell you."

Cain turned and glared at the boy. "I know a pansy-ass crybaby when I see one."

"I ain't no crybaby."

"Some little girl makes you feel bad and you want to shoot yourself?"

"Fuck you, Harley."

Cain jammed on the brakes, slid off the pavement, and the truck spun sideways, coming to rest in a choking wall of dust. He threw the door open, grabbed the pistol, and walked around to Dodger's door. He swung the door open, grabbed the boy by the shirtfront, and jerked him from the truck.

The boy stood wide-eyed, watching as the old man pushed the pistol to him, butt first.

"Here, it's loaded. Go ahead and do it."

The boy hesitated. Cain shouted.

"DO IT!"

The gun rattled in the boy's hands. He looked at Cain, racked back the slide, chambered a round, and considered taking them both out. Cain stood firm. The boy fumed.

He looked down at the gun, looked at Cain, and then pointed the gun downward and squeezed the trigger over and over again until the slide locked back. He stood veiled in the blue smoke until it drifted out into the desert. He threw the gun down into the dirt and limped off, cursing over his shoulder as he disappeared into the dark.

"Fuck you and your horses and your cows and all your bullshit about knowing everything. Fuck you."

Cain picked up the pistol and watched the boy limp away. He slipped back behind the wheel and gazed out into the headlight beam until the boy simply disappeared into the darkness beyond it.

He sat there with the engine running. He wondered if he and the boy wouldn't have both been better off if things had gone differently the night they met. His eyes turned to the .45 on the seat and remained there a long time before he shifted the pickup into gear and began to roll forward.

A quarter mile down the road, the boy's image materialized at the outer edge of his lights and grew larger as he overtook him. Cain rolled to a stop a few yards ahead of the boy, and he waited.

Dodger limped past the truck without looking in at Cain, and continued walking.

Cain waited and then turned the truck out onto the pavement, watching the reflection of the boy in the rearview mirror, standing in the moonlight, his middle finger stuck up in the air.

CHAPTER THIRTY-THREE

In the morning, Cain stood in the kitchen. He looked through the glass in the door. There, on the porch steps, sat the boy looking out over the patched fences, the barn, and the livestock.

He poured two cups of coffee, rolled and lit a cigarette, and then pushed the door open with his boot. Dodger turned at the sound of the door. Cain handed him a cup. The boy took the cup and nodded.

Cain sat in his customary chair and hoisted his boots up on the rail. He smoked his cigarette. They both looked out at the desert a long time. Neither said a word.

Finally, the boy spoke without turning to face the old man.

"I didn't mean what I said last night."

Cain sat gazing over the railing without responding or looking at the boy.

"I'm sorry."

Cain took a long drag and blew the smoke out into the morning air.

"It just all hit me at one time."

"That happens," Cain said. He was resigned, not encouraging.

The boy stood. He turned and extended his hand. Cain hesitated, and then he shook it.

"I wanted to thank you for all you done for me before I leave. I didn't want you to think last night meant I didn't appreciate it."

Dodger tipped his head toward the house.

"Is it okay if I go in and get my stuff?"

Cain raised his eyes to the boy. He stared at him, wondering where things had gone so wrong. A flashing image of his wife and child blurred through his mind.

"You know where it's at."

When Dodger came out, he carried a paper grocery bag packed with what clothes he owned.

"Need a ride?" Cain asked.

"I'll be okay. I'll catch me a ride out there."

Dodger motioned in the direction of the highway. He started down the steps. When he got to the gravel, Cain called out to him.

"Hey."

The boy turned, his expression hopeful.

"You're overdue for a better hand. Good luck to ya, Dodger."

The boy nodded and headed off.

He stopped at the pavement, looked north and south, and then parked his bag on the shoulder and waited. An hour passed and then two. He picked up his bag, walked a hundred yards to a spot of shade, and took up his post again.

By noon, not a vehicle had passed. An hour later, a pickup with a load of hay in the bed and five people in the seat slowed; the driver shrugged, and they continued on. By early evening, Dodger sat cross-legged in the dirt with his arms crossed and his head down. When the sun set and darkness cast everything in the shadow of the moon, Dodger picked up his bag and limped north down the middle of the lane with no hope for a ride.

He followed the highway divider lines in the moonlight,

thinking about Bufort and Bobby and all that had happened. Things had just unraveled.

Lights behind him cast his shadow before him. He moved to the shoulder and looked back with his thumb out. A big rig flashed its lights but did not stop.

Well past midnight, another set of lights approached from the south, casting his long shadow out before him. He moved out of the lane and off the road without looking back or waving for a ride. A pickup swung wide to pass him, then the taillights brightened and the pickup pulled up ahead of him.

Dodger limped his way to the waiting truck, opened the door, and looked inside.

"Hey, Harley."

The old man looked at him.

"Come on, cowboy. Let's go home."

Neither Cain nor Dodger spoke again of the night in the desert.

The following week, the old man and the kid left the ranch and followed a dirt road north as the sun came up. Cain intentionally skirted Bufort.

"Where we going, Harley?"

"Fort Stockton. This is a shortcut. I want you to meet someone there."

"Who?"

"His name is Robert Tarrant. He's an old army friend of mine."

For the next hour, Dodger slept with his head on his arm, leaning against the window. When he awoke, he yawned, stretched, and nodded generally in the direction of the endless desert to his right.

"Can you pull over somewhere, Harley? I gotta pee."

Cain pulled the pickup over to the shoulder and waited. Dodger climbed back in and slammed the door shut.

"Feel better?"

The boy grinned.

"Yessir, I feel just dandy now. We almost there?"

"Another three quarters of an hour, maybe."

• •

When they entered Fort Stockton, they passed oil rigs and storage tanks. The town itself lay on both sides of the main highway, giving it the appearance of a sprawling rest stop rather than a destination.

Cain drove down the main street and pulled into the dirt parking lot of Tarrant's Gym.

Inside, they walked back to a corner office. Cain leaned in and knocked on the open door. The dark-skinned man behind the desk looked up and smiled as he rose to greet them.

"Look what the cat drug in," the man behind the desk said to Cain as he extended his left hand. Cain shook it with his left hand and then turned and nodded toward the boy.

"Sergeant Tarrant, I'd like you to meet Dodger Cooper."

Dodger extended his right hand. Tarrant grasped it with his left hand while his right one hung slack, pinned to his shirt at his side. Tarrant sat down and told Cain and the boy to sit. Dodger tried not to be conspicuous as he stared at the safety pin that held the sleeve of Tarrant's limp arm fast to his shirt.

"Good to meet you, Dodger."

"Thanks. Good to meet you too."

"What brings you to town, Captain?" Tarrant asked.

"I was hoping you could show the boy around and let him see what you got going on here."

Tarrant looked over at Dodger.

"You interested in boxing?"

"I don't know nothing about it, sir."

"Would you like to take a look around?"

Dodger looked at the wall crowded with black-and-white photos of fighters and a shelf full of trophies.

"Yessir, I'd like that a lot."

Tarrant stood again and this time walked from behind the desk, awkwardly favoring the right leg with the heavy brace that held it. Tarrant noticed Dodger's fixation on the leg and the brace.

"I got that and the arm in Normandy—Dubya Dubya Two."

"Sorry."

"Nothing to be sorry for."

"I meant sorry for staring. I know what that feels like."

They walked past the weight room, where a young fighter worked out. They stopped at the ring to watch two fighters in headgear as they sparred. Tarrant observed the fighters with great intensity before he shouted into the ring.

"Jimmy, keep your elbows in and your hands up, and jab. You're leaving yourself wide open."

"Is all this yours, Mr. Tarrant?"

"Yes, it is, Dodger."

"How did you get it?"

Tarrant hesitated.

"You mean how did a crippled colored man get enough money to pay for it?"

Dodger didn't flinch or acquiesce.

"Yessir, that is what I meant."

Tarrant stood to his full height, and there was no arrogance or defiance about him.

"I worked for it. I started here as the janitor. I wasn't too proud to work, and I never complained about having one bad arm and one bad leg."

"What happened to you?"

"You mean how did I get injured?"

"Uh-huh."

"A guy next to me stepped on a land mine. I was luckier than him."

The boy nodded as though he understood.

"I don't know nothing about boxing, but I know some about horses."

"What are you planning to be?"

"I aim to be a vet."

"How you going to do that?"

"I don't know yet."

"Don't matter that you don't know—get it fixed in your mind first, and you'll find a way."

Cain nodded. "He's a hard worker. He will find a way."

• •

Cain and the boy took Tarrant to lunch and then left for Bufort in the early afternoon. The boy rode in contemplative silence until Cain spoke.

"You still feel like half a man?"

"No, sir. That was plain ignorant of me."

Dodger sat back and furrowed his brow as he appeared to be processing the significance of the lesson Cain hoped he had learned. The boy leaned forward.

"You know something, Harley?"

"What's that?"

"I have two Negro friends now, and I look up to both of them."

Cain nodded.

"And they're both named Robert."

Cain shook his head and smiled. "I'm sure that's just a coincidence."

"Yeah, I reckon it is," the boy said. "Is Mr. Tarrant married?"

"He is. He has a pretty wife and three real nice kids."

"So maybe there's hope for me too."

"I'd say there's lots of hope for you."

"Hey, there's a Tarrant County in Texas. They didn't name that after him, did they?"

Cain laughed. "No, I'm reasonably sure they didn't."

"I thought maybe he was famous."

The boy laid his hat on the seat between them and scratched his head. "I reckon I need to come up with a plan," he said.

"What kind of a plan?"

"Well, I'm going to need me a job."

"What's wrong with the one you got?"

"You mean fixing fences?"

"That and other things that need doing around the ranch."

Dodger sat quietly with his face leaning against his fist.

"I got two years of high school to finish, I need to get my driver's license and get me a truck . . . and I need to find me a place to stay."

"I've been giving that some thought. I can put you on at full pay, and you can stay at the ranch as long as you like. If you pass your driver's test and promise not to run into any more bridges, we can work out a loan against your wages to get you a work truck."

Dodger shook his head. "Ain't no way. I can't ask you to do that, Harley."

Cain was careful not to make the job offer sound like charity. "You didn't ask me—I brought it up. Besides, I got other business to attend to. I could use the help. If you don't take the job, I'll have to find someone else anyway. At least I won't have to train you."

"You sure about that, Harley?"

"I am."

Dodger stuck out his hand, and Cain shook it.

"I'll try not to be no bother."

"If we find you a truck, you ain't going to drive it into a bridge, are you?"

They laughed.

"No more bridges, I promise."

Dodger grew silent.

"The way things are going, Harley . . . I can't picture either one of us dead, can you?"

Cain hesitated before he responded. He coughed deeply and cleared his throat before he spoke.

"No, sir . . . we got too much work to do."

They stopped in Bufort at the Department of Motor Vehicles and picked up a study guide for the boy. Two weeks later, he had his learner's permit, and a week after that, he and Cain searched the newspaper for used trucks.

"Here's a bunch of them oilfield trucks they got for sale, Harley."

"We'll steer clear of those, Dodger. Them ol' boys drive the snot out of their trucks before they trade them in."

The boy looked from ad to ad, holding his spot on the page with his finger as he turned to Cain.

"I reckon I need one that'll hold up. Do you favor a Ford over a Chevy?"

"I've had both . . . and had a Dodge too. Mostly I'm partial to a Ford truck."

“That’s what I think I want too. Here’s one. It’s a four-speed, V-8, three-quarter-ton flatbed for four hundred dollars.”

He looked up at Cain with uncertainty. “That’s too much money, ain’t it?”

Cain set his coffee cup on the table and sat next to the boy.

“That is a lot of money, but if it’s a good truck, it’s worth it.”

The boy read the rest of the ad carefully and then leaned back in his chair.

“I guess this one’s out. It’s in Fort Stockton.”

Cain smiled. “Let’s give them a call and see if we can go look at it.”

They drove to Fort Stockton and paid $375 for a well-used but clean flatbed the dealer told them ran “like a top.” It broke down halfway between Fort Stockton and Bufort. Cain repaired the clogged fuel filter, and they made the rest of the trip without incident.

When they pulled into the yard, the boy parked the truck next to the porch and spent the balance of the day cleaning it up and working on it.

The old man and the boy sat on the porch after supper with their boots up on the rail, drinking iced tea.

“That’s a good-lookin’ truck, ain’t it, Harley?”

“It’s a fine-looking truck. I especially like the picture of the longhorn bull on the doors.”

“Do you really like it?”

“I do.”

Dodger grinned. “Me too. Makes it look like a real cowboy truck, don’t it?”

“It for sure does.”

The boy stood and turned toward Cain. He extended his hand, and Cain shook it.

“There ain’t no words to thank you for buying that truck, Harley.”

Cain sipped his iced tea and shook his head.

“I didn’t buy it. You did. I’m deducting ten dollars a month out of your pay until it’s paid for.”

"Well, you didn't have to, and I appreciate that. I'll pay back more each month if I have some left over."

Dodger sat back down in his chair, tilted it back on two legs, and then crossed his boots on the railing.

"I reckon I should take that truck for a ride soon, just to get used to it."

"I reckon you should."

"Maybe I'll do that tomorrow after I finish my work."

"Where you thinking of going in it?"

Dodger shook his head. "I was thinking about driving in to Bufort and showing it to Bobby . . . I think I'm pretty much used to it already."

Cain stood and nodded in the direction of the elevated fuel tank near the barn.

"When you finish up tomorrow, go ahead and fill up at the tank. Keep track of the gas you use, and we'll settle up at the end of the month."

Dodger finished his iced tea, picked up both glasses, and spoke over his shoulder as he entered the house. "Is it okay if I borrow some wrenches? I'm gonna tighten everything up on my truck."

"You know where they are."

My truck . . . sounds funny to say that, he thought as he passed the flatbed on the way to the barn and admired the shadow it cast as he walked by it.

When he returned with the wrenches and a rag, he sat in his truck a long time and imagined himself pulling a trailer loaded with cattle and headed for the sale. He pushed in the clutch and went through the gears, watching the aftermarket tach mounted on the steering column, and pretending to shift each time the needle breached the yellow-zone just below the red line.

Neither Cain nor the boy gave any thought to the legality of the boy driving on his own, and the subject never came up between them. There was no talk of the right or wrong of the boy driving without insurance or a license. There was no cautionary discussion about the responsibility of operating a motor vehicle on public roadways. Both the man and the boy held the unspoken acknowledgement that life is a temporary and short privilege revocable without notice. Neither chose to dwell on the finer details of social conduct, most of which they felt did not apply to them anyway.

Cain had long ago outlived any compulsion he had to conform to the rules of the masses, and the boy, with his all-but-feral upbringing, had avoided all but the most basic of compliant behavioral restraints. The night Cain and the boy had each taken control of his own destiny separated them from normal society. Each bore the burden, as well as the freedom, of that choice.

That night they sat on the porch after dinner, both with their boots up and a tall glass of iced tea in hand. The boy stared at his truck with the moonlight reflecting off the windshield.

"When you see Bobby tomorrow, ask him if he's interested in helping you get on those fences again," Cain said.

Cain imagined himself looking down upon his new world—lights on in the house, cooking smells, conversation—all of it like a dream. For the first time in more years than he could remember, everything and everyone had a purpose, a reason to live.

"I already know he is. Should I bring him back with me?"

"Call him tonight and make sure it's okay. He can stay the week if he likes. It'll take you that long."

CHAPTER THIRTY-FOUR

The two boys walked up the street to the corner where Dodger's truck was parked out of view from the Washington house. Dodger hobbled along as fast as he could, anxious to show Bobby his new flatbed.

They stopped when they got to the truck. Bobby stood speechless and wide-eyed. He looked at Dodger and then back at the truck. Dodger stood there beaming.

"Is that really yours, Dodge?"

"Seriously, it is."

"You're so lucky. Man, I love them longhorns on it."

"I know—looks cool, huh? I can't even believe I got it."

Bobby looked at Dodger and grinned. He held out his hand. "Well?"

Dodger threw him the keys.

"Let's roll, bud."

Bobby and Dodger drove through Bufort hoping to be seen by someone they knew. They stopped by the Conoco and each got a Dr. Pepper for the road. They talked with Mickey, and Dodger showed him the truck.

"Them two girls y'all are always talkin' about was just here. They said they'd be right back," Mickey told them.

Dodger and Bobby looked at each other.

"Who?" Dodger asked.

"Malia and Jackie," Mickey said. "If I was you'ns, I'd hang around so they could see me in my new truck."

The boys stared at the worldly ex-high school jock, as though he had just shared one of the insider-elite's secrets with them.

Bobby turned to Dodger. "Want to wait?"

Dodger grinned. "Heck, yeah. They're only the two cutest girls in the whole school!"

Mickey pointed to the street. "That's them now."

Dodger elbowed Bobby. "Gimme the keys. Hurry."

Bobby turned and held the keys away from Dodger. "Why?"

"I wanna drive."

Bobby reluctantly handed the keys to Dodger. "Geez, not like it's a big deal or anything."

The girls approached. Their dark hair was pulled back into matching ponytails that swung side to side in perfectly choreographed rhythm. They both wore oversized letterman sweaters with *BHS,* a football, and *1957* embroidered across the front that suggested they were going steady with upperclassmen from the varsity football team.

The boys knew that, for the moment at least, the Ford flatbed trumped the sweaters.

Malia flashed her engaging smile and spoke first.

"Hi, Dodger. Hi, Bobby."

"Hi, Malia. Hi, Jackie," they both said in unison.

Jackie checked the truck out first, barely noticing the boys.

"Hi," she said smiling. "Is that your truck?" Her tone was at once condescending and flirty.

Dodger chose flirty. "Yeah, I just got it."

Bobby, thinking much faster than Dodger, opened the passenger door and held it.

"Want to go for a ride?"

"We're going to my house. Can you drop us there?" Malia said.

Dodger nodded. "Sure. Hop in."

• •

The boys dropped the girls off, giddy with excitement. They changed drivers at the end of the block, with Bobby now behind the wheel as they headed south to the ranch.

Dodger leaned forward, turned the knob on the radio, and waited as the dim display light brightened and the crackling of a distant station played mariachi music. He turned the station-selector knob past the few static-choked stations he could find and stopped on the weak signal of a country station broadcasting out of Odessa. He reached out the window and pulled the antenna up to its full extension. He grinned at Bobby when the music blasted through the cab of the truck.

"It works good, huh?" he shouted at Bobby.

"It's the best one I ever heard," Bobby shouted back as he shifted through the gears and marveled at the rumble of the loud exhaust thundering away into the gray of evening.

They rode that way until a commercial break in the music. Dodger reached forward and turned the volume down. He sat back and crossed a boot over one knee. He watched the road through the windshield, deep in thought.

"Do you know anything about boxing, B-Bob?"

"Yeah, some."

"Like what?"

"Well, I know Sugar Ray Robinson just beat Carmen Basilio a while back, and now he's the champ."

"I didn't know you was up on boxing."

"It's just something that appeals to me, I guess. You know that television set they leave playing at night in the window of Gambles?"

"Yeah."

"I watch the fights there when I can—seen a bunch of 'em."

"You ever think about being a boxer?"

"I thought about it, but I wouldn't know how to go about doing it."

"Mr. Tarrant could tell you all about it."

"Who's he?"

"He's the guy that owns a gym up in Fort Stockton. Mr. Cain took me to meet him. He has a boxing ring there with weights and stuff."

Bobby sat up straight, and he looked over at Dodger with his full attention directed toward him. Dodger reached over and punched him on the arm.

"Hey, man, watch the road."

"A real boxing ring?"

"Yeah, there was two guys with helmets on inside the ring going at it."

"Seriously?"

"Seriously."

Dodger smiled. "Want to go up there sometime and see for yourself?"

"Wouldn't I."

"Wooden eye? No, they both had good eyes."

"Funny. I really do want to go see it, though."

Dodger could not remember a time he'd felt more proud. Two of the most popular girls in school talked to him, he had his truck, his best friend was driving it, and he knew a man with a boxing ring.

"We'll see if we can get Harley to take us up there."

Bobby drummed his fingers on the top of the steering wheel, adjusted his hat, and smiled.

"Good deal, Lucille. I hope he'll do it. If not, maybe we could take your truck."

"If he'll let us," Dodger said.

Friday afternoon, Cain called the boys in from their work. They cleaned up, ate a late lunch, and were on the road to Fort Stockton with Cain driving, Dodger in the middle, and Bobby riding shotgun—because he called it first.

"I don't mind riding in the middle," Dodger said as they pulled out onto the blacktop.

"Why's that?" Cain asked.

"My daddy told me that's how you can tell who the real cowboy is in the bunch. The guy in the middle don't have to open and close no gates."

Bobby hung his arm out the window, turned his head, and

looked at Dodger from under the brim of his hat. "We ain't going through no gates."

Dodger shot him a sarcastic look. "It don't matter if we are or we ain't—it still works the same."

"Okay, then, you can be the real cowboy every time, and I'll ride shotgun," Bobby said.

Dodger pushed his hat back. "It don't work like that neither."

"Seems like you've put some deep thought to the matter, Dodger," Cain said.

"No, sir. It's something all cowboys know about."

They parked at the side of the gym and entered through a back door. Bobby could already feel the air of familiarity that comes from being part of something and knowing about a special entrance.

Inside, Tarrant turned when he heard the door open. He greeted the trio as they approached.

"This is getting to be a regular occurrence," he said as he extended his hand to Cain and Cain shook it.

"I brought someone I'd like you to meet, Robert," Cain said as he coughed into a rag he carried. Tarrant waited.

Bobby looked at Tarrant and back at Dodger and whispered, "Is that him?"

Dodger nodded.

"He's colored."

Dodger nodded again. "I know."

Tarrant shook Dodger's hand, told him it was good to see him again, and then waited for Cain to introduce him to Bobby.

"This is Dodger's friend Bobby," Cain said, his eyes still watering from the coughing fit he took.

Tarrant extended his left hand, and Bobby shook it with his left hand. Dodger did not say anything, but he admired Bobby's quickness in catching on.

"Good to meet you, Bobby."

"Thanks. Good to meet you too, sir."

Bobby appeared somewhat ill at ease, not knowing exactly how to relate to the articulate and confident colored man who made no concession to the braced leg he favored and the slack arm pinned to his shirt. He tried not to stare. Dodger nudged him with his elbow.

"A guy next to him stepped on a mine."

Bobby tried to remain inconspicuous—that wasn't helping.

Mercifully, Dodger changed the subject.

"Look at all them boxing pictures up there."

Bobby stepped in closer and put his finger on one, pointing to a man in a suit standing next to Tarrant.

"Mr. Tarrant, ain't that Sugar Ray?"

Tarrant smiled. "Sure is. That was taken in New York at Madison Square Garden two years ago."

They spent the rest of the afternoon with Tarrant. Bobby lifted weights, got a few quick lessons on the speed bag from one of the boxers, and then watched the sparring while he hung on the lower rope and imagined himself in the ring. Before they left, Tarrant gave Bobby an old pair of boxing gloves, a worn-out speed bag, and a new pair of satin boxing shorts with tarrant's gym silk-screened on the leg. He gave Dodger a Tarrant's Gym baseball cap, and the boys promised to come back every chance they got.

On the ride home, the sun settled onto the desert floor and the sky changed from turquoise to crimson red and finally grayed into a blanket of black, shot full of holes where the light of the stars shone through. The boyish banter this night took on a serious tone as Bobby and Dodger talked of the future and Cain spoke of the past, an age when he'd believed himself invincible and exempt from the effects of time.

For the first time in their young lives, Bobby and Dodger dared to dream of a future beyond the boundaries of Bufort. The more they spoke of what could be, the deeper grew their conviction. Cain envisioned them all at the edge of a frontier to a journey none understood. Theirs would take them to places they could not imagine. His would take him to a place he dared not imagine.

Bobby wore the boxing gloves, and Dodger wore the baseball cap. They sat in the dark of that pickup cab staring out into their future, while Cain glanced into the rearview mirror and stared back at his past.

Bobby held up his gloved right fist. "Think it would hurt if I hit you with this?"

Dodger looked at the big, padded glove and then shrugged his shoulders. "I don't think it would hurt much."

"Want me to try?"

"From right there?"

"Yeah."

"Not in the face."

"Okay, one shot to the shoulder."

Bobby nodded and cocked his arm as best he could in the tight confines of the pickup. Cain watched them through the corner of his eye. Dodger braced for the hit.

Bobby connected, and the force of the impact slammed him into Cain and jacked his baseball cap sideways on his head.

"Well, shit, B-Bob, just give it all you got, why don't you?"

Dodger straightened up his cap and apologized to Cain. Bobby laughed.

"Let me try one on you," Dodger said.

Bobby slipped the glove off, handed it to Dodger, turned his shoulder, and waited for Dodger to put on the glove and wind up. Dodger turned in the seat. The seat back prevented a full swing, but he fired anyway. The shot landed solid but weak, and Bobby started laughing. Cain laughed and Dodger fumed. He slipped the glove off and tossed it on the floor. He looked at Bobby, and then he looked at Cain. The infectious laughing took hold, and they all three laughed until their eyes watered.

"Next time I'm gonna hit you in your head so hard you won't even recognize your momma."

Bobby grinned. "If Mr. Cain wasn't sitting there, I'd'a hit you so hard we'd have to go get you."

Cain shook his head slowly side to side. "If you two had put this much effort into fixing them fences, you'd have been done a long time ago."

Then he coughed into his rag and bent over the wheel as he caught his breath, and both boys watched in silence.

CHAPTER THIRTY-FIVE

Bobby stayed in Bufort during the week. Dodger picked him up and drove him to the ranch every Friday. They finished the fence work around the house and barn. Then Cain put them to work repairing the age-damaged wood siding on the porch.

Cain helped less often with the heavy work outside, preferring to stay inside and do the light electrical and plumbing repairs. He made several trips into Bufort to tend to business with the bank, and he visited the man who did his taxes. On two occasions, he traveled to Odessa to take care of paperwork with an attorney there. He made another trip to Houston and reported when he returned that he would not have to go back again, which Dodger interpreted as good news.

Cain's coughing spells occurred more frequently. He appeared older, Dodger thought. But Cain did not slow down. When he returned from his most recent trip to Bufort, he brought paint, drop cloths, rollers, and brushes. They unloaded the supplies, and Cain announced to the boys they were going to paint the house, inside and out.

He handed the boys scrapers and wire brushes for the outside. He began on the inside. "Everything's going to be eggshell white, trimmed in saddle brown," he said.

They finished on a Sunday afternoon. They showered and drove into Bufort, where they stopped for supper at the local café. Cain ordered a T-bone steak and iced tea, and the boys followed suit. He wore his hat low over his eyes and did not remove it while he ate. The boys kept their hats on and ate french fries with their calloused fingers, just as did Cain. When Cain ordered apple pie with vanilla ice cream, both boys grinned and ordered apple pie as well.

When they talked, they talked like three cowboys, comfortable in the understanding one was of no more importance than the other. They laughed when they talked, and the conversation skipped randomly from topic to topic with the good-natured ease of those who have gone beyond the need for formality of any kind.

The waitress stopped at their table to offer more iced tea, and Dodger referred to her by name and asked if the chocolate shakes were any good there; she said they were. He looked at Cain and then at Bobby, who both nodded, and he ordered three shakes and thanked her. She smiled and noted it on the small pad she carried in the pocket of her apron. Bobby watched the entire exchange as though it were a movie and he was in the front row.

Dodger seemed older to Bobby, and he felt older himself. Maybe it was the work, he thought, or maybe it was being treated like a man. Maybe it was Mr. Tarrant; he was not sure.

Yesterday he and Dodger had been kids playing in the dirt with toy trucks. Today they drove a truck and had jobs—it was more like a dream.

Bobby sat with his legs extended beneath the table and his boots crossed. He looked directly at Cain, and Cain looked at him back.

"I been meaning to thank you for everything you done for me and him, Mr. Cain," Bobby said, tipping his head toward Dodger. "I ain't sure you know how much it means to us."

"It's worked out good all the way around, Bobby. By the

way, seems like it would be easier if you just called me Harley, like Dodger does."

"Yessir, Harley. Anyway, thank you."

Cain paused, and then he smiled. "Reckon I should call you B-Bob now?"

They all laughed, and Dodger covered his eyes with his hand as he shook his head. Then he looked through his fingers at Cain, still grinning.

"I'm the only one that calls him that, and he hates it."

Bobby raised a hand and shrugged. "It ain't all that bad. He's been doing it so long, I'm used to it now."

They drove Bobby home. The following morning, before dawn, Cain and the boy decided to take a ride out into the desert. They saddled their horses in the breezeway of the old barn, with its timber construction and the ancient smell of horses, dust, and time about it. Wall pegs held rusty bits and leather harnesses cracked and dried from lack of use and inattention. Old tools and implements the boy did not recognize lay scattered about.

Standing there made the boy feel he was in a world from long ago and, for some reason he could not explain, it felt right to him.

"This might sound strange to you, Harley, but I like the smell of horses and cows. It makes the barn and the corrals feel like they have a use."

"For some of us, standing in an old barn is like watching a fire. You can't explain what it is about it, but you do it anyway because it wouldn't feel right not to," Cain said.

Dodger stood beside his horse and pulled the cinch up tight and then reached under and pulled the back cinch up and buckled it close, but not tight.

"What do you suppose it is about a fire?"

The old cowboy pulled the stirrup leather down from across the saddle and let it drop without hitting the horse.

"I reckon it goes back to a time man first came onto this earth with nothing to wear but the hide of whatever animal he could kill with his hands or a rock. Fire changed everything for them."

"So you think it's bred into us then?"

"I'd say it is."

The boy thought for a moment. "If you think about a newborn calf, it hits the ground, opens its eyes, and then stands up—first thing it does is get up under its momma and looks for a teat, and it ain't ever even seen a cow before."

"That's about the size of it."

They led the horses out of the barn. When they mounted up and rode out, the sky had already begun to gray in the east. Dodger's truck stood next to Cain's, the house shone with new paint, and all the fence wires ran tight and true from post to post.

"See those shiny staples on the posts with old wire restrung on them?" Cain asked.

The boy nodded.

"That's how you tell if your hired help is doing his job. If you ride old fence and don't see them shiners, he's probably crimping the wire somewhere, and that's a shortcut. It weakens the fence. You're just as well to let that man go."

"What if he don't know better?"

"Then you didn't teach him right."

They rode through the cows and headed for the gate at the back of the small pasture that opened out onto the endless desert.

"What do you make of that brockle-faced cow there?" Cain asked.

The boy tilted his head, looked the cow over, and then turned to Cain. "She's bagged up, got an extended vulva, and she's switching her tail—I bet she has a calf at her side when we get back."

Cain smiled. "Think we'll need to pull that calf?"

"No, sir. She's an older cow in with a longhorn bull. She's got a good spread between the hooks and pins. I'd say she won't have no problem."

"What if it's a breach?"

"Then not much of that counts. You thinking we should wait?"

"I think she'll be fine."

They rode for an hour before either spoke again.

"Do you miss your family, Harley?"

Cain took a long drag on the cigarette he held in his teeth and then exhaled the smoke on either side of it as he held the reins in one hand and rested the other on the rump of his horse.

"I miss not having been a father to my son."

"And you never heard from him?"

"Not one time."

"And your wife neither, huh?"

"Her neither."

The boy rode in silence a long time, and then he spoke as though the conversation had never slowed.

"I never missed my momma much until the other day. It made me cry thinking about her. But now, seems like I'm past that and I just feel like there's an empty spot inside me, but it don't hurt."

"Are you glad she's gone?"

"I ain't glad, but I don't believe she's hurting anymore."

"There's a lot to be said for going sometimes."

"You mean dying?"

"Yep . . . you and me both tried it."

"Yeah, we did."

"You know that bullet hole in the ceiling . . . I was going to take that one the night you hit the bridge."

"I knew it wasn't no damn fly, Harley."

Cain smiled.

"You was really going to off yourself that night?" Dodger asked.

"I had it done, 'til you messed it up."

"I knew you tried, but you never told me it was that same night. Would you think about doing it again?"

"Would you?" Cain asked.

The boy shook his head. "No way, Harley."

He looked over at the old cowboy with an expression of grave concern. "So, would you?"

Cain snuffed the cigarette out on the sole of his boot and flicked the butt out into the desert.

"No. No, I wouldn't," he lied.

"Bobby wants to be a boxer," the boy said.

Cain didn't respond.

"He's been beatin' up guys older'n him since fifth grade. He ain't scared of nobody."

Cain shifted his weight in the saddle, coughed and spat, and then looked at the boy, his eyes still watering.

"I talked to Robert on the phone the other day, and he said he thinks Bobby has the makings of a good boxer."

"Boy, that would make his day. Can I tell him that?"

"Sure."

"He hung that punching bag up, and he's out there hittin' it all the time. I gotta admit he's getting pretty good at it."

"He put a good one on you in the truck the other night."

Dodger laughed.

"I know . . . don't tell him, but he hits really hard."

"Does he like to fight?"

"No, sir, he don't like it a bit."

"But he wants to be a boxer?"

"He don't like to fight, but he's real good at it. He said it would be different in a ring with gloves on. That would be his job."

Dodger stretched his back and unbuttoned the top button of his jacket as the sun came up.

"One time on the first day of school, the seniors were making the freshmen walk down the edge of the main hall and punching on them if they stepped on any white tiles. I walked on some white ones and Donnie Lee Horton—he was a senior—he punched me in the side of the head and made me bump into Bobby. Bobby stepped around me, and he hit Donnie Lee so hard it broke his nose and they both got suspended." Dodger made a fist and grinned. "We been best buds ever since."

"Think you could whip him?"

"Donnie Lee, or Bobby?"

"Either one."

"No, not really. Donnie's too big, and Bobby's too tough."

They rode the morning out and rested the horses at an unlikely spot where Cain showed the boy how to find water where none appeared to be by following a trickle to its source at a small spring protected in the rocks. They pulled the bridles and hobbled the horses to graze while they drank of the water. Then they sat in what shade there was, and the boy watched the old man smoke a cigarette and cough into his rag. This time he spat out onto the rocks, and there was blood in the spittle.

"That don't look too good, Harley."

Cain's eyes watered, and he shook his head. He held his hand up in a dismissive manner, caught his breath, and told the boy to catch up the horses. They rode out, the boy following the old man, and the old man following the trail deeper into the desert.

"You reckon we oughta turn back?"

Cain shook his head. "Another half hour."

Thirty minutes later, Cain reined in his horse, stepped down from the saddle, and stood near a survey stake.

"There's several sections of land here, and I own the deed on it," Cain said. "Been piecing it together forever as each parcel came up for sale. It goes from here to the top of that rise and over to about where that tall saguaro stands way off there by itself, and then back over that canyon," Cain said as he waved his hand generally toward the horizon.

"There ain't much on it, Harley. How come you bought it?"

"It ain't much good like it is, but let me show you something."

Cain stepped back up into the saddle, and they rode deeper into the property and into the jaws of a small canyon, rimmed on both sides by a sheer uplift of granite and shale. Just around the turn stood a massive cluster of trees, green and tall, and as out of place in this barren wasteland as the horses they rode.

"Water," Cain said. "There's an aquifer that surfaces right here. They call it the San Jacinto Rift. I had it tested. There's enough water down there to support a city, and to irrigate everything else around here to boot."

"Except there ain't nothin' growing here," the boy said.

"Not yet, but you pump the water to it, and this ground can

grow grass or hay, or crops. It can make this place livable for people who shy away because there's no water the way it is."

"It's a long way back here."

"It is the way we come," Cain said, and then he pointed off to the southeast. "But you go that way a mile and you're back on the highway to Los Caminos. I got the deed to an easement all the way from this property to the highway."

"You thinking about going into farming, Harley?"

"I was thinking about the future. I'm just showing you so you know."

"Why do I need to know?"

Cain stepped down from his horse. Dodger followed suit.

"I won't be here forever, so I been making plans."

Cain stopped to gather his thoughts. The boy waited and jerked his horse's head back when it began to pull away.

"I'm just getting everything set up."

"What do you mean?"

"I got a few bills to settle, then I'm leaving everything else to you, minus what I'm setting aside for Bobby."

The boy's face drained of its color. He shook his head, and his eyes looked wild.

"I don't want to talk about this, Harley. Can we just go?"

"Ain't no need to mention any of this to Bobby just yet—you give me your word on that?"

"Yessir. Let's just leave this alone, please."

CHAPTER THIRTY-SIX

By noon on Saturday, Dodger had packed his tools away for the day, washed his truck, and stepped out of the shower with a towel wrapped around him. He heard Cain in the kitchen.

"Hey, Harley. When did you get home?"

"Just walked in the door."

"All my chores are done, and I changed the leathers on the windmill."

"Don't you wear clothes anymore?"

Dodger laughed. "Guess where I'm going."

"You and Bobby going to Duane's to watch Mickey read dirty magazines?"

"No. Way better than that."

"I don't know what could top that."

"Elena called. She wants to talk. I'm going to Los Caminos to meet her."

Cain hesitated.

"Did she say what she wants to talk about?"

"Said she'd explain when I got there. We're meeting at the Pig Stand."

Cain busied himself about the kitchen as they spoke. Dodger couldn't tell if the old man was distracted or disinterested.

"What are you thinking?"

Cain held the boy in his gaze before he spoke.

"I'm not sure where we stand with the Delgados. Just watch your back."

"You thinking she'd set me up?"

"Do you know she wouldn't?"

Dodger adjusted his towel. "No, I guess I don't."

When Dodger pulled into the Pig Stand, it was early. Three cars full of teenagers sat in the prime parking spaces near the entrance. Elena's wasn't one of them.

Dodger pulled in at the opposite end and waited. He watched the side mirror and turned in his seat every time a car pulled in or out.

A low-slung brown sedan inched out from behind the building, rolling slowly in his direction. His first thought was Umberto Delgado. He bristled and waited.

The car stopped midway across the lot, and two girls jumped out, one with a cowdog on a rope. They giggled and bounced over to the driver's side of Dodger's truck.

He looked at them as they stood at his window.

"Are you Dodger?"

He nodded to the girl with the dog.

"I'm Jordan."

She pointed at the dog.

"His name is Banjo."

The other girl stood back and waved.

"Hi . . . I'm Paige."

The boy gathered himself up.

"Hey. I'm Dodger. I'm from Bufort."

"We know," Jordan said. "Elena said you might be here. She wanted us to tell you she'd be a little late, but to wait for her."

Paige smiled and looked from the truck to Dodger and back to the truck.

"That's a nice truck," she said.

Dodger felt his cheeks heat up.

"Thank you. It's a V-8," he said, stumbling for words.

Jordan raised her finger in mock reprimand. "Don't forget to wait for Elena," she said.

"No, I'll wait as long as it takes. Thanks."

"Okay, bye," both girls said in unison as they walked giggling back to their car.

"See ya, Jordan. See ya, Paige."

Dodger sat and watched the boys and girls laugh and change places in the three cars at the other end of the row. He wondered what it must be like to be so comfortably part of something that it came so natural and easy. Nothing new. On the outside looking in, as usual.

He had turned on the radio and sat back in the seat when the speaker at his window squawked.

"Did you want to order something?"

"Oh, yeah, um . . . could I get a large cherry Coke, please?"

"Will that be all?"

"Yes, ma'am."

Seconds later, a girl on roller skates wheeled up and hooked a tray on his window. She held out her hand.

"Ten cents, please."

He dug in his pocket, pulled out a dime, and handed it to her.

She looked down at the coin in her hand and then back up at him. She did not move. "That's it?"

"Didn't you say ten cents?"

"What about the tip?"

"The tip?"

She cocked her head and shrugged her shoulders. "Well, yeah."

"Sorry."

He dug in his jeans, pulled out a nickel, and laid it next to the dime. He looked up at the carhop and smiled.

"Keep the change."

He nursed the drink for more than thirty minutes before Elena rolled in and parked two spaces down from him. His heart raced.

He looked across at her. She opened her door, stepped out, and walked over to his truck.

She stood at his window, her expression serious, her demeanor difficult for him to read.

"Can we go somewhere and talk?" she asked.

He nodded. When she walked around and stepped up into the cab, she sat close to the door and did not look directly at him. She pointed off in the general direction of the river.

"There's a park down by the river—just go that way."

Dodger waved the carhop over, handed her the tray, and then drove to a point not far from the crossing. He pulled into a secluded clearing nestled in the trees.

"Over there's fine," she said, pointing to a semi-concealed spot scattered with the litter of a favorite teenage hangout.

Dodger pulled in and shut off the engine. He looked about and glanced into the rearview mirror, apprehensive and on guard.

"Are we expecting company?"

She looked at him with surprise and disappointment. "What do you mean?"

"Are your uncles going to come busting out of the brush?"

Elena shook her head. "No, but that's what I want to talk to you about."

Dodger looked at her as she stared down at her cowboy boots with her tight jean bottoms tucked inside. He watched her ponytail bob when her head moved. When her eyes filled with tears, he wanted to hold her, touch her arm, somehow take away some of the pain she felt.

"My father died from infection—not from the gunshot wound. The doctor said the wound would not have been fatal if my father had received medical attention. He said . . ." Her voice dropped off, and she covered her face with her hands and wept.

Dodger reached across and put his hand on her shoulder.

"Elena. I am so sorry. If there was a way for me to undo it, I would."

She nodded, her face still buried in her hands.

"I never meant to hurt anyone."

"I know," she said into her hands. "I have so much pain and so much hate in my heart, I don't know what to do."

"There's no blame in you hating me," he said. "I brought that on myself."

She looked out at him from her open hands.

"Dodger, I am so sorry. I was so wrong for so many things, I can't even explain. I don't hate you. I don't. I just hate all this killing and stealing and lying."

The boy sat back and listened. He patted her shoulder as she talked. Her cathartic outpouring touched him deeply, and he felt his own burdens being lifted as she spoke.

They talked a long time, sharing intimate thoughts and insecurities, the common ground of those who are different. With so much out on the table before them, Dodger grinned.

"Man, I never would have thought you had anything to feel ashamed about. You're so pretty, and so smart. And you have so many friends—I never thought you'd even talk to someone like me."

She smiled, a little self-conscious. "I don't feel sorry for myself. Really. I know I have so much to be thankful for. It's just that it seems like so much at one time."

She caught herself and took a deep breath.

"And I'll never see my father again. You can't imagine how that feels."

Dodger just shook his head.

The afternoon sun traversed the sky and hung above the tree line. They were both exhausted, staring out the window, absorbing all they had shared. Confused about everything.

Finally, Dodger spoke.

"Hey, want to get a pop or something?"

Elena smiled and nodded. She turned to face him, sliding one knee up onto the seat between them as she leaned back against the door and watched him. "That would be wonderful," she said.

When they pulled up onto the pavement, she reached over and snapped the brim of his hat with her finger. "I like your hat."

Dodger glanced over at her and grinned.

"It's one of a kind. My daddy give it to me."

He sat up straight in the seat, hung one arm out the window, and draped his wrist over the steering wheel.

"You want to take the horses out for a ride in the desert sometime?"

"You have horses?"

"Them two of Mr. Cain's. You know about them already."

She nodded, not wanting to revisit any of those memories.

"I love horses," she said.

"Maybe next Saturday when I finish my work?"

"I'll have to check my schedule at the café first but, if I'm off, you got a date."

Dodger's faced flushed red. A *date*? He reached over and turned on the radio.

Jimmie Rodgers came across the airwaves, singing "Oh-Oh, I'm Falling in Love Again." Dodger looked across at Elena and then pulled his hat low over his eyes, fully embarrassed.

Elena saw his reaction and smiled an impish smile.

"Aww, they're playing our song." Then she laughed.

CHAPTER THIRTY-SEVEN

For the next three weekends, Dodger and Elena met in Los Caminos. He was not allowed to visit her house or to call. They took in a movie and then parked at the Pig Stand with the other teenagers, nursing cherry colas—windows down, volume up, all listening to the same radio station while they laughed and talked and the girls flitted from vehicle to vehicle. For Dodger, it was a dream world. Something he had observed all his life from a distance. He'd never expected to be included, and he never assumed that his acceptance into the Los Caminos high school crowd was anything more than their concession to him on behalf of Elena. That was fine with him. He did not feel like an outcast, but he never forgot he was an outsider.

Elena's friends Jordan and Paige flirted and teased and went out of their way to talk to him. It was not lost on the boy that his popularity was either because of Elena or because of the truck, or both. But it was a new experience, and it suited him. Dodger found he fit in easily with the boys—he had a truck. Most of them were not driving yet. It was a macho truck, flatbed and cowboy from bumper-to-bumper. More importantly, it wasn't his *daddy's truck* like some of them drove.

The work at Cain's and his rough childhood gave him a hard edge, and the limp gave him a distinctive trait that made him appear more dangerous than afflicted—a battle scar rather than an impediment. Dodger carried himself with a sense of confidence and a no-nonsense attitude that drew the other boys to him. His hands and knuckles, marked by barbed-wire scars, gave him the appearance of a fighter. The missing tooth only added to his image. For the first time in his life, Dodger felt that circumstances might be working in his favor.

One Saturday night, Dodger and Elena left the movie but did not join their friends at the Pig Stand. Elena sat quietly staring out the window as Dodger pulled into the small parking lot where she had left her car earlier. He backed into the space next to hers, turned off the lights and the engine, and left the radio playing.

He sat back in the seat and rested his arm over the steering wheel. He looked over at her. She reached across and turned the volume down on the radio.

"What's up?"

She shook her head. "Nothing."

"Did you want to go by the Pig Stand?"

"No—I gotta get home pretty soon anyway."

"You still want to take them horses out tomorrow?"

She smiled. "Sure. I told my mother we were going out for a ride. She said it was okay."

Dodger grinned. "What else did she say?"

"She said she's known we've been going out for a long time. She thinks it's not a good idea, though."

"Because of all that's happened?

"No. Because I'm still too young."

"Too young?"

"Too young to start getting serious about a boy."

"Did you tell her we're just friends?"

Elena nodded.

"And what did she say?"

Elena looked down at the floorboard. The light from the

parking lot reflected off her large hoop earrings and her black hair. Dodger watched her and waited.

"She said we're friends now, but eventually we will want more, and that's how young girls end up with babies while they are still in high school."

"Do you think she's right?" Dodger asked.

Elena tipped her head up and down slowly. "I see it all the time. Sophomore and junior girls dropping out of school. Living at home with their parents. Trying to raise a baby. No help from the father. It happens a lot."

"Well, we just won't let it happen to us," Dodger said as he put his hand on her arm, and she covered it with hers and smiled.

"What time are you coming for me in the morning?" she asked.

"Is around eight okay?"

She smiled and flashed her eyes. "Perfect."

She hugged him and reached for the door. "See you in the morning."

As she turned to open the door, Dodger held her arm and looked into her eyes with a deeply serious look she had not seen before.

"That won't be us," he said.

She smiled and thanked him with her eyes and then stuck her head back into the cab and nodded before she closed the door.

"See ya," she said, and the tone of her voice sent the boy's mind soaring.

Dodger grinned. "Later, gator."

Dodger drove by the Pig Stand on his way out of town. He saw several of his friends but did not stop. He settled in for the familiar drive north, preoccupied with the seriousness of his conversation with Elena and the uncertainty about his own feelings, which seemed to him to have no uncertainty at all about them. He had no long-term plans and no thoughts beyond when he would see Elena next. He felt guilty for his desire to push things to the next level with Elena, and he resented Mrs. Delgado's presumption that he would get her pregnant and leave her.

He turned up the radio, stuck his arm out the window, and let his hand ride up and down on the sixty-mile-an-hour wind current as he grinned and thought about tomorrow.

Sunday morning, Dodger stopped by Elena's house. Mrs. Delgado was pleasant but cool toward him. She told him to have Elena back before dark. He promised he would. He resisted the urge to explain himself and his intentions to Mrs. Delgado and, instead, thanked her for giving Elena permission to go with him.

"You were very polite to my mother—thank you."

Elena waited until they were out of sight of her mother's house and then slid over next to him. She looked up at him from beneath the brim of her white hat and smiled.

"Hey, cowboy."

He looked down at her and smiled.

"Hey yourself."

She nodded toward her large straw purse leaning against the door.

"I brought us some lunch."

"Mexican food, I hope."

She shook her head and laughed.

"It's ham and cheese sandwiches, chips, apples, and pop. Does that sound good?"

Dodger pushed his hat back with the tip of his thumb.

"Man, that sounds so good, I could eat it now."

Elena crossed one boot over her knee and hooked her arm in his.

"Sorry, bud, you'll have to wait."

He leaned forward and turned on the radio. They sang along with the country music coming from the speaker and took turns holding the imaginary microphone. The trip seemed to fly by. When they pulled in at Cain's ranch, it seemed that they had just left Los Caminos.

Dodger followed the driveway around and backed up to the trailer parked by the barn. Elena stepped out of the truck and stood by the trailer tongue to guide him in, then she held up her hand for him to stop. She bent down and began cranking the trailer down onto the ball while Dodger brought the horses around. She locked the ball in, hooked up the safety chains, and then walked around to look in on the horses from the side of the trailer.

"Which one's mine?"

Dodger closed the tailgates, latched them, and dropped the pins in.

"The sorrel. I'd ride him, but he ain't broke yet."

"What?"

"I'm kidding, he's a real nice horse. I been everywhere on him. I'm riding the one Harley usually rides—they're both good."

Dodger looked down at her boots.

"Where'd you get them nice spurs?"

Elena looked down and then back up to Dodger.

"From my father, a couple of years ago. They used to belong to my grandfather. He was a *vaquero* in Sinaloa for many years before he came to the US."

"They sure look good on you."

She pulled her hat low over her eyes. Her black hair hung down over her shoulders, blowing up behind her in the breeze as she walked back to the truck. Dodger watched her and gave a wolf whistle. She swung her hips in an exaggerated walk without looking back at him.

They drove three or four miles, and Dodger pulled off the road onto a barren stretch of land and followed the sand into the desert for another three miles before he stopped.

After they unloaded the horses, he divided the food between both sets of saddlebags, handed Elena the bridle for her horse, and slipped his own bridle over the ears of the stocky bay horse Cain normally rode.

He watched Elena slip her foot into the stirrup and lift herself effortlessly into the saddle. She set her heels and looked out at him through her sunglasses. He stepped up and sat in the saddle looking across at her, smiling broadly.

"What?" she asked.

He shook his head.

"No, really. What are you laughing about?" she asked, smiling, with her head cocked waiting for an answer.

Dodger pulled his hat down over his eyes and rode in next to her.

"You really don't have no idea how pretty you are, do you?"

She reached across and pushed him.

"Dodger, Dodger, Dodger." She shook her head and laughed.

They crossed a wide arroyo with a course set for the distant mountains and, when they crossed a dry creek bed, they rode to the south. Dodger found the tracks he and Cain had left on their last visit, windblown and faint but unmistakably theirs. He pulled his horse up in the shade of the willow break where Cain had showed him the water source.

He dismounted, and Elena swung down from her horse.

"We stopping here?"

"Yep. We got water, a little shade, and a little patch of grass for the horses."

Dodger hobbled the horses and hung the bridles from the saddle horns while Elena carried the saddlebags into the thicket.

They talked while they ate and laughed, and Dodger was certain he would awaken at any second to the dark sound of Eugene's obscenities in the kitchen. He hung his hat on a tree, lay back with his head on his saddlebags, laced his fingers behind his head, and closed his eyes. Elena cuddled in next to him with her head on his chest. He draped his arm over her and held her. He spoke without opening his eyes.

"You know, if someone would have told me one day I'd be here with you, like this—there ain't no way I'd of believed them."

"I know. Me too."

They lay there in silence for a long time. For that moment, everything that was wrong in the world righted itself. Every void in their young lives was filled, every wish granted, every dream come true. If life could get any better, neither of them could imagine it. They had no words to explain their feelings and nothing by which to gauge them. They were simply caught in this place at this time, and nothing else mattered.

Dodger felt himself slipping into another dimension, into unfamiliar territory guided by a primitive compass that he gave himself to willingly. He rolled over, supporting himself on one elbow over Elena. She looked up at him, and he pressed his lips to hers. She kissed him and then shook her head.

"No, no, no. Dodger, we can't."

Dodger sat up, leaning on one arm. He looked down at her.

"I'm sorry. I didn't mean to—"

She put her finger to his lips and smiled.

"I didn't mean the kiss. We had to stop there, that's all."

She kissed his fingers, sat up, and took a deep breath. She looked over at him.

"It's not that I don't trust you—I'm just not sure I can trust me."

Dodger laughed. "Well, I trust you, so any time you want to test yourself, you just let me know."

She shook her head. "You're so bad."

They stared deeply into one another's eyes, and she smiled as she shook her head slowly side to side.

Dodger stretched and pointed off to the mountains to the east.

"See that saddle off to the left of the tallest peak?"

"Uh-huh."

"Harley owns from there to across this flat part to the bluffs over there and back to this side of the valley here."

"How much land is that?"

"He told me, but I forgot. It's a lot, though."

"What's he going to do with it?"

"I ain't sure. Build a city maybe."

Elena laughed.

"No, seriously—he's thinking about it."

"I thought you told me he didn't like cities."

"He don't, but he wouldn't have to live in it."

• •

They loaded the saddlebags, unhobbled and bridled the horses, and then stepped up into their saddles.

Dodger sat up straight and looked out into the wastelands before them.

"Want me to show you some things about the desert you might not know?"

Elena smiled. "We have lots of time, and I would really like that. I don't want to ever get off this horse."

They rode at a slow walk for the rest of the day. They talked of the desert and the creatures that lived there—those they could see and those they could not. Dodger told her how the desert was unchanged since before man got there and how it would remain unchanged long after man was gone. He told her how to find water where none appeared to exist. How to eat when there was nothing that appeared edible. But mostly, he told her how the desert and the sun and the moon helped him find a peace he had never imagined existed.

When he told her he was falling in love with her, the words felt right. When she told him how much she wanted to hate him, how much she wanted to hurt him, and how impossible it was for her to deny her feelings for him, he knew nothing to do but to smile and breathe in the soft desert air.

CHAPTER THIRTY-EIGHT

After supper, Cain stood at the sink washing dishes while Dodger dried.

"How'd you and Bobby like to take a ride with me tomorrow morning?"

"Sure. Where to?"

"Fort Stockton. I got to see Robert about a little business and thought you two might like to go along."

"Whoa, buddy. Bobby'd kill me if we didn't take him. Can I call and ask him?"

"Finish that skillet and give him a call. We'll be at his house by eight if that's all right with his folks."

By eight fifteen, they were headed northeast with Dodger in the middle and Bobby sitting with his arm hung out the window. For all to see, they appeared as three seasoned cowboys, hats drawn down, blue long-sleeved snap-pocket work shirts frayed around the collars, each wearing scuffed boots with underslung heels and spur marks.

Cain looked up into the mirror, out across the desert, and then over at the boys.

"Who's ready for some breakfast?"

Dodger raised a finger and smiled. Bobby looked around him and tipped his hat back as his eyes connected with those of the old man.

"I done ate breakfast, Mr. Cain, but thank you."

Cain smiled. "Could you eat another one?"

Bobby grinned. "For real?"

"For real."

"Count me in."

Just outside Alpine, Cain pulled into the gravel parking lot of a small, weathered wood-sided building with LA COCINA DE ROSA painted in red letters on the front. Inside, Cain nodded at two *vaqueros* who touched their hats when he walked in. He picked a table near the window.

"*Buenos dias*," a man said from behind the counter. "Do you need menus?"

Cain turned to the man. "*Buenos dias*. No, I think we know what we want." He looked at the boys for approval, and they both nodded.

A beautiful young girl, maybe eighteen or nineteen, stood smiling as she held her small order pad and waited for them to be seated. She was blond-haired and blue-eyed, a rarity in this part of the country. Dodger looked at her and then nudged Bobby, who stood blocking his way as he stared at her. He jabbed Bobby with his elbow.

"Is it okay if we sit down, B-Bob?"

"Oops. Sorry."

The attractive waitress took Cain's order first. She looked at Bobby. Bobby pushed his hat back with the tip of his finger.

"Same for me," he said, unable to take his eyes off of her.

She looked at Dodger. "And for you, sir?"

Dodger rubbed his chin with his index finger and thumb and looked up at her with a very serious expression.

"Do y'all have scrambled eggs?"

She smiled.

"Of course."

"Okay, Gloria," he waved his index finger to make his point. "I'll have scrambled eggs, bacon, toast, chocolate milk, and . . . umm . . ."

She waited. Cain watched him, and Bobby wanted to hit him. He appeared to be in deep concentration.

"Yes?"

"Gloria," he said in a serious tone. "Do y'all have jelly donuts?"

She shook her head and laughed. "No, I'm sorry. We're all out. We have apple pie, though."

"Hmmm . . . okay then . . . umm . . ."

Bobby backhanded Dodger on the arm. "Will you just order?"

Dodger sat up straight and looked at Bobby with an expression of indignation on his face.

Cain intervened.

"That'll be all for him. Thank you."

Gloria smiled, thanked them, and walked back to the order window.

"Boy, are you guys ever touchy," Dodger said.

Bobby laughed. "We got more to do today than watch you mess with the waitress."

Dodger turned to Cain. "So, what's up in Fort Stockton today, Harley?"

Gloria returned with coffee for Cain and Bobby.

"Well, I got some business with Robert Tarrant—shouldn't take long. I just figured you two would like to ride along."

Bobby nodded. "I sure do want to see that gym again."

"Yeah, me too," Dodger added as he punched Bobby in the shoulder to make his point.

When they arrived at the gym, Robert was sitting in his office with a visitor who appeared to be showing him a collection of spurs and belt buckles spread out across his desk. Tarrant looked up and waved Cain in.

"Harley, come in. I got someone here I'd like you to meet."

Cain went into Tarrant's office while the boys watched two fighters spar in the ring.

"Harland Cain, Kevin Johnson."

"Good to meet you, Kevin."

Johnson extended his hand. "Nice to meet you too, sir."

"Kevin's a bit and spur maker from Clarendon. He's also a pretty damn good silversmith," Tarrant added.

Cain looked down at the spurs and buckles and back at Kevin. "Clarendon's up there in the panhandle, ain't it?"

Kevin nodded. "Yessir. East of Amarillo some."

Cain whistled. "Those are some nice buckles. You make them spurs too?"

Kevin had a quiet but confident cowboy air about him, and Cain liked his straightforward way of talking.

"Yessir. Spurs, belt buckles, pistol grips, handcuffs, bits—you name it."

"Handcuffs?"

"Some of the Texas Rangers have me do up their gear for them. I've engraved a bunch of handcuffs and .45s for 'em."

Cain turned a buckle over in his hand.

"I had me a nice bareback buckle once. Won it in Fort Worth and lost it out in the desert somewhere—ain't had another good one since.

"Give me the word and I'll make you up one."

Cain shook his head. "I expect I'm too far past the age I need a good one now."

He looked down again at the buckle he held and then back up at Kevin.

"How much you reckon two buckles with names on them would cost me?"

Kevin smiled. "I ain't in this to get rich. Let me know what you want, and I'll make 'em up for you priced right."

"I need one with DODGER on it and the other with BOBBY."

Kevin smiled. "Is that them two boys there?" He nodded toward the ring.

Cain nodded without turning. "That's them."

He handed Cain a slip of paper and a pencil.

"Ya just write your name and address down, and I'll send you a drawing before I make them."

"How much do I owe you?"

"Nothing. I'll let you know the cost when I give you the drawing. If you like it, you pay me after you get the buckles."

"That's pretty trusting."

"A handshake tells me a lot about a man. I ain't worried about yours at all."

Tarrant and Kevin finished their business. Kevin shook hands with Cain before he left. Tarrant walked him to the door, and when he returned to the office he sat back in his chair and looked across at Cain.

"I know you ain't here to look at buckles, Harley. What's on your mind?"

Cain looked up from under the brim of his hat, his eyes fixed on those of Tarrant, and his jaw set. He took a deep breath and let it out slowly.

"I need a favor, Robert."

Tarrant nodded. "You name it, you got it."

"I need you to be the executor for my will."

"I ain't sure I know what that means, pardner, but I'll do whatever you want."

"It just means you will be the one who oversees making sure the things in my will go to the right people."

Tarrant did not smile. "How do you know I won't just pack up all the money and light out for Mexico?"

"I've known you too long to worry about that. This is something only a friend would do right, and that's why I picked you."

Tarrant smiled this time. "Judging by your orneriness, it ain't likely we need to worry about all this for a long while yet."

Cain sat back in the chair and crossed a boot over his knee. "I've been going to a doctor in Houston—it might be sooner than we think."

"What do you mean?"

"I got cancer, Robert. They done about all they can for me. We're just waiting now to see how fast things go to hell."

"Is there any chance of recovery?"

Cain shook his head. "The doctor said it's out of our hands now. We just have to wait and see how it goes."

Tarrant looked down at the desk and avoided eye contact with Cain.

"How about pills or radiation?"

"It ain't worth it. Whatever time I got, I won't be spending it trading good days for bad."

"They give you any idea how long?"

Cain looked across the desk, and there was an expression of some relief in his eyes.

"A week, a month, six months . . . they don't know."

Cain cut through the awkward silence that followed. "So, you'll do it?"

Tarrant nodded.

"Of course I'll do it. Get me what paperwork I need and help me understand what it is you want, and consider it done."

"I pretty much just want to take care of them two boys, but there's more there than either of them can handle at this young age. You'll see it all in the will. The house, the land, the property outside Los Caminos, an old truck, and half a century of junk I been collecting."

Tarrant smiled. "I hear ya."

CHAPTER THIRTY-NINE

Tarrant joined the boys ringside while Cain made a few telephone calls from Tarrant's office. He stood and watched the two fighters in the ring until one of the trainers struck the bell with a ball-peen hammer. He looked down at Bobby.

"You been practicing some?"

Bobby nodded and looked up at Tarrant.

"Yessir. I hit that bag almost ever' day."

"Want to show me what you got?"

Bobby's eyes widened, and he tipped his head toward the ring. "You mean in there?"

Tarrant laughed. "No, maybe later. I meant on the speed bag."

Bobby stood and walked toward the bag hanging in the corner. Tarrant and Dodger followed. Bobby looked up at the bag.

"It's kinda high for me."

"We can fix that," Tarrant said as he lowered the frame on the bag and then looked over at Bobby.

"Sit down over there and let me tape your hands."

"Really?"

"Yes, really. Sit down." He looked over at Dodger. "You too."

He wrapped the boys' hands. Then he had them take off their shirts and hats and step up to the bag. Bobby started slow but his rhythm was smooth and the bag bounced against his fists and the top board with a steady staccato thumping that sounded like a marching drum beat. Tarrant watched as the boy increased his speed, rolling the bag off his knuckles as he alternated left, right, left, and then ended the run with a right and a hard left before he stepped back.

"You got a natural talent, Bobby. You need work, but everything is there," Tarrant said.

Bobby grinned. Tarrant waved Dodger up to the bag.

"You're up, cowboy."

Dodger stood. He limped up to the bag and steadied it with both hands. He released the bag, assumed a fighter's stance, and unleashed a blistering right cross that slammed the bag in an explosive drive against the board. The sound reverberated throughout the gym. Dodger stepped back.

Tarrant laughed, and Cain looked up from the desk.

"Is that it?"

Dodger picked up his hat, slipped it on his head, and smiled.

"That's it. My daddy told me if I ever get in a fight there better only be two hits: I hit him and he hits the ground."

"What if you hit him and he doesn't hit the ground?" Bobby asked.

Dodger pulled his hat down low. "Then I just call you."

Tarrant shook his head, and his expression took on a serious edge when he sat on the bench next to Bobby.

"You got a gift there, Bobby. You ever think about doing a little serious training?"

"Yessir, I think about it all the time. But we ain't got a gym in Bufort, and I got no money to pay for it anyway."

"Well, I might have an idea for you. How about we get you set up with a good speed bag and a heavy bag at home? I've got some extra weights laying around here we could throw in. You come up here once a month or so, and I'll give you a training program for the next month. You work on it and I'll help you when you're here at the gym. It won't cost you anything."

Bobby shook his head.

"I can't ask you to do that, Mr. Tarrant."

"I'm offering it to you because you have talent, Bobby—it doesn't come around often. When it does, it deserves to be developed. When you get ready, we'll have you sparring with some of the boys here. We're running out of people to beat up anyway. It'd do us all some good."

Bobby looked at Dodger, and Dodger nodded. "I can give you a ride up here anytime," he said. "That way you'd be no trouble to your daddy."

Bobby grinned and stuck his hand out to Tarrant.

"Thank you, sir. I'll work hard at it—I promise."

Tarrant turned toward Dodger.

"Dodger, that includes you too, if you're interested."

Dodger shook his head. "Thanks, Mr. Tarrant. I believe I'll stick to cowboyin'."

Cain hung up the telephone, made a few notes on the back of an envelope, and then folded the envelope and stuck it in his shirt pocket. He stood at the desk a few moments before he exited the office and joined Tarrant and the boys.

"Which one of you two hooligans made all that racket out here?"

"It was him," Bobby said, pointing his thumb at Dodger. "He tried to kill the bag."

Tarrant addressed Cain directly. "How'd it go?"

"It's all set. I'll have papers for you to sign in about a week. Me and the boys will make a trip back up this way to get that all taken care of with you."

"Good. I'll have a few things for you to haul back with you then."

Cain looked over at Bobby, and Bobby spoke without waiting for Tarrant to fill in the details.

"I'm gonna be training with Mr. Tarrant. We're setting up a little gym at my place."

Dodger interrupted. "And I'm going to drive Bobby up once a month for Mr. Tarrant to straighten out everything he's doing wrong."

Bobby moved closer to Dodger and whispered loud enough for Tarrant and Cain to hear. "Don't make me hurt you—my hands are legal weapons now."

Tarrant shook his head. "I think you mean *lethal*."

Bobby looked at Tarrant and back to Dodger. "Exacto."

They each shook hands with Tarrant. When they got to the pickup, Bobby sat in the middle and stared out the windshield until they were several miles down the road. He nudged Dodger.

"I'm gonna be training to be a fighter," he said.

Dodger's look was serious, and his tone had no-nonsense about it.

"You're gonna be a good one, B-Bob."

Cain held a cigarette in one hand and draped the other over the top of the steering wheel.

"Mr. Tarrant says you got something special, Bobby. He's only seen it in a few other fighters—says it's a God-given gift, what you got."

Dodger looked over at Bobby.

"Geez, B-Bob, if you don't quit grinning like that, they're gonna have to stop-drill your face just to keep it from cracking."

Bobby leaned forward and looked at Cain. "I got lots to think about right now," Bobby said. "The job with you, helping my folks out, school—and now training. I ain't even sure where I can put the bags and weights. We're kinda short on room."

"You'll come up with something," Dodger said.

"I know, but I gotta think about it."

Cain listened as the boys talked and speculated on the future. He felt their excitement. He reveled in their dreams, and he felt a cold emptiness inside knowing he would not be there to see any of them materialize.

They have an eternity ahead of them, he thought. He watched the highway roll by, and he looked out upon the familiar harshness of the desert. It was the everyday things he would miss. The smell of the landscape, the heat, the pickups lined up outside the café, a cigarette in the morning, the relief of sitting down at the end of a long day—so many small things.

Now he had people who needed him—two boys whose lives he could change. The thought of not being there for them weighed heavily on him, and he cursed the inequities of life.

When they saw the city signs at the edge of Alpine, both boys sat up straight, but neither spoke.

"I'm not all that hungry. You boys don't mind if we just skip supper, do you?"

Dodger and Bobby looked at each other, and Dodger answered first.

"I'm fine if you are, Harley."

Bobby nodded. "Me too."

When they approached La Cocina, Cain pulled into the parking lot and slid to a stop near the door. Dodger laughed.

"I knew you were kidding us, Harley."

They entered, sat at the same table, and waited. The same voice echoed out from the kitchen.

"*Buenos tardes*."

They all said *buenos tardes* back, and Dodger grinned when Gloria stepped out from behind the counter.

She got to the table, stood over them, and recognized Dodger.

"Oh, no," she said with a good-natured smile as she shook her head.

She took their orders and brought them their food. After they'd finished eating, Gloria returned with a jelly donut on a saucer with a candle in it and presented it to Dodger.

"I knew I hadn't seen the last of you three," she said.

CHAPTER FORTY

Dodger and Bobby spent the next few days stringing new wire and hauling the old wire and broken posts to the dump. Bobby drove Cain's pickup, and Dodger sat on the passenger side fidgeting with the torn-out fingers on his gloves.

"What'd your daddy say about the gym stuff?" he asked without looking up from the gloves.

Bobby shifted into third gear and settled in for the drive. He glanced up into the rearview mirror and then set his gaze upon the road.

"He said we could set it up in the garage where we sleep. There's room under my bed for the weights, and the bags will hang at the end of the room by the door. We'll just have to walk around them is all."

"Him and your momma okay with you being a fighter?"

"I reckon. I ain't sure my momma knows what to make of it. My daddy told me it's something I need to get on with while I'm young—I guess that means he's okay with it."

"I don't suppose he'd be helping you get a gym set up if he wasn't."

Bobby nodded in agreement, and Dodger looked over at him with a thoughtful expression in his eyes.

"I believe he just wants to do right by all you kids. You're pretty lucky, B-Bob."

"I know."

Dodger leaned back again, propped a boot up on the dash, and continued picking at the fingers of his gloves.

"What're you thinking about doin' after high school?" Dodger asked.

Bobby gnawed at the inside of his cheek.

"Get a job, I guess. I don't know."

Dodger took off his hat, hung it on his boot, and scratched his head.

"I been talking to Harley about vet school," he said, even though Bobby hadn't asked.

"Don't you have to be pretty smart to go to vet school?"

"Well, it's college, so I reckon you do."

"You think you're smart enough?"

"I know some about horses, and Harley's teaching me about cows. That should count for something."

"What about the money? College ain't free."

"That part does bother me some. Harley said he'd set up a fund for me, but I don't feel right about that. He said I could work it off, so that might be a option."

Bobby's voice became soft and thoughtful. "What if something happens to Mr. Cain?"

"Then I reckon I'm back where I started."

"Maybe you and me should start talking to Duane, just in case."

"You mean working at the Conoco?"

"It's something to do—ain't like we got a lot of choices in Bufort."

"Man, B-Bob, if we end up at Duane's, someone needs to take us out and shoot us. Besides, I already asked Duane, and he don't need no help."

Bobby laughed. "I know. We'd probably eat up all the hotdogs and drink up all the RCs the first night."

"You ever think about asking Mr. Tarrant for a job after we finish school?"

"I been thinking about that—I just don't know what he needs done around there. That, and I don't have a way to get there and back every day."

Dodger took a deep breath and resigned himself to looking out the window.

"Well, we got time. Harley'll probably kill us building fences anyway."

They both laughed, but the uncertainty burned long after the discussion ended. They rode the rest of the way to the dump in silence.

On the way back through Bufort, Bobby stayed behind at his place. Dodger drove the rest of the way to Cain's alone. When he pulled into the barn, he saw Cain with the welder working on the squeeze chute. He parked the truck and stood by waiting for Cain to finish the last bead.

Cain turned off the welder and looked up.

"Get it all done?"

"Yessir—a couple more loads and we'll be the dump's best customers."

He watched Cain pick up the cables and helped him roll the welder back into the tool shed.

That night after supper, Cain sat back and lit a cigarette while Dodger cleared the table. He refilled Cain's coffee cup and poured one for himself. He leaned forward with his elbows on the table and sipped his coffee.

"Bobby said you have to be smart to be a vet," he said.

Cain nodded. "I reckon you do."

"I'm not that good at school."

"How do you know? Have you ever tried?"

"Yeah, I tried."

"Well, showing up's one thing. Trying is another."

"What do you mean?"

"Seems to me like you meant well, you just didn't have the kind of a life that actually let you try."

"Gettin' by was about all I could manage, I guess."

"That's what I mean. If you had time to study and a reason to do it, things would be a whole lot different."

"But that doesn't have anything to do with being smart."

"Well, yes and no. You can figure things out. You can fix a motor, work on fences, handle your money. You ain't dumb."

Dodger stared at him.

"You just need a chance and a little practice at studying is all."

"You really think I could be a vet, Harley?"

"There ain't no doubt in my mind. You got a feel for animals, and you got good common sense. All you need is a little education and you could be in there with the best of them."

Dodger grinned.

"When I'm a vet, Harley, I'll get you all vaccinated up so's you never get wormy or catch hoof-and-mouth."

"While you're at it, I'll expect you to do something about this bad knee too."

"I don't know if I'm gonna be working on no knees."

On Friday evening, Dodger and Elena sat on the front porch of the Delgado house. Mrs. Delgado let the screen door close behind her as she came out and set a tray of sugar cookies and lemonade on the flattop steamer trunk they used as a coffee table. Dodger stood until she took her seat in the rocking chair across from the wicker couch. She gestured toward the tray.

"Thank you, ma'am," he said.

She smiled and nodded, and Elena poured them each a glass of lemonade and offered the boy a cookie—a *polvorón,* she called it.

Elena sat down and held the glass on the leg of her jeans as she spoke.

"Dodger's going to be a vet someday, Momma."

"That's nice." She looked at the boy. "Will you stay in Bufort?"

"Yes, ma'am, I intend to."

"Where will you go to school?"

Dodger began to get uncomfortable.

"I ain't sure, ma'am. There ain't no vet schools in Bufort, so I'll have to go where there is one, I reckon."

"Then you plan to return to Bufort?"

"Yes, ma'am, I do."

She nodded her head in a way that suggested she was suspicious of his answers or his intentions, or both. Dodger shifted in his seat.

"Is your family from Bufort?" she asked.

"No, ma'am. I got no family there." He smiled at Elena. "But I do have some good friends here."

He looked back at Mrs. Delgado. "And I got a job."

"Working for Mr. Cain?"

Dodger nodded. Mrs. Delgado turned her head toward Elena and, for the first time, a small smile lit up her eyes.

"Elena is the first in our family who will finish high school."

She looked back at the boy.

"It's good to have plans and to think of the future."

"It's all pretty new to me, ma'am, but I'm working on it."

The talk ran thin, and Mrs. Delgado seemed content to sit and rock with no conversation at all. Dodger and Elena waited a respectable amount of time, and then Elena stood and gathered up the glasses.

"Want to take a little walk?"

Dodger reached for his hat. "Sure."

Elena took the tray and the glasses into the kitchen. When she returned, she stood near her mother and placed her hand on her mother's shoulder.

"We'll be back in a little while," she said, and she patted her mother on the shoulder.

"Don't be too late. Nice talking with you, Dodger."

"You too, ma'am. We won't be long."

At the edge of town, the sidewalk ended. They continued walking into the desert where the land stretched out to the west and the evening sun hung low in the cloudless sky, setting the world before them on fire with blazing shades of crimson, gold, and turquoise. They held hands and walked, comfortable in the silence that surrounded them.

They sat on boulders among the cactus and desert flowers that thrived in that desiccated earth where nothing else grew.

Dodger pointed to the thin purple flowers scattered about in small clumps, balanced on stems so thin they could barely hold the weight of the blooms.

"See them flowers?"

"Uh-huh . . . they're pretty. Are you going to pick one for me?" Elena asked as she fluttered her eyelids and her dark eyes bore into him.

"Mr. Cain told me we should never bother anything that grows out here, 'cause it had such a hard time getting here in the first place."

She feigned disappointment. "Aww."

"No, seriously. He said these plants grow with no water, and they make it in the heat and the dry soil that nothing else can live in. It ain't up to us to take that away."

She took his hand. "I know. I was only kidding. I love the desert and everything about it. It's like some people—beautiful in their own way."

Dodger leaned back against the rocks upon which they sat. He played with her fingers laid flat against the leg of his jeans, gently folding her index finger under, then her ring finger, and finally her pinky finger. He looked over at her and grinned.

"What?"

He laughed.

"What's so funny?"

He looked down at her hand, and her eyes followed his to the obscene gesture posed with her fingers. She withdrew her hand and slugged him on the arm.

"You are so romantic," she teased.

They settled back in, reclining against the rocks, her head on his shoulder and his arm around her.

"What do you reckon you'll do after high school?"

She hesitated and stared off into the sunlit sky, now ablaze with deep blues and golden rays on fire with a crimson glow more vivid than any painting.

"I don't really know. It's not like I have a lot of choices. No college for sure."

"Why not?"

Her expression was one of mild frustration as she became less and less comfortable with the conversation.

"Well, the money for starters. And what's a Mexican girl from a West Texas border town no one ever heard of going to do with a college education, anyway—be the lead waitress at the El Agave?"

Dodger understood exactly what she meant. He knew not to press the issue.

"There's sure a lot more to life than going to college," he said.

She squeezed his hand and kissed the back of it—surrender accepted. She turned her head up to him and pulled his down to her. When their lips met, he knew this moment would remain with him for the rest of his life. He wished it would last forever.

CHAPTER FORTY-ONE

Cain and the boy drove to Bufort and pulled into a run-down truck stop for breakfast while they waited for the Bufort Feed and Seed to open. Cain bought a newspaper from the honor rack near the door as they entered the restaurant.

The high-mileage blond waitress who took their order nodded toward the folded newspaper lying beneath Cain's arm.

"They got their hands full with that one, don't they?" she said through an inappropriately timed smile.

"Ma'am?"

"The police department."

Cain furrowed his brow. She nodded again toward the newspaper.

"They arrested a man for that killing at the Sundowner. It's on the front page. It says they have a witness, but he was drunk, and they might throw his testimony out."

The waitress shrugged her shoulders and then turned and left.

Dodger's eyes widened and his face drained of color as Cain picked up the newspaper and laid it out flat.

ARREST MADE IN SUNDOWNER MURDER

The boy waited while Cain followed his finger along the line of the copy text and read under his breath. He stopped and looked up at the boy.

"It says an intoxicated patron of the Sundowner Lounge stopped to relieve himself outside near the back door when he saw two men leaving the parking lot in a car identified as belonging to Bufort resident Rolando Barone."

"Did they get Eugene?"

"It doesn't say. They questioned Barone and released him. He claims someone stole his car that night. He didn't report it, since a friend spotted it near the highway early the next morning."

"Oh, man, Harley. I'm so dead."

Cain continued reading. When he finished, he stared at the newspaper and then looked at the boy, who sat ashen-faced and nervous.

"It says they are looking for anyone who may have seen Barone's car that night or who might have any information concerning the identities of the two men allegedly in the car."

"I'm the only one who saw it all, Harley."

"Did you see the drunk they're talking about?"

"No, I never seen him, but the back door where he was is on the other side of the parking lot, so I don't know how much he seen neither."

"It says here he saw the car leaving just before the body was discovered by other patrons leaving the establishment at the same time. He admits he did not see the crime in progress or the victim. Somehow he managed to remember the license plate number and the make and model of the car."

Cain leaned back in his chair and shook his head when the waitress lifted the coffee pot from behind the counter and held it up as an offering.

"I been thinking about this one ever since you told me about it," Cain said.

"What are you thinking?"

"It ain't right to let those two get away with murder."

"I know, but if I say anything and it don't go exactly right—Eugene will kill me."

"Well, let's see how this all goes, and we'll talk about it again."

Dodger set his jaw, and there was no give in his eyes.

"I done thought about it, Harley."

"And?"

"I don't need Eugene to have a reason to come looking for me."

"I understand. We'll see how it plays out. You and me been doing the Texas two-step with the law. We don't want to spread our luck too thin, know what I mean?"

Dodger shook his head.

"No, I don't know what you mean."

"That whole thing in Los Caminos, and now this. We don't want to get caught holding more cards than we can handle."

"That don't make no sense, Harley. All's I know is only three of us know about Eugene and Rolando. That's probably two too many as it is."

They dismissed the subject and then drove to the ranch-supply store in silence. After they loaded the pickup with wire, staples, clips, and T-posts, they stopped by and picked Bobby up on the way out of town.

Bobby sat nearest the window, with his arm hanging outside in the hot desert air. He spoke over his shoulder to Cain and Dodger.

"I'm ready for some serious fence work today."

Dodger stuck his chin out. "Kinda hot, don't you think?"

Bobby was on a roll. "When it's too hot for the rest a' y'all, it's just right for me."

Dodger laughed and Cain smiled.

"We'll see who's first to go lookin' for shade after we get about fifty of these T-posts in the ground."

Bobby changed the direction of the conversation without missing a beat. "Did you get a chance to read the paper this morning?"

Dodger stiffened, and Cain looked down at the folded paper tucked in between himself and the boy.

"Why?"

"I was wondering who won the fight last night."

Cain and the boy relaxed some.

"Who was fighting?"

Bobby turned toward Dodger.

"You kidding me?"

"No, I'm serious as a sharp stick in the eye."

"Roy Harris fought Floyd Patterson for the World Championship."

"Who did you want to win?"

"Floyd's the champion, so I'd like to see him not lose. But then, Harris is a Texan, so I kinda hate to see him lose too."

Dodger nudged Bobby with his elbow. "So if you had it your way, they'd both win."

"No, I'm not saying that. I never like to see the champ lose, so I'm hoping Patterson wins."

Bobby leaned forward and noticed the newspaper next to Dodger.

"Is that today's paper?"

"Uh-huh."

"Let me look at it."

Dodger handed the folded paper to Bobby but drew no attention to the front-page story. Bobby shuffled quickly through the pages until he found the sports section, and then he folded the pages back and found the boxing scores. His face brightened and he read aloud.

"Roy Harris dropped the champion to the canvas in round 6, but he found himself the victim of Patterson's blistering right that put Harris on the canvas in round 7 and twice in round 8. Harris went down again in round 11 and was put down to one knee in the 12th, after which his corner stopped the fight. Floyd Patterson retains his crown as World Champion by defeating Harris, the seemingly unstoppable challenger from Cut and Shoot, Texas."

Bobby pushed his hat back and tossed the paper up on the dash.

"Man, that must have been some fight."

Dodger leaned forward and retrieved the newspaper. He shook it out and turned back to the front page. He handed the paper to Bobby and tapped the lead story with the tip of his index finger. Cain watched the exchange between the boys, but did not comment.

"Here's another one for you, B-Bob."

Bobby read the story, and then he reread it. "Holy shit, Dodge."

"I know."

"So what are you gonna do?"

"Nothing. I'm staying out of it."

"They're gonna get away with it, you know," Bobby said.

"I reckon they will. The only thing I can say for them is that I don't believe they set out to kill no one. Not that they wouldn't—I just don't think that was on their mind."

"That don't make it right."

"No, it don't. I know that."

Bobby leaned forward.

"What do you think, Mr. Cain?"

"I think we sit on it for now. There's nothing to be gained by any of us saying anything outside the three of us."

"Okay," Bobby said.

Dodger made a zipper motion across his lips. Bobby punched him.

"What the heck was that?" Bobby asked.

"It means my lips are sealed."

"I never heard that before—I don't believe it means squat."

"It does too. It's a zipper, you knothead."

Bobby turned and leaned his head on the heel of his hand as he gazed out into the windblown landscape that stretched out in all directions until it dropped off the end of that flat plane somewhere beyond the horizon.

"A zipper," he muttered.

A week later, Cain returned from a trip to Bufort. He parked his pickup in the driveway, honked for the boys, and waved them in from the side of the barn where they were cutting and nailing replacement two-by-eights on the loading chute. Bobby turned off the circular saw, and Dodger slipped his heavy framing hammer into the ring on his tool belt. They laid down their tools, picked up their shirts, and walked over to a water trough. Dodger set his hat aside and submerged his head shoulder-deep into the cool water. Bobby did likewise. They shook their heads and carried their hats and shirts as they walked to the house.

Cain was sitting at the old wooden table on the porch when the boys approached the house.

"What's up, Harley?"

Cain pushed the newspaper across the table, and the boys each took a seat. Dodger opened the paper up to the first page and the glaring headline:

WITNESS KILLED

Dodger and Bobby saw it at the same time, and their expressions ran cold as they crowded together to read the story.

"Did you read this?" Dodger asked.

Cain nodded.

"It says he was shot and they don't know who did it," Dodger said.

Cain's eyes were filled with concern, but he did not respond.

Dodger pushed his chair back from the table. Cain and Bobby waited while the boy wrestled with his thoughts. His cheeks flushed red, and he drummed his fingers on the table, nervous, undecided.

"It's back on me," he said.

"It was Eugene or Rolando—I'd bet anything on it."

There was a long silence before Cain offered up the rest of the story.

"You saw where it said he lived alone outside of town. No close neighbors. Of course, no witnesses either. A single shot to the head. Probably someone waiting for him outside in the brush."

"What now?" Bobby asked.

"I don't know much about the law and even less about lawyers, but my guess is the defense attorney would try to discredit Dodger's testimony based on his bad relationship with Eugene. If they can make the jury think there's a personal grudge here, Dodger's testimony might not count for much. My concern is that if they can't find something to tie Eugene and Rolando to either of the crimes, those boys are probably going to get off anyway."

"So you're thinking I should keep quiet about it?"

Cain leaned forward. He lit a cigarette and took a long drag on it before he answered.

"I'm thinking we just hold our cards close to the vest for now."

Dodger nodded, his head bobbing in nervous agreement to the words he wanted to hear.

"Fine by me," he said.

Cain studied the cigarette and then tapped the ash over the rail. His eyes appeared concerned as he looked directly at Dodger.

"Have you said anything about any of this to Elena?"

"No, sir. Not a word."

He questioned Bobby with the same look.

"No sir, Mr. Cain. I haven't said anything to anyone about it, period. Not even my parents."

Cain took another long drag from the cigarette and flicked the still-burning butt off onto the gravel driveway.

CHAPTER FORTY-TWO

Rolando and Eugene laughed and passed a joint back and forth. A six-pack of longnecks sat on the sedan's front seat between them. Rolando was driving. A great moon shone over the sparse Texas landscape and reflected off the glass of the rear window as they made their way through the night along the two-lane stretch of blacktop back to Bufort from Odessa.

Rolando, full of bravado and reeking of arrogance, spoke through the smoke he held in his lungs as he gestured with his free hand.

"That's it, man. No more cops."

He passed the joint to Eugene, and Eugene sucked in a mouthful of smoke, held it, and then let it drift up from his lips as he re-inhaled through his nostrils. He held his breath and then blew the smoke out into a gray cloud that circled above them before it drafted out through the partially open window. He followed the hit with a beer chaser and looked out at the darkness with eyes narrowed and empty.

"*Claro*. No witness, no case, huh?"

He rolled the window down and held the empty beer bottle outside. He threw the bottle high into the air and waited for the sound of bursting glass on the highway behind them. He turned toward Rolando.

"What about the .30-30?"

Rolando furrowed his brow and gave Eugene a condescending look that irritated Eugene.

"Nothing about it, man. We can't sell it and we can't dump it—we keep it."

Eugene's voice showed his impatience with Rolando.

"I need the money."

Rolando smiled.

"We can sell those two Holley four-barrels. They're brand new. We can get good money for those."

Eugene held the last of the joint between the tip of his finger and his thumb. He sucked in the smoke until the ash glowed. Rolando watched him.

"Save the roach," Rolando said.

Eugene snuffed out the tiny butt and dropped it in the ashtray with the others. He held his breath a long time before he exhaled and, as he did so, reached for two beers. He popped the caps and let them fall to the floorboard and then thrust one of the bottles through the darkness to Rolando.

By midnight they'd sold the carburetors. At closing time, they staggered out of an adobe roadside cantina with two middle-aged women reeking of cheap perfume, their peroxide-blond hair back-combed and held up with plastic barrettes, red lipstick running into the creases around their mouths.

They awoke to the glaring sun burning through the side windows and the gagging smell of old perfume and alcohol that hung over the wretched females slumped in the seats beside them, their tight skirts pulled up over their fleshy hips and their lipstick smeared. Rolando pushed the woman who sat next to him away and then reached over the back of the front seat and shook Eugene.

"Come on, man. We gotta go."

He turned toward the groggy-eyed woman beside him.

"Get out."

He reached across, opened the passenger-side door, and pushed her out with his foot.

The floozy in the back seat cursed them both in Spanish as she slid toward the door and fumbled with the handle. She stood outside the car, pulling her skirt down and swinging her purse over her shoulder. She stuck her middle finger into the air at the car as the two men pulled out onto the highway.

That evening in Bufort, Bobby sat at the kitchen table with his family as they finished supper. Mr. Washington took a cup of coffee with him and moved to the large easy chair in the small living room to read yesterday's newspaper.

"Says here the man they found dead the other day was shot with a .30-30, and they're not ruling out the possibility that the killing at the Sundowner and this one could be related." He shook his head. "What is this world coming to?"

Bobby stopped as he cleared the dishes from the table.

"You mean the man that was the witness to the other murder?"

Mr. Washington nodded. "It says they don't have no physical evidence to either murder, but the cases are both under investigation."

"That's it?" Bobby asked.

"That's all it says here."

While Bobby contemplated the complexities of a double homicide, two police patrols had been dispatched to the outskirts of Bufort to pick up Rolando Barone for further questioning. When they arrived at the trailer park, Rolando's sedan was parked near the decaying wooden steps of a single-wide with rusted siding and peeling paint.

A light shone inside. Rolando and Eugene sat at the small table and did not see the patrol cars pull up. Four uniformed officers gathered on the wooden porch of the trailer.

Eugene answered the door. Two officers pushed their way in and had both men in handcuffs before they could protest or demand their rights.

"Who lives here?" the heavyset officer asked.

Rolando shrugged and adjusted his hands against the pressure of the handcuffs.

"I do."

The officer turned toward Eugene and then examined the two men's driver's licenses he held in his hand.

"What about you, Cazares?"

"I'm in between places right now."

"Where are you staying?"

"Here, until I find a place."

He put the licenses in his shirt pocket and addressed Rolando. "Mind if we look around?"

Rolando shook his head in a noncommittal way. "Go ahead."

The heavyset officer stayed with the two men while his partner conducted a cursory search of the disheveled trailer. He returned with a plastic ashtray and set it on the counter in the kitchen area.

"Find anything?"

"Just this—a few smoked-down marijuana butts. Nothing else."

Outside, they placed the two suspects in separate patrol cars. The heavyset officer leaned across the back door and dangled the keys he'd removed earlier from Rolando's pocket.

"These the keys to your car?"

Rolando tipped his head toward the trailer. "For the car and the trailer."

The officer closed the door and motioned to his partner.

"Let's search the car."

They went through the inside, found two sets of Dodge

Lancer spinner hubcaps in the back seat and marijuana butts in the ashtray. The heavyset officer stepped around to the trunk, opened the lid, and whistled.

"Looky here, Roy."

Roy stepped to the back of the car. He grinned.

"A .30-30. What do you want to bet it matches the bullet they took out of the dead guy?"

He reached for the gun.

"Don't touch it. That's evidence. They'll want to dust it and run it through ballistics."

Three days later, Dodger drove into Bufort as the sun began its gray ascent over the eastern horizon. He picked Bobby up, and they stopped at the Conoco to get a newspaper for Cain. They said good morning to Leland and picked up two Slim Jims and an RC Cola each.

Dodger tossed the paper on the seat without looking at it. Bobby opened the colas, handed one to Dodger, and then picked up the paper and set the cola between his legs. He turned immediately to the sports section and began reading in the dim light of the pickup cab.

"Nothing good," he said as he returned the paper to its original order and folded it in half. As he laid it on the dash, Dodger caught the word suspect in the bold headline. He nodded toward the newspaper.

"What does that say?"

Bobby reached for the paper, opened it up, and began reading to himself. Dodger repeated his question, only this time his voice had an unsteady edge to it.

"What's it say?"

"Oh, man."

"What?"

"They arrested Rolando and Eugene. They got the .30-30, and it matches the bullet that killed the witness guy."

Bobby looked slowly up from the paper and over at Dodger.

"The rifle has Rolando's prints on it."

"What about Eugene?"

Bobby continued reading, paraphrasing as he followed his finger down the page.

"It says here the public defender filed for his release . . . then it goes on and says . . . unless new evidence is found to allow the district attorney to file charges, he'll be released tomorrow."

"There ain't no new evidence," Dodger said.

"Nope," Bobby said. "Just you, and this ain't your dogfight."

They drove south and watched the sun clear the earth and wash the land in the bright colors of daylight. Dodger abruptly pulled onto the gravel shoulder and slid to a stop.

"I got no choice, B-Bob . . . I gotta go tell them what I saw." He looked over his shoulder and reached up under the top portion of the steering wheel, preparing to make a U-turn. Bobby grabbed the wheel.

"You gotta talk to Mr. Cain first, Dodge—we promised him."

Dodger pushed Bobby's arm away. "Let go the wheel. This is my problem, not Harley's or yours."

"Well, you're fixing to make it ours," Bobby said.

Dodger shot him a quick look.

"We're partners, Dodge. If something takes a bad turn, we'll all be in the same fix."

Dodger relaxed his grip on the wheel and stared down the highway. "Harley's leaving for Houston this afternoon."

"To the doctor again?"

"Yeah . . . it might not be too good."

Dodger looked across at Bobby, his expression heavy with concern.

"I just want to get all this behind me. Seems like every time I turn around, everything's going to hell on me."

Bobby's voice carried the weight of Dodger's gloom in it.

"It sure seems like it. That's one reason we got to let Mr. Cain know before we do anything."

Dodger nodded in agreement.

"He said you could call him Harley, B-Bob."

"Yeah, I know. But every time I'm around him, he seems so serious I don't want to get out of line."

"He's really a pretty funny guy when you get to know

him—he just seems like he's mad all the time. It's just his way."

Dodger pulled back onto the highway heading south to the ranch. He hung his left arm out the window and draped his right hand over the top of the steering wheel, his hat low over his eyes—looking every bit the cowboy he was becoming. Bobby sat up straight and pulled his hat low over his eyes.

Dodger's voice was low and unsteady.

"You know Harley's dying?"

Bobby's expression was grim, and he waited a long time before he responded.

"How do you know that?"

"We was sittin' on the porch one night, and I asked him why he kept going to Houston."

"What'd he say?"

"At first he wouldn't talk about it, but finally he told me he has cancer." Dodger looked Bobby in the eye as though he was being sworn to secrecy. "He don't want anyone to know."

"Why you telling me, then?"

"I don't know—seems like we're all three in this together. If I was you, I'd want to know."

Bobby paused a long time and then responded with all the seriousness the burden of his new knowledge carried with it.

"How bad is it?"

"I reckon it's as bad as it gets."

"Why's he going back today?"

"He said the doctor told him they don't know what will happen with no treatment. He just wants to know how much time he can count on. They're gonna x-ray him some more."

Bobby sat back in the seat, folded his arms together, and stared at the road ahead, a bit envious of Dodger's relationship with the old man.

"So, he told you all that?"

"Yeah, he did. Him and me talk about a lot of things—like me and you, Bobby . . . we got no secrets."

Bobby looked up from under the brim of his hat. His tone was uncharacteristically dark.

"I might have one or two."

Dodger looked across at him, equally serious.

"Yeah, me too. I reckon everybody does, don't you suppose?"

"I guess."

Dodger turned his attention back to the road. "What's one of yours?"

Bobby grinned.

"If I told you, it wouldn't be a secret."

"No, but what good is it knowing something if you're the only one that knows it?"

Bobby shrugged.

"I don't have no secrets that good anyway. Do you?"

Dodger's head tilted up and down slowly, like the nod itself was a secret.

"I got a head full of 'em, Bobby."

"Tell me one."

"If I do, we got to tell Harley I told you, 'cause it's his secret and I told him I wouldn't say anything just yet."

"So he's okay with you telling me, but not just yet?"

"Something like that."

"Might as well tell me, and we can tell Mr. Cain you did when we get to the ranch. It ain't like he doesn't want me to know—it's just about when."

Dodger raised his eyebrows.

"I don't even know what you just said, B-Bob."

Bobby sat back and crossed a boot over a knee.

"Don't matter to me one way or the other."

"Well," Dodger said with a long drawl as he pushed his hat back. "Harley told me he put you and me in his will. You know what a will is?"

"Yeah, I know what a will is . . . sort of."

"He's leaving a lot of stuff to me and you after he passes . . . which I hope never happens. But we need to be thinking of what to do when it does."

"I'm with you, Dodge—I don't want nothing to happen to Mr. Cain either."

"Just the same, Bobby, we need to sit down with him so we'll know what to do."

CHAPTER FORTY-THREE

When Bobby and Dodger arrived at the ranch, Cain's pickup was gone. There was a note on the kitchen table, folded and tucked under a glass ashtray. Dodger pulled it out and read it.

"It's from Harley. It says stay out of trouble, get the rest of the boards up on the loading alley, and he'll call from the airport in Houston before he leaves to come home day after tomorrow."

"You think he was in a hurry to get out of here, Dodge?"

"No, I reckon he had some stuff to do before he left. He writes all the things he needs to do down in that little notebook he carries in his shirt pocket all the time." Dodger's expression darkened. "You know what that means?"

Bobby waited for the answer.

"Eugene will be out before we get to talk to Harley."

"Well, that might be a problem if Mr. Cain thinks you should go to the cops. But if he don't, then it won't make any difference one way or the other."

Dodger picked his gloves up off the counter and shoved them into his back pocket as he weighed his concerns and indecision about Eugene.

"Best we get started on that lead-up."

Bobby led the way out of the house and spoke over his shoulder.

"Did you remember to buy more nails?"

"Yeah, I got a five-pound bag of sixteen-penny nails. Things should go a lot faster not having to straighten out every other damn one."

Bobby grinned. "I love new nails."

"Yeah, me too. But you know Harley—he don't waste nothing."

"My daddy's the same way. You and me will be acting like that when we get old too, I expect."

Dodger laughed.

"Hell, B-Bob—I'm already like that."

The next afternoon at the Houston Medical Research Hospital, Cain waited for the doctor in a cold and sterile office outfitted in stainless steel, chrome, and black Formica finishes and devoid of pictures or any other humanizing décor. One entire wall was dedicated to an ultramodern light box affair, obviously for viewing a large number of x-ray images side by side. There were no magazines, no framed diplomas, nothing to soften the hard edges for those who waited to hear the final verdict on months of debilitating treatment that ended in the doctor saying *I'm sorry.*

As Cain waited, he thought back to that night on the porch. He knew that, regardless of the doctor's report, he preferred a .45 caliber option to lying overmedicated and bedridden waiting for everything to slowly shut down. It wasn't much comfort, but he'd had some time to think about it, and he convinced himself he would not be a victim as long as the final moment was his call.

When the door swung open, he stood with a start and his heart pounded.

"Harland Cain?"

"Yessir."

"I'm Doctor Vogel."

• •

The next morning, just as the sun began to rise over the edge of the desert, the telephone on Cain's kitchen table rang. Bobby and Dodger looked up from their breakfast. It rang again and Dodger picked it up.

"Oh, hey."

Dodger held his hand over the mouthpiece and whispered to Bobby. "It's Harley."

He held the phone back to his ear.

"So, you'll be back this afternoon late? About what time?"

His head bobbed as he listened.

"Well, what did the doctor say?"

This time he listened a long time, and his expression was blank. Bobby leaned forward in his chair.

"No, sir, I don't know what that means."

He looked at Bobby and shrugged.

"Okay, Harley—we'll see you tonight then. You too. Adios."

He hung up the telephone slowly and his eyes narrowed as he regarded Bobby with concern in his voice.

"Well, what'd he say?"

"He said he'd be back this evening."

"Did he say what the doctor told him?"

"Yeah, sort of."

"Well?"

"He said the x-rays showed it didn't get bigger this time."

"What does that mean?"

"He sounded like it was good news."

"Sounds to me like it just wasn't bad news."

"I guess that's right, B-Bob. He said he'd explain it when he gets home."

"We'll find out tonight, then, I guess."

"We got a lot of talking to do tonight. We better get that lead-up and the loading chute done today for sure, B-Bob."

The boys worked through the day, skipped dinner, and fried up hamburger meat and sliced potatoes for supper. They sat on the front porch with their sweet tea and waited for more than two hours. When they saw headlights slow and then turn onto the gravel driveway, they both stood.

Harley stopped the pickup next to the steps, stepped out of the cab, and reached in across the seat for a heavy shopping bag. When he got to the porch, he looked up, and both boys watched him without speaking.

He handed the bag to Bobby.

"Put this in the icebox."

Dodger grinned at Bobby. "He means the fridge."

Cain walked into the house, and the boys followed him. He hung his hat on the hall tree and then turned to face the boys.

"Well, I ain't dead yet, if that's what you're thinking."

Bobby set the bag in the refrigerator and leaned back against the counter. Dodger straddled a chair and looked up at Cain over the chairback.

He felt it was time to clear the air. "I told Bobby about the cancer."

"I figured you might."

"You ain't mad?"

"I'd a probably done the same in your shoes."

Dodger grinned. "They said it didn't get worse, Harley?"

"The tests indicate no malignant cell growth since the last test."

Dodger looked at him with a puzzled expression. "Yeah?"

"You boys don't know a damn thing about any words more than five letters long, do you?"

Bobby laughed. "No, sir. If a word takes that many letters, there's probably a shorter one that will work just as good."

Cain went to the refrigerator and pulled three beers out of the bag. He popped the caps and passed one to each of the boys.

"This is a celebration. Now, no growth doesn't mean it's gone or that it will get better. It just means it didn't get worse . . . and that's about as good a news as you can get at this stage."

"You mean you're okay?" Dodger asked.

Cain smiled. There was hope in his eyes, and they had a softer look about them. But his voice still had a hard edge of defiance about it—something that came with age, Dodger supposed.

"It could still go either way, but they said it's a good sign."

The boys' eyes were fixed on Cain. Dodger felt his throat tighten. He tried to speak but could not get the words out. He didn't know what to think or feel. He held the bottle out to Cain and Bobby, and they all touched them up. There was no further need for words.

They tipped the bottles back, and the boys waited for Cain to pull down first. They looked from one to the other and watched as Cain continued to drink. There was no give in any one of them as they chugged the beer and shifted their eyes back and forth until Dodger backwashed and began laughing. When he did, Bobby broke and the beer ran down his chin. Cain finally slammed his empty bottle down onto the table.

He looked from Dodger to Bobby and back again. He pulled one more beer from the bag.

"I'd offer you boys another one, but it looks like you got your hands full with what you got."

Bobby held his half-empty bottle in the air.

"I'm good with this."

Dodger ran his sleeve across his chin.

"Me too."

Cain uncapped the new bottle and took a seat at the table. Dodger sat across from him, and Bobby sat between them.

"They let Eugene go, Harley," Dodger said.

"What do you mean?"

"They arrested him and Rolando, but they had to let Eugene go because they didn't have no evidence on him."

"But they did on Rolando?"

"Yeah, his fingerprints were on the .30-30 that killed the witness guy."

"Where did you hear about all this?"

"It was in the paper," Bobby said.

Cain looked across at Dodger.

"Unless you step up and testify, Eugene will most likely get away with murder," Cain said.

"Yessir. Rolando ain't gonna give him up, and now they can't tie either one of them to the deal at the Sundowner," Dodger said, with an air of authority about him. "If Rolando says he found the gun, he might get away too."

Cain pushed his chair back and crossed his arms as he contemplated the whole of it.

"So, what do you want to do?"

Dodger studied his folded hands before him. He raised his eyes to Cain's slowly, and when he spoke his voice had a maturity to it that fell somewhere between resignation and determination.

"I just want to do the right thing for a change. I been ducking guys like Eugene all my life. I'm not gonna keep doing that—I'm done ducking."

"You sure about that?"

Bobby reached over and put his hand on Dodger's shoulder. Dodger nodded.

"I'm sure."

"All right, then. First thing tomorrow morning, we'll drive in and do what we need to do."

Dodger stood, checked Cain's beer, and then went to the refrigerator and pulled two fresh ones out and handed one to Bobby. They popped the caps, and Dodger stuck his bottle, neck first, over the table. Cain and Bobby clinked theirs against his, and Dodger grinned.

"Here's to not getting worse."

"Amen, brother," Bobby said, and he tipped his hat to Cain. "There's one more thing," he said as he looked from Cain to Dodger. "Dodger told me about the will, Mr. Cain."

Cain leaned forward with his elbows on the table.

"I figured he would."

"Are you mad, Harley?"

"No, I ain't mad. How could I be mad? At the rate I'm going now, I'll have it all spent before you two knotheads get anything anyway."

"Fine with me, Mr. Cain."

"Yeah, me too, Harley."

Before they turned in for the night, they called the Bufort police department and made an appointment for the next morning with Detective Nickles.

CHAPTER FORTY-FOUR

After Cain and Dodger dropped Bobby off at his house, they drove to the police station. Cain pulled into the small parking lot and turned off the engine. He left his hand on the key as he addressed the boy.

"Last chance to change your mind."

The boy looked across at the old man.

"Once I do this, you know you and Bobby are going to be on Eugene's list too, right?"

"Yeah, I know. Does Bobby?"

"Yeah. Me and him talked about it a long time. I ain't telling anyone I told you and Bobby what happened, but Eugene will know I did."

Dodger pushed his door open, slid out of the seat, and looked back inside at Cain.

"You comin', or waiting here?"

Cain slammed the door behind him, and the two walked in together. Dodger paused in the hallway and looked over at Cain. The old man touched him on the shoulder.

"Just tell it like you know it to be."
"Yessir, I will."

Halfway down the long corridor, Cain stopped at an intimidating-looking door with CRIMINAL INVESTIGATION painted in gold leaf on the frosted glass pane.

"This is it," he said as he held the door open for the boy.

An unsmiling woman with dark hair pulled back in a tight knot looked up at them.

"May I help you?"

"Yes, ma'am. Me and the boy are here to see Detective Nickles."

"Do you have an appointment?" she asked, looking down at a calendar devoid of entries.

"At nine," Cain said.

The woman glanced up at the wall clock.

"It's quarter to," she said.

Before Cain could respond, a man wearing a white shirt and a wide tie walked up behind the receptionist.

"Mr. Cain?"

"Yessir."

"Bodean Cooper?"

The boy nodded.

"I'm expecting them, Maria. We got busy last night, and I didn't have time to tell you."

Maria raised her eyebrows but said nothing.

"Gentlemen, come on in."

Cain and the boy followed Nickles and Maria to his office. Nickles and Maria sat at a small conference table.

The detective looked directly at the boy. His smile was brief but professionally accommodating.

"Sit down. Make yourself comfortable."

Cain and the boy sat. Dodger looked from Nickles to Cain and then back at the detective, not at all sure he'd made the best decision.

Nickles shuffled pages on his clipboard and then began.

"First of all, I want to thank you for what you are about to do. Without your testimony, Cazares is clearly going to walk on this one."

The boy looked up at him and gnawed the inside of his cheek, not feeling brave or heroic.

"I'm going to swear you in and record your response to my questions. Maria here will stand in as a witness and handle the actual dictation. Do you understand that your word will become legally binding testimony in the state's case against Eugene Cazares for first-degree murder and robbery, and that you will be required to testify accordingly in a court of law?"

Dodger looked surprised. He shot a quick glance to Cain, and then he nodded apprehensively.

Nickles waited a moment.

"Please answer the question verbally—for the record, Mr. Cooper."

"Yessir, I understand."

Nickles excused Cain to wait in the outer office. He then began the questioning in a relaxed manner and a slow but steady cadence. By the time he finished two and a half hours later, the boy sat drained and exhausted. Maria left the room. The detective stood while he looked over the papers before slipping them neatly into the manila folder on the table before him.

"Excellent job, Bodean."

He extended his hand to the boy. Dodger stood, clearly shaken by the experience. He shook the detective's hand.

"Now what?"

"We'll get Cazares in custody and be in touch with you for possible further deposition and ultimately to get you together with the DA's lawyers to help prepare you for your part in the trial."

"My part?"

Nickles's expression seemed cold and indifferent.

"You're the key witness. This entire trial depends on the jury believing you—unless, of course, Barone turns state's evidence, which isn't likely."

Dodger clenched his jaw, but he did not respond. His hands trembled, and his palms ran wet with sweat when he shook the detective's hand again and left the office. Out in the hallway, he wanted to vomit.

"How did it go?" Cain asked.

The boy headed for the door.

"Come on, Harley. Let's get out of here."

They sat in the pickup, and Cain waited while the boy composed himself. He stared out the window a long time before he turned to look at Cain.

"I gotta testify in court."

"I figured you might."

"You didn't tell me that."

"I thought you understood it."

The boy slumped in his seat.

"Well, I didn't. You could have at least said something. I had no damn idea. Now the whole thing's on me."

"If you knew, would you not be here?"

The boy turned, tipped his hat back, and pressed his forehead to the side window. Finally, he turned back to the old cowboy.

"I reckon I'd still be here."

"I figured that too."

"Well, if you got everything so figured out, what happens if they can't find Eugene and he finds out I'm a witness?"

Cain slipped the key into the ignition and fired the engine.

"Then I expect we'll cross that bridge when we get to it."

The boy did not respond, and Cain did not press the issue.

The scent of the desert, sweet and pungent at the same time, drifted in through the open window. The familiarity of it had a settling effect on them both.

They were several miles south of Bufort when the boy turned toward Cain and spoke in a soft voice absent of the anger and frustration he'd felt earlier.

"I didn't mean to be whiny back there."

"I know. There ain't many fifteen-year-olds could hold up under all this—hell, there ain't many full-grown men who could."

Cain laughed that infectious cowboy laugh of his, and the boy smiled.

"One day at a time, just like you always say, huh?"

"That's all we got, Dodger. All we can do is play each day as it comes to us."

Dodger nodded his agreement without comment. He liked the way Cain had of making sense of things that made no sense at all, and he liked the feeling of confidence Cain always seemed to have about him, regardless of which way things were going for him. He'd never seen it in his father, and he did not see it much in the men around Bufort.

"You ain't seen much of Elena lately," Cain said in an obvious turn of the conversation that was not lost on the boy.

"No, sir."

Cain turned his head and looked at the boy as though waiting for the rest of it.

"I'm going down there tonight. We're going to the picture show and then to the Pig Stand after."

"You getting a little sweet on her, are you?"

Dodger grinned. "Why do you say that?"

"I know the signs. I used to be young once too, you know."

"It was different in the olden days, Harley."

"What do you mean?"

Dodger laughed.

"Well, we got cars and telephones and radios and people living in towns. It's just a whole lot faster than it used to be. That's what everybody tells me."

"Some truth to that, I reckon. But one thing hasn't changed."

"What's that?"

"Girls ain't changed a bit. Girls'll make you act silly, say things you don't mean, and generally just keep you off-balance enough that you ain't never sure where you stand with them."

"That's me to a T, Harley. We can have the best time and she'll say something—I'll be the rest of the week trying to figure out what she meant."

"Well, if it helps, there is one thing you can count on when it comes to women."

"What's that?"

Cain looked up, mentally reaching for the right thought. He shook his head.

“Forget it . . . now that I think about it, that one don’t work neither.”

They both laughed and, when they stopped, the boy sat back and looked out ahead at the long stretch of highway before them where it faded into the cross-shadow of the mountains in the flat distance where the jagged horizon seemed to float.

“That’s pretty funny, Harley.”

The evening settled in soft and warm, with a breeze that came in off the desert so subtly that it seemed to come from all directions. Dodger stood on the porch and held the door for Elena. She exited with a mock curtsey to the boy and a quick *good night* to her mother. Dodger followed her across the yard and did a top-to-bottom assessment of her outfit: two-tone cowboy boots, tight jeans, a blue work shirt with long sleeves, and a turquoise necklace that hung at her throat. Her dark hair lay pulled back, exposing ever-present large silver hoop earrings that swayed with the rhythm of her walk.

He smiled and made a conscious effort to minimize the limp that always seemed to be most noticeable when he felt the least deserving.

Elena stopped halfway across the yard and walked back to him. She slipped her arm through his and held his hand with both of hers. She flashed her black eyes and her mesmerizing smile. Dodger pulled his hat low over his eyes and looked down at her.

“Damn, girl.”

“What?”

“I swear—seriously, you just couldn’t be any prettier.”

Elena feigned an insulted expression.

“So, you’re just after me for my looks?”

Dodger held eye contact, and his gaze was determined and confident.

“Yes, ma’am.”

Before she could respond, he placed his index finger against her lips.

"I never knew before what they meant when they said someone is as pretty on the inside as they are on the outside. But that's you all over."

"Aww, thank you, Dodger. That's so sweet."

Dodger grinned.

"I know. I just came up with that."

Elena slapped his arm.

"Jerk."

Dodger held the door as Elena climbed into his truck and positioned herself near the center of the seat. Before he turned the key in the ignition, he paused, contemplating his words.

"What?" Elena asked.

"Do you mind if we skip the show tonight? I got some things I need to talk to you about."

"No, that's fine. Let's stop at the Pig Stand and then we can drive out into the desert, where it's quiet."

They stayed at the Pig Stand just long enough to say hello to friends and get their order to go. Dodger drove south and exited the highway onto a dirt trail. He drove back a mile or so. He backed the truck in between the cholla and the other cacti with a view of the traffic and turned off the lights. He left the radio playing softly in the background. They made small talk, ate their hamburgers, and sipped their sodas. Finally, Elena reached over and turned off the radio.

"So, what's up?"

Dodger balled up the empty food bag and tossed it onto the floor at their feet. His expression grew dark and somber, and his eyes narrowed as he looked over at her a long time before he answered.

"What I'm gonna tell you, I'm only telling you in case something bad happens."

Elena's eyes widened. She sat up straight in her seat and tensed.

"What do you mean, Dodger?"

Dodger looked at her a long time, weighing whether or not to involve her. Finally, he blurted it out.

"I saw who killed the man at the Sundowner in Bufort."

"You *what?*"

"I saw him—I saw it all."

"Did you tell the police?"

"Yeah."

"And?"

"They said they are going to pick him up."

"They don't have him yet?"

"Not yet."

"Did you know who it was?"

Dodger nodded, and this time the expression in his eyes was one of fear.

"It was Eugene."

"Your mom's boyfriend?"

"Uh-huh."

"Oh, no, Dodger. I'm so sorry."

She took his hand in hers.

"If he finds out I saw him before they arrest him, he'll track me down. I'll be a goner."

The boy paused and cleared his throat. "No matter what, you cannot trust Eugene if you ever see him."

"I won't. I promise."

Dodger continued, his thoughts pouring out faster than he could organize them.

"Rolando was with him. He's in jail for killing another man who saw what happened. I think him and Eugene shot that guy, but Rolando was the one that pulled the trigger, so Eugene is still out there."

He turned away from her.

"He's gonna kill me if he thinks I know anything."

She squeezed his hand and shook her head in protest.

"No . . . no, no. I'll tell my mother, and you can come and stay with us until this is over. He won't find you here."

"I can't."

"Why not?"

"I need to look out for Mr. Cain if he shows up at his place looking for me."

Elena's temper and frustration collided in her words.

"Well, that's just crazy. He has no reason to hurt Mr. Cain."

"He'll do what it takes to get to me."

They talked well past dark, and when he dropped Elena off at her home, he promised to consider her offer—if it still stood after she spoke to her mother about it. The drive back to Cain's place was a blur as he considered his options. When he pulled into Cain's driveway, he had no plan and no good choices that came to mind.

CHAPTER FORTY-FIVE

Two police cruisers sat with their red lights flashing and their high beams focused on the mobile home of Rolando Barone. Eugene, driving Rolando's car, arrived in the neighborhood in time to see the police officers circle the place before he got too close. He turned off his lights and sat watching from a distance with the engine running. When he heard the blare of the bullhorn and the voice of the officer manning it, he made a quick but quiet U-turn in the street and waited.

"Eugene Cazares. This is the Bufort Police Department. We have a warrant for your arrest. Step outside with your hands in the air."

Eugene watched the lights of the patrol cars before he turned on his own lights and accelerated away from the scene.

His mind raced as he tried to piece together the events that could have led to an arrest warrant. Nothing fit until he remembered the conversation he'd had with Rolando the day Rolando had found Dodger and Bobby in the Sundowner parking lot. Either one or both of them knew something, and Dodger would be the key to finding out.

He knew the boy was living at Cain's place, but he was not sure of the location. He stopped at Duane's Conoco and pulled in at the gas pumps. He heard the bell ring inside when he drove over the rubber actuator, and he waited.

Mickey nodded as he approached the driver's window.

"Hey, Mickey."

"How's it going, Eugene?"

"You know." He shrugged. "Could be better, could be worse."

"I hear ya."

"Give me three dollars—regular."

Mickey clicked in the last few pennies' worth and then stood at the window.

"That'll be three dollars even. How's that oil?"

"It's good. Hey, I'm on my way to pick Dodger up at that old man's place, but he didn't give me the address. What's the number out there?"

Mickey shook his head.

"I ain't sure the mailbox number, but it's right on the highway, halfway between here and Los Caminos on the left-hand side. Big ol' barn in the back and an adobe and wood-looking house with new white and brown paint up front. It's the only one in the area. You can't miss it."

Eugene stuck three one-dollar bills out the window.

"Thanks, man."

"Any time. Tell Dodger I said hey."

Eugene held a cigarette between his teeth and nodded without responding as he accelerated out onto the street heading for the highway.

At Cain's place, Dodger sat on the edge of the chair in the kitchen and stared up as the old man stood near the table with the telephone receiver pressed to his ear.

"Yeah, I will," Cain said.

A long pause.

"I understand."

Another pause. Cain's head bobbed in response to the unheard side of the conversation.

"All right. Well thanks, Detective Nickles. I appreciate the update."

He hung up the telephone and took his seat across from the boy.

"Well?"

"They tried to serve Eugene a while ago, but they missed him. They're sure he knows about the attempted arrest by now, but they doubt he has any idea you're a material witness."

"So, what does that mean?"

"If you ask Nickles, it means following procedure."

"What if I ask you?"

Cain squinted with one eye.

"If you ask me, it means Eugene is a wild card."

"What do we do?"

"We expect him to show up and be ready for him when he does."

The boy's expression was one of quiet resignation, only this time there was no fear in his eyes and no dread in his heart—nothing left but the dark veil of uncertainty.

He looked down at his hands upon the table. His voice was thoughtful and wrought with conviction.

"Do you reckon all this is our punishment for trying to kill ourselves?"

Cain took a deep drag on the cigarette he held between his fingers and blew the smoke up toward the ceiling, where it drifted and flattened against the yellowed boards. He watched the smoke before he responded.

"If it is, it's a good one."

Cain appeared disengaged and contemplative. The boy knew the look, and he waited. He watched Cain intently, and then Cain stood and poured himself a cup of coffee.

He offered the pot to the boy, and the boy shook his head. Cain sat back at the table and looked up at the electric bulb hanging from a wire and then back down to Dodger.

"Okay, look. Here's what we do. Call Elena and see if her offer to let you stay there still stands."

"I don't want to do that, Harley. I already brought enough trouble on that family."

"Look, we don't have many choices, and we may not have any time. Eugene doesn't know anything about the Delgados, and I don't imagine he knows about your friendship with Elena. We got no choice."

"Okay, Harley, but I don't like it."

Dodger dialed the number and spoke with Mrs. Delgado. She reassured him that he was welcome, but it was Elena's pleading that convinced him. Cain continued with the plan.

"You get your things and drive down there now. I'll set up in the barn where I can watch the house. If Eugene shows up here, you'll be gone. I'll have the upper hand with a rifle from the hayloft."

"What if he don't show up?"

Cain smiled.

"That would be the best news. We'll stick with it until he shows up or gets arrested."

Dodger packed a change of clothes in a paper bag and set it on the table.

"Can I take the .45 with me?"

Cain nodded toward the counter near the sink.

"No argument there. It's in the closet with a new box of ammunition and the extra magazine. Take it all with you."

The boy headed down the hall.

"Thanks, Harley," he said.

The boy helped Cain get set up in the hayloft. When he pulled out of the driveway and turned to the south, he was more uncertain and apprehensive than he could remember ever being. He crested the first dip in the road after he left Cain's place and watched a distant set of headlights coming his way in the rearview mirror. He slowed and waited.

The headlights flickered and then went black about where Dodger estimated Cain's driveway to be. He saw a brief flash of red from the taillights as the vehicle pulled into Cain's place and then stopped. Dodger turned off his own lights. He waited and he watched. When he thought he saw the dim glow of the interior lights flash on and then off in his mirror, he cranked the wheel around and started slowly back toward the ranch with only the thin ribbon of silver moonlight to guide him. There was no other traffic on the road in either direction.

He reached down on the seat beside him and held the steering wheel with his elbows as he held the .45 in one hand and reached for the full magazine with the other. He slammed the magazine home and then laid the pistol between his legs. He felt his stomach turn and his heart pound. When he was near enough to make out Cain's driveway, he slowed to a crawl and listened through the open window.

He watched the driveway but could not see beyond the cover of the house. He looked up at the partially open doors of the hayloft, but he saw nothing.

He struggled with the urge to come sliding hard into the driveway with his horn honking and firing wildly with the pistol. But he was learning patience, a product of his time with Cain. What he had not yet mastered was timing, so he made the conscious decision to pull over to the side of the road and wait, still on the south side of Cain's driveway.

His patience ran out. He slid out of the cab through the passenger-side window to avoid opening the door and lighting up the interior of the truck. Carrying the .45 in his hand and the extra magazine in his hip pocket, he ran into the desert. With his head down and his blood coursing with adrenaline, he ran as fast as his bad leg would allow. He had barely reached the cover of a thin growth of brush when a set of headlights backed out of Cain's driveway and crept down the road in his direction.

The boy cursed and dropped to the ground, hoping the shadows would conceal his position and praying the driver had not seen him. Then he looked back at his truck in full view on the road and felt a chill run through him.

The keys—I left the damn keys in the ignition.

He lay with his cheek against his arms and his eyes following the slow-moving headlights. The lights slunk forward and, when they shone on his truck, they stopped. The lights backed a short distance and then turned to illuminate the desert floor—searching, slowly and methodically. He hunkered down tightly to the ground as the lights cast their beams over him and deep out into the brush beyond. He held his breath, listened as a door opened and closed, and then tensed when a voice called out into the darkness.

"Where are you?"

His stomach knotted and his jaw ached as he gritted his teeth and gripped the pistol. Then the voice called out again.

"It's me—Harley." It sounded like Cain's voice.

The boy stood and waved his arms, blinded by the light and unable to see Cain or anyone who might be there with him.

Dodger dropped to his knees again and did not answer. What if Eugene has him? In his uncertainty, he waited.

"Dodger, it's okay. It's just me."

There was a reassurance in the voice of the old man that overrode any doubt the boy had. He stood again and waved. This time he hollered back toward the bright lights of Cain's truck.

"Could you dim them lights, Harley? I can't see a darn thing."

The headlights went out, and the boy walked toward the parking lights Cain had left on to guide him. Dodger lowered the hammer slowly and slipped the pistol under his belt at the small of his back. He walked toward Cain's truck.

"What are you doin', Harley?"

"I thought you'd be in Los Caminos by now."

"I saw lights. I came back."

"It was Eugene, I'm sure of it," Cain said. "He was driving Rolando's car. He pulled in, turned off his lights, looked around, then backed out and left. It looked like he was coming this way, but it was hard to tell with his lights off."

"I didn't see him come by here. Maybe he went back to Bufort."

"He's too cagey for that. Don't underestimate that one."

Dodger regarded the old cowboy with grave concern. "What now?"

"Same plan. You get on down to Los Caminos, and I'll watch the place from the loft—but keep your eyes open. I don't put anything past Eugene."

The boy, on his way back to his truck, looked over his shoulder.

"Call me at Elena's if there's any news. The number's wrote on the wall by the phone."

"You wrote on my damn wall we just painted?"

Dodger laughed an uneasy laugh. "With a pencil. We can erase it off if you want."

"I guess that'll be fine."

Cain's voice took on an uncharacteristic gentle tone. "You take care of yourself, Dodger."

"You too, Harley."

It was a quarter of an hour later when the boy noticed headlights behind him—not gaining and not falling behind. When he sped up, the headlights sped up. When he slowed, they slowed. He considered pulling over to let them pass but thought better of it. He felt sweat run down his back as he alternately watched the road ahead and the lights trailing in the darkness behind.

When he approached the *mercado*, he figured he'd pull in if there were other cars in the parking lot. He slowed and pulled off the road. The vehicle behind closed the distance some. The parking lot stood empty save the lone pickup of the proprietor positioned under the single lamppost, eerily alone beneath the bright light.

Dodger panicked. He whipped the wheel around and fishtailed in the gravel as he accelerated back onto the blacktop in a desperate attempt to increase the gap between his truck and the vehicle following. The pursuer matched his speed once again. It was now clear to the boy that he had a serious problem.

I can't let him follow me to Elena's, he thought as he gauged the short drive into Los Caminos. He considered driving directly to the police station, but he knew he had no legitimate complaint and could not say for certain that the pursuer was even Eugene.

He reckoned his best chance was to lose the stalker in the side streets of the town and then find a place to hide his truck. He needed to shake him as soon as possible. Los Caminos was a small town laid out on a square grid with very few odd or unpredictably patterned streets.

When the first lights appeared on the outskirts of town, Dodger began to slow, and the vehicle following him did likewise. They entered town together, the pursuit vehicle still too far back to identify. When he approached the first lighted intersection, Dodger moved into the left-turn lane with his left-turn indicator blinking. The traffic light turned red, and Dodger cut across the open lanes to his right, turned off his lights and sped down a dark side street. He turned right, and then left, and waited at the next intersection. Nothing. He took a deep breath and exhaled loudly, intently watching the rearview mirror and seeing nothing.

He did not see the brown-and-tan sedan rolling in his direction from the intersection before him. He sensed the presence of the sedan before he heard it and, when he looked up, Eugene glared at Dodger across the short span from his side window into the side window of the boy's truck.

"You can't hide," Eugene said as his door opened and he leaned to exit the vehicle.

Dodger shifted into gear and stood his right boot against the accelerator pedal, burning rubber all the way across the intersection, driven by panic and fear and the closeness of the face that visited him so many times in his nightmares.

CHAPTER FORTY-SIX

Dodger drove the back streets, wild and aimless, with no plan and no thought beyond distancing himself from Eugene. He watched the side mirrors, and his eyes darted down each dark intersection.

His face was on fire. When he calmed himself enough to take a deep breath, he realized he was lost. He pulled to the side of the street with the lights off and the engine running while he attempted to get his bearings. He watched the street through the windshield and in the mirror, his heart drumming and his chest heaving. He had a sense of where the center of town lay by the concentration of lights illuminating the sky from the Pig Stand and the used car lot adjacent to it.

He squinted into the shadows through the windshield and down the side street just ahead. He shifted into gear and reached for the light switch at the same instant a set of headlights appeared in the mirror through the black void behind him. He slid low in the seat with his foot on the clutch and his hand on the stick shift. The vehicle approached slowly. He waited. The approaching lights drifted to the right, near the curb, and the boy gripped the steering wheel as he waited. His hands shook, and he hung on that fine line near panic.

The lights went black. Dodger leaned out the open window and looked behind him, trying to hear or see anything. A man's voice . . . then that of a woman. One door slammed shut, and the other creaked open and clunked shut as well. In the dim light of the house, he saw two figures walk up the sidewalk and finally stand on the porch of the house he was in front of while the man fumbled with the key in the door lock.

Dodger sat up, pulled on the light switch, and inched slowly away from the curb. He drove with great caution through the residential streets and then pulled into the alley behind the auto-parts store, where there was no light and his truck was not visible to passing drivers.

He backed in close to the store wall and then locked the truck and walked to the end of the alley. Across the street sat the police station. He wanted to go for help, but he chose to stay concealed in the shadows as he began the mile-long walk to the Delgado house.

He looked over his shoulder as he stood on the lighted porch and knocked on the door. A pair of eyes looked out over the small window up high on the door. He heard the lock turn at almost the same instant the door swung open and Elena stood there.

"What's wrong? Come in—come in."

Dodger looked back over his shoulder and then stepped inside and quickly closed the door.

"Eugene's here."

Elena's eyes widened, and she put her hand over her mouth.

"Here? Where here?"

"In Los Caminos. He followed me from Harley's place. He pulled up next to me just as I got into town after I tried to ditch him. I lost him somewhere, but I know he's coming."

Elena turned off the lights in the room and led him to the kitchen.

"We need to call the police."

"Where's your momma?"

"She's in bed."

A voice came from the arched opening of the small hallway behind the boy.

"I'm here."

Teresa Delgado came out wearing a robe that she held close to her. She lit a candle that cast the room in the soft yellow glow of the flame that wobbled and twisted and caused the shadows to move with it. She looked directly at the boy, her coffee-colored eyes hard and unyielding, and locked him in her gaze. She sat next to the boy and placed her hands over his as she spoke. The gesture had a settling effect on him but at the same time subordinated him to the conversation, and he listened accordingly.

"Elena told me what has happened to you. We cannot wait for your Eugene to decide your fate."

"He ain't mine, ma'am."

"Elena, call your uncle Antonio now, please. *Ándale*."

Elena stepped up to the wall-hung telephone, picked up the receiver, and dialed the number.

"Chief Flores, please. This is urgent. I'm his niece. Oh, hi, Doris. Thank you."

Elena looked back at her mother as she waited. She rolled her eyes and drummed her fingers on the wall.

"Hurry, hurry, hurry," she muttered under her breath.

"*Tío*, it's me, Elena. Dodger is here, and there's serious trouble. Dodger, the boy from Bufort."

She nodded. "Yes, Mr. Cain's friend."

Her mother made a *get on with it* gesture, and Elena interrupted her uncle.

"The man who killed the man at the Sundowner in Bufort is in Los Caminos, and he's trying to kill Dodger. Please, can you come now?"

She hung up the telephone and stood behind the boy while she spoke directly to her mother.

"He said he will be here as quick as he can. He said keep the door locked and do not open it for anyone."

Dodger looked up at the plastic kitchen wall clock: 9:35.

At 9:55, he looked over at Mrs. Delgado.

"Antonio will be here," she said.

Dodger's hand shifted down to the waistband of his jeans, and he felt the outline of the .45 grip under his loose-hanging shirttail. He did not want to have to explain the gun to the chief. Dodger looked from Elena to her mother.

"I'm sorry. I wasn't thinking. I never should have come here tonight."

Mrs. Delgado raised a hand in a dismissive manner.

"It's all right. Antonio will be here soon."

Eugene drove the back streets in frustration, his anger building and his resolve hardened beyond question. When he followed the main street back to the center of town, he pulled into the Pig Stand, ordered a soda from the carhop, and called over to a group of kids standing outside a gray primer-painted Model-T roadster.

He smiled and stuck his chin out their direction.

"Y'all seen Dodger tonight?"

His manner was casual and friendly. One of the girls approached his window and leaned on the tray below the pole-mounted speaker. She smiled at the carhop delivering fries and sodas to the car behind her and then turned and looked directly at Eugene.

"Who wants to know?" Her tone suggested more than it said.

"I'm a friend of his. I just wanted to give him his paycheck. He said he needed the money."

"You ain't from around here, are you?"

"No. Me and Dodger's from Bufort—the big city." He smiled again, the forty-year-old charm of a man long past any teenage relatability. Her sixteen-year-old attention span waned as she quickly tired of the banter.

"He's probably over at Elena's."

"That's what I thought. What street is that on?"

"It's on Sixth," she said over her shoulder as she turned to walk back to the roadster.

"What's the number?"

"Four twenty-three."

She did not look back when she answered but exaggerated her swinging hips, to the amusement of everyone except

Eugene, who made a pistol of his fingers and pulled the trigger behind another disingenuous smile.

Eugene watched the street signs in the dim light as he crossed each intersection—Fourth, Fifth, Sixth. He slowed and turned left. The two-hundred block. He checked the house numbers on those he could read. They were going up, and he noticed the even numbers on the right, odd on the left. When he crossed into the four-hundred block, he took his foot off the gas pedal and idled past number 423 with its dark windows and only a dim hint of light from somewhere deep inside the house. He stopped two houses down, turned off the engine, and closed the door, making no sound as he looked up and down the street before he slipped into the shadows and the cover of the untrimmed bushes that separated the Delgado house from that of their neighbor.

He slunk through the bushes and stole down the side of the house, checking the windows and the screen door as he went. Somewhere in the night, a dog barked. Another, more than a block away, answered it. Eugene hunkered back into the branches of the high-growing privets as the headlights of a car passed the house and continued out of sight.

The candlelight filtered through the glass of the kitchen window at the back of the house. Eugene raised up to peer inside. He saw Mrs. Delgado, her back to him, sitting at the table. Across from her sat Elena, neither of whom he recognized. He studied the dark figure in the shadows behind the girl but could not tell if it was Dodger.

Eugene shifted his position for a better look but was unable to get a clear view of the boy. When Dodger leaned forward, his face moved into the lighted glow of the candle. Eugene's expression turned hateful.

His jaw tensed; his eyes narrowed. He felt his breathing become louder and more rapid. Now, with more determination than stealth, Eugene shuffled around to the back door, tried it, and moved on to the next window. Locked.

Inside, the telephone rang. Eugene returned to the kitchen window. He watched the woman pick up the receiver. The boy and the girl listened and waited, apprehensive and uncertain. Eugene strained to hear the muted conversation.

The woman was clearly distressed.

"Momma, what is it?"

Mrs. Delgado put her hand over the mouthpiece of the telephone.

"It's your uncle Antonio. He's at an accident and wants to know if we're okay."

She turned back toward the telephone and removed her hand as she spoke.

"Yes, the doors are locked and the lights are off. No, no one so far. Thank you, Antonio."

She hung up the telephone and addressed the boy in a voice soft and uncertain.

"He will be here when they finish with the accident."

Elena looked up at the boy. The boy was shaken. His apprehension began to unnerve Elena.

"What do we do?"

Dodger blew out the candle.

"Wait."

He whispered to Mrs. Delgado and then to Elena and led them to the bathroom.

"Lock this door and stay inside there."

His eyes adjusted to the dark as he looked about from the narrow hallway into the gloom of the small living room. A dim reflection of the street light cast a yellow beam onto the worn carpet and up onto the wall of the kitchen. The boy stepped past the beam and positioned himself at the window. The heavy drapes reeked of dust and cigarette smoke. He stood there a long time listening, not moving.

His eyes widened and his head snapped around when the house creaked or a new sound disrupted the quiet. He tried to resist the urge to look outside, but he grew impatient. He slid the drapery aside slowly with one finger and peered out through the glass to the yard beyond, where the shadows appeared to conceal every manner of evil.

His chest felt tight, his palms wet, his mouth dry. He dropped his hand from the drape and turned with his back to the wall. He closed his eyes and took a deep breath. He waited a long time, listening, dreading what was coming.

Then he heard it. A car door. Open, then close. He turned and drew the drapery aside just enough to see the hulking form of a man cross the yard and stop in the shadows to light a cigarette. The flare of the flame from the lighter illuminated the face of Chief Flores and, as the boy reached for the door to open it, he heard the hollow, crushing sound of metal to bone. He glanced through the glass to see the unmistakable silhouette of Eugene reach down to drag the slumped body of Flores into the bushes.

Dodger panicked. His first instinct was to throw open the door and start firing. Instead, he pressed his back to the wall and closed his eyes. Images of Eugene, drunk and loud and violent, held him there. He wanted to cover his head with his arms until it all passed. His mind was a blur of unrelated thoughts; and when the vision of his mother's body being carried out of the house flashed before him, he clenched his jaw and looked about the room.

He reached for a cane-back chair near the table and jammed it up under the doorknob. He backed into the kitchen and took up a kneeling stance partially concealed behind the plaster wall that divided the two rooms. He trained the .45 on the door and waited, his stomach in a knot.

He expected a raging Eugene to kick the door off its hinges and come storming into the room as he had witnessed so many times before, but there was only silence and uncertainty, and the dreadful anxiety of waiting. He envisioned Eugene hunkered over Flores, his eyes hot and glazed and blood dripping from his hands.

He heard the bathroom door creak open. He rose up and turned to see Elena looking out from the darkness. He shook his head and waved her back inside, but she stepped into the narrow hallway without seeing him and closed the door slowly behind her.

The boy's heart all but overloaded. His surroundings transcended into some dreamlike state where there was only silence and a tunnel-visioned sense of all about the room.

Everything seemed to move in exaggerated slow motion. He stood. He yelled but could not hear his voice. She turned her head, first to the voice, and then to the explosion of wood and metal as the front door burst inward and the light from the street illuminated the carpet. Wood fragments and the door lock lay scattered about the room, but there was no sign of Eugene.

Elena screamed, held her hands over her mouth, and did not move. The boy stepped across the room and fired a wild shot in the direction of the loose-hanging door, looking for Eugene to follow the debris into the room.

The smoke cleared, the room fell silent, and Elena and the boy stood immobilized until Dodger spoke.

"Where'd he go?"

Elena shook her head. Dodger gripped her arm and forced her to the bathroom door.

"Get back in there, and keep the door locked."

Dodger stood in the hallway waiting as he watched the partially lit opening where the shattered front door hung. Outside, shadows shifted on the porch as the night breeze moved through the trees. There was no traffic on the street and no response from the neighbors. The boy had never felt more alone.

He moved with great caution into the living room and angled for a better view out the front door, but saw nothing. He slid closer, his stomach twisted and his fingers clenched white-knuckled around the grip of the pistol. He took first one tentative step and then another as he inched his way in the direction of the doorway, straining his head right and left to see out into the darkness. Nothing. No sound. No movement. He took another step. His heart was in his throat. He stopped. He balanced himself against the shattered doorframe and waited, listening before he looked out onto the porch.

Dodger strained to see into the dark of the bushes and could barely make out the shoes Flores wore, toes pointed into the grass and one heel cocked off to one side. He sucked in a chest full of the warm night air and was preparing to step out onto the porch when he heard the explosion and saw the muzzle flash that catapulted his body across the room, where it came to rest—blood running out of his shirt and his pistol lying on the carpet—tilted up against the wall in the hallway.

Eugene stood in the backlit doorway, the pistol in his hand trained on Dodger's unmoving body. Elena slammed open the bathroom door and screamed at the sight of the boy soaked in his own blood and Eugene standing over him.

Elena watched Eugene look up at her and then down at the boy as he lined up his next shot. The second explosion lit up the room in an intense flash of muzzle fire that choked the air and made the whole scene feel like a low-budget black-and-white movie.

Elena watched as the world moved in slow motion. Eugene's eyes widened, his thick torso lifted and then catapulted backward. His chest cracked. He lay on his back with blood pumping out of his shirt as he tried to talk. He raised his arm; it dropped. The blood stopped pumping. Eugene's empty eyes stared at the ceiling.

Elena stood with Dodger's still-smoking pistol clenched in her hands.

CHAPTER FORTY-SEVEN

Dodger awoke in the stark whiteness of the recovery room with Elena sitting at his side and Cain looking over him from the foot of the hospital bed. Bobby stood behind Elena's chair. Dodger's eyes had that same wild look as the day he'd stirred from Cain's sofa, but this time he smiled. Elena took his hand.

"Where am I?"

Elena kissed his hand. "You're in the hospital."

The boy raised his head and looked up at Cain. "I didn't wreck my truck again, did I?"

Cain laughed. "No, your truck's just fine."

Bobby leaned forward. "You don't remember what happened?"

Dodger looked down at his bandaged midsection and felt a burning sensation when he tried to turn.

"Did Eugene shoot me?"

Elena hushed him with her fingers over his lips. "We'll talk about it later."

Cain put his hand on the sheet covering the boy's feet and patted him.

"You took a bullet that missed every organ it passed. It blew a hole where it exited, about the size of a silver dollar. But you'll be okay."

"I remember," the boy said, his voice now subdued and tentative. "Eugene was about to shoot me again."

Bobby looked down at Elena and then over at Cain. Elena sat mute, her downcast eyes wet with the tears she was withholding. Cain looked at Bobby and shook his head, as though the gesture were a whisper.

Bobby's eyes acknowledged Cain's signal as he spoke. "You don't have to worry about Eugene no more."

Elena stood and excused herself as she hurried out into the hallway, with Bobby following close behind. Dodger regarded Cain with questioning eyes, and Cain held his hand up and waited for the door to close behind Elena and Bobby.

"What's wrong, Harley?"

"Elena saved your life."

"She did? How did she do that?"

"She picked up the .45 you dropped when you went down. She fired and it hit Eugene square in the middle of his chest. He died almost instantly, but she's taking it pretty hard."

"Oh, man. What about her uncle?"

"Flores? He's fine. He ended up with a concussion, but they released him this morning."

Dodger laid his head back and closed his eyes. When he opened them, he moved himself up slightly on his pillow and grimaced as he did so. He appeared older, more thoughtful as he spoke slowly and carefully.

"So, Elena shot him?"

Cain nodded.

The boy considered all that had happened. Cain could see that he was overwhelmed. He let the boy dwell on it.

Dodger turned back to look up at Cain.

"That don't make her a killer, though."

"No, it don't."

"What'd she say?"

"She thought you were dead. She didn't even remember picking up the pistol."

Dodger winced as he shifted his weight again.

"I knew something bad was gonna happen. I brought all this on her."

"No. No, you didn't. The world is a complicated place with lots of small moving parts. When someone moves one part just a little, it causes all the other parts to move in ways we can't see coming. If you start looking for someone to blame, there ain't no end to the list and there ain't no end to the blame. We ain't at the start of anything, and we ain't likely at the end of it neither. So don't start thinking you're a bigger part of something than you really are."

The boy smiled his half smile.

"You know what, Harley?"

"What's that?"

"I think I understood what you just said."

They both smiled, and the smiles were those of two who have journeyed through hard country together.

Dodger lifted up on one elbow and looked around the room.

"Where's my hat?"

Cain smiled.

"I already checked on that. It's still at Elena's where you left it. She promised to look after it for you."

The boy rested his head back against the pillow. He was quiet a long time before he spoke.

"What do I say to Elena about all this?"

"When the time comes, you just thank her for saving your life and leave the rest of it alone."

"That's it?"

"If she wants to talk about it, she'll let you know. Just give her time."

Cain turned to look out the window. The boy relaxed back against his pillow. His eyes studied the ceiling tiles. He imagined a universe so vast, so dark, and so distant that it defied understanding. This time when he imagined Bufort, Texas, he imagined it in the sunlight with him in it.

He continued to gaze at the ceiling tiles as he spoke to Cain.

"I got my mind set on vet school," he said. His voice had a maturity, a seriousness about it that Cain had not heard before.

The old man stared out the window, across the parking lot below, and far out into the desert, farther than his eye could travel. Elena and Bobby slipped quietly back into the room and stood at the door. Then they moved up to the bed, one on each side. Elena took Dodger's hand. Bobby laid his hand on Dodger's shoulder.

Cain heard the door close. He turned slowly and looked at the three kids a long time. Then he looked down at Dodger and smiled. His voice was thoughtful. He sounded distant when he spoke.

"You'll make a good one," he said.

THE END

AFTERWORD

People came and people went, but the desert never changed much.

Harland Cain lived to see Dodger and Bobby graduate from high school. In 1961, he was killed when his pickup ran off the road at a high rate of speed and struck a concrete bridge abutment a few miles from County Road 37. His grave is situated on the ranch at a remote site out near a desert spring, where a few wildflowers grow and his marble headstone is shaded by a stand of scrub willow.

Bobby Washington never made it into professional boxing. He left Bufort to work for Robert Tarrant in Fort Stockton, where he and his wife raised two sons, Bodean and Harley.

Robert Tarrant looked after Cain's affairs as promised. He took Bobby on as an apprentice and eventually sold him the business before he passed away peacefully in 1969.

Elena Delgado left Los Caminos with Dodger's one-of-a-kind hat to live with relatives in Santa Monica, California, where she finished high school and one semester of junior college. She returned to Los Caminos for Cain's funeral in 1961 and brought Dodger's hat with her. They were married the following year.

Dodger completed one year of veterinary school, but he dropped out after he and Elena married. They raised Santa Gertrudis cattle on the sprawling 14,000 acres irrigated by water from the San Jacinto aquifer. Out of respect for Cain's love of the untouched land, they never developed the place. He and Elena had three sons and two daughters. His eldest son died at seventeen of a drug overdose. He was buried next to Cain. Every couple of weeks, Dodger would saddle a horse and visit with Cain and the boy, until that too ended when, nearly three quarters of a century later, age got the best of him. Elena buried Dodger out there with her son between him and the old man, where she imagined the three talked and laughed and watched the stars together.